WILLOWEND

TESTED BY FIRE
STRENGTHENED BY GRACE

ROBERT GRIFFITH

GRACE AND TRUTH PUBLISHING
P.O. Box 338, Gunnedah NSW 2380 Australia
www.graceandtruthpublishing.com.au

ISBN: 978-1-7642635-6-6

1. THE LETTER ON THE PULPIT

The morning sun spilled across Willowend in long, wavering lines of heat. Even before nine o'clock, the air sat heavy over the town like a woollen blanket that had been left on too long. Heat shimmered off the narrow dirt road that led to the small white weatherboard building standing back from the street with its corrugated iron roof and very modest timber sign:

WILLOWEND BAPTIST CHURCH
Sunday Service 10am

Despite the heat, Pastor Caleb Merritt was feeling a quiet sense of steadiness as he unlocked the front doors and stepped inside the sanctuary. The building was old - older than most of the people who still worshipped there - but it was loved. He flicked on the ceiling fans, which began their usual slow, determined rotation overhead, stirring warm air rather than cooling it. Dust particles drifted lazily through the long shafts of morning light.

He paused halfway down the centre aisle and looked around. This space - with pews varnished long before he ever set foot in Willowend, hymn numbers carefully arranged on a faded board, the wooden cross fixed firmly to the front wall - was familiar in a way that sank into his bones.

He had preached here for nearly fifteen years, long enough to know where the floorboards creaked, which pew dipped slightly on the far-right side, and how the morning sun always seemed to strike the pulpit with a kind of quiet blessing. And yet today, something felt different. Not wrong, exactly - just weighted.

Caleb placed his worn Bible on the pulpit and exhaled slowly. A letter was tucked inside the front cover, the letter he had read and reread since Wednesday. His eyes had skimmed its words so many times he could almost quote them from memory:

"As part of our ongoing commitment to support local congregations, the State Baptist Association is requesting a preliminary review of Willowend Baptist Church's health and sustainability..."

He closed the Bible gently, as though the act of shutting it might muffle the words inside. A review. Discussions about "future viability." He knew what those phrases often meant for small rural churches. He also knew the Association wasn't the enemy. They cared. They wanted health, strength and gospel presence.

But that didn't make it easier to stand before a congregation of twenty-five faithful people who had poured so much love over so many years into this place and inform them that someone, somewhere, may be doubting their future.

"Good morning."

The soft voice behind him brought warmth into his chest. He turned to see Rachel, his wife of almost forty years, stepping through the open doors. She carried her usual quiet confidence with her - shoulders relaxed, a gentle smile, the kind of solid composure that had steadied him more times than he could count. Her auburn hair, now streaked with grey, was pulled into a simple twist at the back of her head, and her eyes - those thoughtful, steady eyes - took him in with immediate awareness.

"You're here early," Caleb said, reaching to take the folder from her hands.

"So are you." She brushed a bit of lint from his shirt. "You didn't sleep much last night."

He smiled faintly. "You always know."

"Of course I know." She touched his arm. "You're carrying that letter again, aren't you?"

He didn't have to answer. She already saw it in his posture. Rachel moved beside him, gazing around the sanctuary with the same tenderness he felt.

"Whatever happens," she said softly, "none of it changes who God is - or who you are to these people."

Caleb nodded, comforted by the truth of her words. She had stood next to him through storms far fiercer than denominational reviews. Through changes and conflicts.

Through the quiet ache of his melanoma scare six years ago, when the doctor's tone had turned too serious and the world had contracted into a series of hospital rooms and appointments, and through the uncertain months afterwards when every freckle on his body seemed suddenly suspect.

Rachel had prayed him through, stayed up with him through anxious nights, grounded him when fear whispered louder than faith. He had emerged from that season with a thin, pale scar on his shoulder and a deeper one inside – a reminder that life could shift suddenly beneath a person's feet.

Rachel squeezed his hand gently. "I'll be praying while you share it with them."

"I know." He bowed his head briefly. "Thank you."

She smiled. "Always."

The first car pulled into the gravel parking area outside - a dusty white ute belonging to Len Harper, one of the deacons. Not far behind came Bev and Mark Chen, then Mary Kline, her floral dress visible even from the doorway. Within minutes, the trickle of arrivals formed the slow, familiar rhythm of Sunday morning.

Caleb and Rachel stood together greeting the people - shaking hands, exchanging hugs, listening to updates about crops that still hadn't seen enough rain, grandchildren enjoying school, a new calf born breech but surviving. Each conversation reminded him why he loved this place. These people trusted God deeply, even when life gave them precious little to hold onto.

By ten o'clock, twenty-three people filled the sanctuary. Fanning themselves quietly, shifting in their seats, greeting one another with soft familiarity. Caleb stepped to the front, opened his Bible, and smiled at them.

"Good morning, church."

A soft echo came back - "Morning, Pastor."

Whether there were few or many, that same sincere warmth greeted him every single week.

He began the service with prayer, then guided them through a couple of hymns. Rachel's voice, clear and steady, blended beautifully with Mary's alto and Graham White's deep baritone. As they sang *Great is Thy Faithfulness*, something inside Caleb loosened, as though the words themselves stitched hope into a seam that was beginning to fray.

After the announcements and pastoral prayer, he took a breath. Rachel watched him from the third row, very calm, present, supportive. She gave him the smallest nod.

Caleb rested a hand on his Bible. "Before we open the Scriptures this morning, there's something I need to share with you."

The sanctuary hushed in expectation and curiosity.

"This week, the State Baptist Association sent us a letter. It's part of their regular process to support churches across the state, especially those in rural areas like ours." His voice didn't falter, but the weight of the moment began to lean into him. "They've requested that we begin a conversation with them about the health and long-term sustainability of Willowend Baptist."

A stillness settled over the congregation. Mary's lips pressed together; Len shifted heavily in his pew. Bev folded her hands tightly. The younger Patel couple looked uncertain but attentive. Caleb continued, gentle but very honest. "This does not mean decisions have been made. It doesn't mean anyone's closing doors. It's simply a review - a chance to talk, pray, and reflect honestly on where we are and where God may be leading us."

He looked around the room, meeting each gaze. The faces he saw were weary but trusting. Older believers who had poured lifetimes into this place. Farmers whose livelihoods rose and fell with the whims of the rainfall. Families who had stayed faithful through droughts, losses, and changes. People who didn't need flashy programs or polished performance - only the quiet, steady presence of God and one another.

"We've walked through many seasons together," Caleb said. "And God hasn't failed us yet. So, we'll enter this process with open hearts, trusting Him."

Mary nodded firmly. Graham exhaled very slowly. Rachel's eyes shone with encouragement.

Caleb opened his Bible. "Let's turn to the Gospel of John."

The Pastor's voice steadied with the Scriptures, as it always did. He preached with tenderness and conviction, focusing not on scarcity or anxiety but on light - the light that shines in darkness and is never overcome. He spoke of Christ's presence in places that feel small, forgotten, or overlooked. He invited his Church family to trust that God sees what others might dismiss.

People lingered for a time after the benediction, as they always did - chatting quietly, promising to pray, offering small smiles of reassurance. Caleb moved among them, listening, encouraging, staying present. But as the sanctuary emptied, he felt the weight of the letter settle again.

Rachel approached, slipping her hand into his. "You handled that beautifully."

"Do you think so?"

"I know so." She squeezed his fingers. "You were honest, gentle, and full of faith. That's all God asks."

They stood together in the quiet of the sanctuary, the ceiling fans turning their slow circles overhead.

Finally, Rachel said, "Come on. Let's head home before the sun bakes us onto the footpath."

He chuckled softly and followed her out through the doors, locking them behind him, wondering how many more times he would be able to repeat that ritual. The heat outside hit them both immediately. A faint smell of smoke lingered in the air - not from any immediate danger, but the kind that travelled for kilometres during dry summers like this. Caleb glanced toward the horizon where the faintest smudge of haze blurred the sky.

"Fires somewhere," he murmured.

Rachel nodded. "We'll pray for them."

They drove the short distance home along the dirt road that wound past parched paddocks and empty water troughs. A pair of kangaroos lifted their heads as the car passed, then bounded away into brown grass that crackled beneath their feet. Dust trailed behind the tyres like a slow-moving cloud.

Their house - a simple weatherboard structure shaded by an old jacaranda - stood as it always had - solid, welcoming, familiar. Rachel went straight to the kitchen to prepare lunch while Caleb stepped onto the back verandah to inhale a bit of fresher air. Except even here, the scent of distant smoke lingered.

He rubbed absently at the faint scar on his shoulder, hidden beneath his shirt. The melanoma had been caught early - thank the Lord - but the experience had changed him. Some days the memory felt like a shadow. Other days, like a quiet reminder of mercy.

Rachel joined him on the verandah with two glasses of iced water. She handed him one and leaned against the railing, watching the dry paddocks.

"You're thinking," she said gently.

"Always."

"Want to share any of it?"

He hesitated. "I think - I think the letter reminded me of how fragile everything feels sometimes. The church. The town. Our health. Our plans."

Rachel turned toward him, her expression soft. "Maybe fragile things show us where God's strength truly holds."

He smiled faintly. "You always know how to say exactly the right thing."

"No," she said with a small laugh. "I just know you."

They stood together in the stillness, sipping cool water while cicadas buzzed like an unending chorus in the trees. A faint breeze whispered briefly across the yard before vanishing again. Caleb felt Rachel's quiet presence - warm, steady, unwavering.

"We will walk through this," she said. "The Association. The review. Whatever comes."

"Yes," he said, believing her. "We will."

And as they stood there, the afternoon sun dipping slightly, a soft gust of wind carried another breath of smoke across the sky. Caleb watched the horizon thoughtfully.

Something - he wasn't sure what - felt as though it was shifting, preparing, waiting.

Rachel followed his gaze. "It's getting smoky again."

He nodded. "There's a fire somewhere out there. Far off, but..."
"But it only takes a change in the wind," she murmured.

He glanced at her. "Let's pray."

And they did - side by side on the verandah, hands clasped, voices quiet but steady - lifting their town, their people, and the uncertain path ahead to the God who had never left them.

2. SMOKE ON THE HORIZON

The smoke arrived almost unnoticed. Not thick or dramatic, not enough to obscure the sun or alarm the town yet, but a faint, persistent haze that hovered against the horizon like the ghost of some far-off memory. It drifted right across Willowend on the Wednesday morning after Caleb's announcement, carried by winds that were hotter than they should have been this early in summer. Smoke was not uncommon in the region - farm burns, distant lightning strikes, the inevitable dry-season flare-ups - but something about this one felt different to him.

Caleb tried not to read too much into it. He had learned over time, especially after his melanoma scare, to resist the reflex that leapt too quickly from ordinary signs to ominous predictions. Still, as he stepped out of the house that morning, the faint tang of smoke caught in his throat, and a subtle awareness stirred within him. Not fear - never fear - but the quiet alertness of a man accustomed to reading the land and listening for its moods.

He drove into town for errands, his ute rattling its familiar tune along the uneven road. Willowend's main street was still waking up - shop doors propped open, the scent of fresh pastry escaping from the bakery, a red van parked halfway onto the footpath outside the hardware store.

Caleb parked outside the post office and stepped into the cool, shadowed interior, exchanging greetings with the clerk who handed him a small stack of envelopes.

When he stepped back outside, he paused a moment. The haze was still there. To most people it would register as nothing more than summer air. But he had lived in rural Australia long enough to know when smoke was simply drifting - and when it was sending a message.

He tucked the letters under his arm and crossed the road to the servo. He found Amelia Patel outside, wiping down the petrol bowser, her long dark hair pulled into a low ponytail. She looked up immediately.

"Morning, Pastor," she said with a warm smile.

"Morning, Amelia." He glanced toward the horizon. "You see the smoke?"

"I've been watching it since seven," she said. "RFS says there are a couple of spot fires north of the ridge. Nothing to worry about. Yet."

Her emphasis on the last word wasn't lost on Caleb.

"Tough weather for it," he said.

"Tough weather for everything," she replied, wringing out her cloth. "Drought's biting harder this year. Even the birds seem crankier."

He smiled at that. "Any news around town?"

You mean besides everyone asking what's happening at the church?" She raised an eyebrow playfully.

Caleb chuckled. "Word travels quickly."

"Faster than your sermons," she said with a grin.

He laughed. Amelia had a way of levelling tension with humour. Many in town felt intimidated by the idea of church, but Amelia treated Caleb like any other bloke - a man doing his best in a hard season. He found her frankness refreshing.

"We've had a letter from the State Baptist Association," he said. "A review of the church's health. Just conversations. Nothing immediate."

"So not closure, then?"

"No. Absolutely not."

"Good," she said thoughtfully. "Because this place is quieter without your lot singing on Sundays."

Caleb shook his head with a soft chuckle. "Noted."

But then Amelia's tone shifted slightly. She lowered her voice. "You know… I'm not much of a believer. Never really have been. But when I drive past that old church building, it reminds me the town isn't empty. Like… someone still cares enough to keep showing up."

Her words landed with more meaning than she intended, and Caleb felt a warmth deep inside.

"I'm glad it feels that way," he said.

She shrugged lightly. "Anyway, don't let them take it away without a fight."

He nodded. "I don't intend to."

Back in the ute, he drove toward the outskirts of town where the paddocks began. The land crackled beneath the sun, grasses pale and brittle. He turned down the gravel track leading to the White family farm, dust billowing behind him.

He found Graham White leaning against a fence, hat pulled low, eyes narrowed at a dam that looked more like a cracked bowl than a water source. Julie White emerged from the farmhouse and waved, ushering him toward a full jug of iced tea on the verandah.

"Hot one today," Caleb said, taking a seat beneath the shade of a gum tree.

"Hotter tomorrow," Graham muttered. "Then hotter again on the weekend."

Julie placed a cold glass in Caleb's hands. "We're praying for rain, Pastor. But it's been so long since we've seen any real clouds that I've forgotten what they look like."

Graham exhaled deeply, running a calloused hand down his face. "The dam's dropped two more feet. At this rate…" He shook his head. "We might have to sell more cattle. Or worse."

Caleb leaned forward. "You've weathered many seasons like this before."

"Not like this," Graham replied quietly. "Nothing like this."

Julie placed a hand gently over her husband's. "We're just tired, Caleb. Tired of holding everything together on hope alone."

Caleb felt a tug deep in his spirit. Their farm, like so many in the region, wasn't just a business - it was identity, heritage, story.

"Let's pray," he said softly.

They bowed their heads. His prayer was simple, but heartfelt: strength for today, rain where rain was really needed, peace that surpassed understanding, and God's presence in their waiting. When he finished, Graham cleared his throat and just nodded, gratitude hidden beneath his rugged exterior.

After leaving the farm, Caleb drove a short way down the track and stepped out to breathe. The heat radiated off the land in flickering waves. The scent of eucalyptus mingled with the faint smoke carried on the breeze.

He touched his shoulder absently - where his melanoma scar rested. It never hurt, but it held memory. A doorway back to a season that had taught him how fragile life could feel.

Rachel often said scars were reminders, not predictions. He held onto that.

When he returned home later that morning, he found Rachel in the kitchen preparing lunch. Her calm presence wrapped around him like a familiar blanket.

"How were the Whites?" she asked.

"Struggling. Tired. But holding on."

She turned, studying him with compassionate eyes. "And you?" He smiled faintly. "I'm all right."

"You always say that," she said with a gentle, knowing look.

He laughed softly. "I know. And then you remind me it's okay not to be."

She touched his arm. "We'll walk through this season one day at a time. God's already ahead of us."

He felt himself breathe more deeply. "I'm grateful for you."

"And I for you," she said simply.

They ate together at the kitchen table, talking about nothing that urgent - Rachel's new book she was reading, a bird nesting near the verandah, Amelia's latest witty comment. These were the small moments which anchored him.

That afternoon, Caleb went to the church to prepare Sunday's sermon. The sanctuary was cool and dim, ceiling fans humming softly. As he unlocked the front door, he noticed someone sitting on the steps.

"Daniel?" Caleb said gently.

The boy lifted his head, eyes shadowed beneath dark hair.

"Hey," Daniel muttered.

"You alright?"

"Didn't feel like being at home." The words were spoken with a kind of defensive honesty.

"You're welcome to sit here," Caleb said, taking a seat beside him. "As long as you want."

Daniel stared at the dusty ground. "You... you don't try to fix everything, do you?"

"No," Caleb replied. "Some things aren't mine to fix. But I can listen."

A long silence followed, the kind that feels more like connection than absence.

Finally Daniel stood, brushing off his jeans. "See you around, Pastor."

"See you, Daniel."

Caleb watched him walk away, sensing a deeper story beneath the boy's restless exterior.

Inside the sanctuary, he placed his Bible on the pulpit and prayed a quiet prayer for the youth of the town, for the families which were just holding on by a thread, for the church stepping into uncertain conversations, and for whatever the smoke on the horizon might be forewarning.

As he prayed, the late afternoon sun streamed through the high windows, casting long beams of gold across the worn timber floor. A peace settled over him - not the absence of concern, but the grounding presence of God in the midst of it.

He had no way of knowing then how much the town would lean on that presence in the weeks to come.

When evening came, the sky settled into a strange palette of soft gold and faint amber, blurred slightly by the distant smoke that was drifting across the horizon.

Caleb and Rachel stood on their back verandah, glasses of cool water in hand, the huge jacaranda above them whispering with whatever breeze still found its way through the heat.

Rachel rested her head gently against Caleb's shoulder. "I've been thinking about the Whites," she said quietly.

"Me too," he replied. "They're carrying so much."

"Most of this town is," she added. "You carry them too. I see it in you."

He looked at her warmly. "I try. But sometimes it feels like not enough."

She turned to face him. "It has never been about being enough, Caleb. It's about being present. God uses presence far more than perfection."

He breathed in her words like fresh, cool air. Rachel had always possessed the gift of clarity - discernment that spoke straight into the heart of things.

They stood together in silence, as they watched the final threads of daylight curl along the treetops.

"You've been noticing the smoke," she said after a moment.

"Yes."

"Do you think it's a threat?"

"Not yet," he replied, though he felt the unspoken: *but it could be*.

"We'll keep watch."

The cicadas grew much louder as the light faded before them. A kookaburra laughed in the distance, its call echoing across the dry paddocks. The familiarity of the sounds secured him, even as a faint unease still tugged at the edges of his thoughts. Smoke meant fire somewhere. Fire meant families were vulnerable, land was endangered, and lives were uncertain. In a community like Willowend, everything was connected.

"We'll pray tonight," Rachel said.

He nodded. "And every night until the danger passes."

Later, before they went to bed, they prayed together, trusting in the unseen hand that had held them through far darker seasons. Caleb whispered prayers for protection over the town, for the farmers, for the firefighters already working long hours. Rachel prayed for wisdom, for rain, for peace to guard the hearts of people who lived close to the edge of uncertainty.

The next morning brought an air heavier than before. Caleb stepped outside and inhaled deeply. Yes - smoke, stronger now. The sky had the faintest yellow tinge. Not enough to cause alarm, but enough that he knew the RFS would be on high alert.

He drove into town for the day's visits. When he stopped at the servo for fuel, he found Amelia standing outside again, hands on her hips, gazing northward.

"See that?" she said, pointing to a faint plume rising in the distance. "It wasn't there yesterday."

Caleb followed her gaze. "No. It wasn't."

"You reckon it's the same fire?"

"Hard to say."

Amelia wiped her brow. "Feels different this summer. Like everything's brittle enough to snap."

"It does," he agreed.

She turned to him suddenly, a seriousness in her eyes he hadn't seen before. "Do you think God warns people? Before things happen?"

Caleb considered the question very carefully. "Sometimes. Not always dramatically. Sometimes it's just a nudge in the spirit... a sense to be attentive."

Amelia nodded slowly, absorbing this. "I've felt that. A nudge, like you say. Don't know what to make of it."

"You don't have to make anything of it," he said. "Just stay open. God speaks gently."

She smiled faintly at that. "Gentle would be nice for a change."

He left her sweeping the forecourt, her expression thoughtful, as though she were weighing truths she'd never considered before.

From there, Caleb drove out to visit an elderly couple living just south of the town. He checked in on them, made sure they had enough water, took note of the brittle dryness in their paddocks. The heat was pressing down relentlessly. Even the birds seemed quieter, conserving energy.

By the time he returned to the church that afternoon, the air had thickened with the smell of burning eucalyptus. He paused at the front steps, noticing again the quiet stillness of the sanctuary within. He unlocked the door and stepped inside, gratitude washing over him. This space, with its familiar old pews and stained-glass windows, never failed to restore him. He spent time studying, praying and re-shaping Sunday's message.

The theme of refuge kept circling in his mind - God as fortress, God as shelter, God as present help. He didn't yet know how the sermon would land, but he sensed it needed to be spoken.

As he worked, he heard the soft creak of the front door opening. He turned to see Mary Kline, leaning on her walking stick, entering slowly but with purpose.

"Afternoon, Pastor," she said. "I saw your ute out front."

"Good afternoon, Mary. Come in. Have a seat."

She made her way to the pew closest to the front. "I just wanted to talk about the review. About the Association."

Caleb nodded and sat beside her. "What's on your mind?"

Mary sighed, folding her hands over the top of her walking stick. "I've been here since the seventies. Seen this church through storms, floods, droughts. We lost half our roof once. Lost half our congregation twice. But God never let this place go. And He won't start now."

Her conviction moved Caleb.

"I believe that too," he said.

She leaned in slightly. "I wanted you to know… you're the right pastor for us, Caleb. God brought you here for a reason. Don't ever doubt that."

Emotion pricked unexpectedly at the back of his eyes. "Thank you, Mary. That means more than you know."

She tapped his knee affectionately. "We all need encouragement sometimes. Even pastors."

He smiled. "Especially pastors."

When Mary left, Caleb lingered a moment before the cross at the front of the sanctuary. He closed his eyes and breathed deeply. The scent of smoke drifted even here. He prayed silently: *Lord, hold this community together. Let us be a refuge of Your peace.*

That evening, he met with the other deacons - Len and Bev - at the church hall. They sat around the old timber table, papers spread out but largely ignored.

Len rubbed his temples. "I had someone ask me today if the church is shutting down."

Caleb shook his head. "We're not shutting down."

"I told them as much," Len said. "But people worry."

Bev leaned forward, her voice calm. "This is a chance to reflect, to grow, to seek God's direction. Reviews aren't threats - they can be opportunities."

Caleb felt gratitude for her steady perspective. Bev had always been a quiet source of wisdom.

"We'll hold a congregational meeting next week," he said. "Be honest, open, prayerful. Nothing good ever came from panic."

Len huffed a breath that was part laugh, part sigh. "That's the truth."

After the meeting, Caleb walked the short distance home. The sky above was washed in muted amber, the colour of sunset filtered through smoke. As he reached the gate, Rachel stepped outside, sensing him before she saw him.

"You're later than usual," she said.

"Long meeting."

"How are you feeling?"

He considered for a moment. "Carrying many things. But not alone."

Rachel smiled softly and slipped her hand into his. "Let's sit a while."

They walked to the verandah, where the air trembled with heat even after sunset. They sat together without speaking, listening to the cicadas, watching the faint plumes drifting far north of town.

After a long silence, Rachel whispered, "Something is shifting."

"Yes," Caleb replied.

"But God's still here."

"Always."

They rested in that truth, letting it settle in their hearts. Whatever lay ahead - fire, drought, denominational reviews, unexpected change - they would face it together, anchored by faith and by one another.

The smoke on the horizon lingered well into the night, thin yet undeniable, like the first quiet note of a much larger song the land was preparing to sing.

3. QUIET WORK IN DRY SOIL

The following week settled into a rhythm of heat, dust, and quiet concern. Willowend was accustomed to hard summers, but this one carried an edge that people felt even if they didn't speak about it. The smoke on the horizon became part of the landscape - never thick enough to alarm yet never absent long enough to forget. It seeped into conversations, into prayers, and into the subtle way people glanced at the sky whenever a gust of wind changed direction.

Caleb rose early each morning to walk through the sanctuary before the day began. He had done this ritual for many years - unlocking the main doors, turning on the lights, opening the windows, checking hymnbooks, placing his Bible on the pulpit - but lately the act felt more significant, almost protective.

The church felt fragile in a new way. Perhaps it was the letter from the State Baptist Association still folded inside his Bible. Perhaps it was the shrinking weekly attendance. Or perhaps it was something deeper, a sense that the land and its people were entering a season that required a much gentler, more deliberate shepherding.

He spent a good portion of Wednesday visiting homes on the outskirts of town. The petrol in his tank was running low by the time he pulled into the servo mid-morning, and Amelia came out to meet him with a wave.

"You're doing your rounds early today," she said as she replaced the fuel nozzle.

"Trying to catch some of the older folk before the worst heat sets in," he replied.

"Good idea. It's going to be just awful by midday." She glanced toward the distant smoke plume that had grown slightly in height. "Still burning out there. The radio says they are working to contain it, but the wind keeps changing."

"I'll check the RFS page again later," he said.

Amelia nodded, then hesitated.

"I'm not a church person," she added quickly, as if needing to qualify the moment. "But things feel… off lately. Not just the smoke. Everything."

He nodded. "A lot of people are carrying heavy burdens."

She folded her arms. "It's weird. When you're around, it feels less… hopeless."

He was touched by her honesty. "Hope doesn't depend on circumstances," he said gently. "Sometimes it starts with simply knowing we're not alone."

Amelia looked at him as though considering something very important. Then she nodded and stepped back. "Well… your fuel's done. Go on before I say something too sentimental."

He laughed. "I appreciate you, Amelia."

She rolled her eyes but smiled as she headed back inside.

As Caleb drove toward the south end of town, he felt the land's dryness more intensely than ever. Dust billowed behind his ute in long, swirling clouds. The paddocks he passed were more brittle and bare than he remembered, the dams all shallow and cracked around their edges. Even the gum trees looked weary.

He spent the next few hours visiting families who rarely asked for help but who welcomed prayer: an older couple whose son lived far away; a widow whose health had been declining; a young mother doing her best to raise two children while her husband worked long shifts out west. He listened, prayed, lifted groceries from the back of his ute, offered encouragement where it was needed, and simply sat quietly when silence felt holier than words.

These visits reminded him why he still felt called to Willowend. Ministry was rarely glamorous and often unseen, but it mattered deeply. Quiet work in dry soil could still bear fruit.

By early afternoon, the heat had become really punishing. Caleb returned to the church to prepare some notes for the upcoming congregational meeting about the Association review. He sat at the old timber table in the hall, papers spread out in front of him, but his thoughts kept drifting toward the smoke outside.

He finally stood, stretched, and walked into the sanctuary for a moment of prayer. The stillness there had become his refuge. The fans hummed softly overhead. Light streamed through the tall windows in angled shafts that made the air look almost tangible. "Lord," he whispered, "please give us wisdom in this season. Strengthen this little church. Guide us gently."

As he was praying, the front door creaked open and footsteps approached. He turned to see Daniel Reid standing hesitantly inside the doorway.

"Hey," Caleb said, offering a warm smile. "Didn't expect to see you today."

Daniel shrugged, avoiding eye contact. "Mum's working. Dad's away again."

"You're welcome here any time," Caleb said. "Sit if you'd like." Daniel wandered down the aisle and dropped into the nearest pew. His lanky frame slouched forward, elbows on knees, hands tangled together.

"You okay?" Caleb asked.

"Not really," the boy muttered.

Caleb took a seat beside him, leaving enough space not to crowd him. He waited. Silence usually worked better with Daniel than questions. After a short while, Daniel said quietly, "People at school… they don't get it. They think because Dad works away, I'm lucky. Like I don't have anyone breathing down my neck." He shook his head. "They don't know what it's like when no one's around."

Caleb's heart tightened. "That sounds lonely."

Daniel shrugged again, but his voice wavered. "Mum's tired all the time. She doesn't need me being… whatever I am."

"She needs you to be honest," Caleb said. "And she needs you to know you matter."

Daniel sniffed, swiping a sleeve across his eyes. "You don't even know me."

"I'd like to," Caleb replied.

The boy didn't answer, but he didn't leave. That alone felt like a step forward.

They sat together for some time, the sanctuary wrapping them both in its gentle quietness. When Daniel finally stood, he mumbled, "Thanks… I guess." Then he slipped out the door before emotions could escape any further.

Caleb remained seated for a long moment, praying silently for the boy - for direction, for stability, for the sense of being seen.

That evening, all the deacons gathered in the church hall: Len Harper already looking worn from tending his property in the heat; Bev Chen calm and resolute as always; and Mary Kline bright-eyed despite her walking stick and years.

Caleb opened with a simple prayer, then walked them through the Association's initial steps in the review. The deacons listened intently, though the weight of it settled differently on each of them.

Len frowned deeply. "Feels like they're checking whether we're worth keeping open."

"That's not the aim," Bev said. "Reviews help churches see reality clearly. We don't need to fear that."

Mary tapped her stick lightly. "God has kept this church through worse times than this. It's never been about how many sit in the pews."

Caleb nodded. "This process isn't about closing doors. It's about asking the right questions. We'll be honest, we'll be prayerful, and we'll trust God with whatever comes."

They agreed to hold a congregational meeting the following week. Caleb took note of questions the deacons thought might arise, and afterwards, they shared a simple, but special moment of companionship - three faithful people committed to a small church in a forgotten corner of the state.

When the meeting ended, Caleb found Rachel sitting on the front steps of the hall. She stood as he approached.

"How did it go?" she asked.

"As well as it could, I think" he said. "People are worried. But not panicking."

"Good," Rachel said. "Worry we can always work with. Panic just scatters people."

He smiled at her wisdom. "You always know how to interpret things clearly."

"I just listen harder than most," she replied with a small grin.

As they walked home, the air still radiated warmth from the day. They paused at the gate to look at the darkening horizon where a faint orange flicker appeared and disappeared behind the ridge. Rachel slipped her hand into his. "We keep watch. We stay faithful. And we pray."

"Yes," Caleb said softly. "Always."

Thursday brought with it a restless kind of heat, the sort that settled into the earth and refused to lift. By midday the air shimmered above the bitumen on Willowend's main street, and even the tough old gum trees looked more stressed, their leaves now hanging limp and motionless.

Caleb made several shorter visits that morning - checking on a man recovering from surgery, dropping in on a widower who hadn't been eating well, calling briefly on a young couple whose toddler had been very sick.

These small acts of presence, though unremarkable to most people, formed the quiet backbone of his ministry to this special town.

By early afternoon the heat was oppressive, stealing breath and motivation in equal measure. He stopped by the bakery to buy a loaf of bread for a housebound church member, and while he waited, he noticed how many people kept stepping outside to look toward the north. The smoke was more visible now - a faint but distinct plume rising beyond the ridge. No one panicked; this was rural Australia, after all. Fires ignited and burned every year. Still, there was something unusual in how often people glanced skyward, as though they were listening for something they couldn't name.

With bread in hand, Caleb returned to the ute and drove toward the home of Mr. Foster, an elderly man whose eyesight had worsened in recent months. When Caleb arrived, Mr. Foster was sitting on his verandah with a radio playing softly beside him.

"I smelled smoke out there," the concerned old man said as Caleb approached. "Is it close?"

"Not too close," Caleb assured him. "Fires north of the ridge, but the RFS says they're monitoring it."

"Well, that's something, I guess" Mr. Foster replied, though the uncertainty in his voice betrayed lingering worry.

They spoke for a while about the old days, rain cycles, past fire seasons and the ones people still spoke of almost with a tone of reverence. When Caleb prayed with him, Mr. Foster squeezed his hand tightly - grateful, lonely, aware of his frailty in a way that pierced Caleb's heart.

Later, as Caleb drove back toward town, a gust of wind carried the scent of smoke more sharply than before. He slowed the ute, his eyes scanning the distant tree line where the faint plume rose against the washed-out sky.

It was still far enough away not to endanger Willowend, but fire was unpredictable - danger could travel with a single spark riding the wind.

At home, he found Rachel in the kitchen, peeling carrots for dinner. She glanced at him, reading his expression instantly.

"You've smelled it too," she said.

"Yes," he replied, setting the bread on the counter. "It's stronger today."

Rachel nodded calmly. "I saw people talking about it outside the grocer. This town remembers fire seasons. They're cautious, but they're steady."

"They're strong," Caleb agreed. "But quite tired. Everyone feels stretched thin."

Rachel smiled, "This is why God placed you here. Not when everything was comfortable, but when the land and its people are worn. You're a calming presence, Caleb."

He swallowed softly. "I hope so."

"You are," she said without hesitation.

After dinner, the wind seemed to pick up a little, rustling the gum leaves around their home. The air felt charged - not storm-charged, not rain-charged, but something dry and restless.

Caleb stepped outside to bring in the washing, but paused with the basket in hand. Rachel joined him, her gaze fixed in the same direction.

"Look," she murmured.

Beyond the ridge, a faint, flickering glow appeared - small, distant, but visible in the darkening sky.

Flames.

Not towering infernos, not sweeping walls of fire, but a controlled burn gone restless or a lightning strike awakening in the dry brush. Whatever it was, it pulsed like a heartbeat against the horizon.

Caleb exhaled slowly. "It's far enough for now."

"Yes," Rachel said. "But we pray."

They stood outside for a few minutes, listening to the sounds of the land - cicadas, wind brushing dry grass, the distant hum of a lone vehicle on the highway. The glow flickered again, then faded behind the rise.

Inside, after dishes were done, Caleb sat at the dining table with his notes for the upcoming church meeting spread before him. He wanted to prepare the congregation well - to be open about the review but not alarmist. Willowend Baptist had weathered many seasons; he believed it would weather this one too. And yet he felt the responsibility deeply. The church was not just a collection of ministries and Sunday services - it was the spiritual heart of a community that needed stability now more than ever.

As he reviewed the Association's documentation, Rachel came to sit beside him with a cup of tea.

"What's on your mind?" she asked.

He tapped the papers. "I want to explain this clearly on Sunday. I don't want anyone to feel blindsided or anxious."

"You have a gift for clarity," Rachel said. "But even more, you have a gift for peace. Your way of delivering news has always helped people breathe."

He smiled softly. "I suppose that's half the job."

"It's more than half," Rachel replied.

They worked side by side for a little while - Caleb making notes, Rachel reading through a draft he'd prepared. Occasionally she offered a suggestion or offered a reassuring smile when he grew too focused and his thoughts tightened.

She was not just his companion; she was the steadying centre of his life, the quiet voice of discernment that helped him walk confidently when the path grew uncertain.

Later that night, as they lay in bed, the breeze rattled the window frame. Caleb listened to the faint rumble of wind moving over the dry paddocks. Somewhere far away, a dog barked.

The smoke smell was now drifting intermittently through the open window.

"Can't sleep?" Rachel whispered.

"Just thinking about the church," he murmured.

"About Sunday?"

"About everything."

She placed a warm hand on his chest. "You're not carrying it alone."

He closed his eyes, letting her reassurance settle into the spaces where worry had begun to creep. "I know."

"God is with us," she whispered. "And we're with each other."

He smiled into the darkness. "That's enough."

When he finally drifted into sleep, he dreamed of Willowend - of its dusty streets, its ageing church building, its resilient people. He dreamed of the glow on the horizon and the sound of wind stirring dry grass. He dreamed of a town holding its breath, waiting for something to break or shift or renew.

And through it all, he dreamed of Rachel walking beside him, steady and certain, her presence always the quiet assurance that whatever came next, they would meet it together.

The next morning dawned with an intensity that hinted at the coming weeks. The air was already warm by six. Caleb stepped out onto the verandah and saw the smoke standing taller now, a more defined column rising against the sky.

He knew then - without panic, but with a sure certainty - that Willowend's season of testing was approaching. And he also knew, without doubt, that God was already preparing the way.

4. A TOWN ON EDGE

By Sunday morning, Willowend felt different.

Not in dramatic ways - not in evacuations or sirens or flames leaping across the horizon - but in the subtle shifts that only those who lived close to the land would notice. The air hung heavier, the smoke lingered much longer, and conversations carried an undercurrent of watchfulness. Even the birds seemed unsettled, their calls sharper, more frequent, as though they too sensed a change moving quietly through the valley.

Caleb rose before dawn, stepping outside with his first cup of tea. The eastern sky glowed pale pink above the distant ridge, and the smoke was a faint, wavering veil along the horizon. He stood barefoot on the verandah, listening to the faint crackle of dry leaves in the breeze. In another season, he might have found the morning peaceful. But today, that peace was tinged with unease - not fear, but a readiness, an awareness that Willowend was entering a time when attentiveness mattered.

Rachel came out to join him, wrapping a light shawl around her shoulders. "How's the sky looking?"

"Smokier than yesterday," he replied. "But still distant."

She leaned against the verandah rail. "The church will need steady leadership this morning."

He nodded. "And so will I."

She smiled at him, reassuring and certain. "God hasn't brought us this far to abandon us now."

At eight-thirty, they drove into town. The ute rumbled along the well-worn road, dust lifting behind them. As they approached the church, Caleb noticed clusters of people outside - more than usual for that hour. Some leaned against cars; others stood in small circles, all glancing at the haze drifting above the ridge.

A few farmers had arrived early straight from their morning chores, boots still dusty, shirts sweat-marked by work done before sunrise.

He saw Graham and Julie White among them, standing close, their expressions guarded but hopeful when they saw him. Caleb stepped out of the ute and greeted each one with warmth.

"Good morning. Glad to see you all."

Graham nodded. "Bit of smoke up there."

"More than a bit," someone added.

Caleb followed their gaze but kept his tone steady. "The fire's still a long way off. RFS has crews monitoring it. We'll stay watchful, but the situation is under control for now."

People relaxed slightly - only slightly, but enough. Rural folk didn't panic quickly, but reassurance from a trusted voice carried weight.

Inside the sanctuary, the air was very cool, the fans clicking rhythmically. People filed in slowly - more than usual for an ordinary Sunday. Whether they came because of the smoke, the congregation meeting later, or the growing sense that Willowend needed anchoring, Caleb wasn't really sure. But he felt a deep responsibility settle onto his shoulders as he stepped toward the pulpit.

Rachel touched his arm before he walked up the steps. "Speak from peace," she whispered. "Not from pressure."

He nodded, inhaled deeply, and began.

The worship service unfolded gently - familiar hymns, subdued voices, a sense of collective attention. When Caleb stepped up for the message, he felt the weight of the congregation's eyes upon him. These were people who had weathered droughts, floods, crop failures, economic downturns - and now, once again, a season of uncertainty. They didn't need grand speeches; they needed truth spoken quietly but firmly.

He opened to Psalm 46.

"God is our refuge and strength," he read, "an ever-present help in trouble."

He paused before continuing, letting the words settle into the room.

"Therefore," he said, "we will not fear."

The sermon was not very dramatic nor filled with theological intricacy. Instead, it spoke of steady trust, of God's presence in dry seasons, of courage rooted not in outcomes but in deep faithfulness. He spoke gently about the Association's upcoming review - not with anxiety but with transparency.

"This church is not defined by numbers," he said. "It's defined by faithfulness. By the love you have for each another. By the quiet work you do day after day. A review does not threaten that - it simply helps us see where God is leading next."

Heads nodded, and some eyes glistened. When he finished, the congregation sat for a moment in reflective silence. Then they rose together for the final hymn, voices carrying a little stronger than usual.

After the service, people were heavily engaged as conversations buzzed in low, but earnest tones. Caleb moved among them, offering encouragement, listening to their concerns, answering their questions with steady clarity.

Near the back pew, he saw Mary Kline approaching with her walking stick, her expression firm.

"You spoke well, Pastor," she said. "You steadied everyone."

"I'm glad it helped," he replied.

"It did," she said, touching his arm. "You keep your eyes on the Lord. The rest will sort itself out."

He promised he would.

As he made his way outside, the door opened just as Amelia approached the steps. She wore a clean shirt for once, her hair brushed back, and she hesitated when she saw the crowd dispersing.

"Oh. Sorry," she said. "Didn't mean to interrupt."

"Not interruption at all," Caleb said, smiling warmly. "Good to see you."

She didn't step inside, but she stood with him on the steps.

"I... uh..." She looked down at her feet, kicking lightly at the concrete. "I've been thinking a lot about what you said last week, About hope."

He nodded, listening.

"And today - well - I nearly came in." She laughed awkwardly.

"But I'm not quite there yet."

"That's all right," Caleb said gently. "You don't have to rush anything. Just know you're welcome. Anytime."

She nodded, visibly relieved. "Thanks." Then she added, after a pause, "Also... the smoke's thicker near the servo. People are talking."

He looked at her more closely. "Are they worried?"

"Not panicking..." She sighed. "Just very unsettled."

"So are you," he said softly.

She didn't argue.

Caleb promised to check the fire updates again and thanked her for letting him know. As she walked away, he felt the nudge of something significant beginning in her life, a softening, a searching, a tentative reaching toward God.

The congregational meeting began shortly after most people had returned from grabbing a quick morning tea. The sanctuary, though still warm, felt safe - its familiar walls echoing with decades of prayers, laughter, grief, and worship.

Caleb opened with prayer, then laid out the details of the review clearly: timelines, expectations, discussions which would be held, assurances from the Association.

He explained that this was not a judgement but a reflection tool, a chance to discern the future with wisdom.

Hands went up. Questions ranged from practical to emotional - How long will this take? What will they assess? What happens if we don't meet their guidelines?

Caleb addressed each one calmly.

"We will be treated with respect," he assured them. "We are not alone in this. And God's plans for this church are not threatened by process or paperwork."

By the end of the meeting, people seemed steadier. Not carefree, but more grounded. They sensed the leadership was prepared, prayerful, unshaken.

When the final questions were answered, people drifted out slowly, many staying to chat in the shade of the old gum tree beside the church.

Caleb stepped outside last, exhausted but peaceful. The breeze carried the distinct scent of smoke. It was stronger now - no longer a distant suggestion but a more discernible presence threading through the air.

He stood for a moment, letting the reality of it settle. Willowend was entering a new chapter. Rachel walked up beside him, sliding her hand into his.

"Long morning," she said.

"Yes."

"Good morning," she corrected gently.

He smiled. "Yes. Good morning."

They looked together toward the north ridge, where the plume of smoke rose in a thin but unwavering line.

A farmer's ute rumbled past them on the road, heading in that direction.

The land was quiet.

Watchful.

Waiting.

The hours after the congregational meeting moved more slowly than usual, as though the whole town was holding its breath. Caleb and Rachel returned home for a light lunch and a brief rest, but neither of them fully relaxed. Every gust of warm wind carried a reminder of the dry land and the fire smouldering beyond the ridge.

After lunch, Caleb stepped outside again. The sky held a muted, washed-out quality, as though someone had taken a soft charcoal pencil to the horizon. It wasn't oppressive, not yet, but it hinted at something building. He closed his eyes, breathing in deeply. Even the breeze had changed - no longer clean and warm but tinged with that unmistakable smell of burning earth.

Rachel joined Caleb on the verandah and stood there - looking toward the ridge. "You're listening for something," she said.

"Maybe I am."

The land is speaking," she added. "Just quietly."

He nodded. Rachel had always been able to sense the ebb and flow of creation with a clarity he admired. "It feels like we're in a waiting season," he said. "Like something is shifting under the surface."

Rachel rested a hand on his arm. "Whatever happens, God has already prepared the way."

Her insight calmed him more deeply than he expected.

He spent the early afternoon visiting a few more church folk who hadn't made it to the meeting - those who lived further out of town, where properties stretched wide and loneliness pressed closer. One was Mrs. Hartley, an elderly woman whose arthritis made walking difficult.

"Pastor," she said as he stepped inside. "I could hear something on the wind this morning. Like a whisper of trouble."

Caleb smiled kindly. "A whisper isn't a prophecy, Mrs. Hartley. It might just be the land feeling tired."

She reached out and patted his hand. "Even so, you be careful. And tell the town to be careful too."

"I will."

On the edge of town, he stopped by to check on the Reid home. Daniel opened the door only partway, peering out with that familiar guarded look.

"Oh. Hi… Pastor."

"I was in the area," Caleb said gently. "Just wanted to see how you were going."

Daniel shrugged. "Fine."

Caleb gave a soft smile. "That's one of your favourite answers."

Daniel looked at the ground. "Mum's asleep. She works late shift tonight."

"I won't disturb her," Caleb said. "Just checking in."

Daniel hesitated, then stepped outside, closing the door quietly behind him. They stood together on the front step, neither rushing to fill the silence.

"You know," Daniel said eventually, "I never really liked church stuff."

That's all right," Caleb replied. "A lot of people don't at first."

Daniel shifted his weight. "But the other day, when I sat in there… it felt… quiet. Not like the world was judging me."

Caleb nodded. "It's meant to be a place of rest."

"Is it always like that?"

"Only when someone lets their guard down long enough to notice."

Daniel nodded slowly. "Well… thanks."

"For what?" Caleb asked.

"For not... I don't know... pushing too hard."

Caleb smiled warmly. "Daniel, you're welcome at the church anytime. Even if you sit at the back and leave before anyone sees you."

The boy almost smiled. "Maybe."

It was enough.

As evening approached, the temperature dropped only slightly, and the wind picked up again - still dry, still hot. Caleb and Rachel drove back into town for the late afternoon prayer meeting, a weekly rhythm that usually drew a small handful of faithful attendees. Today, however, more people arrived than usual.

Some came because they sensed the town was on edge. Others because they'd been moved by the morning sermon. Still others because smoke in the sky had stirred old memories - of past fires, of nights spent watching for embers, of losses narrowly avoided. Inside the sanctuary, the atmosphere held a soft intensity. People prayed with earnestness, with tenderness, with a sense of communal dependence. Caleb led them gently.

"Lord," he prayed aloud, "we entrust this land to You. You know its needs far better than we do. Please keep safe those who are responding to the fires. Strengthen our community. Give us peace that steadies hearts."

Rachel prayed beside him with her quiet authority. "God, give us eyes to see Your presence even in uncertainty. Let compassion deepen, not fear. Let faith rise, not anxiety. Hold us close as You always have."

Others offered prayers in their own words - simple, heartfelt, sometimes trembling, but sincere. After the gathering, people lingered again. Conversations turned, inevitably, to the smoke.

"It's stronger than yesterday," Bev observed as she joined Caleb near the front steps.

"Yes," he said. "But still not a threat to the town."

"I believe you," she replied. "But we'll stay alert."

Down the street, the fading sunlight cast long shadows across the old buildings. A faint orange flicker appeared again behind the northern ridge, slightly brighter than the night before. Caleb watched it silently.

Bev followed his gaze. "You're thinking about 2005?" she asked quietly.

He exhaled. "I wasn't here then, but I've heard the stories."

"It wasn't like this," she said. "But… it has that feel. The waiting. The uncertainty."

Caleb nodded, grateful for her honesty, even though it pressed gently on his spirit. As dusk settled, he and Rachel walked home through the quiet streets. The air was warm, the cicadas loud, and the smell of smoke unmistakable.

"What are you thinking?" Rachel asked softly.

"That the land is asking for rain," he replied. "And we don't know when it will come."

Rachel squeezed his hand. "We pray. And we prepare."

He looked at her, appreciating her certainty. "You've always had a gift for simplicity in complex seasons."

"I just listen," she said. "To God. To people. To you."

When they reached home, they sat again on the verandah, exactly where they'd begun their morning. The world was dark now, save for the faint glow beyond the ridge - a quiet warning, a distant reminder.

Rachel rested her head against his shoulder. "Do you think the fire will come closer?"

"I don't know," Caleb said honestly. "But if it does, we'll face it with wisdom and courage."

"And together," Rachel added firmly.

"And together."

They sat until the stars emerged - dimmed slightly by smoke but still shining through. Caleb felt the weight of the season pressing upon Willowend: the dryness, the denominational scrutiny, the brewing uncertainty in both land and hearts.

Yet sitting beside his wife, the sky shimmering faintly with starlight, he also felt something else:

A stillness that held him.

A peace that did not depend on circumstances.

A quiet conviction that God was already moving in ways none of them yet understood.

When he finally rose to go inside, he glanced once more at the ridge.

The glow flickered, faint but insistent.

A reminder that seasons of testing do not arrive all at once. They begin with murmurs. With hints. With smoke on the horizon.

And Willowend was listening.

5. EMBERS IN THE MIND

Monday rolled in without ceremony, wrapped in heat and grey-blue sky. The smoke that had hovered on the horizon over the weekend now rested more visibly across the valley, a pale filter over the sun that turned its light a muted, weary gold. The radio spoke of fires in the wider region, controlled burns that had broken their lines, pockets of bush alight far from towns but uncomfortably persistent.

Caleb stood at the kitchen sink after breakfast, looking through the window toward the distant ridge. The plume that had been slender now seemed fatter, less polite. Not urgent, but insistent. He poured the kettle's leftover water into the pot of herbs by the window, then glanced at the calendar pinned beside the fridge. "Three weeks until the first Association visit," he murmured.

Rachel, who was washing the last of the dishes, glanced up. "Is that worrying you more than the fire?"

He considered. "I wouldn't say more. Just differently."

She smiled at the distinction. "The Association comes with forms and questions. Fire comes with wind and embers. God is bigger than both."

"That He is," Caleb said softly.

They finished cleaning up, and he gathered his notebook and Bible for the day. Monday was usually quieter in terms of visits; it was his day to catch up on planning, reading, administration - the unglamorous tasks that kept the machinery of small-church life turning. But lately, nothing felt entirely ordinary. The town was too watchful. The land too tense.

On his way into town, he switched on the radio. A regional news bulletin reported several fires burning in bushland to the north, with crews working long shifts to contain them. No immediate threat to any populated areas yet, but conditions were being monitored hour by hour. He listened carefully, then switched the radio off and let the silence settle.

At the church, the sanctuary welcomed him with its familiar coolness. He opened a window slightly, letting in a thin stream of warmer air and a faint scent of smoke. The pews sat in their usual rows, quiet witnesses to years of worship and worry and joy. He walked slowly between them, praying under his breath - not eloquent prayers, not sermon prayers, but simple phrases of trust and intercession:

"Lord, give us wisdom."

"Hold this community steady."

"Keep our firefighters safe."

"Let Your peace root deeper than fear."

He spent the morning at his small office desk working through the practicalities of the upcoming review. He drafted a summary of the church's ministries - small but sincere: a weekly prayer gathering; occasional food hampers for families in need; pastoral visits; a modest youth gathering that came and went with the school terms; cooperation with other churches in the district for Easter and Christmas events. Nothing flashy, but real.

As he wrote, a thought occurred to him: most of what mattered in Willowend Baptist would never fit into neat categories on a form. The faithfulness of Mary's prayers. The tears he'd seen in Graham's eyes when he prayed over his bone-dry dam. The way Amelia, who wasn't sure she believed at all, brightened when she heard words like hope and refuge. The quiet way Rachel moved among people, speaking encouragement so gently they barely knew they were being strengthened.

He rubbed his shoulder absentmindedly, fingers brushing the spot where his melanoma scar rested. The review forms and the smoke outside triggered similar feelings in him - memories of vulnerability, of being observed and measured, of hearing phrases like "prognosis" and "assessment" and wondering what they might mean for the future.

He placed the pen down and took off his glasses, closing his eyes for a moment. That hospital season had changed him more than he ever spoke of.

He'd learned then that life could narrow in an instant, that plans could dissolve under a single phone call, that the illusion of control was just that - an illusion.

But he had also learned something else: that God did not shrink in those corridors of uncertainty. He expanded.

"Lord," he whispered now, "help me remember that."

By late morning, he decided to walk up the street for some fresh air before lunch. The main road through Willowend hummed with its usual quiet routine. A truck rolled past carrying hay bales; two teenagers sat outside the bakery sharing chips; an older man hosed down the footpath in front of the grocery store, even though the water restrictions technically frowned on such things.

Caleb stopped outside the servo. Amelia was inside restocking a fridge, but she saw him and waved him in.

"Pastor," she greeted him. "You here to check on your unofficial parish?"

"Just stretching my legs," he replied. "How's business?"

"Steady. People might skip holidays, but they can't skip fuel."

She stepped back from the fridge and wiped her hands on a cloth. "Smoke's thicker again, isn't it?"

"It is," he said. "How are you feeling about it?"

She shrugged, but it was half-hearted. "I've seen worse. But I've never liked this feeling - you know, when the sky goes weird and everything is too quiet."

He nodded. "Makes people remember they're not in charge."

"That too," she said dryly. Then she added, after a pause, "I heard you had a meeting about the review."

"We did."

"Are people okay?"

"They're concerned, but hopeful." He smiled faintly. "In their own cautious way."

Amelia leaned on the counter. "I might not go to your church, but I've noticed something. People here talk about it like it's... a kind of anchor. Like even the ones who don't attend think it should stay."

"That's kind of you to say," Caleb replied.

"It's true," she said. "If they disappear you, we'll have less to hang on to."

Caleb absorbed the comment quietly. "The Association isn't here to disappear anyone," he said. "They're here to help us discern the future. Whatever that looks like."

"And what do you think it looks like?" she asked.

He smiled gently. "I think God isn't finished with Willowend."

For some reason, that answer satisfied her. A slow, thoughtful look crossed her face. "Keep an eye on that fire," she said. "The firies were in this morning to fill up. They looked really tired."

"I will," he promised.

He left the servo feeling both heavier and lighter – heavier with the knowledge of the town's underlying anxieties, lighter with the sense that quietly, God was stirring hearts in unexpected places.

On his way back to the church, he noticed Daniel sitting on the low brick wall outside the pharmacy, headphones around his neck. The boy's gaze was distant, fixed on nothing in particular. Caleb approached at an angle that wouldn't startle him.

"Afternoon, Daniel."

The teenager glanced up and gave a small nod. "Hey."

"You all right?"

Daniel shrugged, as he often did. "I came to get something for Mum. She's got headaches again."

"I'm sorry to hear that," Caleb said gently. "How's she coping with the heat?"

"Not great," Daniel replied. "She doesn't say it, but… I can tell." Caleb nodded. "You're attentive. That matters."

Daniel shifted, uncomfortable with the compliment. "People don't usually say that."

"Maybe they should," Caleb answered.

For a moment, the boy's guard slipped. "You think the fire will come here?" he asked.

"I don't know," Caleb said honestly. "Right now, it's still some distance. The RFS is doing good work. But we stay alert."

Daniel looked toward the ridge. "I remember when I was little, Mum taking me outside one night because the sky was orange. She said it was just back-burning, but… it scared me. Fire that big, close to town. Felt like the whole world could go."

Caleb listened. "Memories like that stay with you."

"Do they go away?" Daniel asked.

"Not entirely," Caleb admitted. "But they don't have to control you. Sometimes they can help you be wise and compassionate."

Daniel didn't answer, but his posture softened slightly. Small shifts, Caleb thought. Small, but real.

Back at the church office, he spent the afternoon refining the notes for the review and sketching out ideas for next Sunday's sermon. He felt drawn toward passages about perseverance - about God's people remaining faithful in seasons where nothing seemed to change, where the soil stayed dry and the skies stayed empty. Late in the afternoon, the phone rang. It was Bev.

"Sorry to bother you," she said. "I just spoke to someone on the brigade. They said conditions might deteriorate tomorrow. Nothing official, but… worth knowing."

"Thank you," Caleb replied. "We'll keep praying. And keep watch."

He hung up, then sat for a moment, listening to the quiet hum of the ceiling fan overhead. His mind wandered – unbidden - back to a hospital room six years ago.

The biopsy result had come back positive for melanoma. He remembered the doctor's compassionate yet clinical tone, the explanations about thickness and staging and margins. He remembered seeing Rachel's eyes fill with tears, even as she squeezed his hand and said, "We'll get through this. One day at a time." He then remembered the tightness in his chest as he contemplated endings he had never imagined arriving so soon.

Those months had been full of waiting - waiting for surgery dates, waiting for scan results, waiting through the long stretch of follow-up appointments where each "all clear" felt like a borrowed piece of future.

Now, sitting in his small office in Willowend with smoke on the horizon and a review looming, he recognised a similar pattern: uncertainty, waiting, learning to trust God without knowing the outcome.

He rested his hand again on his shoulder, feeling the faint ridge of scar beneath his shirt.

"Thank You," he whispered, "for bringing me through that. Help me to remember Your faithfulness as we walk through this."

He gathered his things and locked the church for the day. As he stepped outside, the late afternoon sky had taken on a strange shade of light - washed, diffuse, the sun a pale coin behind a veil. Ash hadn't started falling; the fire was still too far for that. But the atmosphere carried a hint of something approaching.

At home, Rachel greeted him with a gentle kiss on the cheek and a knowing glance.

"You've been thinking about the scar again," she said softly.

"Yes," he admitted.

She took his hand and pressed it briefly over his heart instead. "This scar," she said, "is the one that defines you most."

He smiled, touched by her simple wisdom. "How do you always know what to say?"

She shrugged lightly. "The Spirit is kind," she said. "And I've had nearly forty years of practice reading you."

They ate dinner quietly, the clink of cutlery punctuated now and then by the creak of the house in the heat. Later, they carried their cups of tea onto the verandah and watched as darkness folded over the valley.

The glow on the ridge pulsed faintly again, like the slow beating of a heart somewhere beyond sight.

Caleb felt the weight of many things - smoke, review, memories - but he also felt something else: an invitation to trust. To keep walking, step by step, into whatever lay ahead.

Beside him, Rachel leaned against his shoulder. "Embers can be dangerous," she said, looking toward the horizon. "But they can also be the start of something new."

He thought about that for a long time.

Tuesday dawned with a stiffness in the air, the kind that hinted at rising winds and unpredictable shifts in the atmosphere. Caleb stood on the verandah before breakfast, noticing the smell of smoke was no longer something carried on occasional breezes - it rested permanently in the air now, faint but persistent, like a reminder that something unseen was moving closer.

He watched the sky for several quiet minutes before Rachel stepped out, tying her hair back as she walked.

"Sleep any better?" she asked gently.

"A little."

"Your mind is working overtime again."

He gave a small, weary smile. "You know me well."

"I do," she said, sliding an arm around him. "But even your mind needs a Sabbath."

He let her comment sink in and then said, "Feels like the whole town is holding its breath."

"It is," Rachel replied. "But breath held long enough becomes prayer. Willowend is praying, even if it doesn't know it."

The thought settled warmly into him.

After breakfast, he headed into town to check on several families who lived closer to the northern boundary. The road cut through long stretches of dry grass that crunched under the weight of the ute's tyres. The ridge, always a comforting silhouette, now looked mysterious and shadowed behind the haze.

He stopped first at the O'Neil property. Martin O'Neil was outside checking sprinklers, his movements tense, his shirt already damp with sweat despite the early hour.

"Morning, Pastor," Martin called without pausing from his task.

"Morning, Martin. You preparing things?"

"Just making sure the pumps still work. If the fire turns south, we'll need every ounce of pressure this place can give."

Caleb walked closer. "RFS say anything new?"

"No official warnings," Martin replied, tightening a valve. "But unofficially? They're nervous. The fuel load this year is nasty - thick scrub, too much dry growth."

"How's your wife?" Caleb asked.

"Worried," Martin admitted. "But trying not to show it. She's baking scones right now like it's any other Tuesday."

"That's her way of keeping steady."

Martin nodded, his face softening. "Would you pray with us? I know you probably have a dozen other visits."

"I'd be honoured."

They went inside, the air cooler in the kitchen where Mrs O'Neil hovered over a tray fresh from the oven. She welcomed Caleb warmly, though her fingers trembled faintly as she reached for plates.

They prayed - not with dramatic pleas, but with quiet trust: for safety, for strength, for peace, for wisdom in the face of uncertainty. When he finished, Mrs O'Neil dabbed at her eyes.

"You always bring calm," she whispered.

He shook his head gently. "That's not me. That's God doing what He does best."

From there, he visited two more homes before heading back toward town. As he drove, he noticed the plume rising more distinctly now, darkening at its base. An uneasy knot formed in his gut. Fires could be unpredictable; he knew that. Wind was a dangerous companion in seasons like this.

Around midday, he stopped at the servo for fuel and a bottle of water. Amelia was outside again, watching the horizon with her arms folded.

"I thought you'd come by," she said.

"Why's that?"

"Because you're the town barometer," she said with a half-smile. "If you're calm, people stay calm."

"I'm calm," Caleb replied. "Concerned, but calm."

"That's pretty much everyone in town," she said. "The firies came by earlier. They didn't look panicked, but they looked more tired than the last time."

He nodded. "Long days ahead for them."

Amelia hesitated, then spoke in a quieter voice. "Pastor… do you ever worry that God goes quiet? Especially when things get dangerous?"

Caleb studied her face. She wasn't being rhetorical - she was genuinely asking.

"He's never quiet," he said softly. "But sometimes His voice comes through stillness, not noise; through presence, not thunder. You might not hear Him loudly, but you'll sense Him." Amelia exhaled shakily. "I think… I think I need whatever that is."

He placed a gentle hand on her shoulder. "He's closer than you think."

She didn't respond right away, but she didn't brush aside the comment either. A seed had been planted - Caleb felt it.

By mid-afternoon, the heat was intense. Caleb returned to the church to prepare for evening prayer, but as he approached the building, he saw someone sitting on the bottom step.

Daniel.

The boy had his backpack beside him, knees drawn up, head resting on folded arms.

Caleb approached quietly. "Hey, Daniel."

The teenager lifted his head. His eyes were red - not from smoke, but from something deeper.

"Dad rang," Daniel muttered. "Said he might be away longer. Maybe a month."

"I'm sorry," Caleb said, sitting beside him.

"It doesn't matter," Daniel mumbled. "He's always away."

"It still matters. Your heart doesn't get used to absence the way your head pretends it does."

Daniel rubbed his face with both hands. "Mum's stressed. Bills are piling up again. She won't say it, but I see it."

"You're carrying a lot," Caleb said gently.

Daniel's voice broke. "I don't know what to do."

"You start where you are," Caleb replied. "With the strength you have today. And you let others help where they can."

"No one helps," Daniel whispered.

"I'm here," Caleb said. "Not to fix everything - but to walk alongside you."

Perhaps for the first time, Daniel didn't pull away. He leaned his shoulder very slightly against Caleb's, just enough to suggest trust.

They sat together without words for several minutes, the quiet of the sanctuary behind them and the haze of smoke before them.

Before leaving, Daniel said, "Can I… come to the prayer thing tonight? Maybe sit at the back?"

Caleb smiled warmly. "You're welcome anywhere you feel safe."

"I don't want people staring," he muttered.

"They won't," Caleb assured him. "They will just be glad you're there."

Daniel nodded and walked away slowly, shoulders slightly less hunched.

As evening approached, the wind shifted again, carrying a more noticeable layer of smoke across the town. As Caleb and Rachel opened the church doors for the prayer gathering, a few flecks of ash drifted in on the breeze - tiny, harmless, but undeniable.

People arrived with subdued expressions, each aware of the fire, aware of the uncertainty, aware of the collective weight the town carried. And yet, they came. They prayed. They leaned into hope.

Daniel slipped in halfway through and sat quietly near the back, head down but present. Rachel caught Caleb's eye and smiled - a knowing, grateful smile.

Afterward, several people spoke to Caleb about their concerns, but no one panicked. They simply wanted prayer, reassurance, or someone to listen.

Willowend was anxious, but Willowend was also steady. This was a community used to long roads of waiting.

As Caleb stepped outside after the last person had left, he noticed the sky glowing more distinctly now behind the ridge. It was not dangerously bright, but brighter than before.

"You're thinking again," Rachel said softly, joining him.

"Always," he replied.

She touched his arm. "Whatever comes, we walk through it with God. And with these people. And with each other."

He wrapped an arm around her shoulder. "You're my anchor."

"And you're mine."

They stood there together, the warm wind brushing past them, carrying the smell of distant fire and something else - something intangible, something like change.

"Embers are unpredictable," Rachel said quietly. "But God is not."

Caleb closed his eyes, letting the truth of her words settle deep. "Tomorrow might be harder," he murmured.

"Then we meet it with grace," Rachel answered.

The glow on the ridge flickered once more, steady and slow, like a distant pulse.

Willowend felt poised on the edge of something - not disaster, not yet - but a turning point. A moment that would test its heart, its resilience, its faith.

And as Caleb and Rachel slowly walked inside, he whispered a final prayer into the smoky evening air:

"Lord, make us ready."

6. WHEN THE WIND TURNS

By Wednesday morning, Willowend had slipped fully into that strange, suspended state between normal life and alertness. People still went to work, opened shops, tended stock, checked rainwater tanks, packed school lunches, and paid bills - but always with one eye turned toward the north. Conversations at the bakery, the post office, the servo, and even the school gate began with the same question:

"Any updates?"

Caleb woke early again, long before dawn. He hadn't slept poorly - only lightly, as though his mind had chosen to rest in shifts. He stepped onto the verandah with his cup of tea and gazed toward the ridge.

The smoke was a lot heavier today, building in slow, unsettling layers. It didn't obscure the ridge entirely, but it dulled its shape.

The plume rose more vertically now, suggesting activity rather than drift. And although the fire was still miles beyond the ridge, the land itself felt different beneath this kind of sky.

Rachel joined him a few minutes later.

"It thickened overnight," she said.

"Yes."

"The wind hasn't picked up yet," she added, "but it will. You can feel it in the air."

Caleb nodded. He could feel it too. A kind of dryness that hinted at movement. A waiting in the trees. A heaviness in the sky.

They stood in silence for several minutes, letting the morning speak its own language.

After breakfast, Caleb left early to visit Graham and Julie White. Their farm lay closer to the northern boundary than most, and he wanted to see how they were faring. The drive took him past expanses of parched paddock where grass had thinned to the colour of ash.

The land, beautiful even in drought, now seemed to tense its shoulders against the coming heat. When he reached the Whites' property, Graham was already outside near the old water tank, checking hoses and clearing away dry debris.

"You're out early," Caleb called.

"So's the smoke," Graham replied, wiping his brow with a dusty sleeve. "Julie saw the glow before sunrise. She's rattled."

"Understandably."

Graham exhaled deeply, leaning against the tank. "This season has been hard, Pastor. Really hard. The dam is nearly gone. The cattle are thin. And now this." He gestured toward the ridge.

"Feels like we're running out of buffer."

"You're not alone," Caleb said.

"Some days it doesn't feel that way."

Caleb stepped closer. "What can I help with?"

Graham pointed toward the old pump. "Could use an extra pair of hands. You any good with stubborn machinery?"

"No," Caleb admitted. "But I can hold things, fetch tools, and offer moral support."

Graham cracked a smile. "Moral support is really what most machinery needs."

They worked together for nearly an hour, tightening fittings, clearing out leaves, checking pressure. The pump wheezed reluctantly at first, then groaned back to life with a stuttering rumble.

Julie came out with a tray of cold water and biscuits. She looked tired.

"Thank you for coming, Pastor," she said softly. "It's strange - I keep praying for rain, but with the fire out there, I'm almost praying more for calm winds."

"We pray for both," Caleb said. "Rain comes in its season. Protection comes daily."

Julie nodded, though her eyes lingered on the ridge.

Before leaving, Caleb prayed with them again - a prayer for peace, for strength, for protection over their land and livestock, and for hope that didn't rise or fall with the weather.

When he returned to the ute, he paused and looked toward the distant fire line. It was invisible behind the ridge, but the plume told its story. Something was burning with determination.

On his way back into town, he stopped at the servo to refuel. Amelia stepped out as he pulled up, her expression more tense than the day before.

"You've seen it?" she asked immediately.

"Yes."

"The firies were through again just after sunrise," she said. "They didn't say much. Just filled the truck and left in a real hurry."

"That's not unusual," Caleb said gently. "They work very long hours."

"Long hours mean something's not going that smoothly," she replied, her voice low.

He didn't contradict her. "How are you holding up?"

She shrugged. "I told myself last night not to think about it too much. Then I woke up thinking about it anyway."

"That happens," he said. "We're made to care."

Amelia leaned her hands on the counter. "People are starting to worry quietly. Not panicking - but worrying."

"Worry is natural," Caleb said. "Fear doesn't have to be."

She gave him a thoughtful look. "How do you separate them?"

"With prayer," he answered honestly. "And perspective."

Amelia breathed out slowly. "Well… if you see God around the place, tell Him to send some rain."

Caleb smiled. "I'll be sure to pass it on."

As he left the servo, he noticed something he hadn't seen before - a darkening smudge at the far-left edge of the plume. More smoke. Another flare-up, perhaps.

Rachel was waiting for him at home when he returned for lunch, although she rarely came back before midday.

"I thought you'd be out longer," he said.

"I was heading to visit Mary," she replied, "but I felt a nudge to come back first."

"A nudge?"

"You know - the kind the Spirit gives when words haven't formed yet."

He nodded. They'd lived long enough with the Spirit's leading to recognise these moments. "What do you sense?"

"That the day isn't finished with us yet," Rachel said quietly.

"Nor the fire."

He sat beside her at the table. "The wind will turn this afternoon. I could feel it near the Whites' place."

Rachel's reassurance came as always, "Whatever happens, we're walking into it with peace, not panic."

"Agreed."

They ate simply – some cold chicken, salad, bread. But every few minutes, one of them glanced toward the window. The smoke thickened perceptibly after lunch. By early afternoon, sunlight took on a copper shade, and the air smelled less like distant burning and more like burning nearby. Still not threatening - not yet - but close enough that Caleb found himself stepping outside repeatedly, scanning the horizon, reading the land with pastoral instinct and a growing rural familiarity.

He visited the church briefly and noticed the sanctuary felt unusually still. Even the air inside carried the faintest trace of smoke. He opened a window, then closed it again after only a moment.

Something tugged inside him - not fear, but anticipation.

Just after three o'clock, as he was leaving the church office, Daniel appeared at the doorway again, out of breath as though he'd walked quickly.

"Pastor," he said, "Mum asked if you could come by. She's not feeling great."

"Of course," Caleb replied immediately. "Is she all right?"

"Just overwhelmed," Daniel said, rubbing the back of his neck. "And... the smoke doesn't help."

They drove together to the Reid home. Daniel led him inside quietly, where Mrs Reid sat at the kitchen table with a damp cloth pressed to her forehead.

"Pastor, I'm sorry," she said weakly. "I didn't want to bother you."

"You're never a bother," Caleb said, kneeling beside her. "Tell me what's happening."

"Headache," she murmured. "And everything feels... heavy." Caleb spoke gently. "You've been carrying a lot for a long time." She nodded, tears threatening. "I try not to worry Daniel ..."

"You're not alone," Caleb assured her. "Let's pray."

He prayed softly, compassionately, asking for relief, for calm, for strength, for breath in her spirit that didn't feel weighed down by circumstance. When he finished, she exhaled slowly, almost in release.

"Thank you," she whispered.

Daniel hovered awkwardly in the doorway, but there was real gratitude in his eyes.

After ensuring Mrs Reid was comfortable, Caleb walked outside with Daniel.

"You did the right thing calling me," Caleb said.

Daniel shrugged. "I just… didn't know who else to ask."

"You asked the right person," Caleb said gently.

For a moment, Daniel looked away toward the ridge. "It looks worse today."

"It does," Caleb said honestly. "But we keep steady. One day at a time."

Daniel nodded, though his expression remained troubled.

When Caleb returned home just after four, the wind had begun to shift - a subtle but unmistakable change. Leaves on the gum trees whispered with a new urgency. The ridge looked blurred behind a growing curtain of smoke. Light took on a deeper, more uneasy shade.

Rachel was on the verandah, watching the horizon calmly.

"It's turning," she said.

"Yes," Caleb replied, standing beside her.

They watched together as the wind pushed the plume sideways, spreading it wider across the valley.

"It's not threatening the town yet," he said. "But conditions are changing."

Rachel nodded quietly. "And when the land shifts, the soul often does too."

He turned to her. "What do you sense coming?"

She exhaled softly. "Not fear. Not disaster. But a moment. A moment where everything comes into sharper focus."

For several long minutes they stood in silence, the wind rustling, the smoke drifting, the land speaking in ways only those who loved it could hear.

The fire had not arrived.

But the wind had turned.

And that meant everything that followed would begin to unfold differently.

By late that afternoon, Willowend had shifted from unease to vigilance. Not panic - not even close - but the quiet, practical alertness of a town that understood fire seasons and respected the land's unpredictable moods.

Caleb and Rachel sat on their verandah for just a while longer, watching the plume grow darker at its base. The shifting wind carried the scent of burning eucalyptus straight through the valley now. They spoke little; presence was enough.

Just after five o'clock, Caleb's phone buzzed with a message from Len Harper: RFS update meeting at 6pm in the hall. Thought you'd want to know.

He showed the message to Rachel.

"We should go," she said.

"We will," Caleb replied. "It'll help people feel grounded."

They ate a quick dinner - soup and bread, the simplest meal they'd prepared in weeks - then walked hand-in-hand toward town. The air felt charged, the wind steady but restless. As they approached the church hall, they saw a small but growing cluster of townsfolk gathered outside. Some wore work boots and broad-brim hats; others still had aprons from the bakery or dust from the stockyard on their clothes. A fire truck was parked off to the side, its engine cooled but ready.

Inside the hall, two RFS volunteers stood near a whiteboard - one middle-aged with sunburnt cheeks and a clipped manner of speaking, the other younger but sharp-eyed, clearly absorbing everything from his senior.

The older volunteer nodded at Caleb as he entered. "Pastor. Good to see you."

"Good to see you too, Murray," Caleb replied.

Murray cleared his throat and began, his voice firm but calm. "Right. Here's the situation. The fire's still on the far side of the ridge, around fifteen kilometres from the town boundary. It's classified as 'being controlled,' but we've had several flare-ups today, and the wind's not doing us any favours."

A few murmurs rippled through the room.

Murray continued, pointing to a map. "There's no immediate threat to Willowend. I want to be clear about that. But conditions are unpredictable. We need people to be aware, keep properties clear, know their plans, and listen for updates. If anything changes, we'll get the word out fast."

People nodded - some gravely, some with forced confidence. Caleb watched the room. Anxiety, yes. But not fear. These were people shaped by seasons, by resilience, but also by God's quiet sustaining grace.

After the briefing, a few approached the RFS volunteers with specific questions - livestock evacuation routes, water access points, the placement of fire breaks. Caleb moved among the group, offering quiet encouragement where needed.

He found Mary Kline seated alone at a table, gripping her walking stick tightly.

"You all right, Mary?" he asked, sitting beside her.

She nodded, but her voice shook slightly. "I'm not afraid, Pastor. But I feel... unsettled."

"That's human," Caleb said. "Even faithful people feel the tension of uncertain days."

Mary leaned back. "I was here during the fires in '91. The sky went black. People prayed like I've never heard before."

"And God carried you through," Caleb reminded her.

Mary patted his hand. "And He'll carry us through this too. But I wanted to see your face tonight - to be reminded."

Caleb smiled gently. "Then I'm glad we're here together."

On the other side of the room, Daniel had slipped in quietly, sitting near the wall with his backpack at his feet. Caleb saw him and gave a small nod. Daniel offered a timid one in return. Slowly, deliberately, the boy was stepping toward trust.

When the meeting wound down, Caleb and Rachel walked home in the deepening dusk. The sky was smoky, the stars weaker but still present. The ridge glowed faintly - not bright, not alarming, but alive.

Rachel laced her fingers through Caleb's. "How are you feeling now?"

"Grounded," he said. "Concerned … but grounded."

"Concern is responsible," she replied. "Fear is not."

They walked in silence for a while before Rachel said, "You know… this fire season is waking something in people. I can feel it. They're more tender. More open. Even Amelia."

Caleb smiled softly. "She's surprising me."

"She's searching," Rachel said. "Quietly. Carefully. But she's searching."

He nodded. "I felt that too."

"And Daniel," she added. "His heart is bruised, but softening."

"There's a lot happening beneath the surface," Caleb said.

They reached their gate just as another gust of wind carried ash across the yard - only a few specks, harmless, but unmistakable. Caleb brushed one from his sleeve.

"The fire's still far," Rachel said calmly. "But it's speaking."

"Yes," Caleb replied. "And the town is listening."

Inside, they settled briefly before bed, but the evening felt too alive to retire early. Caleb walked through the house turning off lights, pausing at each window to look out toward the ridge.

He wasn't looking for danger - he was listening for God.

Rachel found him standing at the back door, gazing into the night.

"What do you hear?" she asked softly.

"Not fear," he said. "Just… expectancy."

Rachel nodded, stepping up beside him. "Then let's sit with it. Not run from it."

They moved to the verandah again, wrapped in the warm, smoky air. Willowend lay quiet, but not asleep. A dog barked once in the distance. A motorbike rumbled faintly somewhere on the highway. A single bird called out, unsettled by the wind's shifting voice.

Caleb and Rachel sat close, letting silence do its work. The glow beyond the ridge pulsed faintly again, steady and slow.

After a long minute, Rachel spoke.

"Do you remember the year after your surgery?" she asked.

He turned to her. "I do."

"Everything felt uncertain," she continued. "Like the future was foggy, undecided. But you said something then that I've never forgotten."

"What was that?"

"You said, 'God does His best work in me when I'm walking through a season I didn't choose.'"

He exhaled. "I did say that."

Rachel smiled gently. "And it's still true."

He leaned his head back against the post behind him. "Maybe Willowend is walking through a season it didn't choose."

"But God is doing His best work," she said.

He thought about the Whites, holding on through drought.

About Daniel, finally letting someone see his worries.

About Amelia, drawn toward God by questions she couldn't name.

About the congregation, standing steady in the face of a review and a fire.

About himself - remembering past valleys and finding faith renewed.

"Maybe He is," Caleb whispered.

The wind shifted again, rustling through the trees in a way that made the whole night feel alive. Not dangerous. Not yet. But alive in a way that pulled every sense toward attention.

Rachel placed her hand over his. "Whatever unfolds next - we're ready."

He squeezed her hand gently. "Yes. We are."

They sat until the first hints of cooler air brushed against their skin. The glow dimmed again behind the ridge. And though the fire still burned somewhere beyond sight, peace settled over their verandah like a quiet benediction.

The wind had turned.

But so had the town's heart.

7. ASH ON THE DOORSTEP

Thursday morning greeted Willowend with a sky the colour of tarnished metal.

The sun rose as it always did, but its light was dulled and diffuse, a pale disc behind a veil of smoke that now settled low across the valley. The hills were still visible, but only faintly, their outlines softened as though sketched in charcoal and then smudged. The air smelled distinctly of burning eucalyptus, and even inside the house, Caleb and Rachel could taste it.

Caleb stood at the kitchen window, mug in hand, watching a few ash flecks drift lazily past the glass. They were small, grey, seemingly harmless. But he knew what they meant.

"Embers," he murmured.

Rachel, buttering some toast at the bench, glanced up. "Started already?"

"A few specks," he said. "Nothing more. But they've crossed the ridge."

She set down the knife and joined him at the window. Together they watched in silence as another tiny fragment of ash floated past, turning slowly in the uncertain light.

"Still a long way off," Caleb said after a moment. "But today will matter."

"Yes," Rachel replied. Her voice was calm, but her eyes were alert. "The town will feel this."

They ate breakfast quietly, the small sounds of spoons and plates amplified against the backdrop of soft, smoky stillness. The routine helped - toast, fruit, tea, Rachel's gentle humming - but underneath it all, both of them felt the day's weight.

"What's on your list this morning?" she asked.

"Check on a few of the older folk," he said. "Drop in on the Patels. Call Graham. And stop by the church. I'd like to keep it open today, just in case people need somewhere to come and sit."

"Good," Rachel said. "People will need places that feel safe."

"And you?" he asked.

"I'll visit Mary," she replied. "She'll be praying, but she'll also be remembering. I want her to have company in both."

Caleb smiled, warmed by her insight. "She'll be grateful."

Outside, the air felt heavier than the days before. The smoke didn't sting his eyes yet, but it coated every breath with a faint bitterness. As he walked to the ute, he noticed a single, fragile strip of ash resting on the bonnet. It disintegrated under his fingertips.

The fire was still far enough away not to threaten homes, but it was near enough now to send its messengers.

He drove first to the outer edges of town, checking on those most isolated. At the Hartley place, Mrs Hartley met him at the door clutching her Bible to her chest.

"I heard embers on the roof earlier," she said, wide-eyed. "Just little ones. Nothing stayed. But I heard them."

"That's why the RFS has their patrols out," Caleb reassured her. "They're watching the ridges and the roads closely. You're not forgotten."

"I am not afraid," she said, though the tremor in her voice suggested otherwise. "But I don't like being alone when the sky looks like that."

"That's why I'm here," Caleb said gently.

He sat with her for half an hour, listening to stories from past summers, from fires that had never quite reached the town but had branded themselves into people's memories. When he prayed, he asked not only for physical protection, but for peace that could sit beside old fears without letting them take over.

From there, he drove to the edge of the industrial area - a grand term for just a cluster of sheds and workshops.

The mechanic waved, the panel-beater lifted his chin in greeting, and someone outside the storage yard called out, "Keep praying, Pastor!" He raised a hand in response.

At the servo, Amelia was already outside, sweeping stray ash from the concrete.

"Got yourself a new job?" Caleb asked as he stepped out.

"Apparently." She flicked another fleck of ash from her sleeve.

"If I keep sweeping it away, maybe the fire will take the hint and stay where it is."

He gave a small smile. "I don't think it works quite like that."

"Worth a try," she said. Her humour was still there, but her eyes were serious. "They're telling us on the radio the fire's still classified as being controlled. But this wind…" She shook her head. "It's the wrong kind."

"It's not ideal," he agreed. "But the crews know what they're doing."

Amelia stopped sweeping and turned to face him fully. "You keeping the church open today?"

"Yes," he said. "Door will be unlocked. Anyone who wants to sit, pray, or just breathe in a different space is welcome."

"Good," she replied. "I'm not saying I'll come. But it's good to know."

He met her gaze gently. "You are welcome anytime, Amelia. Whether you sit at the front or the very back. Or just stand at the door."

She looked away, swallowing. "If I came… I wouldn't know what to say to God."

"He already knows," Caleb said. "Sometimes turning up is the prayer."

Her eyes glistened unexpectedly, and she quickly turned back to her broom. "I'll … keep that in mind."

He left the servo with a quiet sense that something deeper had shifted in her - not dramatically, not theatrically, but like a door being left on the latch rather than bolted shut.

Next, he called Graham. The farmer's voice sounded strained but steady.

"We had a few embers on the back paddock," Graham reported.

"Nothing caught, thanks be to God. But I've got sprinklers going and hoses out. We're ready as we can be."

"Do you need help?" Caleb asked.

"No," Graham replied. "Just prayer."

"You have plenty of that," Caleb assured him. "I'll check in again this afternoon."

At the church, the sanctuary felt different again. Smoke had seeped further into its quiet air, and the light coming through the windows was dimmer, softer. Caleb opened the front doors wide and set a small table just inside with a jug of water, some glasses, and a few simple printed prayers for people who might struggle to find words.

He knelt briefly at the front, resting his hand on the pulpit.

"Lord, let this place bring peace today," he whispered. "Not because the world is safe, but because You are near."

People began to drift in gradually. Mary arrived mid-morning, leaning heavily on her walking stick.

"The sky reminds me of '91," she said. "But my heart doesn't feel the same. I'm less... frantic. More rooted."

"Age brings perspective," Caleb said kindly.

"Faith brings perspective," she corrected with a small smile.

She took a seat halfway down the aisle and bowed her head, her lips moving silently. A young mother came next with a toddler on her hip, both of them restless from being cooped up at home.

She didn't speak much - just sat near the back, letting the boy clamber over the pew beside her while she stared ahead, eyes darting now and then toward the windows.

Around lunchtime, to Caleb's quiet surprise, Amelia appeared at the door.

She didn't come all the way in - not at first. She hovered in the doorway, hand resting on the frame, eyes scanning the room as though expecting judgment or spectacle. She found neither.

Caleb walked toward her slowly. "Good to see you."

"I was on my break," she said, looking awkward. "Thought I'd… check if you needed anything."

"We're fine," he said. "But you're welcome to sit."

She hesitated, then stepped inside and chose a pew near the back, just as he'd said she could. She didn't kneel or fold her hands; she just sat, staring at the cross on the front wall with an expression that was half wary and half searching.

Caleb returned to the front and stayed quiet. The sanctuary didn't need filling with words. The Spirit was already busy in the silence.

Later in the afternoon, Daniel slipped in, shoulders hunched, cap pulled low. He gave a tiny nod to Caleb and slid into a pew not far from Amelia, though they barely acknowledged each other. Two different lives, two different sets of burdens, drawn into the same space by the same smoky sky.

Time moved gently in the sanctuary. People came and went. Some prayed. Some cried quietly. Some simply sat, breathing slowly, letting peace work its way back beneath their ribs.

Throughout it all, Caleb moved quietly - refilling the water jug, checking on people with a word or a glance, praying in his own heart for each face he saw. He didn't make speeches. He didn't force conversations. He simply stayed present. By late afternoon, he stepped outside for a moment to stretch his legs.

As he did, a gust of wind blew a small cluster of ash onto the church steps, scattering grey fragments over the old timber boards. He bent down and brushed them aside gently.

Ash on the doorstep. Not danger in itself, not yet, but a reminder that whatever was happening beyond the ridge was no longer entirely distant.

Rachel arrived not long after, having spent the day with Mary and then visiting a few others on the congregation's fringe.

"The town is tired," she told him quietly.

"I know," he replied.

"But also softer," she added. "Like soil after it's been broken up. It hurts, but it's ready for something new to grow."

He looked at her, absorbing the phrase. Ready for something new to grow.

They stood together in the doorway, watching as a few last people came to sit in the sanctuary's fading light.

The fire had not reached them.

The Association had not yet arrived.

But ash now lay on the doorstep, and Caleb sensed that in ways only God could fully see, Willowend's inner landscape was already beginning to change.

The late afternoon light dimmed as smoke thickened in the sky, and by the time Caleb closed the sanctuary doors for a brief moment of quiet, the interior had taken on a muted, amber tint. The air was still breathable, but heavy - the kind of heaviness that made people speak softly, as though raising their voice might disturb something delicate in the air.

Caleb walked slowly down the centre aisle, pausing beside each pew as though checking on an old friend. Today had been different from any day since he'd arrived in Willowend. People had come not out of routine or obligation, but out of longing - for steadiness, for refuge, for a sense of God's nearness when the land felt unsettled.

He reached the front of the sanctuary and rested his hand on the pulpit again.

"Lord," he whispered, "thank You for drawing people here. Keep doing what only You can do."

Outside, a car pulled up, and moments later, Rachel stepped inside, brushing a thin dust of ash from her jacket. She found him at the front and offered a gentle smile.

"You've had a steady stream today," she said.

"More than I expected," he replied. "People came quietly, but they came."

"Well," Rachel said, slipping her arm through his, "smoke has a way of making souls reflective."

They walked slowly toward the back of the church. Amelia was still sitting in the same pew near the rear, her hands clasped together loosely, her gaze outward but unfocused. She looked up when she sensed them.

"Oh - I should get back," she said quickly, standing as though caught somewhere she didn't belong.

"You can stay as long as you like," Caleb said gently.

She hesitated. "I… didn't really do anything. I just sat."

"Sometimes sitting is the bravest thing a person does," Rachel said, her tone warm.

Amelia's eyes softened, and she exhaled a breath she seemed to have been holding all afternoon. "It felt… quieter here," she said.

"Even though the world outside doesn't."

"That quiet comes from God," Caleb said. "Not from the walls." She nodded, her expression troubled but thoughtful. "I'll… maybe come back tomorrow, if that's all right."

"It's more than all right," Rachel said.

Amelia gave a faint smile and slipped out quietly, brushing ash from her sleeves as she stepped into the smoky air.

As she left, Daniel looked up from where he'd been sitting across the aisle. He hadn't moved for nearly an hour, his posture drooping with the weight of thoughts he didn't know how to handle.

Caleb walked toward him. "Do you need a lift home?"

Daniel shook his head. "Mum's picking me up later. She said she might come too."

Caleb felt a warm swell in his chest. "Tell her she's welcome."

Daniel swallowed. "Pastor… do you think God listens even if you don't know what to say?"

"Yes," Caleb said without hesitation. "He listens to silence. To sighs. To tears. To whatever honesty we bring."

Daniel bit his lip. "I tried praying. It felt… weird."

"That means you were doing it right," Caleb said with a small smile.

The boy's shoulders eased a fraction. "Thanks."

Rachel approached him as well, speaking to him with a kindness that felt like cool water. "Daniel, you can always sit here, even if we're not around. The church will stay open."

Daniel nodded and looked away quickly, not out of dismissal but out of emotions he wasn't used to managing.

When he finally stood and slung his backpack over one shoulder, he gave Caleb a quiet nod before leaving. The gesture held more trust than words could have offered.

As the last footsteps faded, Caleb turned to Rachel. "Something's happening."

"In the town?" she asked.

"In them," he clarified. "In their hearts."

Rachel studied him. "Then the fire isn't just in the bush."

He considered that. "You think God might be stirring something deeper?"

"Yes," she said with certainty. "Smoke brings people inward. Fire draws them to reflection. And ash on the doorstep reminds them how small they are."

"And how much they need Him," Caleb finished.

They stepped outside together into the cooling evening. The air was thicker than it had been that morning; even the gum trees appeared hazed by drifting smoke. A few neighbours were outside sweeping ash from verandahs or checking their gutters, quietly talking across fences.

At the end of the street, someone was hosing down their roof.

"People are preparing," Rachel said softly.

"It's wise."

He brushed more ash from the step with the side of his shoe. "Even small things help people feel less helpless."

Rachel looked toward the ridge. "The glow is stronger."

He followed her gaze. The faint orange pulse was indeed more pronounced - not dangerously bright, but steady, insistent, like a beacon meant to be noticed.

They walked home slowly, their steps easy even if their thoughts were not. The streets of Willowend were quiet, but not empty. The town felt alive in a subdued, contemplative way - as though everyone had become aware of unseen layers of their own lives. Fire seasons did that.

When they arrived home, the scent of smoke filled their yard. Caleb checked gutters and downpipes, not out of panic but responsibility. Rachel wetted the garden beds nearest the house. They worked together smoothly, comfortably, as they had in so many seasons before.

"This reminds me of the storm season six years ago," Rachel said as she coiled the hose. "When you were still recovering from surgery."

Caleb chuckled softly. "I remember. You were climbing ladders faster than I could supervise."

"You were banned from ladders at the time, remember." She tapped his shoulder lightly. "Doctor's orders."

"And your orders," he said, with a cheeky smile.

They returned to the verandah as dusk settled into night, the horizon glowing faintly like a coal cupped in the hand of the hills.

"Do you ever wonder why God lets people walk so close to danger sometimes?" Caleb asked quietly.

Rachel thought for a long moment. "I used to. But not so much anymore."

"Why?"

She leaned her head on his shoulder. "Because I realised the point isn't the danger. It's the closeness. When valleys deepen, God draws closer. He doesn't promise skies without smoke - He promises presence within it."

He breathed that in, letting it settle. "And He always keeps His promises."

"Yes," she said. "Always."

They sat until well after dark, the breeze whispering through the gum leaves, the valley holding its breath, the glow flickering like a heartbeat beyond the ridge.

Finally, Caleb stood. "Tomorrow might be harder."

Rachel rose with him. "Then tomorrow, God will be nearer still."

They went inside together, closing the door gently against the smoky air, leaving the ash on the doorstep - both as a warning of what lay beyond the ridge, and as a quiet sign of how deeply Willowend was being stirred.

Not just by fire.

But by God.

8. THE FIRST NIGHT WATCH

Thursday night passed uneasily for Willowend.

Some slept, but lightly. Some lay awake listening to the rustle of dry leaves, the shift of the wind, the soft crackle of ash drifting against windowsills. Others kept radios on low volume beside their beds, tuned to emergency frequencies though no alert had been issued. The fire remained distant – just a restless presence beyond the ridge - but the wind was unpredictable, and the land knew how quickly "distant" could change.

Caleb didn't sleep fully. He drifted in and out, waking each time the wind rattled the edge of the guttering. Beside him, Rachel lay still, not restless exactly, but attentive even in her rest. Just before dawn, she turned slightly and whispered, "It's stronger."

He sat up. "The smoke?"

"The feeling," she murmured, then opened her eyes. "But also the smoke."

Caleb rose quietly, put on his dressing gown, and stepped onto the verandah with bare feet. The sky was still dark, but the horizon glowed faintly with a murky, diffused light - the kind of light created not by sunrise but by smoke reflecting the first hints of dawn.

The smell was unmistakable. Stronger than yesterday. A steady reminder of what lay beyond the hills.

He remained outside for several minutes before Rachel joined him, wrapping a shawl around her shoulders.

"Did you hear anything overnight?" she asked.

"No," he said. "Just the wind shifting. And the occasional leaf skipping across the verandah."

They stood together watching the horizon. It wasn't fear that stirred in Caleb, but a quiet, alert compassion - the kind that made shepherds keep watch through long nights, even when danger was still far away.

"We'll check in on people early today," Rachel said. "Before the heat rises."

"Yes," Caleb replied. "Today will be a long day for Willowend."

They shared a brief prayer, simple and steady, like breathing: "Lord, guide us. Guide the firefighters. Hold this town in Your hands."

By the time they finished breakfast, the sky had grown a pale, troubled amber. The smoke wasn't choking, but it was thick enough to shift the colour of light inside the house. When Caleb drove toward town, ash flicked against the windscreen like errant snowflakes.

At the servo, Amelia had the doors propped open, sweeping again though it hardly seemed to help.

"You back already?" she called as Caleb stepped out of the ute.

"Thought I'd check in."

"Well," she said, gesturing grandly at the air, "the sky's decided to give us a theme today."

He gave a small smile. "How are people feeling?"

"Like they're waiting for someone to announce something," she replied. "Even if they don't know what."

"Waiting can be its own burden."

Amelia shrugged. "Better than panic. But still not great for business. People keep popping in just to stand under the air-conditioning for a minute and sigh."

Caleb chuckled softly. "We all cope in different ways."

She lowered her voice. "Is the church open again today?"

"Yes. It will be, all day."

She nodded, swallowed, then said quietly, "I might duck in later."

"You'd be welcome."

Before he could leave, an elderly farmer approached the servo, brushing ash from his hat brim. "Pastor," he said, tipping his head. "Looks like a day to stay close to home."

Caleb agreed. "Keep hydrated. And call if you need anything." The man nodded, his weathered face tight with the memory of summers long past.

As Caleb drove through town, he felt the shift more keenly. People were not fearful, but they were introspective. Families stood on verandahs watching the hills. A group of teenagers sat outside the bakery in silence - not scrolling through their phones, but simply staring at the sky. A dog barked intermittently at nothing visible.

He stopped first at Mary Kline's home. She was already on her porch, Bible open on her lap.

"I knew you'd come," she said.

"How are you this morning?"

"Steady," she replied. "The world doesn't feel steady, but God does."

He sat beside her for a few minutes, listening to her reflections. She wasn't anxious, but she remembered seasons where fire had tested the town's resilience. After a short prayer together, he moved on.

Next, he visited the Patels at the general store. Mrs Patel looked weary but calm.

"People buy little things," she said, "tea, batteries, snacks. As if they need to do something with their hands."

Her husband added, "And they look for reassurance, Pastor. Even if they don't say it."

He chatted with them for several minutes, prayed briefly, then continued.

By mid-morning, the smoke thickened again. The sun was a strange, pale disc, visible through the haze like a lantern behind frosted glass.

The wind came in intermittent bursts - not strong, but shifting. A few leaves spiralled awkwardly across the road.

At the church, he found that Rachel had already unlocked the doors. A soft light glowed inside. Two or three people were seated in quiet reflection, their silhouettes still against the pews. Caleb whispered a greeting to Rachel as she handed him a jug of fresh water.

"No one wants to be alone today," she murmured.

"No," he agreed. "Nor should they."

Together they tended the sanctuary - refilling water, adjusting fans, offering gentle conversation to those who needed it while leaving space for those who preferred silence.

Shortly after midday, a sudden gust rattled the windows and sent a flurry of ash tumbling through the open doors. Caleb stepped outside to sweep the steps again.

That was when he saw Graham and Julie driving slowly toward the church, their ute covered in dust and their faces drawn.

He walked to meet them.

"Everything all right?" he asked.

Graham shook his head. "We lost the back paddock for an hour this morning - embers landed in the dead grass. Thank God Julie saw it early. We got it out, but Pastor… it happened fast."

Julie's voice trembled. "We thought we'd lose the shed."

"You didn't," Caleb said gently. "You acted quickly. And you're safe."

"But it shook us," Graham admitted. "We needed to come somewhere that didn't feel… on edge."

"Then you've come to the right place," Caleb said.

They entered the sanctuary, and Caleb watched as they sank into a pew. Julie bowed her head immediately; Graham rested his hands on his knees, breathing deeply.

Just then, Daniel slipped in through the side door, looking agitated. He hesitated when he saw the Whites but walked to Caleb.

"Hey," Caleb said softly. "What's the matter?"

Daniel swallowed. "Mum's at work. She rang me and said the smoke's making her chest tight. She told me to stay inside, but... I didn't want to be at home alone."

"You can stay here as long as you need," Caleb said.

Daniel nodded, then sat near the back, hugging his backpack to his chest.

Throughout the afternoon, people came and went freely. A few hardened farmers sat in silence, not moving. A young woman cried quietly in the corner. Someone Caleb barely knew lit one of the small candles near the front and sat staring at it for nearly half an hour. The sanctuary became a place of unspoken prayers - breaths held, hearts opened, burdens shared with God in whispers or in silence.

At one point, a faint siren could be heard in the distance, not rushing toward town but reminding everyone that others, somewhere, were fighting hard.

Caleb stood near a window, watching the plume as it expanded and contracted with the shifting wind. He prayed silently: "Lord, hold them. Hold us."

By late afternoon, a quiet exhaustion settled over the sanctuary - not the exhaustion of despair, but of shared weight.

Rachel returned to his side. "It's time to take a short break," she said. "You've been standing all day."

"I'll sit once the last person leaves."

She shook her head, smiling. "Shepherds always say that."

He gave her hand a gentle squeeze. "How are you?"

"Steady," she said. "Concerned, but steady."

They stepped outside together as the sun dipped lower, turning the smoke into a strange mosaic of orange and grey.

"That's new," Rachel said softly.

Caleb followed her gaze. A faint line of darker smoke curled along the base of the plume - denser, heavier, more concentrated.

A flare-up.

He inhaled deeply. "It's still far enough not to threaten the town tonight. But tomorrow… we'll see."

Rachel tucked her arm through his. "Then tonight we pray."

"And tomorrow we watch."

"And through it all," she added, "we trust."

He nodded, feeling the weight of the day settling over him like ash - fine, real, unavoidable, but not suffocating.

They stood for a long moment on the church steps, watching the smoke paint the horizon in troubled colours. Behind them, the sanctuary glowed warm with soft lamplight, a refuge amid the gathering tension. Before they closed the doors for the evening, Caleb whispered a final prayer into the smoky air: "Lord, draw near tonight."

It was both request and declaration.

And as darkness settled over Willowend, the faint glow beyond the ridge pulsed like a heartbeat against the sky - foretelling a night in which every soul in town would sleep half-awake, listening, waiting, trusting.

The sun slipped behind the hills early, swallowed by smoke before it could colour the sky in its usual evening hues. What should have been a golden dusk became instead a gradual dimming of a world already muted.

By six o'clock, Willowend was wrapped in a strange half-light - neither day nor night, but something in between, as though time itself had paused to listen.

The valley felt quieter than usual. Dogs barked less. Cars moved more slowly. People spoke in low voices as they stood on verandahs or wandered their yards, checking hoses, clearing leaves, glancing toward the ridge with expressions that held more contemplation than fear.

Caleb and Rachel returned home briefly in the early evening to rest and share a simple meal. They ate soup again - this time pumpkin - and neither apologised for its simplicity. They were too tired for elaborate cooking, and both knew they needed their strength for whatever might unfold in the next twenty-four hours.

After dinner, they stepped outside onto the verandah. The glow beyond the ridge was stronger now, not alarmingly bright, but steady - pulsing faintly with the shifting wind.

It reminded Caleb of a lantern carried by someone walking behind the hills. Not rushing, not threatening, just... moving.

"It's like the fire is breathing," Rachel murmured.

"It is," Caleb said, watching the plume.

He noticed that the valley was unusually still for a summer evening. Usually, dusk brought the distant rumble of farm utes returning home, the sound of neighbours chatting across fences, the occasional laughter of teens walking to the servo for ice creams. Tonight there was none of that. People were home, doors closed, routines disrupted.

Rachel rested her hand lightly on his arm. "We should go back into town soon."

"Yes," he said. "People will gather - even if they don't plan to."

They walked back toward Willowend just as the streetlights flickered on, their glow cut through the haze like soft amber halos.

A few silhouettes moved along the footpaths - neighbours walking pets, farmers checking on sheds, older residents stepping outside to feel the wind direction for themselves.

At the church, they found a small group of people already waiting on the steps. No one had been invited, yet here they were - drawn by instinct, worry, prayer, or simply the need for shared presence.

Graham and Julie approached first.

"Sorry to bother you at dinner time," Graham said quietly, "but Julie didn't want to be alone at home tonight."

Julie managed a soft, apologetic smile. "I keep hearing embers that aren't there."

"You're not bothering us," Caleb said. "Come in."

Behind them, Mary Kline approached slowly with her walking stick, breathing heavily but determined.

"Couldn't rest at home," she said. "Thought I'd try resting here instead."

"You're always welcome," Rachel told her, guiding her gently inside.

Soon others trickled in - a young couple new to town; a widower who rarely spoke; a teenage girl Caleb recognised from school assemblies, still wearing her sports hoodie; a family of four who slipped in quietly and sat near the side wall, the father's arm around both children.

It wasn't a meeting. It wasn't formal. It wasn't planned.

It was a watch. The First Night Watch, though no one called it that aloud.

Inside, the sanctuary glowed softly with warm lamplight. Caleb dimmed the overheads, leaving only the lamps lit. The effect was calming - less like a service and more like a hearth, a gathering place where anxieties could exhale.

Rachel moved among the people with gentle ease. A hand on a shoulder here, a whispered question there. Her presence alone seemed to settle the room.

Caleb sat on the front pew for a moment, just taking it in. He didn't feel pressure to lead anything, to preach, to deliver a message. He simply needed to be present.

After a while, he rose and walked to the middle of the space. "I don't plan to make a speech," he began, voice soft but steady. "But I want you to know that God is not far from us tonight."

A murmur of agreement moved through the room.

"He hasn't been pushed away by the fire. He isn't blocked by smoke. He's as close now as He ever is - maybe even closer in our awareness."

He looked at each face, letting his eyes rest on every person just long enough to communicate something steady.

"We won't pretend this is nothing. But we also won't pretend that we're alone."

That was enough. He stepped aside, and silence reclaimed the sanctuary - a gentle, gathered silence that felt like prayer even when no one spoke.

Amelia slipped in then, moving quietly into a back pew. She avoided attention, but when her eyes met Caleb's, he offered a small nod. She returned it, her expression grateful but guarded. Next came Daniel, more restless than he'd been earlier. His hair was mussed from running his hands through it, and his backpack hung loosely from one strap. He walked straight to Caleb.

"Is it okay if I stay a while?" he asked.

"Of course."

"It's just… weird at home. Mum's trying not to freak out, but she keeps checking the news. And I don't like the way the smoke looks tonight."

"You're safer here than sitting with your thoughts alone," Caleb said gently. "Stay as long as you need."

Daniel nodded and sat near the aisle, tapping his foot anxiously against the timber floor.

The hours passed slowly but not painfully. Some prayed. Some simply sat. Some whispered to each other. A few stepped outside intermittently to look toward the ridge, then returned inside with quiet updates.

"The wind's changed again."

"The glow's lower."

"I can hear choppers."

"No, maybe that was just a truck on the highway."

Around nine o'clock, a distant helicopter thudded faintly, its blades muffled by smoke and distance. People looked toward the windows instinctively, though nothing could be seen from this angle.

Graham cleared his throat. "Air crews must be doing night monitoring."

Julie squeezed his hand tightly. "Good."

Caleb noticed how many people were leaning on one another tonight - literally or figuratively. Married couples held hands. Strangers exchanged soft nods. A teenage girl offered a tissue to the widower sitting beside her. Even Amelia accepted a cup of water from Rachel with a soft "Thank you," as though it cost her something to accept kindness.

Just after ten, someone outside called lightly, "Pastor."

Caleb stepped out and found Murray, the RFS volunteer from the earlier briefing, standing near his truck. His uniform smelled of smoke, but his face remained composed.

"Evening," Murray said. "Didn't mean to interrupt."

"You're not interrupting," Caleb replied. "How's the fire?"

"Still holding," Murray said. "But the wind's tricky tonight. Not dangerous yet, not for here. Just… unpredictable. We'll know more in the morning."

"Is your crew okay?"

"Tired," he said honestly. "But steady."

"We're praying for you."

Murray nodded, visibly moved. "I figured. It helps."

He looked toward the sanctuary and seemed surprised to see how many people were inside.

"People always come together when the sky looks like that," he murmured.

"They come together when they remember how much they need each other," Caleb said.

Murray tipped his head. "Just keep doing what you're doing. It matters."

He drove off slowly, the red tail-lights fading into the smoky darkness.

Inside, the atmosphere had softened again. People were weary but calmer. The communal presence had steadied them - the reminder that fear diminishes when carried together.

Shortly before eleven, Rachel whispered to Caleb, "We should let people go home soon. They need rest."

He nodded. "Just a few more minutes."

Then he stood near the front.

"Friends," he said quietly, "thank you for keeping watch tonight. Let's head home, gently, knowing that God has been with us in every breath. The fire has not reached us, and we will face tomorrow as it comes - together."

People rose slowly, stretching, gathering bags and jackets. Some hugged. Some shook hands. Some simply gave soft nods and stepped out into the cool, smoky evening.

As they left, Caleb saw Amelia linger at the door.

"You okay?" he asked.

"Better than I would've been at home," she admitted. "Thanks... for keeping the doors open."

"They'll be open tomorrow too."

She hesitated, then whispered, "I might... come earlier next time."

He smiled warmly. "Anytime."

Daniel approached next. "Pastor... thanks for tonight."

"You don't need to thank me," Caleb said. "Just come back when you need to."

Daniel nodded, then ran a hand through his hair. "I probably will."

When the last of the congregation had gone, Caleb and Rachel stepped outside, locking the doors gently behind them.

The glow beyond the ridge pulsed steadily through the smoke.

"How do you feel?" Rachel asked.

"Grateful," Caleb answered. "And watchful."

She took his hand. "Then we're ready for tomorrow."

They walked home under the dim, smoky sky, side by side, hearts steady even as the land held its breath for morning.

9. A DAY OF WARNINGS

Friday dawned without colour.

The sky held no pinks, oranges, or gentle gradients announcing the sun. It was simply grey-brown, heavy, and low, as though someone had draped a blanket of smoke over the valley during the night and forgotten to lift it. The sun was a pale coin above us, invisible but inferred. Everything outside looked subdued - the trees, the paddocks, the gravel road - as though Willowend had been rendered into a faded photograph.

Caleb woke with a start, unsure at first what had roused him. Then he heard it - the faint, distant thump of a helicopter, barely audible through the thickened air.

Rachel was already awake beside him, lying on her back, eyes open.

"Morning," she said quietly.

"Morning," he replied. "You didn't sleep much."

"Neither did you."

He swung his legs over the side of the bed and sat for a moment, feeling the weight of the night's watch still lingering in his body. The First Night Watch, as his mind had begun to call it, had not been that dramatic. There had been no evacuations, no sirens, no urgent alerts. Yet something had certainly shifted. The town had crossed a threshold - from watching the horizon to living in its shadow.

He stood and walked over to the window. The garden looked oddly dull, its colours leached out by the smoke-filtered light. A light dusting of ash covered the outdoor table, the steps, the top of the letterbox.

"More ash," he said.

Rachel joined him at the window. "It looks like it's snowed in sepia," she murmured.

They dressed in comfortable, practical clothes - the kind suited for long days where anything might be required - and shared a quick breakfast. Toast, fruit, tea. Neither felt particularly hungry, but routine mattered.

"What do you sense today?" Caleb asked as he rinsed their cups.

"That we'll need extra gentleness," Rachel said. "People are worn thin from the inside out."

He nodded. "And you?"

"I'm steady," she replied. "Not relaxed, but steady."

He smiled at the distinction. It sounded like his own heart.

On the way into town, the ute's headlights looked strange in the thickened air, beams cutting through haze rather than darkness. Ash blew across the road in slow, random patterns. The world felt muffled, as if sound itself had softened.

The regional radio bulletin came through with the morning forecast. Caleb turned up the volume.

"Total Fire Ban continues across the region," the announcer said.

"The incident north of Willowend remains classified as being controlled, though difficult conditions are expected today with rising temperatures and variable winds. Residents are urged to stay informed and have their fire plans ready. Rural Fire Service crews will continue to work on containment lines throughout the day."

Caleb listened carefully. No evacuation orders, no emergency-level alerts. But the phrase "difficult conditions" lodged in his mind.

At the servo, Amelia had propped the doors open again, even though it let the smoky air inside.

"Everything smells like a barbecue gone wrong," she said as he approached. "I'm starting to forget what clean air felt like."

"How did you sleep?" he asked.

She snorted lightly. "Badly. But coming to the church last night helped. I didn't expect that."

"I'm glad you came."

She hesitated, then added, "I… might come again tonight. If you will be open."

"We will be," he said. "For as long as people need it."

Amelia looked toward the north. The ridge was barely visible through the haze now. "They said on the radio the fire's still under control," she said. "But this doesn't feel like control."

"Control doesn't always look calm," Caleb replied. "Sometimes it looks like persistence."

She considered that. "I like that word better than 'fight.'"

"Me too," he said.

As he left, an elderly man filling his tank muttered, "Feels like we're living inside a warning sign."

Caleb's heart resonated with the phrase. A day of warnings. Not panicked alarms, but steady, repeated reminders to stay alert, to prepare, to lean on something larger than themselves.

At the church, the sanctuary felt more enclosed than before. The light that filtered through the windows had taken on an orange tinge, and the faint smell of smoke clung to the fabric of the pew cushions. Caleb switched on the lamps again, filling the space with warm, human light.

He walked slowly down the centre aisle and prayed aloud in a voice just above a whisper.

"Lord, be our clear air in thick days. Be our horizon when smoke hides what's ahead. Be our strength when our own feels thin."

He knew Rachel would be visiting people who couldn't easily leave their homes today. Her quiet ministry threaded through the town as surely as his, sometimes more effectively, because she moved with a rare gentleness that disarmed defences.

By mid-morning, a few people began to arrive.

Mary came first, as he had expected. "I thought about staying at home," she said. "Then I remembered that worry grows in small rooms."

"The doors here are wide," he said, smiling. "So is God's peace."

Next came the young mother with the toddler. This time the boy clung more tightly to her leg, unsettled by the very strange light outside.

"He keeps asking why the sky looks wrong," she said. "I told him the air needs prayer."

Caleb laughed softly. "That's one of the truest explanations I've heard."

He knelt down to the boy's eye level. "It does look a bit strange, doesn't it?"

The child nodded solemnly.

"Well," Caleb said, "when things look strange, we can always remember that God hasn't changed. He's the same, even when the sky looks different."

The boy seemed to think about this, then asked, "Can we talk to Him now?"

"Yes," Caleb said. "We can."

They prayed a simple, child-sized prayer together. Something inside Caleb settled more deeply as they did.

As the day wore on, text messages and murmured conversations brought small updates. Someone had seen more fire trucks on the highway. Someone else had received a call from a cousin in a neighbouring town where the smoke was even thicker. The local school adjusted its schedule, keeping children indoors for most of the day.

Just before midday, a shrill, unfamiliar sound cut through the sanctuary. Caleb startled slightly before realising it was his phone vibrating with an emergency text alert. He glanced at the screen.

"Watch and Act," it read. "Bushfire north of Willowend. No immediate danger to the town at this stage, but conditions may change. Monitor media, follow instructions of authorities."

He read it twice, then carried the phone to Rachel, who had just arrived from her morning visits.

"Watch and Act," she said, after reading the message.

"Appropriate words."

"Not yet 'Emergency,'" he said. "But more than 'Advice.'"

"It tells people what they need to know," she said calmly. "That we're not in crisis, but we're not in comfort either."

They decided to put a printed copy of the alert on the table just inside the church door, so people could see it clearly on arrival. Around one o'clock, Graham walked in, dust in his hair, his shirt smelling strongly of smoke.

"They've given us the same alert on the outer properties," he said. "Our fire plan's in place. We're ready to stay and defend if it comes to that. But I needed a few minutes where my hands weren't holding a hose."

"You're welcome to lay them down here," Caleb said.

Graham sat heavily, rubbing his palms together as though trying to scrub off the morning. Julie arrived shortly afterwards with a bottle of water and sat beside him, leaning her shoulder gently against his.

Later, Daniel slipped in again, his eyes rimmed with tiredness.

"How's Mum?" Caleb asked quietly.

"She's okay," he said. "Her boss let her finish early. She's resting. She told me to come here if I wanted to." He paused, then added, "She called it 'the calm place.'"

Caleb's heart warmed. "She's welcome too."

"She said she might come tonight," he added quickly, as though not wanting to commit her on her behalf.

"I'll be glad to see her, whenever she's ready."

In between arrivals, Caleb found moments to sit, to breathe, to let his own soul rest. He felt the weight of responsibility, but not as a solitary burden. God had shared it across the town - through Rachel, through the deacons, through those whose quiet prayers never made it into reports or meetings.

By late afternoon, the smoke outside thickened further. The view of the ridge almost vanished altogether, leaving only a vague sense of distance. The radio spoke about the "challenging but manageable conditions." The emergency app remained at "Watch and Act."

Warnings. Nothing more. Nothing less.

Inside, as people came and went, a different kind of watch continued - one that didn't involve maps and wind charts, but hearts and souls.

"Do you think this will change the town?" Rachel asked him quietly during a rare pause.

"It's already changing it," he answered. "I see it in their faces. In who's walking through the doors. In who's staying longer than they used to."

Rachel nodded. "Fire seasons always leave marks. But they can also expose roots."

"Roots of what?" he asked.

"Of what people really trust," she said.

He thought of Amelia, sitting at the back pew, eyes fixed on the cross. Of Daniel, finding courage to name his fears. Of Mary, steady but tender. Of the Whites, exhausted yet determined. Of himself, standing between his own memories of illness and the present uncertainty.

"What do you think God is showing us?" he asked.

"That we're more fragile than we like to think," she said. "And that His presence is more solid than we sometimes remember."

He let the words really sink in. They felt like truth buried deep in smoky air.

As the afternoon slid slowly toward evening, the valley waited. Warnings hung in the air - in conversations, on phones, on radios, in the colour of the sky.

But so did something else.

Hope. Quiet, steady, not loud - but there.

And Caleb sensed that whatever tomorrow brought, Willowend would not face it as the same town it had been just a week before. By late afternoon, the ash was falling more steadily, though still light - scarcely more than scattered flecks drifting like strange summer snow. Yet to the people of Willowend, each fragment felt like a message carried on the wind. Not a message of doom, but of caution. Of attention. Of preparedness.

The church remained open, its soft lamplight a stark contrast to the murky glow outside. People came in quietly, staying only a few minutes at times - just long enough to breathe differently, to recalibrate their thoughts, to gather a sense of peace before stepping back into the haze.

Shortly after five, Amelia slipped in again, her hair dusted faintly with ash.

"I didn't think I would come today," she said sheepishly as she approached Caleb. "But the air at the servo smells like someone burnt toast in the microwave of the whole district."

Caleb smiled gently. "You're welcome here as often as you want."

She hesitated, then added in a low voice, "I … didn't want to be alone with the smoke."

"That's a wise instinct," he replied. "None of us are meant to face heavy days alone."

Amelia nodded and drifted to the same pew she had occupied the previous night. But something was different.

She didn't sit rigidly this time. Her shoulders had loosened. Her breathing steadied. It was as if her soul had recognised a place where it felt safe to lower its guard.

A few minutes later, the door opened again and Daniel hurried inside. His face was flushed, his breathing rapid.

Caleb walked toward him. "Daniel, what's wrong?"

"I just …" The boy stopped to cough lightly from the smoky air outside. "The radio said something about spotting overnight. About conditions changing quickly. Mum's worried. And when she's worried, I get… I don't know. All churned up."

"You came to the right place," Caleb said. "Sit for a moment."

Daniel nodded and dropped onto a pew near the centre, elbows on his knees, head in his hands.

Rachel approached him with a bottle of cool water. "Here," she said softly. "Sip slowly."

He drank gratefully, and some of the tension in his shoulders seemed to ease.

At six o'clock, a notification tone echoed through the sanctuary - not one, but several, rippling from phones across the room as an updated alert came through. The atmosphere shifted instantly, the way a room changes when a doctor enters with test results.

People checked their screens.

A few held their breath.

Caleb read his own.

"Watch and Act remains in place," the message said, "with increased fire activity expected overnight due to rising winds. Crews are strengthening containment lines. Residents should monitor conditions and be ready to enact their fire plans if needed. No evacuation order at this time."

Rachel read over his shoulder. "Still holding," she murmured.

"Yes," he said. "But the language is firmer."

The people in the sanctuary reacted quietly - a few anxious glances, a mother gathering her children closer, an older man folding his hands in prayer without a word. No sign of panic. Just a deeper awareness.

Caleb knew he needed to address them, not with a speech, but with clarity.

He stepped to the front.

"Everyone," he said softly, "we've received the updated alert. Nothing has changed for the town in terms of immediate danger. But tonight will be a serious night for the firefighters. Let's pray for them. And let's stay prepared in our hearts and minds."

There were nods right across the room. People trusted him, not because he had all the answers, but because he refused to speak more than he knew.

After a short collective silence, Caleb brought out a large jug of cool water from the kitchen and began filling glasses. It was a small act, but in smoky air, it felt sacramental.

As he returned to the pews, Graham and Julie walked in again. Graham's shirt was still streaked with ash, and his eyes showed the deep fatigue of a man who had worked past what his body preferred.

"How's the property?" Caleb asked.

"Holding," Graham said. "But we've had embers most of the afternoon. Nothing caught, thank God. But I didn't want to leave Julie alone tonight."

Julie touched his arm. "And I told him he needed to sit before he went back out again."

"You're going out again?" Caleb asked gently.

Graham nodded. "Just for a bit. I want to check the back fence after sunset. Embers travel differently at night."

"Wait until you've rested," Caleb said. "Your judgment will be clearer."

Graham exhaled. "That's what Julie said."

Julie offered a small, understanding smile. "Common sense is a partnership."

They sat together for a brief rest. Julie bowed her head; Graham closed his eyes, his hands unclenching for the first time that day. Outside, a gust of wind rattled the eaves. Several people looked toward the door instinctively. The sanctuary's warm light felt even more precious in that moment - a soft refuge from a restless world.

Around seven-thirty, a faint orange flicker appeared at the far end of the northern windows - not flames, but reflection. The fire must have reached a higher patch of trees on the ridge, bright enough now to paint the smoke with colour.

Rachel noticed first.

"Look," she murmured to Caleb.

He turned toward the window. The glow was clearer than it had been all day. Not threatening. But undeniably present.

"I think," Rachel said softly, "this is the fire's way of saying we are on its mind."

Caleb nodded. "And we are on God's."

The sanctuary filled with a deeper hush.

Mary Kline whispered, "Lord have mercy."

Amelia looked down at her hands, turning them slowly as though suddenly aware of how fragile they were.

Daniel swallowed, eyes fixed on the window.

Graham and Julie clasped hands more tightly.

Rachel leaned her head against Caleb's arm for a moment.

The moment seemed to hold - not fear, not dread, but reverence. A recognition of the seriousness of the night ahead.

Caleb breathed deeply, sensing the weight and the holiness of it. "Friends," he said gently, "we don't know what tonight will bring. But we do know this: God is not shaken by smoke or wind. And whatever unfolds, we will face it together."

A soft murmur of assent rose across the room.

They stayed for another hour, some praying, some resting, some quietly talking in corners, others staring at the shifting orange glow outside.

At last, as night deepened and the air cooled slightly, people began to disperse. Not hurriedly, but gradually - like a tide drawing back.

Amelia paused at the door before leaving. "Pastor… if the fire… if it comes closer …"

"We'll be here," Caleb said.

She nodded, exhaling. "Good."

Daniel lingered last of all. "Thanks for today," he said. "And yesterday. And… probably tomorrow too."

"You're welcome," Caleb replied. "And tell your mum she's also welcome anytime."

"I will."

Then the boy left, disappearing into the smoky twilight like a small figure navigating a much larger story.

When the sanctuary was empty, Caleb and Rachel stepped outside and looked toward the ridge again. The glow seemed much stronger now - not rushing toward them, but stretching, reaching, growing.

Rachel spoke softly. "The town will need strength tomorrow."

"And God will supply it," Caleb replied.

She slid her hand into his. "He already has."

They walked home in silence, the night cool but laced with the scent of burning eucalyptus. Above them, the stars were faint, blurred behind the haze.

Tomorrow was uncertain.

But tonight - tonight Willowend was watchful, prayerful, and held firmly in hands far greater than its own.

10. THE HEAT BUILDS

By Saturday morning, the heat arrived early.

It wasn't just temperature - though the air was already warm by seven - but the kind of heat that felt purposeful, determined. A heat with intent. The smoke had thinned slightly overnight, enough to let in a weaker form of daylight, but the sun rose through a veil of haze, casting a strange copper glow across the land.

Caleb stepped out onto his verandah and looked at the withering grass which had felt brittle underfoot. The trees hung motionless, as though waiting for something. Even the birds were subdued - only a few tentative calls echoed through the valley, muted by the thickness of the air.

Rachel joined him, holding two mugs of tea.

"It's going to be a hard day," she said, handing him his cup.

"Yes," he replied. "I could feel it before I opened my eyes."

"Has there been an update yet?"

"Not since last night's Watch and Act," he said. "But they should issue one soon."

They stood for a few moments, sipping their tea, watching the light grow over a land that seemed, in its own quiet way, weary.

"Whatever today brings," Rachel said softly, "we will walk into it with God."

He nodded, taking strength from her steadiness.

They drove into town earlier than usual. Along the way, Caleb noticed signs of preparation everywhere: hoses stretched across yards, sprinklers set near sheds, fuel tanks cleared of debris, gutters checked and rechecked. People had already begun the many rituals of defensive hope. At the servo, Amelia was outside again, sweeping ash from the concrete as though this was her assigned task for the season.

"You're out early," Caleb said.

"So's everyone else," she replied, nodding at a couple across the road hosing their front garden. "The air just feels wrong today. Tight."

He knew what she meant. The town felt wound up like a spring.

"You heading to the church?" she asked.

"Yes."

She hesitated, then said quietly, "I'll come later. If I can close for a break."

"You're welcome anytime."

Her eyes flicked to the north. "Is the fire closer?"

He shook his head. "Not significantly. But the wind today might test the lines."

"Right," she said. "Well… I'll try not to think about that while selling meat pies."

Caleb chuckled softly, but her eyes showed real tension. The fire was no longer a distant story; it had now become an uninvited character in everyone's day.

At the church, the sanctuary once again felt like a place separate from the outside world - not untouched by smoke, but gentler somehow. Caleb turned on the lamps, opened the doors, set water out, and prayed a simple prayer for strength.

Soon, people trickled in.

Mary arrived first, leaning more heavily on her walking stick than usual.

"I didn't sleep," she admitted. "The wind kept changing."

"You're safe here," Caleb said.

"More than safe," she replied. "Centred."

Next came the young mother and her son. The boy clung tightly to her hand, eyes wide.

"He had a dream last night that the fire was in our yard," she whispered to Caleb.

He knelt beside the child. "Dreams can feel big when we're small. But the fire isn't anywhere near your house. And God is watching while we sleep, even when our dreams aren't kind."

The boy nodded slowly, reassured.

By mid-morning, the church was fuller than it had been in previous days. Not crowded, but steadily attended - a quiet stream of people seeking the steadying presence they could not find at home.

Rachel spent the morning visiting two elderly women who couldn't leave their homes because of the smoke. She returned shortly before noon, pale but composed.

"How are they?" Caleb asked.

"Tired," she said. "But grateful. Everyone's grateful for any sign of God's nearness today."

He nodded. "We are, too."

As noon approached, a faint breeze stirred the air. It wasn't particularly strong, but it felt sharp, as though it was carrying something edged. The plume beyond the ridge began to shift again, the smoke rising more vigorously.

Rachel noticed immediately. "The wind's changed earlier than yesterday."

"Yes," Caleb said quietly. "And the smoke is darker."

Still, there were no sirens. No urgent alerts. Just the steady hum of a day inching toward its hottest point.

Around one o'clock, Daniel arrived at the church, his backpack slung over one shoulder.

"Mum's at home resting," he said. "She said I could come here. Said it's better than me pacing around the house all day."

"How are you holding up?" Caleb asked.

Daniel shrugged. "Fine. I mean… not fine. But not as bad as yesterday."

"That sounds like progress."

"Maybe." Daniel looked toward the window. "I hate the colour of the sky today."

"Most of the town does," Caleb said. "But we face it together." Daniel sat deeper in the pew, letting out a long breath.

Around two o'clock, the emergency alert tone sounded again — not from one phone, but from several.

This time the tension in the sanctuary rose instantly.

People checked their screens. A few held their breath. Caleb read his first.

"Watch and Act - elevated conditions. Fire remains north of Willowend but has increased in intensity. Residents should stay alert and enact fire plans if conditions deteriorate. Prepare for possible further updates."

Rachel read her own and looked up at him.

"It's shifting," she said.

"Yes," he replied. "But not toward us yet."

"We need to stay open all afternoon."

"I wasn't planning on closing."

People asked quiet questions - not panicked, but searching.

"Does this mean we should leave town?"

"Is the wind heading this way?"

"What are the firefighters saying?"

Caleb answered each one gently, giving only what he knew, and no more.

"The fire is still at a distance."

"The RFS is working hard."

"We will be informed if anything changes."

"There is no evacuation order."

"And God is with us."

Each phrase seemed to settle something, even if only briefly.

Mid-afternoon brought a sudden spike in heat. The temperature rose sharply, and the air seemed to press down on the valley with palpable weight. The breeze became inconsistent, flickering between stillness and sudden, jarring gusts.

A new sound joined the day - the constant low throb of aircraft. A helicopter flew overhead, barely visible through the haze, its rotors muffled by smoke.

People stepped outside instinctively to watch.

Caleb and Rachel joined them.

The sky looked bruised - brown, grey, and dull orange blending into each other like smeared paint. The sun appeared only as a pale disc suspended in murk.

"This day feels stretched," Rachel said. "Like the hours are heavier than usual."

"Yes," Caleb replied. "It's a day waiting for a decision."

"Whose?" she asked quietly.

"God's," he said. "And the wind's."

Shortly before four, Graham appeared again, his shirt stained with sweat and soot.

"Containment lines are holding," he reported. "But it's shifting east. Not toward us - not yet. But it's started spotting again."

Julie followed behind him, her face drawn. "I hate the way fire thinks," she murmured. "Sneaky. Quick."

"It's not thinking," Rachel said softly. "It's reacting to the wind. God is thinking."

Julie breathed out slowly. "Yes. That helps."

Inside the sanctuary, people prayed quietly in corners. The toddler slept in his mother's lap. Mary rocked gently as she recited Psalm 121 under her breath. A few farmers sat with heads bowed, hands clasped, their rugged faces softened by the lamplight.

Caleb felt the weight of responsibility rising within him - not the pressure to fix anything, but the call to stand steady while others leaned.

He could sense, in the quiet of his spirit, that Willowend was approaching a threshold. Not yet danger - but certainly gravity. A seriousness that would shape the next hours.

As afternoon stretched toward evening, the light outside shifted again, growing darker, heavier, more foreboding.

"Tonight will be different," Rachel said softly.

"Yes," Caleb whispered. "Tonight, the fire tests the lines - and the town."

He wasn't afraid.

But he was watchful.

And he felt God drawing close.

Very close.

By early evening, the heat felt unnatural - as though the sun had settled lower than it should, pressing its weight directly onto the valley.

The breeze came and went in strange bursts, gusting hard enough to stir dust from the roadside, then stopping abruptly, leaving a jarring stillness in its wake. Willowend felt suspended in a moment that was not yet crisis, but no longer ordinary.

At the church, people had begun gathering earlier than the night before, arriving in ones and twos from just after five. Some came directly from work, faces tense but relieved to be somewhere anchored. Others came from their homes, having spent the day checking roofs, clearing dead leaves, listening compulsively for updates.

Caleb watched them enter, each one carrying a mix of fatigue, uncertainty, and quiet courage. Rachel had spread the chairs slightly wider this time, sensing people needed room to feel the space breathe. She lit a few small candles on the front table - not as ritual, but as a symbol. Light in smoke-fogged days felt precious.

Amelia slipped in wearing a jacket still dusted with ash. She sat in her usual place, less guarded now, her expression open but weary.

Daniel arrived soon after, followed by three of his schoolmates who trailed behind him awkwardly, unsure whether they should enter or not. Daniel glanced back at them and said, "It's fine. He won't make us pray or anything."

Caleb laughed quietly at that and came to greet them.

"You're welcome here," he said. "However you come."

The boys nodded, relieved.

As the gathering grew, the sanctuary took on a different tone from previous days. No one was panicking. No one was frantic. But there was *anticipation* - an unspoken recognition that the fire and the valley were now in a kind of delicate conversation, and the wind would translate the next line.

Just after six, the emergency alert tone chimed again.

Phones buzzed. Heads lifted. Conversations paused.

A shared breath held.

Caleb read the message first.

"Watch and Act - conditions worsening. Significant fire activity on northern flank. Spotting occurring. Residents should enact fire plans and remain prepared. No evacuation order at this stage."

Rachel read hers and nodded slowly. "A firmer warning. But still no call to leave."

Caleb stepped gently to the front and addressed the sanctuary.

"The update is serious, but predictable. Conditions are difficult. But the RFS is strong, and the containment lines hold. The town is not under evacuation orders. And we will face the night together."

He didn't raise his voice. He didn't dramatize anything. He simply anchored the room.

The tension softened, if only a little.

Mary leaned heavily on her walking stick as she whispered, "The Lord is my refuge." Caleb placed a gentle hand on her shoulder. Graham and Julie entered then, looking exhausted from work on their property, but grateful for the steadiness of the room.

"How's the back paddock?" Caleb asked.

"Holding," Graham said. "But the wind's unpredictable."

"The whole day feels unpredictable," Julie murmured.

Rachel offered them both water. "Sit. Rest your minds before you go back out."

"We're not going out again tonight," Graham admitted. "The RFS advised us to stay put for a while. Embers are coming from too many directions."

"That's wisdom," Caleb replied. "Let others carry the hoses tonight."

As dusk approached, the glow beyond the ridge brightened noticeably. Not racing toward them - not a wall of flame - but a clear, pulsing reminder that the fire had woken with the heat.
A few people stepped outside to look. Even through the thick smoke, the light flickered with unsettling beauty.

"It's like the hills are breathing fire," one man whispered.

"It's like the world is holding its breath," someone else said.

Rachel stepped beside Caleb, watching the sky ripple with orange through to grey. "Tonight feels like hinge-time," she murmured. "A turning point."

He felt it too. The season, the fire, the town, even his own heart - everything felt poised.

Back inside, he found Daniel pacing near the rear pews.

"You okay?" Caleb asked.

Daniel nodded, then shook his head. "I don't know. My chest feels tight. Not from the smoke… just from thinking."

"It's a heavy night," Caleb said. "But you're not alone."

Daniel swallowed. "Mum almost came tonight. She got dressed and sat by the door and then said she wasn't ready."

"She doesn't have to rush her steps," Caleb replied. "Coming to the edge is still movement."

"Yeah," Daniel whispered. "I guess so."

He sank onto a pew, his foot tapping anxiously until Rachel placed a calming hand on his shoulder. "Breathe," she said softly. "Slowly."

He obeyed, tension easing from his shoulders.

Around seven-thirty, the sanctuary had settled into a kind of quiet rhythm. People prayed in silence.

A few whispered to one another. Others simply sat still, listening to the shifting wind outside.

Then, without warning, the breeze hit the building hard, rattling the windows.

Everyone looked up.

The sudden gust passed quickly, but its message lingered.

"That was a change," Graham said under his breath.

"Wind's turning south-easterly," Julie added. "Not the worst direction, but not the one we want."

Caleb stepped outside to check the sky. The ridge flickered more brightly now, the fire's movement harder to ignore.

Murray, the RFS volunteer, pulled up in his truck and climbed out swiftly.

"Pastor," he called.

Caleb walked toward him, heart steady but firm.

"Can I share something indoors?" Murray asked quietly.

"Yes," Caleb said. "They need clarity."

Inside, the room hushed as the firefighter entered. Murray removed his hat, ran a hand through soot-streaked hair, and stood near the centre of the sanctuary.

"I won't be long," he began. "But I want you to know what's happening."

Solemn faces turned toward him.

"The fire *is* more active tonight," he said. "We've got spotting ahead of the main front. Crews are working the lines. It's challenging, but manageable. The important thing is this: right now, Willowend is not in direct danger."

A collective breath eased out of the room.

"But," he continued gently, "this is a night to stay purposeful. Keep your fire plans in mind. Check your radios. Keep your phones charged. If anything changes, we will let you all know immediately."

Mary nodded appreciatively. Julie breathed out. Daniel's foot stopped tapping.

Murray looked around, softened by the faces watching him.

"And keep praying," he added. "We feel it on the lines."

A small murmur of warmth rippled through the sanctuary.

He nodded once more, then left to return to the fire ground.

As the night deepened, the sanctuary took on the tone of quiet endurance. People stayed not because they feared the flames, but because they feared being alone with their thoughts.

At ten o'clock, after several hours of stillness and whispered prayer, Caleb stood and spoke softly.

"Friends, it's time to head home and rest. The fire has not changed direction. We are safe tonight. Let us sleep in God's keeping."

People rose slowly, gathering jackets and bags.

Amelia approached him near the front door. "Thanks for not pretending everything's fine," she said. "And thanks for not making it sound worse."

"We walk in truth," Caleb replied. "That's all God asks."

She nodded and slipped into the smoky night.

Daniel came last, as he often did. "Mum says thank you," he whispered. "She said being at home tonight didn't feel as scary because she knew I was here."

"She's welcome tomorrow," Caleb said gently.

"I'll tell her," Daniel replied.

He left with a small wave.

As Caleb and Rachel stepped outside for the final time that night, the glow beyond the ridge felt sharper, more defined.

"It will test them tonight," Rachel whispered - meaning the firefighters.

"Yes," Caleb said. "But God will hold them."

She leaned lightly into him. "And tomorrow?"

"Tomorrow," he said, "God will hold us, too."

Together they walked home under a sky that flickered with warning and with hope - a sky that invited both caution and trust.

Saturday night arrived like a held breath.

The heat did not ease after sunset as it normally would; instead, the air stayed warm and restless, as though the land itself hesitated to cool. Smoke hung thick across Willowend, thinning at times, rolling in at others, shifting unpredictably with each unsettled gust.

Caleb and Rachel stepped outside their home around seven o'clock, intending to walk into town together before the night watch began. As Caleb locked the door, they both turned instinctively toward the northern ridge.

They stopped in their tracks.

The hills glowed.

Not with towering flames - nothing so close or dramatic - but with a long, bright contour of orange light that pulsed behind the crest like an ember-streaked horizon. It wasn't raging. It wasn't rushing. But it was alive.

Rachel exhaled slowly. "This is the first time we've seen it like that."

Caleb nodded. "Yes."

"It's beautiful," she whispered.

"And terrible," he replied.

Together, they stood for a long, quiet moment, watching the hills in their fiery silhouette. It really felt as though the land were illuminated from within, like stained glass lit by a hidden lamp.

"It's not coming toward us," Caleb said softly. "But it's awake."

Rachel slipped her hand through his arm. "Tonight, the town will feel the weight of that."

"Tonight," he agreed, "the town will need the church more than ever."

As they walked toward Willowend, the smoky air thickened slightly, carrying the scent of burning eucalypt and something deeper - the dry, ancient smell of heated earth. The glow flickered behind them like a slow-moving heartbeat.

At the servo, Amelia was locking the doors.

"You're closing early tonight," Caleb observed.

"Yes," she said. "My boss said we could. Said it wasn't worth staying open when everyone's eyes are glued to the ridge."

She brushed ash from her sleeves. "I'm coming up to the church. I'd rather sit there than stare at the glow from my kitchen window."

"You're welcome," he said warmly.

Amelia hesitated, then added, "It looks closer tonight. Even though I know it's not."

"Perception changes when the sky lights up," Rachel said gently.

"I don't like that," Amelia admitted. "But I guess it's human."

"It is," Caleb replied. "And God meets humans where they are." Her shoulders loosened a fraction. "Then I hope He's meeting Willowend tonight."

"He is," Caleb said simply.

At the church, people were already gathering, earlier than the previous nights. Some arrived in pairs, some alone, some with quietly worried children in tow. No one looked panicked, but everyone looked *awake* - more alert, more sober, more aware of the thin line between safety and vulnerability.

Daniel was there, sitting on the steps with his backpack at his feet.

"Hey," he said as Caleb approached. "I got here early."

"How's your mum?"

"She said she might come later." He paused. "She keeps standing at the back door looking at the ridge."

"Does she know she's welcome here?" Caleb asked.

"I told her," Daniel said earnestly. "She just… she needs time."

"That's all right," Caleb said.

Inside, the sanctuary filled quickly. Candlelight flickered softly at the front. The air had a faint scent of smoke, but the lamplight made the space feel warm rather than claustrophobic.

Mary Kline sat near the front, her hands folded tightly, her expression resolute.

Graham and Julie arrived soon after, walking slowly, as though they were carrying the weight of the whole valley. Graham looked exhausted - lines of tension around his eyes, his shirt still marked with the day's sweat and ash. Julie sat first. Graham hovered at the end of the pew until Caleb approached.

"You all right?" Caleb asked.

Graham shook his head slightly. "I'm stretched, Pastor. I'm not ashamed to say it."

"Stretching isn't failing," Caleb said. "It's being human."

Graham pulled in a breath. "The embers were bad this afternoon. Nothing caught, but we had to run the sprinklers constantly. And the fence line …" His voice broke slightly … "It's strange, seeing your land glow like that. Like it's lit from the wrong side."

"It's unsettling," Caleb said. "But you're not alone." Graham nodded, his jaw tightening. He sat beside Julie, who took his hand without a word.

At eight-thirty, the church was almost full. Not in a crowded sense - there was still room for people to breathe - but full in the sense that the community had gathered. Even those who rarely stepped inside had come tonight.

Caleb stood at the front, not to preach, but to ground the room.

"Thank you for coming," he said softly. "Tonight, the hills look different. Tonight, we see what has been there all week - just hidden until now. But I want you to remember something: nothing about the fire surprises God. Not its movement. Not its glow. Not the heaviness we feel."

He let that settle.

"We gather tonight not because we fear the fire, but because we trust the One who walks with us through it."

Heads nodded. A few eyes glistened.

"The fire is still distant," Caleb continued. "The RFS is working tirelessly. And we have not received any warning to leave. But it is right to be wise, to be prepared, and to keep watch - together."

A gentle murmur of agreement rippled through the sanctuary. Caleb stepped back. "This space is yours tonight. Pray, sit, talk, rest. We are held."

Around nine o'clock, the glow on the ridge intensified briefly. Someone near the window gasped softly.

"It's flared," they whispered.

Caleb walked outside with several others. The breeze was warm and erratic, pushing smoke in uneven waves across the valley. The fire's light flickered between trees like distant lightning, but steady.

"It's not racing," Rachel said after studying it. "It's burning high fuel. The ridge is dry."

Caleb nodded. "It looks closer than it is."

"Doesn't matter," someone murmured. "It feels close."

That was the real truth of the night.

The fire had not physically advanced — but the *feeling* had.

People returned inside more quietly than before.

Just before ten, a car pulled into the church yard. The headlights illuminated the smoke in eerie cones of light.

Daniel sat up straighter.

"Mum," he whispered.

A slender woman stepped out, hesitant at first. She kept one hand on the open car door, eyes fixed on the sanctuary as though assessing whether she was allowed to enter.

Caleb walked toward her.

"You're welcome," he said gently.

She swallowed, her voice barely audible. "He said... people weren't judged here."

Caleb smiled softly. "People aren't judged here."

She nodded, breathed out shakily, and entered - her shoulders sagging with relief as soon as she stepped through the doorway. Daniel ran to her and hugged her tightly. She held him for a long moment before sitting beside him.

Amelia watched the scene from across the room and wiped her eye discreetly.

Around ten-thirty, the emergency alert tone chimed again - sharp, piercing, immediate.

Phones lit up. The room stilled.

Caleb checked his screen quickly.

The message was firm but not alarming:

"Watch and Act — increased activity overnight. Spotting ahead of main front. Monitor conditions. Firefighters conducting night operations. No evacuation order."

He read it aloud. People exhaled, some with relief, some with unease.

"It's the same alert level," Rachel said quietly. "Just updated."

"Yes," Caleb replied. "And still no call to leave."

He stepped forward.

"Friends, the fire is active, but we are not in danger tonight. We will continue to pray for the crews. But we will also rest in the fact that God has not changed."

The sanctuary softened again. Tension ebbed, if only slightly.

As the night deepened, a profound stillness settled over the room. The glow flickered through the windows. The candles burned steadily. People leaned on each other's presence.

A holy quietness descended.

Even the smoke outside seemed to pause, hanging heavy but unmoving.

Rachel whispered to Caleb, "This is the night when Willowend remembers. The night hearts crack open."

He nodded slowly. "And God slips in through the cracks."

The night deepened slowly, as though reluctant to reveal its full weight. Outside, the air was warm and unsettled; inside, the sanctuary held a quiet that felt almost ancient.

The lamplight flickered softly across bowed heads and still hands, illuminating the faces of people who had not gathered for a sermon, or a meeting, or an event - but simply to *be* together.

The hills continued to glow beyond the ridge. Not fiercely, not urgently, but insistently - a steady orange pulse against the smoky dark. A reminder. A boundary. A warning.

Around eleven o'clock, a light gust rattled the windows. Not hard, but sharply enough that several heads turned instinctively. Daniel's mother, now seated beside him, tightened her grip on his hand. She had barely spoken since entering, but her presence alone was an answered prayer no one had prayed aloud.

Caleb watched the room gently, sensing the subtle waves of emotion that moved through it - fear in some, fatigue in others, but mostly something deeper: a longing for assurance. A longing not to be alone in the face of uncertainty.

He didn't stand to address it. He didn't feel led to. Instead, he walked quietly through the pews, kneeling briefly beside those whose breaths trembled, praying unspoken prayers with nothing but the pressure of a hand on a shoulder.

Rachel moved similarly, her gentleness like a balm. When she sat beside Amelia, she didn't say a word. She simply rested her hand on the woman's arm. Amelia inhaled shakily, then whispered, "I don't feel silly for being here. That's... new."

"You belong here," Rachel answered softly. "You always have." Amelia wiped her eye and nodded.

At eleven-thirty, a faint, muffled rumble echoed across the valley - not thunder, not trucks, but the distant shift of fire finding new fuel. The sound rolled like a low drumbeat beneath the hills.

Someone near the window whispered, "Did you hear that?"

Caleb stepped outside briefly, scanning the ridgeline. The glow had intensified again, stretching much further across the crest, flickering with new life and intensity. Still far. Still not racing. But unmistakably active.

Murray's words from earlier echoed in his mind: *Challenging, but manageable.*

He breathed deeply and whispered, "Lord, strengthen them." When he returned inside, people watched his face. He offered a steady smile - honest but reassuring.

"It's more visible tonight," he said. "But it's still burning along the ridge, not toward us."

A soft, collective exhale moved through the sanctuary.

Just before midnight, the most unexpected moment of the night arrived. Mary Kline, who had been sitting quietly near the front, struggling with the weight of memory and age, slowly stood without her walking stick. She braced herself on the pew, turned toward the room, and said in a voice both trembling and strong:

"May I pray?"

The room hushed instantly.

Mary lifted her chin, eyes bright with unshed tears.

"Lord God," she began, "we have walked these valleys for many years. We have seen drought and flood, sickness and loss, joy and laughter, fear and faith. And You have never left us. Not once."

A few heads bowed deeper.

"We stand tonight in the glow of a fire we cannot see fully. But You see it. We breathe in smoke we cannot avoid. But You breathe life into us. We feel the weight of uncertainty - but You feel none of it, because You hold every tomorrow in Your hands."

Her voice wavered, but she continued.

"Make us brave, Lord. Not foolish. Not proud. Just brave enough to trust You. Brave enough to care for one another. Brave enough to keep our hearts open. And grant strength to those out there fighting the flames we only watch from afar. Bless their hands. Bless their families. Bless their courage."

She paused, tears spilling freely now.

"And bless Willowend - small as we are, tired as we are - that we might remember tonight that You are our refuge."

A chorus of quiet *amens* rose from the congregation. Some whispered, some choked with emotion, some spoken only in breath.

Caleb felt his own eyes burning, and not from smoke. "That," he whispered to Rachel, "was the sermon no one needed me to preach."

Rachel smiled softly. "The Spirit speaks through the willing."

After Mary's prayer, the sanctuary's atmosphere changed. Not lightened - the glow on the ridge still pulsed, the smoke still shifted - but deepened. Strengthened. Like a cord drawn tighter through many hands.

For a while, no one moved. The silence felt sacred.

Then gradually, slowly, the night settled again. People prayed quietly. A few cried softly. Graham held Julie's hand with renewed steadiness. Daniel rested his head on his mother's shoulder, her fingers gently tracing circles on his sleeve.

Even Amelia closed her eyes and breathed deeply, letting the quiet work its way into the corners of her heart.

Around twelve-thirty, the emergency app buzzed again.

Caleb checked it immediately.

No escalation.

No evacuation.

Only a status update:

"Watch and Act - fire behaviour variable. Containment lines holding. Crews conducting active night operations. Residents advised to stay alert."

He read it aloud. Relief - quiet, restrained, but real - moved through the room.

"Thank You, Lord," Mary murmured.

As the approach of one o'clock softened the edges of the night, people began preparing to leave. Not because the danger had passed - it had not - but because their souls were steadier than they had been at sunset.

The glow still burned behind the ridge, but its presence no longer felt like a threat pressing against their breath. It felt like a reminder: life is fragile, and God is faithful.

When Amelia rose to leave, she approached Caleb hesitantly.

"I never prayed before," she said quietly. "Not really. But when Mary prayed tonight... I felt something."

"What did you feel?" Caleb asked.

Her eyes filled with emotion she didn't try to hide.

"Like the air inside me was different from the air outside. Like… peace."

Caleb nodded gently. "That's God drawing near."

"Will He… draw near again?" she whispered.

"He never stopped," Caleb said.

He expected her to look away, but she didn't. She nodded slowly and walked into the smoky night with more steadiness than she'd carried in.

Daniel and his mum were next. The woman approached with tentative courage.

"Pastor," she said softly, "I … needed tonight more than I knew."

"I'm glad you came," he replied.

Her voice cracked. "It's been so long since I sat in a place where people weren't angry."

"Church is not for anger," Caleb said. "It's for refuge."

She nodded, wiping her eyes. "Thank you."

"You're welcome here anytime," he said gently.

When the sanctuary finally emptied and the lamps were turned off, Caleb and Rachel stepped outside into a night that glowed faintly along the ridge. Smoke drifted like pale ghosts across the streetlights. The wind, though softer now, carried the warmth of burning trees far away.

Rachel leaned lightly into him. "Tonight … changed people."

"Yes," Caleb said. "Tonight, God breathed through a smoky valley."

"And tomorrow?"

"We'll meet tomorrow as it comes."

They began the walk home, hand in hand, the glow behind the ridge flickering like a distant lantern guiding them through the dark.

Willowend was still safe.

The fire was still contained.

God was still near.

And the night the hills glowed would not be forgotten.

Sunday morning rose through smoke.

The sun, weakened by haze, appeared as a pale disc suspended behind a muted sky. Though the night's glow along the ridge had faded with dawn, its memory lingered - in the air, in the land, and especially in the hearts of the people of Willowend.

Caleb woke before his alarm. He lay still for a few moments, listening. No helicopters. No sirens. Just a quiet, oppressive stillness that felt almost reverent.

Beside him, Rachel stirred. "You're awake early."

"So are you."

"That was a long night," she whispered.

"Yes," he said softly. "And a holy one."

They dressed slowly, neither speaking much. A Sunday morning always carried a certain weight, but this one carried more - not because the fire threatened them, but because the town had stepped closer to its own soul the night before.

At the kitchen window, Caleb paused, watching ash drift lightly across the yard.

"It's falling again," he murmured.

"Softly," Rachel replied, joining him at the window. "Like a reminder, not a warning."

He nodded. "People will come tired today."

"People will be coming different today," she said. "God did something last night."

Caleb felt that truth resonate deep in his spirit. He didn't know exactly what God had stirred, only that hearts had shifted - some gently, some profoundly. The glow on the ridge had illuminated more than land; it had illuminated lives.

They shared a simple breakfast, then walked slowly toward the church. The sky hung heavy with smoke, but the path felt familiar, steady beneath their feet.

As they neared the building, Caleb saw something that made him stop for a moment.

People were already arriving.

Not just the usual early faithful. People who rarely came. People he'd never seen on a Sunday morning. Amelia. Daniel and his mum. Even two of the boys who had followed Daniel the previous night, awkward and unsure.

They weren't just drifting in; they were *seeking*.

Rachel smiled softly. "They're coming because they found refuge here."

"And because the valley breathed fear last night," Caleb said.

"And God breathed peace."

The congregation gathered in small clusters near the entrance - tired, subdued, but open. Graham and Julie stood hand in hand, faces lined with exhaustion but relief. Mary sat on the bench by the door, walking stick in one hand, prayer book in the other. She looked up when she saw them.

"Pastor," she said gently, "today is not a day for long sermons." Caleb laughed quietly. "I wasn't planning one."

"Good," she said. "Today is a day for rest."

She tapped her chest lightly. "The kind only God can give."

Inside, the sanctuary felt both familiar and new. The lamplight from the night before had been replaced with the soft, filtered daylight pushing through the smoke. The cross at the front stood steady, unaffected by the haze. Caleb walked down the aisle slowly, letting the space breathe with him. He could sense the quiet expectancy - not the kind that comes before a polished service, but the kind that comes after a shared experience of vulnerability.

As the time for worship approached, the congregation settled. No chatter. No bustle. Just a deep, communal stillness.

Rachel leaned toward him and whispered, "Lead softly today."

He nodded. "Softly."

He stepped to the front and looked out at the faces before him. Weary faces. Honest faces. Faces carrying traces of smoke and traces of grace.

"Good morning," he said gently.

A soft murmur of response echoed back.

"It feels strange to say 'good,' doesn't it? After a night like last night."

Several people nodded. Amelia wiped her eye.

"But it *is* good," Caleb continued. "Because God held us. He held our town. He held the firefighters. He held the night."

He let the silence hold that truth.

"He isn't done holding us yet."

He opened his Bible, not to a carefully prepared passage, but to Psalm 46 - a familiar psalm, but more alive today than ever.

He read slowly, without embellishment:

"God is our refuge and strength,
an ever-present help in trouble.
Therefore we will not fear, though the earth give way
and the mountains fall into the heart of the sea,
though its waters roar and foam
and the mountains quake with their surging."

People breathed the words in as though they were fresh water.

"There is a river whose streams make glad the city of God," he continued. "God is within her, she will not fall; God will help her at break of day."

At break of day.

As he read the line, Caleb felt the weight of it settle over the congregation. Break of day. The morning after. The moment when light emerges through smoke, not because the danger is gone, but because God has not left.

He closed the reading gently.

The service continued, but not in its usual form. There was no formal structure, no strict order of worship. People shared brief prayers. Someone requested a hymn. Someone else asked for silence instead. The room moved like a body - breathing, resting, trusting.

Daniel's mother sat still throughout, tears running silently down her cheeks. When the first hymn began - "Be Still, My Soul" - she closed her eyes and mouthed the words, though her voice made no sound.

Amelia sang quietly, barely audible, but with sincerity she had never felt before.

Mary prayed with her hands lifted slightly, palms open.

Graham and Julie leaned together, heads touching lightly.

And Caleb, standing at the pulpit, knew without doubt: this was not a Sunday service. This was a gathering of people who had met God in the flicker of firelight and now came seeking His rest. People lingered long after the benediction.

Nobody seemed in a hurry to leave, as though stepping back into the smoky air too quickly might undo the tenderness God had stirred inside them. Conversations formed in quiet clusters - not loud, not hurried, but warm and genuine, like neighbours reacquainting themselves with hope.

Daniel stood with his mother near the back pew. She looked different today - softer, less guarded, as if last night had loosened something she had held tight for years. When Caleb approached, she offered him a shy smile.

"Thank you for reading Psalm 46," she said. "I'd forgotten how strong those words feel when the world's... uncertain."

"They feel different," Caleb replied, "when you've lived them." She nodded. "I think I needed to hear it today."

Daniel shifted awkwardly, then said, "Mum might come again next week."

She shot her son a direct look, half embarrassed, half grateful. "I might," she admitted.

"You'll be welcome," Caleb said warmly. "Anytime."

As they stepped away, Amelia approached, hands in her jacket pockets, her hair still faintly dusted from the morning ash.

"That was... good," she said, struggling for words. "Simple. Honest."

"That was the goal," Caleb answered.

Amelia hesitated, then added, "When Mary prayed last night... I didn't know prayer could sound like that. Like someone talking to a Friend who was already listening."

"He was," Caleb said.

She exhaled. "I think I want to learn how to pray. Properly, I mean."

Caleb didn't rush his response. "Prayer isn't about being proper.

It's about being honest."

She nodded slowly. "Then... maybe I'm closer than I thought."

He smiled, and Amelia's eyes softened. She didn't linger; she simply dipped her head in gratitude and walked out into the hazy sunlight.

Graham and Julie stayed behind to help tidy the sanctuary. Graham gathered hymnbooks with a care that revealed how fragile he felt himself.

"How's the back paddock?" Caleb asked.

"Holding," Graham said. "The RFS gave us an update this morning. They got ahead of the spot fires overnight. The winds settled around three a.m. Made their lives a lot easier."

"Thank God for that," Caleb said.

"Yeah," Graham replied. "I had an hour's sleep after that. Best hour of sleep I've had all week."

Julie smiled gently. "I think the fire's given Graham a new prayer life."

Graham shrugged. "If last night didn't make a man pray, then nothing will."

By early afternoon the smoke began to thin. Not disappear - that would take days - but lift enough for the hills to appear in fuller silhouette again. The orange glow had faded entirely. Only a faint grey smear marked the place where the fire worked along the ridge.

Relief moved through Willowend like a quiet breeze. Not a celebration, not a triumph - just a softening.

Caleb and Rachel walked home slowly after the last people had left the church. The air still tasted of ash, but less acrid than the night before. The sunlight filtering through the haze was warmer now, more golden than copper.

"They're exhaling," Rachel said as they walked. "The whole town."

"Yes," Caleb agreed. "Last night tightened everyone's hearts. Today, they loosen."

"They loosen," Rachel said, "but they also open."

He nodded, thoughtful. "It feels like a turning - not of the fire, but of the people."

They reached their gate just as a faint breeze stirred the gum leaves overhead.

"Do you remember," Caleb said, "when we first prayed about coming to Willowend? When we asked God to give us a place where our ministry would be less about busy work and more about hearts opening?"

"I do," Rachel said.

Caleb looked toward the hills, now clearer than they'd been in days. "I didn't expect God to use a fire to do it."

Rachel's expression softened. "Sometimes He uses heat to reveal what's underneath the dust."

They stood quietly for a few moments, reflecting. Then Rachel slipped her hand into his.

"Come on," she said gently. "Let's rest a while."

The afternoon passed in a soft haze. Caleb lay on the sofa reading messages from neighbouring pastors checking on Willowend. Rachel prepared a light lunch. The simple domestic rhythm felt almost sacred after days of tension.

Around three o'clock, Caleb stepped outside to check the sky. He expected ash - and it was there - but what surprised him was the clarity of the horizon. The main smoke plume had shifted east. The ridge still held faint wisps, but nowhere near the dramatic glow of the previous night.

He whispered, "Thank You."

When he turned, he saw Rachel watching him through the doorway.

"Better?" she asked.

"Better," he confirmed.

She stepped onto the verandah, her face calm but reflective. "It feels like God said, 'Rest today. Tomorrow will bring its own needs.'"

Caleb nodded. "And tomorrow we begin again."

But not as the same town.

As evening approached, the temperature finally eased. The air settled into a warm, smoky dusk, but gentler than before. The wind, once restless, grew mild.

Caleb and Rachel walked once more toward the church to lock up fully for the night. The path felt lighter. The air easier. Even the birds had returned to their usual chatter, tentative but growing in confidence.

When they reached the churchyard, they found someone sitting on the steps.

It was Mary.

She had her Bible in her lap, her walking stick leaning beside her. "Mary?" Caleb asked gently. "Everything all right?"

She looked up and smiled. "I came to sit here awhile. I wanted to see the church in daylight after the night God gave us."

Caleb and Rachel sat beside her.

"I've lived a long time," Mary said quietly. "And I've seen a lot of nights. But last night…" She shook her head softly. "God was closer than the fire."

Rachel nodded. "He was. And He still is."

Mary closed her Bible. "This town is changing, Pastor. People will look back on last night as a night God reached out His hand."

Caleb felt that truth settle deep within him.

Mary took his hand. "And they will look to you. You and Rachel. For what comes next."

He didn't respond immediately. The words were weighty, not in expectation, but in blessing.

At last he said, "We'll walk wherever God leads."

Mary smiled. "Then Willowend will be all right."

They stayed there together until the light dimmed and the smoky dusk turned to night.

No glow danced on the ridge.

No sirens cut the air.

No alerts sounded.

Only the quiet hum of a town held in God's hand, catching its breath after a night of firelit prayer.

When Caleb and Rachel finally rose to leave, Mary called after them softly.

"Pastor? Tonight… sleep deeply. God is keeping watch."

Caleb smiled, his heart full.

"Yes," he said. "He is."

They walked home under a sky softened by smoke, but not threatened by it - a sky that carried the scent of both fire and mercy.

And for the first time in days, Caleb felt his soul rest.

Monday morning arrived with a surprising coolness, the first genuine relief Willowend had felt in weeks. A southerly change overnight had pushed the heaviest smoke eastward, leaving the valley breathing a little easier. The hills were still shrouded in a soft grey veil, but the sky above them held traces of blue - muted but present, like hope beginning to show its face again.

Caleb stood on the verandah with a mug of tea, savouring the crispness in the air. Rachel joined him with her own cup, leaning lightly against the railing.

"It feels different today," she said.

"It does," Caleb said. "Like the whole valley is finally exhaling."

A kookaburra called from the gum tree across the road - a sound they hadn't heard since before the smoke thickened. It made them both smile.

"I think people will come alive again this week," Rachel said.

"I think they already are," Caleb replied softly.

He thought of the faces gathered on Sunday morning - weary, expectant, softened - and he sensed that something had shifted, not just in the atmosphere but in the spiritual soil of Willowend. Something tender. Something ready. He didn't know yet what shape it would take, but he had learned not to rush what God was unfolding.

After breakfast, they walked slowly toward the church, enjoying the novelty of clearer air. A few people were out sweeping ash from verandahs or washing down cars left dusty from the last few days. Everyone they passed gave a tired but genuine wave.

Outside the servo, Amelia was hosing down the footpath. She looked up as they approached and lifted the nozzle in greeting.

"Morning," she said. "Feels almost normal today."

"Almost," Caleb replied. "And how are you?"

"Better," she said, surprising herself with the confidence in the word. "Yesterday helped. And last night... I slept."

She said it with a kind of wonder, as though sleep had reclaimed her unexpectedly.

"That's a gift," Rachel said warmly.

Amelia nodded. "I was thinking... would it be weird if I came to the midweek Bible study? Not to say anything. Just to listen."

"It wouldn't be weird at all," Caleb said. "It would actually be wonderful."

A faint smile tugged at her mouth. "Good. Then I'll try."

The hose water splashed at her feet as she returned to her work, but her expression held a new brightness - small but unmistakable.

At the church, Caleb sorted through the mail that had collected over the weekend. As he flicked through envelopes, he paused at one bearing the letterhead of the State Baptist Association.

Rachel noticed immediately. "Is that what I think it is?"

"Yes," he said quietly.

The pastoral review.

He had almost forgotten it in the haze - literal and figurative - of the previous week. He didn't open it immediately. Instead, he placed it on the desk, letting its presence settle without allowing it to settle too deeply.

Rachel stepped behind him, resting her hands gently on his shoulders. "One thing at a time, love. Last week was about fire. This week is about people. The review will have its place."

Caleb nodded. "You're right. I just... wasn't ready for it today." "You don't have to be," she said calmly. "God will walk with us through that too."

He breathed out slowly, letting her words anchor him.

Later that morning, he visited Graham and Julie's property to check on them after the long night. The drive out was peaceful, the countryside tinged with ash but not with fear. When he arrived, he found Graham checking fences while Julie tended to the garden beds near the house.

"How're things holding up?" Caleb asked.

Graham removed his hat and wiped his brow. "Better than expected. The wind change helped. They got on top of the worst spots."

Julie nodded. "We were blessed, Pastor. Honestly blessed."

Caleb walked with them a while, listening to their reflections, offering reassurance where needed. Graham spoke openly about the strain he'd been under - something he rarely allowed himself to admit.

"It's funny," Graham said quietly, "but Saturday night... I felt God closer than I've felt in years. Closer than during any sermon or song."

"God often comes close when the sky glows," Caleb said. "Not because of the fire, but because we're finally ready to listen." Graham nodded deeply, understanding the truth behind the words.

As Caleb left, Julie called after him. "Thank you for holding the town together, Pastor."

He smiled gently. "God did the holding. I just kept the doors open."

By midday, the temperature was still pleasantly cool, and Caleb found himself drawn to walk through the centre of town. People weren't bustling - Willowend didn't bustle - but there was a liveliness in their steps. Less heaviness in their shoulders. A readiness in their expressions.

Something was awakening.

As he passed the bakery, the owner, Sheila, waved him inside.

"I've got fresh scones," she said. "And Pastor - they're on the house. For everything you've done this week."

Caleb protested lightly, but she shooed away his objections with a flourish of her tea towel.

"Sit down. Eat. You look like you could use a bit of spoiling."

He sat. He ate. And he listened as Sheila told him how her sister in the next town had prayed for Willowend during the glow night, how neighbours had checked on neighbours, how fear had turned unexpectedly into kindness.

"Makes you think," Sheila said thoughtfully. "A fire can bring out the worst... but it can also bring out the best."

"It brings out what's already there," Caleb said. "Sometimes hidden until the smoke clears."

She nodded, her eyes soft. "I think you're right."

That afternoon, while Rachel prepared for the midweek program, Caleb visited Mary Kline. She greeted him at the door with her walking stick in one hand and her Bible in the other.

"I thought you might come," she said. "Come in, Pastor. I've brewed tea."

Inside, her small lounge room felt timeless - lace curtains, polished wooden frames, knitted blankets draped neatly over chairs. On the table lay her open Bible and a notepad filled with handwritten prayers.

"You carried the town on Saturday night," Caleb said sincerely.

She shook her head. "No, Pastor. I just spoke the prayer everyone else had inside them. Sometimes it takes an old woman to give words to the young people's hearts."

Caleb smiled.

Mary took her cup of tea and sat across from him. "God is stirring something here," she said plainly. "I felt it in that sanctuary. This wasn't just fear. This was awakening."

"I've sensed that too," Caleb replied. "But I don't want to force anything."

"No," Mary said firmly. "You won't. That's not your way. But you must be ready for what comes."

She leaned forward, her eyes bright.

"The town will need more from you in the weeks ahead - not bigger sermons, not louder words, but deeper presence. The kind of presence you and Rachel already give."

Caleb absorbed the words. They were weighty, but gentle.

"When God breathes on a dry valley," Mary said softly, "the ground softens before it grows."

He nodded. "Then we will walk with whatever grows."

"Good," she said. "Because it's coming."

As he walked home through the soft afternoon light, Caleb felt a strange mix of responsibility and peace.

Responsibility - because Mary was right.

Peace - because none of it depended on him alone.

The fire still smouldered beyond the ridge, but even more importantly, something had ignited within Willowend - something quiet, something holy. And this time, it was not smoke that drifted through the valley, but the first stirrings of renewal.

The rest of Monday unfolded quite slowly, as if the valley was reluctant to rush into normal life too quickly. Caleb spent much of the afternoon responding to messages from church members - brief check-ins, offers to help neighbours, quiet admissions of lingering fear. Each message felt like a small window into a heart softened by the weekend.

By late afternoon, he sat at his desk with the unopened letter from the State Baptist Association still resting beside his Bible. He touched the envelope, not to open it, but to acknowledge it.

Rachel appeared at the doorway, reading his posture instantly.

"You don't need to open that now," she said.

"I know," he replied. "But I also can't pretend it isn't there."

She walked in, placed a hand on his shoulder, and said, "There's a time for every task. The fire gave way to rest. Rest will give way to clarity. And clarity will give way to decisions. One step at a time."

He nodded, grounding himself in her steady wisdom. They had been through reviews before - some gentle, some difficult - but this one had arrived at an unusually tender moment, just as Willowend was beginning to stir spiritually. Caleb could sense that timing was no accident, though he didn't yet know why.

The next morning brought an unexpected knock at the church office.

Caleb opened the door to find Daniel standing there, hands in his pockets, backpack slung over one shoulder. His expression was unusually earnest.

"Got a minute?" he asked.

"Of course."

Daniel stepped inside and perched awkwardly on the edge of a chair. He looked around the office, taking in the bookshelves, the soft lamp, the framed Psalm on the wall.

"Mum wanted me to thank you," he said. "For Sunday. For… everything."

"How's she doing today?" Caleb asked.

"Better," Daniel said. "We talked for the first time in ages. Real talking, I mean. She told me she used to go to church when she was younger. Before… everything got hard."

Caleb waited, giving the boy space.

"She said last night was the first time in years she felt like God wasn't angry with her."

Caleb's heart softened. "God has never been angry with her."

Daniel nodded. "I told her that. She cried."

He glanced toward the window, embarrassed by his own emotion. "She wanted you to know she's thinking about coming on Sunday again. And maybe... maybe joining something during the week."

"That's wonderful," Caleb said gently. "Tell her she's welcome at anything - even if she only wants to sit and listen."

Daniel cracked a faint smile. "That's probably how she'll start."

He stood to leave, then paused. "Pastor?"

"Yes?"

"Thanks for not making church weird."

Caleb laughed softly. "I'll take that as a high compliment."

Daniel nodded once more, then left, his steps lighter than when he arrived.

Late that morning, Amelia knocked on the open church door and called, "Anyone home?"

Caleb waved her in. "Come in. How's your day going?"

"Good," she said, sounding almost surprised by her own answer. "Really good, actually."

She sat down, elbows on her knees. "I've been thinking about prayer. You said it isn't about being proper. Just honest."

"That's right."

"So..." She took a breath. "How do I start? I mean, what do I even say?"

Caleb smiled warmly. "Say whatever's true. If you're tired, say you're tired. If you're grateful, say you're grateful. If you're confused, say you're confused. God isn't waiting for perfect words - just open hearts."

Amelia absorbed that with a seriousness he hadn't expected.

"Could you… maybe write something simple for me? Something I can say until I find my own words?"

Caleb nodded. "Of course."

He took a small card from his desk drawer and wrote:

God, I don't have fancy words.
But I want to talk to You.
Thank You for being near, even when life feels hard.
Help me trust You.
Help me find peace.
Amen.

He handed it to her. She read it quietly, her eyes softening.

"This… this I can say," she whispered.

"That's enough," he said.

She stood to go, gripping the card tightly.

"Pastor?" she said at the door.

"Yes?"

"I don't think I came to Willowend by accident."

Caleb's heart warmed. "I don't think so either."

That afternoon, Caleb made home visits - brief conversations, cups of tea, reassurances that the worst of the fire threat had eased. Each home carried the same sense of quiet gratitude and lingering vulnerability.

At the Thompsons' farm, an elderly couple who rarely came to church, he found them sitting on their verandah, watching the hills.

"Pastor," Mr Thompson said, "we heard the church was open during the fire. We didn't come, but… it meant something knowing it was there."

"That's what it's for," Caleb replied.

Mrs Thompson added, "We might come one Sunday. Not sure when. But we might."

Caleb smiled. "Whenever you're ready."

They nodded, the invitation settling into their hearts like seed on soft soil.

As he walked back toward town, Caleb finally felt the full weight of what Mary had sensed - the valley was ripe for something new. Not revival in the dramatic sense, not crowds or noise or spectacle, but renewal. Quiet. Steady. Rooted.

People who had been closed were opening. People who had been distant were drawing nearer. People who had been alone were seeking community. And somehow, a fire on the ridge had been the catalyst.

When he returned home, Rachel was sitting at the kitchen table with the envelope from the State Baptist Association in her hand. She looked up, her expression calm.

"I didn't open it," she said. "I just thought… maybe today is the day."

Caleb sat across from her. His heart wasn't anxious - not truly - but aware.

The review wasn't punitive. It wasn't an accusation. But it was scrutiny, and scrutiny always carried weight for a pastor.

Rachel reached out and took his hand. "Whatever is inside, we face it together."

He nodded. Then he opened the envelope. He unfolded the letter slowly, scanning it once, then again more carefully.

Rachel watched his face, searching for signals.

At last, he placed the letter on the table.

"Well?" she asked gently.

"It's… official," he said. "They're scheduling the review visit. Two representatives. Within the next fortnight."

"Two weeks," Rachel murmured.

"Yes."

He leaned back, thinking.

Suddenly the fire, the glow, the spiritual shifts - all of it - took on a new dimension. Not threatened, not overshadowed, but… contextualised.

Whatever God was doing in Willowend would unfold in the very season when Caleb's ministry was being examined by the Baptist Association.

Rachel exhaled slowly. "Interesting timing."

"Very," he said.

But his heart was steady.

"Whatever this review brings," he said softly, "it won't stop what God is doing."

Rachel smiled. "No. If anything, it might reveal it."

They sat quietly for a moment, absorbing the convergence of events. Outside, the sky had cleared further, the ridge now visible in its full outline.

A smoky valley awakening.

A church stirring.

A pastor facing evaluation.

A movement growing in unexpected soil.

And Caleb knew - the real story of Willowend was only just beginning to unfold.

Tuesday morning broke clearer than any day in the past week. The sky, washed pale from days of smoke, stretched over Willowend with a faint blue that felt almost indulgent. The air still carried the scent of burnt eucalyptus, but the heaviness had lifted. People breathed more deeply, walked more lightly, moved as though the valley itself had taken a small step toward healing.

Caleb sat on the verandah with Rachel, enjoying the cool shade before the warmth settled in. They didn't speak for a while.

Eventually, Rachel said, "Do you feel it?"

Caleb nodded. "The stillness?"

"The softness," she clarified. "Like the ground of people's hearts is ready. More ready than before."

"Yes," he said quietly. "Something has shifted."

Rachel took a slow sip of tea. "I think the fire made people listen. Not to the danger, but to their own longing."

Caleb looked out over the valley, thoughtful. "There's a hunger here. Not dramatic. Not loud. But real."

"And now," Rachel said, "the question is what we do next."

He nodded. "We'll follow gently. Not push. Not organise something clever. Just… respond."

She smiled knowingly. "Which is your strength."

Caleb laughed softly. "Only because I've learned that forcing God's timing never works."

Around mid-morning, a knock sounded at the church office door. Caleb opened it to find Julie standing there, dust from the paddocks still on her boots.

"Sorry to drop in unannounced," she said, pushing a loose strand of hair behind her ear. "But I thought… maybe today needed a visit."

"You're always welcome," Caleb said warmly. "Come in."

She stepped inside, taking the seat nearest the window.

"I won't take up very much of your time," she began. "But something's been on my mind since Sunday."

Caleb waited.

"It's Graham," she said. "Something shifted in him on Saturday night. He won't say it outright, but I can see it. He's quieter. Softer. And last night he asked if we could pray before bed."

Caleb felt a warmth spread through him. "That's wonderful."

"It is," she agreed, "but he's… unsure. He hasn't prayed out loud in years. Maybe decades. He says he doesn't know how anymore."

Caleb nodded gently. "It's not about knowing how. It's about being willing."

Julie smiled. "That's what I told him. But he asked… would you mind coming by sometime this week? Not to make it formal. Just to talk. He trusts you."

"Of course," Caleb said. "Whenever suits."

Julie exhaled with relief. "Thank you. He's been carrying so much. Maybe this is the start of him letting God carry some of it."

As she stood to leave, she added, "The town's changing, Pastor. People feel safer speaking about faith now. You and Rachel… what you did during the fire… it mattered."

Caleb shook his head lightly. "All we did was open the doors." She smiled. "Sometimes open doors change more than sermons."

Later that afternoon, Caleb walked into town to pick up a parcel from the post office. The streets felt lively - not bustling, but awake. Shop owners were sweeping pavements, chatting with customers, and leaning on broom handles to watch the newly cleared sky.

At the bakery, Sheila called through the open window, "Pastor! Try the apple scrolls! I've perfected the recipe!"

He laughed. "I'll take your word for it - for today."

As he continued down the street, Amelia stepped out of the servo, waving him over.

"Pastor! Got a minute?"

"Always."

She held up the small prayer card Caleb had written for her the day before.

"I've been saying it," she said. "Every night. And... something's happening."

Caleb listened carefully.

"I don't know how to explain it," she continued. "It's like... like when I say the words, the air in the room changes. Not dramatically. Just... gently. Like I'm not alone."

"You're not," Caleb said.

She looked almost amazed. "I've never felt that before."

He nodded. "Prayer opens the heart. And God meets us there." Amelia tucked the card carefully into her jacket pocket. "Is it too soon if I come to the Bible study tomorrow night?"

"Not too soon at all," Caleb said with genuine joy. "Come just as you are. Sit, listen, ask nothing of yourself."

She nodded. "Then I'll be there."

As she turned back toward the servo, Caleb felt the quiet certainty grow stronger - Willowend was waking.

That evening, as the sun dropped behind the western hills, Caleb and Rachel took a walk along the back road behind their home. The air was still warm, but the breeze held a refreshing cool edge. Birds returned to their usual chorus, filling the trees with life not heard in days.

Rachel said, "Have you noticed how many people are stopping you in town this week?"

Caleb smiled. "You too."

"They're not just making small talk," she said. "They're asking real questions. Sharing real things."

He nodded. "Something's thawing."

She looked at him thoughtfully. "And the review?"

He sighed softly. "It feels secondary... but still present. Like a shadow at the edge of things."

"Not a threatening shadow though," Rachel said. "More like a responsibility."

"Yes," he agreed. "And I want to handle it well. But I don't want it to distract from what God is doing here."

"It won't," Rachel said. "Because God knew the timing before they even scheduled it."

Caleb looked at her with gratitude. "You're good for me."

She smiled. "I know."

They walked in companionable silence for a few minutes before she added, "Do you think Willowend is ready for something new? Not a program. Just... a deeper seeking?"

"Yes," he said quietly. "I think they already started without us."

After dinner, Caleb sat at his desk, rereading Sunday's Scripture - Psalm 46. The words resonated differently now than they had even two days earlier.

"God is our refuge and strength..."

The fire had proven that, not by threatening the town, but by revealing its hunger for refuge.

"Therefore we will not fear..."
Fear had knocked loudly, but faith had answered quietly.

"There is a river whose streams make glad..."

Willowend had begun to feel those streams - not rushing, not dramatic, but steady.

As he closed his Bible, he felt a quiet prompting - not a voice, not a command, just a sense:

Prepare.

Prepare for what?

He didn't know yet.

A change in people?

A shift in the church?

A new season of ministry?

Something entirely different?

Whatever it was, it was gentle, like the way morning dew covers the paddocks - unnoticed until the sun touches it.

Before bed, Caleb stepped outside once more. The sky above the ridge was dark but clear, no glow on the horizon. Only the faint smell of lingering smoke remained.

Rachel joined him, standing with her head resting lightly against his shoulder.

"No fire glow tonight," she said.

"No," Caleb replied. "But there's another kind of glow rising."

She looked up at him. "You feel it too?"

"Yes," he said. "God is preparing something in this town."

"And in you," she added softly.

Caleb breathed deeply, letting the cool air settle in his lungs.

"If He is," he said quietly, "then I pray I'm ready."

Rachel wrapped her arm through his and whispered, "You will be."

They stood together under the quiet sky, the town resting beneath them like a field ready for planting.

No urgency.

No panic.

Just expectancy - the gentle kind that grows without sound.

Something was awakening in Willowend.

Something rooted.

Something quiet.

Something holy.

And Caleb knew - the next steps would matter.

Wednesday arrived with a gentle warmth and a clearer horizon. Though faint wisps of smoke still drifted from the far side of the ridge, Willowend felt more like itself again - grounded, peaceful, touched by collective gratitude. The fire crews remained vigilant, but the immediate threat had eased.

Caleb sensed it the moment he stepped outside. The valley was breathing again.

He and Rachel spent the morning preparing the hall for the midweek Bible study. They set out chairs in a semi-circle, placed a jug of water and cups on the side table, and opened the windows to let the fresh air filter in.

"This might be the largest group we've had in months," Rachel observed.

Caleb nodded. "People are hungry. The glow night changed something."

Rachel paused, looking at him with a soft, discerning expression. "And it changed you."

He smiled. "In ways I'm still discovering."

Before the study began, Caleb visited Graham and Julie's house as promised. Graham was sitting at the outdoor table, a mug of black tea in hand. He rose as Caleb approached.

"Pastor," he said, almost shyly.

"Graham," Caleb greeted, shaking his hand. "Julie said you wanted to talk."

Graham nodded and gestured for him to sit. His eyes were clearer than they had been in weeks, but there was vulnerability there too - the honest kind that comes not from weakness, but from finally setting down the weight of pretending.

"I'm not sure where to start," Graham admitted. "Saturday night… something broke open in me. Fear, maybe. Or pride. Or both."

Caleb listened without interrupting.

"I realised I've been carrying everything on my own shoulders for years. The farm. The drought seasons. The finances. Even my walk with God. I just… kept going. But I wasn't actually walking with Him anymore. I was just walking."

His voice tightened.

"Then that glow lit up the sky and… I don't know. It felt like God was near and I wasn't ready."

Caleb's reply was gentle. "God draws near even when we aren't ready."

Graham nodded. "I felt that. For the first time in a long time."

He hesitated, embarrassment flickering across his face. "I want to start again, Pastor. But I don't know how."

Caleb leaned forward. "You start where you are. You pray with whatever words you have. You open the Scriptures even if you don't understand them at first. And you let God meet you in the small, ordinary moments."

Graham swallowed hard. "Could you… pray with me now?"

Caleb smiled. "I'd be honoured."

They bowed their heads. Caleb prayed simply, asking God to renew Graham's heart, to lighten the burdens he carried, and to strengthen the faith already stirring within him. When they finished, Graham's eyes were damp but peaceful.

"Thank you," he said quietly. "That was… different from what I expected. Softer."

"God is soft with the humble," Caleb said.

Graham nodded again. "Then I'll keep showing up."

The Bible study that evening drew nearly twice the usual number of people. New faces mingled with familiar ones. Chairs were added quietly around the edges. The room hummed with something gentle but unmistakable - expectancy.

Amelia slipped in just before they began, taking a seat near the back. She clutched the small prayer card Caleb had given her, using it like a touchstone. Daniel sat nearby with two of his friends. Even Mary attended, walking slowly but radiating quiet authority.

Caleb welcomed them with his usual warmth but sensed the room needed something deeper than casual pleasantries.

Before opening Scripture, he said, "I know many of you have had sleepless nights this past week. Fear does that. But God has been close in the midst of it. Let's enter tonight with open hearts — not for answers, but for presence."

The study centred on John 14:27: *"Peace I leave with you; my peace I give you."*

They discussed peace not as a feeling but as a Person. Not as calm circumstances but as Christ's nearness.

Amelia listened intently, occasionally nodding, her face alight with curiosity. When Caleb invited reflections, she surprised herself by speaking.

"I always thought peace was something you had to create. Like you had to work for it," she said slowly. "But… maybe it's something you receive."

Heads nodded around the room.

"That's exactly it," Caleb said softly. "Peace isn't born in us - it's given to us."

As the study continued, the room filled with vulnerability. People shared fears they had rarely voiced. Others spoke of the unexpected comfort they'd found in the sanctuary during the glow night. There was no rush, no force - only authenticity.

Rachel watched from the side, her heart full. She could see what Caleb saw: Willowend wasn't asking for programmes or polished theology. It was asking for presence - God's and each other's.

After the study dismissed, people lingered again, forming small groups of conversation. Amelia approached Caleb with hesitation replaced by something more confident.

"I didn't think I'd say anything," she admitted. "But it just came out. Like something unlocked."

"That's how God works," Caleb said.

"Do you think," she asked quietly, "that He would want to use someone like me? Someone who's... well, not put-together?"

Caleb smiled gently. "God delights in using people who know they're not put-together. Because they lean on Him."

A soft smile touched Amelia's lips. "Then maybe there's hope."

"There's more than hope," Caleb replied. "There's purpose."

Her expression softened further. "I'd like to keep learning."

"You will," he said. "One step at a time."

As Caleb locked up the hall, Mary approached with her walking stick tapping lightly against the tiles.

"Pastor," she said in her firm but affectionate tone, "the river is rising."

He chuckled. "You and your metaphors."

She raised an eyebrow. "This old woman has lived through more seasons than you, young man. I know when a river of the Spirit is rising."

"I know," he said softly. "And I agree."

Mary leaned forward just enough to press her hand to his arm. "Protect it. Don't smother it. Don't rush it. And don't let outsiders trample it."

Caleb knew the last part was about the impending review.

He nodded solemnly. "I'll do my best."

"You won't do it alone," Mary said. "None of this depends on only you."

Her words were both encouragement and warning.

That night, back at home, Caleb sat at his desk reading over the State Baptist Association letter again. Official, polite, and precise - outlining the scope of the pastoral evaluation, the interview schedule, the conversation points.

Rachel entered quietly, carrying two cups of tea.

"Thought you might need this."

He accepted the cup and set the letter aside.

"Do you think the review will be difficult?" she asked.

"I think," Caleb said slowly, "that we're in a delicate season. And I'm not sure the review team will understand what God is doing here."

She nodded. "Probably not at first."

"But," he continued, "I'm not afraid of their presence. Only of distraction. I don't want the church to lose its tenderness, its openness."

She touched his arm. "You won't let that happen."

Caleb sighed softly. "I hope not."

Rachel smiled. "No - you know."

And he did know. Deep down.

Whatever the review held, Willowend's awakening belonged to God alone.

Later, standing outside beneath the cool night sky, Caleb looked toward the ridge. No glow. No smoke plume. Just the faint outline of the hills against the starlit horizon.

It was the first truly clear night in over a week.

And Willowend was much clearer too - hearts softening, faith awakening, relationships mending, and the Spirit moving quietly through conversations and prayers.

A subtle awakening had begun.

And Caleb could feel - as surely as he felt the cool air on his skin - that this awakening would shape everything that followed.

15. STIRINGS AND SHADOWS

Thursday dawned warm, with a gentle breeze moving through the valley. It was the kind of morning that made the gum trees shimmer softly in the light. The hills stood quiet, no longer glowing or smoking, only holding the memory of the week that had unsettled the entire community.

Caleb and Rachel shared breakfast on the verandah, listening to the magpies' morning warble. For a few precious minutes, it felt as though life had returned fully to normal.

But as Caleb reached for his tea, he felt that quiet nudge again - the sense of a new season emerging, both beautiful and weighty.

Rachel noticed his contemplative expression. "You feel the shift again, don't you?"

"Yes," he said. "Something is growing in people. But at the same time…" He hesitated.

"The review," she finished gently.

He nodded.

"It's like two currents running beside each other," Caleb said. "One full of life, the other carrying questions."

Rachel reached across the table and took his hand. "You don't have to fear questions."

"No," Caleb agreed. "But I want to steward the awakening here carefully. I don't want anything to interrupt it."

Rachel smiled. "The Spirit's work is not so easily interrupted."

That truth settled him.

Later that morning, Caleb went into town to buy supplies for the weekend service. As he walked along the footpath, Sheila waved him over from the bakery window.

"Pastor, come taste this batch - I've been experimenting again," she said, holding up a tray of steaming cinnamon scrolls.

Caleb laughed. "You're soon going to have me preaching about gluttony."

"You preach about love," she retorted. "Leave the gluttony to the big city Baptists."

He chuckled and stepped inside.

The scroll was excellent - soft and sweet with just the perfect amount of spice.

As he finished, Sheila leaned on the counter and lowered her voice. "You know, Pastor, I've been thinking... that night the hills glowed? I expected chaos. Fear. But what we got was... unity. Quiet unity."

"Yes," Caleb said. "God met us in it."

She nodded. "I never thought I'd say this, but... I might come along this Sunday. Haven't been in that church since my niece's baptism fifteen years ago."

Caleb felt a rush of warmth. "You'd be most welcome."

"Don't make a fuss if I turn up," she warned.

"No fuss," he promised.

Sheila winked. "Good. I don't do fuss."

As he left, he realised - this was happening everywhere. People who hadn't been near the church in years were feeling drawn.

Not by programs or pressure, but by something deeper.

Something holy.

On his way to the grocer, Caleb spotted Amelia sitting on a bench outside the servo, reading the prayer card again. She looked up immediately.

"Pastor!" she said, brightening. "I'm doing it. Twice a day now."

"That's wonderful," Caleb said sincerely.

"And I've started writing down things I'm thankful for," she added. "It's strange, but… it makes the day feel different."

"Gratitude does that," he said.

Amelia hesitated, then asked, "Do you think God hears me even when I feel awkward?"

Caleb smiled warmly. "God hears awkward prayers better than polished ones."

She laughed. "Good. Because mine sound like someone learning to drive a car for the first time."

"You're doing beautifully," Caleb assured her.

Amelia folded the card carefully. "Bible study was good. I didn't understand everything, but… I understood enough. Enough to want more."

"You're on the right path," he said.

She nodded slowly. "For the first time in years, I feel… steady."

He felt his heart lift. "That's God's peace."

As Caleb approached the grocer's, he noticed an unfamiliar car parked outside the church - sleek, silver, and out of place among the dusty utes and hatchbacks of Willowend. Two people stood beside it, examining the exterior of the building.

A man in a navy blazer and a woman holding a clipboard.

Caleb's steps slowed.

Rachel, who had caught up with him on her way from the hall, also paused.

"Do you think…?" she began.

"Yes," Caleb said quietly. "I think the State Baptist Association has arrived early."

They approached the pair with calm, measured steps.

"Good morning," Caleb said with a friendly but cautious tone.

The man turned, smiling politely. "Ah, Pastor Merritt. Good to meet you. I'm Mark Ellis, and this is my colleague, Sarah Penman. We're with the State Baptist Association."

Rachel offered a gracious nod. "Welcome to Willowend."

"Thank you," Sarah said warmly. "We've driven up today to familiarise ourselves with the town before the formal review meeting next week."

Caleb kept his expression open. "How can we assist you?"

"Oh, nothing formal today," Mark said, brushing the air lightly. "Just getting a feel for the place, you know? Understanding the context of your ministry."

His tone was friendly, but Caleb sensed an analytical edge beneath the warmth.

Sarah added, "We've heard interesting things about Willowend lately. A lot of community engagement. A full church on Sunday after a difficult week."

Caleb nodded. "Yes. It's been a unique and tender season."

Mark glanced toward the church doors. "May we walk through the building? Just a brief look."

Caleb hesitated - only for a heartbeat - then smiled. "Of course." He opened the doors and led them inside. The sanctuary still held the lingering sense of Sunday's gathering - quiet, holy, alive.

Mark paused at the front pew. "This is a lovely space," he said. "Simple. Warm."

"It fits the town," Caleb replied.

Sarah studied the room with thoughtful eyes. "We've read your ministry reports. They're thorough. But reports never tell the whole story. We like to see the living context."

Caleb nodded. "Understandable."

She leaned slightly toward him. "We're not here to catch you out, Pastor. The review process is meant to strengthen churches, not burden them."

Caleb smiled politely. "I appreciate that."

But he felt Rachel's quiet presence behind him - steady and discerning. She sensed what he sensed: this review was not hostile, but neither was it light.

After a few minutes of casual conversation, Mark extended his hand. "We'll see you next week for the formal meetings. In the meantime, keep doing what you're doing. The Association is hearing good things."

Caleb thanked them, saw them to their car, and watched it pull away.

When the sound of the engine faded, Rachel exhaled.

"Well," she said softly, "that was sooner than expected."

"Yes," Caleb agreed. "And more pointed than expected."

She stepped closer. "You handled it beautifully."

He nodded, but his gaze was distant.

"I just wonder," he said quietly, "what they're really looking for."

Rachel touched his arm. "Whatever it is, truth will serve us best."

He smiled, the tension easing slightly. "Always."

They walked back toward town together, hand in hand, the breeze carrying the scent of gum leaves.

The awakening in Willowend continued. But the shadow of scrutiny had now entered the story. And Caleb sensed - with that quiet intuitive awareness God often gave him - that the two currents would soon meet.

The next morning, Caleb woke unusually early, long before the sun had fully coloured the eastern horizon. He lay still on his back, listening to the faint rustling of trees in the cool breeze.

It was peaceful, but his mind was already turning.

Rachel stirred beside him. "You're awake early."

"So are you."

She smiled in the dimness. "I felt you thinking."

Caleb chuckled softly. "Sorry."

"No need," she said gently. "Is it the review team?"

"Partly," Caleb admitted. "Their early visit yesterday… it felt intentional."

Rachel sat up against the headboard. "What do you think they were looking for?"

"Tone," Caleb said quietly. "Atmosphere. A sense of the church beyond the reports."

She nodded slowly. "And what did they find?"

Caleb considered this carefully. "A church that is softening. A town that is waking. A pastor who walks gently."

"And is that something they will question?"

"Or something they will celebrate," Caleb said. "I just don't know which."

Rachel reached for his hand. "Whatever they bring, we'll face it with honesty."

That settled him.

He got up, showered, and dressed with quiet purpose. Today would be a day of simple ministry - the kind that grounded him.

Late that morning, Caleb visited the aged-care wing of the town's small medical clinic. He went every fortnight, reading Scripture or simply sitting with the residents who no longer remembered names but remembered voices of comfort.

As he walked through the corridor, Nurse Heidi waved him over.

"Pastor, good timing. Elsie's been asking for you."

Caleb's face warmed. "How is she today?"

"Calm," Heidi said. "But thoughtful. You'll see."

Elsie sat by the window in her armchair, blanket over her lap, sunlight catching the silver in her hair.

When she saw him, her face brightened. "Pastor Caleb! I've been thinking about God this morning."

"That's always a good start," Caleb said, pulling a chair beside her.

She nodded vigorously. "The sky looks different today. Like it's been washed. And it made me wonder… does God sometimes wash skies because people finally look up?"

Caleb smiled deeply. "I think God washes skies because He loves beauty. But people looking up is its own gift."

Elsie nodded, satisfied with the answer. "Read me something peaceful."

He read Psalm 121. She closed her eyes as the words flowed over her.

"I lift up my eyes to the hills…"

When he finished, Elsie whispered, "Those hills have fire behind them, but God is still my help."

Caleb gently touched her hand. "Yes, Elsie. He is."

When he left the clinic, his spirit felt steadied again. Ministry at its simplest always reminded him why he was called.

After lunch, he stopped by the servo to refill his car. Amelia was inside, sorting stock with surprising energy.

When she noticed him, she waved excitedly. "Pastor! Guess what I bought?"

Caleb stepped inside. "What?"

She held up a small paperback Bible - crisp, new, and blue. "My first one. Well… my first one in a long time."

Caleb smiled, the kind of smile that reached all the way to his heart. "Amelia, that's wonderful."

"I started reading it this morning," she said proudly. "John chapter one. Had to read some bits twice - okay, three times - but it clicked. And the words… they felt alive."

Caleb nodded. "That's God speaking through Scripture."

She grew quieter then, more reflective. "Do you think… one day… I could help others like you help me? Not preaching or anything - just… being there?"

"Absolutely," he said without hesitation. "God works through willing hearts, not perfect ones."

She beamed. "Then maybe I'll start by helping at the church breakfast next month. Sheila said she'd show me the ropes."

"That would be perfect," Caleb said warmly.

Amelia returned to stacking shelves with a lightness that hadn't been there a week ago. Willowend was indeed changing.

In the mid-afternoon heat, Caleb drove to Graham and Julie's property for a follow-up chat. He found Graham near the machinery shed, repairing a fence post that had been loosened during the windy days of the fire.

"Pastor!" Graham called out, wiping his hands on his jeans.

"Good to see you."

"You too," Caleb replied, stepping out of the car.

Graham leaned against the fence, his expression open. "I've been thinking about what you said yesterday - starting where I am. I tried praying again last night. Just simple."

"How did it feel?" Caleb asked.

"Like I was talking to someone patient," Graham said slowly. "Someone who doesn't rush me."

"That's exactly who God is."

Graham nodded firmly. "Julie and I also talked. Properly talked. First time in weeks. We're… we're stepping into this together."

Caleb smiled. "That's a blessing."

Graham glanced toward the hills. "Pastor, do you think God used the fire to wake us up?"

"I think," Caleb said gently, "that God used the fire to remind you that you're held."

Graham swallowed, emotion catching in his throat. "Yeah. That's what it felt like."

They talked a while longer - practical things, spiritual things, things men rarely say unless trust has been quietly built.

As Caleb left the property, he felt the weight of something Mary had told him days earlier:

The river is rising.

He could see it now - in Graham's softened heart, in Amelia's awakening faith, in Daniel's restored relationship with his mum, in the growing attendance at Bible study, and even in Sheila's tentative return to church.

The Spirit was moving, quietly but unmistakably. But not all movement was gentle. Late afternoon brought an email notification on Caleb's phone. He opened it while sitting at his desk, expecting something routine. Instead, he found a message from the State Baptist Association:

> *Pastor Merritt,*
>
> *We appreciated the informal opportunity to view the church and meet briefly yesterday. Our team is looking forward to the upcoming review and commend you for your pastoral care during recent community events.*

Caleb read the email twice. Rachel, who had been preparing dinner, noticed the hush and came to his side.

"What is it?" she asked.

He handed her the phone.

She read the email, then set it down slowly. "This is… detailed."

"Yes," Caleb said. "More detailed than I expected."

"They want clarity," she said.

"They want oversight," he replied gently but honestly.

She nodded. "Both, perhaps."

He leaned back in his chair. "I don't mind transparency. I just worry about timing. Willowend's awakening is fragile. Tender. I don't want bureaucratic scrutiny to disturb it."

Rachel sat beside him. "Then we pray. And we answer with truth. And we stay steady."

He exhaled, letting her words ground him.

"They are not our enemies," she added softly. "They're just… cautious."

"Yes," Caleb agreed. "And perhaps God is going to use even their caution for good."

That night, after dinner, Caleb stepped outside alone. The sky above the ridge was clear again, stars scattered like quiet promises across the dark.

He breathed in deeply, sensing both currents:

The rising river of renewal.

And the approaching scrutiny of man.

He lifted his face toward the heavens. "Lord," he whispered, "let me shepherd Your people gently. And let me face this review with grace."

A soft breeze stirred the leaves.

And Caleb knew - without any dramatic sign - that God had heard him.

16. THE SUNDAY OF SOFTENED HEARTS

Sunday morning dawned with a clarity Willowend had almost forgotten. The sky was washed clean, the light soft and warm, and the ridge stood firm and unscarred against the horizon. The fires had not reached the valley, but the valley had nonetheless been changed.

Caleb stepped onto the verandah with his Bible under his arm and paused. He could *feel* it - something in the air, something in the land, something in the hearts of the people. An expectancy that wasn't loud or dramatic, but quietly alive.

Rachel joined him, fastening her earrings as she stepped outside.

"It's a beautiful morning."

"It is," Caleb said. "And I think the church will be full today."

Rachel smiled knowingly. "You're not the only one who sensed a shift this week."

They walked toward the church together. The path felt lighter, familiar and yet new. Birds were out again, swooping low over the paddocks. A slight breeze rustled the gum leaves overhead. As they rounded the corner toward the church, Caleb slowed.

Cars were already gathering outside. Not the usual handful of early arrivals, but many - perhaps twice the number he normally saw before the service began.

Rachel exhaled softly. "They're coming."

Caleb felt his heart swell. "Yes. They're coming."

Inside, the sanctuary hummed with quiet conversation. People filled the pews: regulars, newcomers, faces Caleb had only seen in passing around town, even a few who hadn't crossed the threshold of a church in years.

Julie waved from the second row. Graham gave a small nod, his eyes steady and open. Mary sat near the front; hands folded in serene expectation. Daniel sat with his mum, who offered Caleb a shy smile as he approached.

Amelia slipped in next, clutching her brand new Bible with the reverence of someone holding a treasure. She chose a seat not at the back, but in the middle - close enough to feel included, far enough to breathe freely.

Caleb noticed the many subtle signs of awakening. Hearts were softening. Faces were opening. People were leaning toward hope.

Rachel whispered, "Be gentle today."

"I will," he said. "Today isn't a day for big words."

"No," she agreed. "It's a day for warm ones."

When the service began, Caleb didn't start with announcements or explanations. He simply stepped forward, rested his hands lightly on the pulpit, and let the silence settle.

"Good morning," he said - not loudly, but with warmth.

A soft chorus answered. Even that felt different - more unified somehow.

"I don't know what each of you carried this week," he said.

"Fear. Weariness. Questions. Relief. Gratitude. But I know this: God was near. In the smoke. In the glow. In the stillness. And He is near this morning."

He let his eyes move across the room. Faces met his, some tearful, some hopeful, all attentive.

"Our Scripture today," he continued, "is from Matthew 11."

He opened his Bible.

"'Come to me, all you who are weary and burdened, and I will give you rest.'"

A hush followed. Not silence – a hush. The difference was subtle but unmistakable. Silence is empty. Hush is full - of awareness, of presence, of anticipation.

"No one in Willowend escaped weariness this week," Caleb said gently. "But weariness is not failure. It's an invitation. Jesus does not say, 'Become strong so you can come to Me.' He says, 'Come to Me so I can give you rest.'"

Several people nodded, including some who rarely reacted.

Caleb continued, speaking with tenderness rather than passion. "We learned something in the glow night. Not about fire, but about refuge. Not about fear, but about comfort. Not about danger, but about presence."

His gaze drifted naturally toward Amelia, toward Daniel and his mum, toward Graham and Julie.

"When uncertainty surrounds us, the invitation of Jesus becomes clearer: *Come to Me*. Not when you're brave. Not when you're perfect. But now. As you are."

He paused again, sensing the Spirit working quietly in the room. "Rest," he said softly. "Hope. Peace. These are not things we create. They are gifts we receive."

The sermon continued for only fifteen minutes - unusually short for Caleb - but every word felt weighted, precise, intentional. Not because he was trying to impress or inspire, but because the room needed simplicity, not speeches.

When he prayed at the end, he prayed for the firefighters, for those who had feared losing their homes, for the weary, for the awakening of hope, and for hearts carrying hidden burdens. Quiet sniffles were heard throughout the sanctuary.

After the sermon, the congregation sang "It is Well," and something unplanned happened. Halfway through the first verse, voices that usually murmured began to strengthen. The harmonies grew. The singing lifted. It wasn't polished; but it was earnest.

Daniel's mum wiped tears from her face. Amelia's voice cracked but did not falter. Graham sang in a voice Caleb hadn't heard in years.

By the final chorus, the whole room was singing with a conviction that came not from vocal strength, but from lived experience:

"When peace like a river attendeth my way..."

It was, in every sense, a moment of spiritual alignment.

After the benediction, people lingered as though reluctant to leave. Conversations sparked easily. Laughter bubbled in corners. A few tears were shed, but they were gentle tears - of relief, release, or recognition.

Caleb moved through them slowly, talking with each person who reached for him.

Sheila approached, arms folded in self-consciousness. "Well," she said, "you didn't embarrass me in front of everyone."

"I said I wouldn't," he replied, smiling.

She nodded. "It felt... right to be here today."

"You're always welcome," Caleb said.

Sheila nodded again, more softly this time.

Daniel's mum approached next, her eyes shimmering. "Pastor... today felt like something I've been missing for a long time."

"God has been waiting for you," Caleb said quietly.

She blinked away a tear.

Amelia came last, her Bible pressed to her chest. "I understood things today," she said. "Real things."

"God opens hearts slowly," Caleb replied. "And beautifully."
She smiled shyly. "I'll be back next week."

But as the last few people drifted out, Caleb noticed something out of place. A car parked discreetly under the trees across the road. The same silver vehicle he had seen earlier that week.
Two figures sat inside, watching the congregation leave.
Rachel followed his gaze. "Do you think...?"

"Yes," Caleb said quietly. "The review team."

"Observing," she murmured. "Taking notes, perhaps."

"Perhaps," Caleb said, though no anxiety coloured his voice.

He looked back at the church - at the doorway through which softened hearts had just passed, at the sanctuary that had become a refuge, at the community God was shaping.

Let them watch, he thought.

Let them take notes.

Let them see what God was doing.

Because whatever they evaluated, counted, or measured would never fully capture the Spirit's quiet work in Willowend.

Rachel touched his arm. "Are you all right?"

"Yes," Caleb said, feeling peace settle in him like a steady hand on his back. "Because the One who called us here is watching too."

They walked home hand in hand, leaving behind a church buzzing with holy possibility - and a pair of observers who would soon realise they were witnessing something deeper than a pastor's performance.

They were witnessing the beginning of renewal.

The rest of that Sunday unfolded like a slow exhale across Willowend. People drifted home from the service with a quiet sense of fullness - not excitement exactly, but a gentle settling in the soul, the kind that follows an encounter with peace.

Caleb and Rachel walked the short path back to their house, hands intertwined. They didn't speak much at first. They didn't need to. They had shared that room, that atmosphere, that sense of God moving in ways neither of them could manufacture.

Eventually Rachel said softly, "You preached as though you were holding something delicate."

Caleb nodded. "Because I was."

"Their hearts?"

"And mine," he admitted.

She leaned her head briefly on his shoulder as they walked. "It was exactly what the church needed."

He paused, then added, "And exactly what I needed."

Later that afternoon, after a simple lunch, Caleb sat at his desk intending to rest. But his thoughts returned to the silver car he had seen parked discreetly across from the church. Mark Ellis and Sarah Penman had made it clear the review was scheduled for later in the week, but their quiet observation that morning had carried… something.

Curiosity?

Caution?

Concern?

Interest?

He wasn't sure.

He opened his journal and wrote a single line:
Lord, let my heart stay soft and my steps stay true.
He closed the journal again. That was enough.

Mid-afternoon, there was a gentle knock at the door. Rachel opened it to find Daniel standing awkwardly on the porch, looking as though he wasn't sure whether he should leave or run. "Come in," Rachel said warmly.

Daniel stepped inside, removing his cap out of instinctive politeness. "Sorry to drop in," he said. "Mum sent me. Well… she asked me if I'd mind coming. She didn't want to bother you."

"You are certainly not bothering us," Caleb said, joining them in the kitchen. "What's on her mind?"

Daniel scratched the back of his neck. "She wanted me to tell you… thank you. For the way you spoke this morning. She said it felt like you were talking *to* her, not just to the room."
Caleb nodded gently. "Tell her I'm glad it reached her."

"And she said…" Daniel hesitated. "She said she wants to meet with you sometime this week. She wants to talk about… faith. And coming back to it."

Rachel's eyes softened. "That's beautiful."

Daniel nodded, relief visible in his posture. "She wasn't ready to ask herself. She didn't want you thinking she'd fallen apart."

"No one comes to God because they're put together," Caleb said.

"They come because they finally know they need Him."

Daniel exhaled as though he'd been holding the breath for hours. "I'll tell her."

He lingered a moment longer, then added quietly, "And Pastor? Thanks for seeing me too. I don't feel like a background character anymore."

The words struck Caleb tenderly.

"You never were," he said.

Daniel nodded, eyes glistening, then left quickly before emotion caught up to him.

As the afternoon light shifted into the golden haze of early evening, Caleb and Rachel took a walk along the back road. The air smelled faintly of eucalyptus and warm dust, with no trace of smoke.

"Today felt like a beginning," Rachel said.

"Yes," Caleb replied. "Like God is preparing something gentle, but real."

Rachel gave him a knowing look. "And yet?"

Caleb sighed softly. "And yet the review sits in the background. I don't want it to colour how I shepherd this church."

"It won't," Rachel said firmly. "It may test you a little. But it won't change what God is doing."

He glanced at her with a quiet smile. "Your faith steadies mine."

"That's how marriage works," she replied.

They walked in silence for a while as the warm afternoon settled around them.

At dusk, after dinner, Caleb heard a knock at the door again. This time it was Graham.

"Evening, Pastor. Hope I'm not imposing."

"Never," Caleb said. "Come in."

Graham stepped into the living room, hat in hand, expression earnest but uncertain.

"I didn't come for anything complicated," he said. "Just wanted to tell you… thank you. Today's service… it did something in me. I can't explain it, but it felt like God put His hand on my shoulder."

Caleb nodded, touched by the sincerity.

"And I wanted to say," Graham continued, "that I'm ready to step forward again. To lead my home spiritually. To be the man God wants me to be."

Caleb felt a lump rise in his throat. "Graham, that's a holy desire."

Graham's eyes glistened. "I haven't felt it in years."

"You're not returning to God," Caleb said gently. "You're remembering Him."

Graham nodded slowly, deeply. "Yes. That's it."
Before he left, he handed Caleb a folded sheet of paper.

"What's this?" Caleb asked.

"A prayer," Graham said shyly. "I wrote it last night. Thought you might… look it over."

Caleb unfolded it. The handwriting was rough, but the words trembled with earnest humility:

Lord, teach me to walk with You again.
Teach me to trust.
Make me steady.
Make me gentle.
And bring peace to this house.

Caleb looked up. "This is beautiful."

"You think so?" Graham asked, incredulous.

"I know so," Caleb said.

Graham left with a lighter step.

Rachel emerged from the hallway, having overheard the end of the conversation.

"That prayer," she said softly, "is a sign."

Caleb nodded. "Yes. A sign of the river rising."

Just as they were settling down for the evening, Caleb's phone buzzed with a text from an unknown number. He opened it.

Pastor Merritt,

We appreciated observing the service today.
Looking forward to our meeting on Thursday.

Warm regards,
Sarah Penman

Caleb read it, exhaled, and handed the phone to Rachel.

"They were there," she said quietly. "Inside the car."

"Yes."

"Do you feel uneasy?"

Caleb thought for a moment. "Not uneasy. Just… watched."

Rachel stepped close, resting her forehead lightly against his.

"Then let them watch. What they see is God's work, not yours."

Caleb nodded, a steady peace settling over him.

"Yes," he said. "Let them watch."

He turned off his phone, set it aside, and took Rachel's hand. Together, they stepped out onto the verandah. The sky above Willowend was unusually clear, dotted with stars that shimmered like promises.

No glow on the ridge.

No smoke in the air.

Only hope rising in quiet ways.

Something was awakening - slowly, tenderly, unmistakably.

And even under scrutiny, the Holy Spirit's work would not be dimmed.

Monday morning arrived warm and bright, with a breeze that rustled the tops of the gum trees and carried the comforting scent of eucalyptus through the town. Willowend had begun the slow work of returning to rhythm - not the old rhythm, but a new one shaped by the glow night, by shared prayers, by softened hearts.

Caleb felt it the moment he stepped outside. Something in the spiritual atmosphere was alive. Quiet, but unmistakably alive. He walked to the church with a lightness he hadn't felt in months, greeting people along the way. Sheila waved from the bakery window. Daniel cycled past with a grin. Amelia stepped out of the servo, her new Bible tucked under her arm.

"Good morning, Pastor!" she called.

"Good morning, Amelia," he replied with genuine joy.

She jogged over. "I read John 3 last night. Twice. The bit about being born again? I never really understood that before. Now… somehow I do."

"That's God giving clarity," Caleb said. "He opens the heart and the mind."

She nodded. "It's like someone turned on a light in a room I always thought was dark."

He smiled warmly. "Keep walking in it."

Later that morning, Caleb met with Rachel in the church office to prepare for the week. They reviewed the schedule: pastoral visits, the Wednesday Bible study, and - looming like a quiet shadow - Thursday's review meeting.

Rachel noticed Caleb glancing at the calendar more often than usual.

"You're thinking about it," she said gently.

"I am," Caleb admitted. "Not with fear. Just with… awareness."

"Awareness is good," she replied. "Worry is not."

He smiled. "I'm not worried. Only… attentive."
Rachel leaned against the desk. "What do you sense?"

"That they're curious," he said. "That they've heard things. Good things, perhaps. But maybe also concerns."

"Concerns about what?" she asked.

"That I don't know," Caleb said honestly. "It could be anything. Attendance patterns. Financial reports. My pastoral style. My age. Or simply that things are changing here and change always makes someone uneasy."

Rachel nodded thoughtfully. "Well, we'll meet it together."

Always those words - steadying, grounding, true.

In the afternoon, Caleb drove out to visit a retired couple, the Winchesters, who had attended church sporadically over the years. Their property sat on a slight rise overlooking the valley. When Caleb arrived, he found Mrs Winchester sweeping ash from the verandah.

"Pastor!" she called. "Come in, come in. We were just talking about the service yesterday."

Caleb smiled. "Good things, I hope."

"Oh yes," she said emphatically. "Harold hasn't stopped humming since we got home."

From inside the house, Harold shouted, "It's a catchy hymn!"

Caleb laughed. "It is."

They sat together on the verandah for nearly an hour - talking about the fire, their family, their memories of the church. At one point, Harold grew unexpectedly serious.

"Pastor," he said, leaning forward, "I've lived in this valley all my life. I've seen droughts, floods, plagues, and fires. I've seen churches rise and fall. But I haven't seen hearts soften like this in a long time. Not since the revival meetings in '78."

Caleb felt a stir in his spirit.

Harold nodded slowly. "Don't lose whatever this is. Don't let anybody squash it. Not even the Baptist Association."

Caleb blinked in surprise. "You've heard about the review?"

Harold snorted. "Small towns hear everything. And I'll tell you this: the Holy Spirit is doing something here. And I trust that more than any clipboard."

Caleb smiled gently. "Thank you, Harold."

"No, thank *you*," Harold said. "For opening the doors when the smoke was thick."

Caleb returned to town with Harold's words lingering in his mind like a quiet prophecy.

By late afternoon, the temperature had risen, but not the oppressive heat of the fire week. The sky held a gentle haze. Caleb and Rachel took their usual walk to clear their heads.

They passed Mary Kline's home. She stood at the gate, as though expecting them.

"Pastor," she said, "I have something to give you."

She handed him a small, folded piece of paper. Caleb opened it. A simple handwritten verse looked back at him:

"Be still before the Lord and wait patiently for Him."
(Psalm 37:7)

Caleb exhaled. "Mary…"

"It's for Thursday," she said softly. "Whatever questions they ask, whatever they misunderstand - be still. God will speak through calm hearts."

Rachel nodded. "Thank you, Mary."

Mary's wise eyes watched them. "Do not fear men with forms to fill," she said. "Fear only losing the tenderness God has grown here."

"We won't lose it," Caleb said firmly.

Mary pointed her walking stick toward the hills. "Then stay steady as the land."

That evening, Caleb received a text from Sarah Penman.

Pastor Merritt,

Just confirming Thursday's meeting at 10am. Looking forward to hearing your reflections on the ministry landscape in Willowend.

Warm regards,
Sarah

Caleb showed the message to Rachel.

"It's polite," Rachel observed. "But formal."

"Yes," Caleb agreed. "They want to know how I see things."

"Then tell them truthfully," she said. "Let them see the real Willowend. And the real you."

Caleb nodded. He wanted that too. But a small question flickered in his mind: *Will they understand what God is doing here?*

He hoped so.

He prayed so.

But not all movements of the Spirit are easily documented.

As night fell, Caleb stepped outside once more. The stars shimmered softly through the faint haze. The ridge lay quiet, no longer glowing, no longer threatening, simply resting.

He stood there for a long time, listening to the hum of insects, the distant bark of a dog, the rustling of leaves. Willowend felt peaceful.

Alive.

Tender.

Open.

Yet beneath the peace, he sensed the approaching tension - not dramatic or ominous, but present. Like the early shadow of a cloud drifting toward the valley.

Rachel joined him, slipping her arm through his.
"Whatever Thursday brings," she murmured, "it cannot undo what God has begun."

"No," he agreed. "It can only reveal where we stand."

"And we stand," she said softly, "on holy ground."

Caleb breathed deeply, letting peace settle his spirit.

"Then let Thursday come."

They stood side by side under the night sky, the quiet valley resting around them - a valley on the brink of something both spiritual and scrutinised.

And Caleb knew:

God had prepared him for both.

Tuesday dawned cool and still, the kind of morning that seemed to invite reflection. A faint mist settled in the hollows around Willowend, softening the edges of fences and gum trunks, as if the valley itself were preparing for a moment of clarity.

Caleb woke early, feeling unusually calm. Not indifferent - simply rooted. The Sunday service lingered in his memory like a warm hand resting on his shoulder. Even the thought of Thursday's meeting didn't disturb him the way it might have a week earlier.

Rachel made tea while he read a Psalm at the kitchen table. When she sat down across from him, she studied his face with quiet affection.

"You look peaceful," she said.

"I feel peaceful," he replied, surprised by the truth of it.

She smiled. "Then God has already gone ahead of you."

Caleb's first visit of the day was to the bookstore café - a small, cosy place run by an elderly couple, Doris and Len Murray. They had been pillars of the church in decades past, but age and mobility had limited their participation recently.

When Caleb entered, Doris looked up from behind the counter, eyes brightening.

"Pastor! I hoped you'd stop in before the review."

Caleb blinked. "How did you …"

"Oh don't be silly," she chuckled. "News travels in Willowend faster than a bushfire."

Len emerged from the storeroom carrying a box of books. "We're praying for you," he said with no preamble. "Not because we're worried, but because God seems to be stirring the pot around here."

Caleb laughed. "Stirring the pot?"

"Yes," Len said firmly. "Not trouble - renewal. And whenever God stirs renewal, someone inevitably sends a committee."

Doris shot him a playful glare. "Don't say it like that. They're not the enemy."

"I didn't say they were," he replied. "Only that they rarely see the whole picture."

Caleb leaned on the counter. "Do you think renewal is happening?"

Doris nodded softly. "Oh yes. Haven't you noticed how much? People are speaking differently. Softer. More honest. Even the air feels gentler."

Len gestured to the small stack of Bibles behind him. "Sold six of these since Sunday. Six. That hasn't happened in years."

Caleb lifted an eyebrow. "Six?"

"People are waking," Len said simply.

The words settled into Caleb's chest like a seed falling into fertile soil.

Late morning found Caleb back at the church preparing for Wednesday's Bible study. He printed some new study sheets, arranged chairs in a circle rather than rows, and prayed briefly over each seat as he passed.

Halfway through his preparations, his email pinged. He opened it, expecting a message from a church member.

Instead, it was from someone in the State Baptist Association office - but not Sarah Penman or Mark Ellis.

The subject line read: *Request for clarification — Willowend.* Caleb frowned slightly and opened the email.

Dear Pastor Merritt,

In advance of the review scheduled for Thursday, our administrative team has noted some discrepancies between reported attendance data and your previous quarterly returns. To ensure accuracy, could you please provide a brief explanation of these variations?

Warm regards,
Administrative Support Team

Caleb read the message twice.

Discrepancies?

Variations?

He checked the quarterly reports stored in his filing drawer. The attendance fluctuations had been small - nothing unusual for a rural church. If anything, the last two quarters had shown a slight increase.

So why the question now?

He forwarded the reports with a simple note:

Attendance patterns reflect natural variations common in rural settings, with a modest upward trend in recent months.
No concerns identified. Happy to clarify further on Thursday.

Yet something about the request stayed with him - not alarming, but peculiar.

Rachel arrived while he was closing the email.

"Something wrong?" she asked.

"No," he said slowly. "Just… curious."

In the afternoon, Caleb visited Sheila at the bakery. The moment he stepped inside, she waved him over with a dishcloth in hand.

"I've been thinking about what you said Sunday," she began, leaning on the counter. "That church is a place for the weary. Not the sorted."

"It's true," Caleb said.

"Well… for what it's worth," she continued, "I felt … not judged. Not even a little. And that hasn't happened to me in a church since I was a teenager."

Caleb smiled gently. "You belong in the family, Sheila. Always have."

She exhaled heavily. "Keep doing what you're doing, Pastor. Willowend needs it."

He thanked her, and just as he was about to leave, Sheila added,

"Oh - and two people were in here yesterday asking about you." Caleb paused. "Two people?"

"Yes," she said, wiping the counter. "City types. Smart clothes. Didn't buy anything. Just asked questions."

Caleb exchanged a look with Rachel, who had walked in behind him.

"Visitors?" he asked.

Sheila shrugged. "Said they were 'looking at the town.' But they asked specifically about the church. And about you."

Caleb's stomach tightened slightly. "Did they give names?"

"No," Sheila said. "But they asked a lot of questions about how involved you are in the community."

Rachel met Caleb's eyes.

Reviewers?

Or something else?

"Thank you for telling us," Caleb said calmly.

But as he left the bakery, he felt a faint shift - like a breeze that hinted at a change in weather.

That evening, as the sun dipped behind the ridge, the midweek Bible study group began arriving.

Something was different.

More people came than usual - not for spectacle, but for nourishment. Chairs filled quickly. People greeted each other with a warmth rarely seen on a Tuesday night.

Caleb led the study through Psalm 34:

"The Lord is close to the broken-hearted..."
People shared openly.

Mary reflected.

Amelia asked sincere questions.

Graham offered thoughtful insights.

Even Sheila slipped quietly into the back row.

Rachel watched it all with tender awe.

After the study ended, people lingered again - not rushing home, but soaking in the peace.

Daniel approached Caleb as the room emptied.

"Mum wants to meet you Thursday afternoon," he said. "She said she's ready."

Caleb felt his heart swell. "Tell her I'd be honoured."

Daniel nodded, then added, "Pastor... those two city people Sheila mentioned? I saw them yesterday too. They were near the lookout. Watching the valley. And writing things down."

Caleb absorbed that news with quiet seriousness.

"Thank you for telling me," he said.

Daniel nodded again, then left with a small wave.

Rachel stepped to Caleb's side. "Something's happening," she murmured.

"Yes," Caleb said softly. "Good things. And… other things."

"Do you feel unsettled?"

"No," he replied truthfully. "Just aware."

She slipped her hand into his. "Whatever comes, God has prepared your heart."

Caleb looked around the room - the empty chairs, still warm from the people who had filled them; the Bibles left open; the echoes of renewed faith in the air. He felt it again - that deep, quiet certainty.

God was moving in Willowend. And on Thursday, when the review team arrived with questions and forms and assessments, they would walk into a story much larger than they expected. A story God Himself was writing.

18. THE DAY OF THE REVIEW

Thursday morning arrived with an unusual stillness - as though the valley itself was holding its breath. Soft light spilled across Willowend, brushing the roofs and paddocks with gold. Birds called from the gum trees. A faint cool breeze moved gently across the yard.

Caleb woke early, not from anxiety but from readiness. He had slept deeply, held by a sense of quiet strength. Today would require clarity, patience, and grace - but nothing in his spirit resisted it.

Rachel watched him dress, her expression calm and supportive.

"You're steady," she observed.

"I feel steady," he replied.

"That's the Spirit's work," she said, fastening a button on his shirt with tender precision. "Not confidence in yourself – but a confidence in Him."

He kissed her forehead. "Walk with me to the church?"

"Always."

They walked together along the familiar dirt path. There was dew on the grass, and the air smelled clean. As they approached the church, Rachel squeezed his hand once.

"You do not walk into that meeting alone."

He nodded. "I know."

"And whatever they bring," she continued, "it cannot erase what God has begun here."

He smiled gently. "You sound like Mary."

"Mary's right," Rachel said simply.

Caleb unlocked the church and stepped inside. The sanctuary was cool and quiet, washed with soft morning light through the stained-glass windows. Dust motes floated like slow-moving stars in the beams of sun.

He took a few minutes to pray, not for success, but for alignment with God's purposes.

"Lord," he whispered, "let me speak truthfully. Let me remain calm. Let me honour You in how I respond."

Rachel waited respectfully at the back.

After a few minutes, Caleb rose.

"Coffee?" she asked.

"Please."

They shared a simple breakfast in the fellowship room - toast, fruit, and the strong black coffee Caleb always preferred on days requiring clarity.

At nine forty-five, the sound of tires crunching over gravel drifted through the open window.

They exchanged a glance.

"They're early," Caleb said.

"So are we," Rachel replied.

Two cars pulled into the church grounds - the silver sedan Caleb had noticed earlier in the week, and a dark blue hatchback following it. From the first car stepped Mark Ellis and Sarah Penman, dressed neatly and carrying folders. From the second emerged a third person Caleb had not met.

A man in his early forties, sharp-featured and impeccably dressed, with an expression that suggested cautious distance rather than warmth. He carried a slim laptop bag.

Sarah greeted Caleb with a polite smile. "Good morning, Pastor Merritt."

"Good morning, Sarah … Mark."

Mark shook Caleb's hand. "Thank you for meeting with us. This shouldn't take too long."

Caleb nodded. "You're welcome. And this is…?"

The unfamiliar man stepped forward.

"Justin Strickland," he said crisply. "Administration."

The tone was professional, but neither warm nor unfriendly - simply efficient.

"Welcome, Justin," Caleb said gently. "Please come inside."

Rachel stayed in the foyer as the team entered, offering them refreshments. Mark accepted some tea. Sarah requested water. Justin declined everything.

"Thank you," he said curtly. "I prefer to begin promptly."

Rachel met Caleb's eyes briefly. She didn't need to speak. He understood: *Be steady.*

They moved into the fellowship room, where Caleb had chairs arranged in a circle. The setup seemed to surprise them slightly. Sarah offered a polite smile. "A circular layout. That's very refreshing."

"I find it encourages conversation rather than interrogation," Caleb replied.

Justin made a small note on his tablet.

Mark cleared his throat. "Pastor, we appreciate your hospitality. Our purpose today is simply to gain a deeper understanding of your ministry context and the dynamics of Willowend Baptist."

"Of course," Caleb said. "I'm happy to share openly."

The conversation began cordially. Sarah asked about Caleb's personal ministry philosophy. Mark asked about community engagement, pastoral care patterns, and the town's response to recent events.

Caleb answered with calm clarity, speaking honestly about renewal, fragility, and the gentle spiritual movement he sensed in the valley.

Then Justin spoke for the first time.

"We've noticed a significant shift in attendance in recent weeks," he said. "Some might call it irregular. Can you account for these fluctuations?"

Caleb's eyebrows lifted slightly. "Attendance has risen slightly, yes. But irregular? Not unusually so for a rural church."

Justin's expression didn't change. "And what steps have you taken to ensure accurate reporting?"

"My reports have always been accurate," Caleb said calmly. "I submit them faithfully."

Justin made another note.

Mark interjected with a soft chuckle. "To be fair, Daniel is meticulous. Sometimes too meticulous."

Justin did not acknowledge the comment.

Sarah leaned forward. "Pastor, from our observation on Sunday, the congregation seemed deeply engaged. That's not always the case in rural churches. What do you attribute that to?"

Caleb answered honestly. "People are weary. The fire reminded them of their vulnerability. And God used that to soften hearts. I didn't cause it. I only opened the doors."

Sarah nodded thoughtfully.

"Would you say the church is experiencing renewal?" she asked.

"I would," Caleb said quietly.

Justin's fingers tapped his tablet again.

After nearly an hour, the tone shifted subtly. Sarah glanced at Justin. "There's another item we need to discuss."

Justin sat forward. "Yes. We've received informal feedback from a few sources indicating concerns about *pastoral boundaries.*"

Caleb blinked, surprised. "Boundaries?"

"Yes," Justin said. "Comments suggesting your approach may be overly personal. Too involved perhaps. Potentially blurring professional lines."

Rachel stiffened in her chair.

Mark cleared his throat. "We're not making accusations. Only following up on remarks."

"What remarks?" Caleb asked gently.

Justin's tone remained clinical. "Community observations. Some suggesting your availability is… unusually high."

Caleb paused. "Availability is a core part of rural ministry. People need presence."

Justin made another note. "Some also suggested you spend a significant amount of time with individuals going through personal crises."

Caleb frowned slightly. "That is pastoral care."

Sarah intervened kindly. "Justin, I think the point is simply to understand the balance."

Justin nodded but did not soften. "We must ensure pastors maintain emotional health and avoid becoming overly enmeshed."

Caleb breathed slowly, recalling Mary's verse: *Be still before the Lord…*

"I appreciate that concern," he said calmly. "But if people feel safe enough to seek help, that is pastoral fruit, not pastoral drift."

For the first time, Justin's expression seemed to shift now - not disagreement exactly, but recalculation.

Mark smiled reassuringly. "Pastor, please understand - we're not here to critique your heart. Only to ensure clarity."

"Clarity is welcome," Caleb said.

Sarah leaned in. "And for what it's worth, Sunday felt... alive. We don't often see that."

Justin glanced sideways at her. "We must remain objective."

Sarah nodded. "Of course."

When the questioning paused, Caleb spoke gently.

"May I ask something in return?"

Mark nodded. "Certainly."

"What is the purpose of this review? Truly. Beneath the formal language."

For a moment, none of them spoke.

Then Sarah answered quietly, almost reluctantly.

"There have been concerns at the Association level about pastors nearing retirement age. Questions about longevity. Succession. Resilience."

Justin added, "We need to ensure churches remain sustainable."

Caleb absorbed their words with calm understanding.

"So this is about age," he said softly.

"Not only age," Mark said. "But yes - it's a factor."

Rachel's eyes flashed, but Caleb reached for her hand.

He remained steady.

"Thank you for your honesty," he said.

The review continued, but the atmosphere had certainly shifted. Questions became more nuanced. Observations more open. Even Justin seemed slightly less rigid.

And as they moved toward their closing remarks, something unexpected happened.

Sarah spoke quietly, almost to herself.

"Whatever concerns exist," she said, "there is surely something happening in this valley that we cannot quantify."

Mark nodded slowly. "Something good."

Justin hesitated a little, then added, "Something worth paying attention to."

Caleb felt the Spirit stir within him.

Not defensiveness. Not triumph.

Only peace.

By the time the meeting adjourned, the sun was high and bright, casting long beams into the sanctuary.

Rachel squeezed his hand.

"You were steady," she whispered.

Caleb exhaled. "God carried me."

But as the review team packed their folders, Caleb sensed something else too: The meeting was not finished. Not truly. There was more beneath their questions - something not yet spoken, not yet revealed. And that revelation was coming.

Soon.

As Mark called the formal portion of the review to a close, the atmosphere in the fellowship room shifted from structured assessment to something looser, more human. The papers were stacked, laptops closed, pens set aside. But Caleb sensed, as clearly as if he had heard a whispered warning, *this is not finished.*

Rachel excused herself to prepare tea for the group. Caleb followed the review team into the sanctuary, where they wanted a final look at the space - the heart of the church's life.

Morning light streamed through the stained-glass windows, bathing the front of the sanctuary in a gentle warmth. Dust motes drifted in the beams, slow and unhurried. It was peaceful, prayerful - almost sacred.

Sarah paused at the pulpit, running her fingers lightly along its edge.

"You preached with such... softness on Sunday," she said quietly.

"Softness?" Caleb asked.

"It was strength," she clarified. "But it was gentle strength. People listened differently."

Mark stood near the front pew, taking everything in. "We saw something rare," he said. "A congregation leaning forward, not out of duty, but desire."

Justin stood further back, arms folded, expression unreadable.

"Engagement is important," he said neutrally.

But something in his tone betrayed thoughtfulness.

Rachel returned with a tray of tea, placing it on a side table near the front. Mark and Sarah thanked her warmly. Justin gave a polite nod.

As Rachel stepped back, Caleb felt her presence like a quiet anchor behind him.

Mark sipped his tea. "Pastor, I want to acknowledge something. These reviews can feel clinical. Impersonal. But your ministry here is clearly relational, deep, and grounded. That comes through even in how you answer questions."

"Thank you," Caleb said genuinely.

Sarah added, "You shepherd gently. That's... rare."

Justin finally spoke. "Gentleness can be misinterpreted."

Sarah turned to him, surprised. "How so?"

He hesitated - a rare crack in his composure.

"Some might see it as passivity. Or as being too close. Too available. Boundaries can blur."

Caleb nodded slowly. "I understand the concern. But availability is essential in this rural context. People don't need a distant shepherd. They need a present one."

Justin didn't reply, but he didn't argue either. His gaze drifted toward the cross at the front, and something in his posture softened.

After a few moments of thoughtful quiet, Sarah set her cup down.

"Pastor," she said carefully, "there is something we need to discuss. Not formally - not as part of the official report - but as a matter of pastoral wisdom."

Caleb felt the atmosphere shift again. Rachel stepped a little closer.

"Of course," he said gently. "Speak freely."

Sarah glanced at Mark, then at Justin. Mark gave an approving nod. Daniel's expression tightened, then settled.

"During the review process," Sarah began, "we sometimes receive … additional feedback. Not complaints. Not accusations. Just observations from people who care about their church and want to ensure pastoral longevity."

Caleb waited calmly.

"This time," she continued, "we received comments expressing concern for *your* wellbeing. Your emotional load. Your pastoral weight. The amount of crisis care you've carried."

Caleb blinked, surprised. "Concern for me?"

"Yes," Mark said gently. "Not criticism. Concern."

Justin added quietly, "Some worry you bear too much alone."

Rachel inhaled softly, emotion stirring behind her eyes.

Sarah explained, "We heard from a few community members - not church members necessarily - that you seem increasingly tired. That you hold others' burdens deeply. That the fire week, the pastoral crises, even the quiet renewal happening now... all of it may be taking a toll."

Caleb exhaled slowly. He had not expected this.

Mark stepped closer. "Pastor Merritt, your ministry is beautiful. Truly. But renewal brings weight. And sometimes churches awaken faster than pastors can carry."

Justin added, his tone unexpectedly gentle, "You don't need to be a solitary shepherd."

Caleb felt a strange mixture of humility and warmth rise within him. He had anticipated the scrutiny, the evaluation, perhaps a questioning of competence or longevity - but not this.

Not concern for *his* soul.

"I didn't realise people noticed," he said quietly.

Rachel touched his arm. "I've noticed," she whispered.

Caleb looked at her, tenderness in his eyes. "I know. But hearing it from others... it's different."

Sarah nodded. "We're not recommending anything drastic. We simply want you to have support. Mentoring. Companionship in ministry. Rural pastors can become isolated without realising it."

Mark added, "We also want to understand your own sense of calling long-term. Not because we believe you're near the end, but because sustainability matters - for you and the church."
Caleb absorbed this with deep thoughtfulness.

"My calling has not wavered," he said slowly. "But I see now that perhaps I've held too much quietly."

Rachel nodded firmly. "You have."

Justin said softly, almost cautiously, "Strength doesn't mean silence."

The words landed gently but powerfully.

Caleb took a moment before responding.

"Thank you," he said. "Truly. I certainly wasn't expecting this perspective, but I receive it with humility. I love this church. I love this valley. And I always want to serve faithfully - not just passionately."

Sarah smiled warmly. "Then we're on the same page."

Mark nodded. "Excellent. Because the State Baptist Association wants to support you, not pressure you."

Even Justin's posture eased a little. "Rural ministry is complex. You're doing well. Better than many realise."

It was, for a man of his disposition, high praise.

As the conversation wound down, Rachel spoke up - something she rarely did in formal settings.

"If I may," she said softly, "Caleb carries this community in prayer every day. He gives more than people know. And I believe with my whole heart that what's has been happening in Willowend is God's work - not Caleb's burden."

Her voice trembled slightly, not with fear but with conviction.

Sarah nodded with deep respect. "Thank you, Rachel. That's important for us to hear."

Mark added, "Your partnership as a couple is evident. It's a gift to the church."

Justin simply said, "Strong marriages steady churches."

Rachel smiled appreciatively.

They closed in prayer - initiated by Mark but joined by all.

And as they prayed, something happened that none of them commented on, but all silently felt:

The atmosphere shifted again.

The room warmed.

Peace settled.

A quiet sense of God's presence rested upon them.

Not the presence one feels in a large gathering - but the intimate nearness that surrounds honest conversation and humility.

When the prayer ended, there was a moment of shared stillness.

Then Sarah exhaled softly. "Thank you, Pastor. This was quite different from most reviews."

"I hope that's a good thing," Caleb said gently.

"It is," she answered.

Justin extended a hand - firm, respectful. "You're not what I expected."

Caleb smiled. "Neither are you."

Justin allowed the smallest hint of a smile.

As they packed their things and prepared to leave, Sarah paused at the door.

"One last thing," she said. "We still have a few questions to process. A few conversations to have. But my impression is this: Willowend is healthy. And so is its shepherd."

Caleb felt a wave of gratitude rise within him. "Thank you."

"We'll be in touch soon," Mark added.

Rachel walked them to the doorway, saying her goodbyes with grace. When the cars finally disappeared down the road, the church grounds fell into silence again.

Caleb turned to Rachel, exhaling slowly.

"Well?" she asked.

He nodded, emotion softening his features. "It wasn't what I feared. And it wasn't what I expected. But I think…"

He paused, searching for the right words. "I think God used it."

Rachel slipped her arm through his. "Of course He did."

They stood together on the church steps, letting the stillness wash over them.

The review was over.

The truth had surfaced.

And the deeper work - in Caleb, in the church, in the valley - had only just begun.

The morning after the review broke bright and clear, as though the valley were offering a soft, reassuring nod to the day before. Sunlight poured across the ridge, warming the gum leaves and dappling the ground. There was no heaviness in the air. No lingering tension. Only a calm sense of continuation - the quiet rhythm of a place that had learned to hold both vulnerability and hope.

Caleb stepped outside with his coffee, breathing deeply. He felt… lighter. Not because the review had been easy - parts of it had touched tender places - but because it had been honest. And honesty, he realised, had brought clarity rather than burden.

Rachel joined him on the verandah, her hair pulled back, her Bible open in one hand.

"How's your heart this morning?" she asked.

"Settled," he replied.

"And your mind?"

He chuckled. "Also settled. Mostly."

She leaned her head gently on his shoulder. "Then yesterday served its purpose."

Caleb nodded. "It did. But I want to be wise about what they shared - especially about carrying too much alone."

Rachel lifted her eyes to him. "That wasn't a criticism, Caleb. It was care."

He smiled softly. "I know."

Their first stop of the morning was the general store. Caleb needed milk, and Rachel wanted stamps. But the moment they walked inside, they were greeted with something unexpected.

A handwritten sign on the noticeboard read:

"Thank you, Pastor Caleb - for being here this week."
- From a grateful community

Beneath it were several smaller notes - anonymous but sincere.

"Your doors being open saved us from panic."
"Your prayer on glow night brought us peace."
"We saw God in your gentleness."

Caleb paused, touched. "Who - ?"

The store manager, Donna, emerged from the aisle with a knowing smile.

"People needed to say something," she said. "Everyone knew the review was happening this week. Folks wanted you to know you're valued."

Rachel's eyes shimmered. "That's incredibly kind."

Donna shrugged lightly, but her voice held feeling. "It's true. This town trusts you. You don't always see it - but they do."

Caleb felt warm gratitude settle over him. "Thank you. Truly."

"And Pastor," Donna added, lowering her voice, "those review people? They came in here afterwards. Asked a few questions. But they seemed impressed."

Caleb smiled with a mixture of amusement and relief. "Good to hear."

Next, Caleb visited Graham's property. He hadn't seen him since the Bible study, and something in his spirit nudged him to check in.

He found Graham near the shed, repairing a gate latch. When he saw Caleb, he wiped his hands and grinned.

"Well, if it isn't the man of the hour," he joked.

"Don't start," Caleb said with a laugh. "I'm still regaining my equilibrium."

Graham clapped him on the shoulder. "Word around town is you did well."

Caleb raised an eyebrow. "Word gets around quickly."

"Faster than the post," Graham replied. "And Pastor? Julie and I wanted to say… we're proud of you."

Caleb's chest tightened slightly. "Thank you."

"And one more thing," Graham added, pointing with his spanner. "Yesterday's reminder? About not carrying everything alone?" He paused. "Take it seriously. You are allowed to rest too."

Caleb nodded, moved by the sincerity. "I will."

Graham grinned. "Good. Now help me with this latch - because I'm carrying *too* much alone."

Caleb laughed and stepped forward to help.

Later that morning, Caleb returned to the church to do some light administrative work - review attendance sheets, update pastoral care notes, and prepare Sunday's message. But something unexpected awaited him.

A small package sat on the front pew, wrapped in brown paper with a note attached.

"Pastor Caleb - thought this might help.
From someone grateful you're here."

He opened the paper carefully. Inside was a beautiful leather-bound journal - rich brown, soft, and embossed with a simple cross.

Caleb ran his fingers across it, deeply touched by the intimate thoughtfulness.

He sat down in the pew, opened the journal to the first blank page, and wrote:

"Lord, teach me to share the weight You never asked me to carry alone."

He paused, then added:

"And thank You for this valley - Your valley - where hearts are softening like dawn."

Around midday, he visited Mary Kline. She was sitting on her verandah as though waiting for him.

"I knew you'd come," she said before he even greeted her.

"How?" Caleb asked with a smile.

"You always check on those who prayed for you," she replied.

"Come sit."

He sat beside her, grateful for the quiet wisdom she carried.

"Well?" she asked. "Did they tear you apart?"

"Not at all," Caleb answered. "In fact, they expressed concern for my wellbeing."

Mary nodded as though she had known that would happen. "Of course they did. God gave them eyes to see what you hide well." Caleb chuckled. "What do I hide?"

Mary turned her gaze toward the ridge. "Your weariness. Your compassion. Your quiet ache for this town. You carry people deeply - and that's good. But deep carrying tires the heart."

He exhaled. "That was part of their concern."

"And rightly so," she said. "Even shepherds need shepherding."

They sat in silence for a long moment.

Then Mary spoke again. "Pastor, renewal is coming. You can feel it, can't you?"

"Yes," Caleb said. "It's gentle, but real."

"It will grow," Mary said. "But so will the weight. So learn now to share the load - before the river becomes a flood."

Caleb considered her words deeply.

"Thank you," he said. "I'll take that to heart."

"I know you will," she replied.

In the late afternoon, as Caleb and Rachel walked home together, they passed the servo. Amelia rushed out to greet them.

"Pastor! Mum wants to meet you tomorrow, just like she said. She's ready."

Caleb smiled warmly. "That's wonderful."

"And… I wanted to give you something," Amelia added shyly, holding out a bookmark she'd made from thick card. On it she had written a verse in her neat, careful handwriting:

"The Lord is my strength and my shield…"
(Psalm 28:7)

Caleb felt unexpectedly moved. "Thank you, Amelia. That really means a great deal."

She grinned. "You look less tired today. Mum said it was because 'the review people didn't give you a hard time.'"

Caleb laughed softly. "She may be right."

That evening, after dinner, Caleb and Rachel sat quietly on the verandah. The sky blazed orange and pink as the sun dipped behind the ridge.

Rachel reached for his hand.

"What are you thinking about?" she asked.

"Balance," he said truthfully. "Rhythm … learning to share the emotional weight of ministry without stepping back from its heart."

"And?" Rachel prompted.

"And that maybe," he said softly, "this review wasn't a warning - but an invitation."

"To what?"

"To ministry that is lighter, wiser, and more shared."

Rachel's thumb brushed his hand. "I am completely with you in that."

He smiled. "I know."

They watched the colours fade into twilight, the valley resting around them.

The review had ended.

The community had spoken.

God's Spirit was stirring gently.

And Caleb sensed that Willowend was moving - slowly, steadily - toward something deeper.

Friday morning dawned soft and cool, the kind of morning that seemed to wash the valley in reassurance. A thin mist hovered above the grass, slowly dispersing as the sun warmed the landscape. Willowend breathed quietly, steadily - a town settling into its new spiritual rhythm.

Caleb woke with a sense of purpose, not urgency. The review was behind him, but the encouragement and cautions it brought were still tender in his mind. He felt no dread, no heaviness - only a gentle awareness that something was shifting in him, and perhaps in the church as well.

Rachel handed him a mug of tea, watching him with perceptive eyes.

"You're thinking," she said.

"I'm always thinking," he smiled.

"But today it looks kinder," she replied.

He chuckled. "Maybe because today is about people rather than paperwork."

"Ah," she said knowingly. "Daniel's mum."

"Mm," he nodded, feeling a warm anticipation. "She asked for this meeting. That alone is… significant."

Rachel leaned closer. "You'll walk gently."

"I usually do."

"Yes," she said softly. "But today, walk gently with *yourself* too."

He didn't dismiss the comment. He took it with him.

Caleb met Daniel's mum - Karen - at the picnic tables behind the local hall. The area overlooked the river, where water shimmered in the morning light. Karen arrived a few minutes early, hands clasped nervously, eyes soft but unsure.

"Good morning, Pastor," she said.

"Good morning, Karen. I'm glad you came."

She exhaled shakily, sitting down. "I wasn't sure I should. I wasn't sure I'd know what to say."

"You don't need to come with words prepared," Caleb said gently. "Just honesty."

Karen nodded, looking toward the river. "Sunday… something happened in me. I felt… seen. Held. Like God was close again, but not in a frightening way."

Caleb remained quiet, letting her speak.

"I always believed," she went on. "But somewhere along the way

I decided God probably didn't want much to do with me anymore. Life got messy. Choices got complicated. Shame… grows faster than weeds."

She wiped a tear quickly. "But Sunday, when you spoke about Jesus' invitation - 'Come to Me as you are' - it undid something. I don't know how. But it did."

Caleb nodded slowly. "Karen, God never steps back from us. But we often step back from Him - usually because we think we've disqualified ourselves." He leaned forward slightly. "But grace doesn't work like that. Grace draws close."

Karen's tears flowed freely now, but quietly. "I want to come back to faith. I want to come home. I don't know how."

Caleb's voice remained soft. "You just did."

She inhaled sharply, hand clasped over her mouth, emotion overwhelming her.

After a long, quiet moment, she whispered, "Thank you."

Caleb shook his head gently. "Don't thank me. Thank the One who's been calling your name all along."

Daniel appeared on the far side of the field, watching from a distance. When he saw his mum crying, he hesitated, unsure whether to approach. Caleb gave him a small encouraging nod. Daniel walked over slowly.

"Mum?" he asked softly.

Karen turned to him and smiled - a real smile, fragile but glowing. "It's okay," she said. "It's good. Really good."

Daniel sat beside her, and the three of them talked for nearly an hour. Not about theology or rules or expectations - about grace, hope, and the slow rebuilding of things once thought lost.

As they parted, Karen squeezed Caleb's hands.

"You've given us a chance," she said.

"No," Caleb replied. "God did that. I just stood nearby."

Late morning, Caleb returned to the church to prepare the weekend service. As he walked down the aisle, he noticed the leather-bound journal he had left on the front pew. He picked it up, running his hand over the smooth cover. A gentle prompting stirred in him.

You don't have to carry all of this inside your heart alone.

He sat down and opened the journal.

For the first time in years, he wrote not as a pastor recording tasks or prayer needs, but as a man speaking honestly with God.

Lord, teach me to find rest in You.
Teach me not to confuse calling with strain.
Help me to shepherd without absorbing every sorrow.

He paused, letting the stillness of the sanctuary settle around him.

And thank You for this valley. For renewal that whispers rather than shouts. For people awakening to Your presence. For grace unfolding gently.

When he finished writing, he closed the journal with a quiet sense of release.

That afternoon, Amelia knocked on the church door.

"I'm not interrupting, am I?" she asked.

"Not at all," Caleb smiled. "Come in."

She held up her Bible. "I've been reading every night. But..." She hesitated. "Some parts I don't understand. Could we... meet sometimes? Just to talk about it? Not formal. Just... learning."

Caleb felt a deep, warm gratitude rise in him. "Yes, Amelia. Absolutely. We can walk through Scripture together."

Her face brightened. "Really? I thought maybe pastors are too busy for that."

Caleb's smile softened. "If I'm too busy to walk with someone who is seeking truth, then I've misunderstood ministry."

She let out a breath she hadn't realised she was holding.

"And," Caleb added gently, remembering the review, "I'm learning to share the journey rather than carry it alone. You're part of that."

Amelia nodded, eyes shining. "Then I'll bring biscuits."

Caleb laughed. "Perfect."

Later, Graham pulled up in his ute as Caleb was locking the church.

"Pastor," he called, leaning out the window. "Julie made too much lasagne. Thought you and Rachel could use an easy dinner."

Caleb accepted the container gratefully. "Thank you, Graham."

Graham hesitated. "You seemed lighter today."

"I am," Caleb said. "A bit more at peace."

Graham nodded thoughtfully. "Good. Because Julie and I were praying for just that."

Caleb placed a hand on the side of the ute. "Thank you. Your prayers matter more than you know."

Graham smiled. "Thursday felt heavy around town. But today feels steady."

"Steady is good," Caleb said.

"Yes," Graham agreed. "Steady is the ground God builds things on."

That evening, Caleb and Rachel sat on the verandah again, the valley bathed in warm twilight. The glow behind the ridge had long since faded, but a new kind of glow - deeper, spiritual - had taken its place within the community.

Rachel leaned her head on Caleb's shoulder.

"How did your meeting with Karen go?" she asked.

"Gracefully," he said softly. "She's finding her way home."

"I could see something different in Daniel today," Rachel said.

"Yes," Caleb said. "Hope looks good on him."

They fell into a comfortable quiet, watching the sky shift from orange to deep blue.

After a while, Rachel said, "So... are you going to make any changes?"

Caleb thought for a moment.

"Yes," he said finally. "Small ones. Intentional ones. Not because the review told me to - but because God is nudging."

"What kind of changes?"

He smiled gently.

"Sharing the emotional load. Making space for rest. Asking for help when needed. And letting others walk their journeys without me carrying every step."

Rachel squeezed his hand. "That sounds like wisdom."

"It feels like obedience," he whispered.

The night settled around them, soft and peaceful.

Renewal was unfolding - not only in the town, but in Caleb's heart.

And he sensed, deeply and quietly, that Willowend's awakening was just beginning.

Saturday arrived with the gentlest of breezes, carrying the scent of freshly cut grass and warm soil. Willowend felt unusually alive - not bustling, not noisy, but quietly vibrant, as though something beneath the surface had begun to stir in earnest.
Caleb felt it too.

He woke before dawn, a soft hum of expectancy settling in his spirit. It wasn't the weight of a sermon or the anxiety of a meeting. It was the sense that something new had begun - something subtle and tender, like the earliest bud on a winter branch.

Rachel noticed immediately.

"You're smiling," she said as she handed him his tea.

"Am I?" he asked, surprised.

"Yes," she replied. "And not the 'I hope today goes smoothly' smile. The other one."

He raised an eyebrow. "The other one?"

"The one you get when God has whispered something," she said gently.

Caleb laughed under his breath. "Perhaps He has."

Later that morning, Caleb headed into town to visit the Saturday markets - a modest collection of stalls on the oval that sold everything from homemade jams and second-hand books to knitted scarves and freshly baked bread. He usually walked through quietly, greeting people, offering a word of blessing here and there.

But today felt different.

People greeted him not with routine politeness, but with softness. Gratitude. A sense of shared understanding.

"Morning, Pastor," one man said as he passed.

"Good to see you, Caleb," a woman added.

"Beautiful sermon last Sunday," another remarked.

It wasn't flattery. It was connection.

Connection deepening.

At the far end of the markets, near the eucalyptus grove, Caleb noticed a small gathering around one of the picnic tables. Young people - teenagers mostly - sitting in a loose circle. At first he thought it was just friends catching up.

But then he noticed Daniel standing at the edge of the group, Bible in hand.

Curious, Caleb approached.

Daniel brightened when he saw him. "Pastor! Um - do you have a moment?"

"Of course," Caleb said. "What's going on here?"

Daniel glanced at the group awkwardly. "We... well, after the glow night, and then Sunday, and then Bible study, some of us were talking - just casually - and a couple of the guys asked if we could meet sometimes. Not in the church. Just... here. To talk. And maybe read something. Nothing formal."

Caleb's eyebrows lifted with gentle surprise. "A gathering?"

Daniel nodded. "We're not calling it anything. Just meeting. Talking. Listening. Figuring stuff out."

One of the boys - a lanky teenager named Archer - raised his hand shyly. "We don't want to do, like, sermons. We just want to ask questions and not feel dumb."

Another girl added, "And we thought Daniel should lead it. Since..." She gestured vaguely. "Since things have changed."

Daniel flushed. "I'm not leading," he said quickly. "I'm just... starting the conversation."

Caleb smiled. His heart warmed. "This is beautiful. Truly."

Daniel shifted nervously. "Is it… okay?"

"More than okay," Caleb said. "God loves when people gather sincerely. Don't force it into something else. Don't turn it into a program. Keep it simple. Keep it honest."

Archer grinned. "That's the plan."

Daniel exhaled with relief. "We weren't sure if we needed permission."

"You don't," Caleb said warmly. "Just keep your hearts open."

He stayed for a few minutes, listening as the group shared quiet reflections. They weren't polished or theologically sharp — but they were real. Honest. Fresh.

Renewal was always gentlest among the young.

After leaving the markets, Caleb made his usual Saturday visit to the aged-care wing. He often read Scripture to the residents or chatted about simple things - gardens, memories, grandchildren.

Today, however, he was met with a surprise.

Elsie - the soft-spoken woman who always sat by the window - had her Bible open. Wide open. Not on her lap, but spread in front of her as if she'd been searching earnestly through its pages. When she saw him, her eyes sparkled.

"Pastor! Sometimes I forget things these days, but today I remembered a verse from long ago." She tapped the open page.

"Here it is. 'He restores my soul.'"

Caleb sat beside her. "A beautiful reminder."

Elsie nodded. "It's what He's doing with this town, isn't it? Restoring souls?"

Caleb felt that truth land deeply within him. "Yes, Elsie. I believe He is."

She closed her Bible with trembling hands. "Well then… don't you go getting tired before He's finished."

He laughed softly. "I'll do my best."

By midday, Caleb returned home where Rachel was preparing lunch.

"How did the markets go?" she asked.

Caleb leaned against the counter, marvel still evident on his face.

"Something unexpected is happening."

Her eyes lit with curiosity. "Tell me."

So he did - about Daniel, about the group gathering under the trees, about the softening among the residents, about the sense of God whispering renewal across the valley.

Rachel listened with growing joy. "Caleb… this is the beginning of something. You've felt it for weeks, but today it's visible."

"Yes," he said quietly. "Visible and real."

She placed her hand over his. "Then let's be faithful to walk with it but not control it."

He nodded slowly. "That's exactly what we must do."

Later that afternoon, Caleb sat on the back verandah with his journal. The breeze carried the smell of warm earth and gum leaves.

He wrote slowly:

Lord, something is stirring.
Not loudly. Not dramatically.
But gently - like dawn spreading across the hills.
Teach me to shepherd without clutching.
Guide me to support without stifling.
Let renewal rise as You choose, in Your way.

As he set down his pen, he sensed - not heard, but sensed - that God was preparing Willowend for something more. Something not yet visible. Something that would need Caleb present, but not controlling; guiding, but not driving; supporting, but not exhausting himself.

A whisper of renewal.

A hint of grace.

A stirring of hearts.

It was coming.

And it was good.

Sunday morning arrived with a clarity that seemed almost symbolic. The sky was high and blue, the air cool but promising warmth, and the ridge glowed softly in the early light. It was the kind of morning that felt like a fresh page.

Caleb sensed it before he stepped outside – like the hush of expectation, the gentle tension that falls over a valley when God is preparing something. Not dramatic. Not storm-like. Quiet. Patient. Real.

Rachel met him at the door, Bible in hand, wearing a smile he had seen only a few times in his ministry - the smile of someone waiting to witness something holy.

"Ready?" she asked.

"As ready as I can be," he replied.

As they approached the church, Caleb slowed.

Cars lined the roadside far beyond the usual stretch. Some he recognised. Some he didn't. People were gathered near the entrance in small clusters, talking with an openness that didn't feel forced or polite.

Daniel stood near the steps, greeting people - awkwardly but earnestly. Amelia and Sheila were speaking together as though they had been friends for years. Graham had his arm around Julie, and both radiated a quiet hope.

Even Mary was outside, leaning gently on her walking stick, eyes bright as she watched everyone arrive.

When she saw Caleb, she gave a small nod and said quietly, "The river is rising."

Caleb felt a chill - not of fear, but of awe.

Inside, the sanctuary filled much more quickly than usual. The murmured conversations had a different tone - softer, warmer, threaded with anticipation. A few visiting faces sat among the regulars: an older couple from out of town, a young family, two of Daniel's friends from school, and, unexpectedly, the Murrays from the bookstore café.

"Didn't want to miss what God's doing," Doris whispered as she took her seat.

Caleb moved to the front, greeting people gently as he passed. When he reached the pulpit, he paused, letting the room settle into quiet.

The sanctuary grew still. Not a stiff stillness - a weighted one.

The kind that comes when hearts lean forward.

"Good morning," he said softly.

The response wasn't loud, but it was unified.

He opened his Bible.

"Today," he began, "we read from Isaiah 43."

He paused, letting the rustle of pages settle.

"See, I am doing a new thing;
now it springs up, do you not perceive it?
I am making a way in the wilderness
and streams in the wasteland."

The words fell into the room with unexpected force - not because he inflected them dramatically, but because they resonated with what was unfolding in the valley.

Caleb continued, voice steady and gentle.

"This is not a declaration of grand events or noisy miracles. Isaiah speaks here of God doing something *new* - something that begins quietly, almost imperceptibly. Renewal rarely shouts. Most often, it whispers."

Several people nodded - Mary, Graham, Amelia, even Sheila, who usually resisted emotional expressions.

Caleb continued.

"A week ago, our valley faced fire. Fear spread quicker than flames. But God met us - not in the blaze, but in the stillness that followed. And in that stillness, something has begun to grow."

He felt the truth settle into the room like sunlight.

"I see it in conversations. In acts of kindness. In unexpected courage. In softened hearts. I see it in you."

He didn't preach long - fifteen minutes, perhaps a little more. But every word felt aligned with what God was already doing, not what Caleb was trying to accomplish.

He ended simply:

"If God is doing a new thing among us, let us not rush it. Let us not control it. Let us not fear it. Let us only open our hearts — and watch what grace does."

When the time came for prayer, something quite unexpected happened. Caleb invited the congregation to bow their heads. But before he could begin, Karen - Daniel's mum - stood. Slowly. With trembling hands. But determined.

The room froze.

She took a quiet breath and said, voice steady but emotional, "I… need to thank God. Out loud. For the first time in years."

Caleb stepped back from the pulpit, giving her the space.

Karen's voice softened as she prayed.

"Lord… thank You for calling me back.
Thank You for lifting shame.
Thank You for giving my boy hope.
And thank You for not giving up on me."

A small sob came from someone in the pews. Then another. But these weren't sobs of sorrow - they were the release of long-held burdens.

When Karen finished, she sat down quickly, embarrassed but peaceful.

Before Caleb could say a word, Graham stood.

"I need to say something too," he said, voice rough with emotion.

"Julie and I… we found our way back to prayer this week. Proper prayer. And I want to thank God for not letting me drift too far." Julie took his hand and nodded, tears in her eyes.

And then - almost hesitantly - Amelia stood.

"I don't know what I'm doing," she said, cheeks flushed. "But… I'm reading the Bible again. And it's making sense. And I'm grateful."

A soft ripple of laughter - gentle and warm - moved through the congregation. The atmosphere shifted. Something opened. Breath deepened. Hearts relaxed into something holy.

Caleb stepped forward again, voice tender.

"This… this is what renewal looks like. Honesty. Gratitude. Return. Rest."

He prayed briefly - thanking God, blessing the congregation, asking for tenderness to remain.

After the service, people lingered even longer than before. Conversations blossomed naturally. The young people from Daniel's new group huddled together excitedly. Karen's eyes shone with new clarity. Even visitors stayed, drawn into the warmth of a community waking up.

As Caleb stood near the doorway, greeting people, Sarah's words from the review echoed gently in his mind:

We saw something rare.

She had been right. And today he understood why.

Rachel squeezed his hand. "You felt it too, didn't you?"

He nodded. "Something shifted. Not wildly - but deeply."

She smiled softly. "A whisper becoming a breeze."

"Exactly."

Then, to Caleb's surprise, Justin Strickland - the administrator from the review team - stepped out of a car parked across the road. He must have attended discreetly, unseen.

He didn't approach. He only paused, looked at the church full of life, and gave Caleb a small, respectful nod before driving away. Rachel noticed. "They're still watching."

"Yes," Caleb said, not troubled. "But so is God."

They walked home along the familiar path, sunlight warm on their shoulders. For the first time in a long time, Caleb felt not just hope - but joy.

Real joy.

Something was happening in Willowend.

Something precious.

Something growing.

And he sensed deep in his spirit:

This was only the beginning.

By Monday morning, Willowend felt different in a way that was hard to articulate but impossible to miss. The quiet spiritual movement that had begun in the sanctuary was now rippling through the valley in unexpected places - in homes, in workplaces, in conversations between neighbours who had rarely spoken.

Even the air felt changed. Not lighter exactly, but clearer.

Caleb noticed it the moment he stepped outside with his coffee. The magpies were singing their looping, liquid call. Sunlight warmed the dew. And something in the atmosphere was whispering, *'Pay attention.'*

Rachel joined him on the verandah, hair still damp from the shower, holding her favourite blue mug.

"You feel it, don't you?" she asked.

He nodded. "It's like the whole town is exhaling."

She sipped her tea thoughtfully and then said, "Renewal begins in the sanctuary, but it grows in kitchens and paddocks."

Caleb smiled. "You should preach next Sunday."

She laughed softly. "You would never let go of the pulpit long enough."

He grinned. "Fair point."

Caleb's first stop that morning was the servo. Amelia had grown used to his Monday visits, but today her smile held something brighter - a sense of belonging rather than politeness.

"Pastor! You won't believe what happened last night."

He leaned on the counter. "Try me."

"My mum asked if she could read the Bible with me," Amelia said, eyes shining. "She hasn't touched a Bible in years. But she said after church yesterday, something… shifted."

Caleb felt warmth bloom in his chest. "How did it go?"

"Awkward," Amelia admitted with a laugh. "We didn't know where to start. We read Psalm 23 because it was familiar. Then we talked about what it meant to have a Shepherd."

Her voice softened. "Pastor... we haven't talked like that in years. Not about anything real."

Caleb nodded gently. "This is how God works - not through grand events, but through small openings."

Amelia exhaled deeply. "It feels like we've been walking in darkness and someone finally lit a candle."

"That's renewal," Caleb said.

As he left, he noticed Archer - one of the boys from the market gathering - sitting outside on the bench with a notebook open, writing something with deep focus. He looked up briefly, gave Caleb a small nod, and returned to his work.
Seeds everywhere. Quietly taking root.

Late morning, Caleb visited the primary school. The principal, a warm and practical woman named Lynette, had invited him to stop by. She met him near the gate.

"Pastor, something interesting is happening here," she said as they walked toward the staff room.

"Oh?"

"Teachers are reporting calmer classrooms," she said. "Children more patient with each other. Parents sending notes thanking staff for 'hope' of all things."

Caleb raised an eyebrow. "Hope?"

"Yes," she said. "Hope. And get this - two teachers told me they want to start a morning prayer group again. It's been dead for years."

Caleb felt the familiar stir in his spirit. "God is moving."

"Looks that way," she said with a half-smile. "Though some people prefer to call it an 'atmospheric shift.' We'll let them use their terms."

He chuckled. "Whatever they call it, the fruit is undeniable."

Around midday, Caleb returned to the church to prepare for several pastoral visits. But as he stepped inside, he noticed someone sitting quietly in the back pew.

It was Justin Strickland.

The last person he expected to find alone in the sanctuary.

Justin sat stiffly, hands clasped, shoulders tense. He wasn't praying exactly - more like trying to anchor himself. For a moment, Caleb simply watched him, choosing not to interrupt. Daniel had the look of a man unfamiliar with vulnerability.

Finally, Caleb approached quietly. "Justin?"

Justin startled slightly, then composed himself. "Pastor. I... apologise for dropping in unannounced."

"You're welcome here anytime," Caleb said gently. "How can I help?"

Justin hesitated - visibly torn between professionalism and honesty.

"I was just passing through the area again," he said at first. "I thought I'd... check on something."

Caleb sat beside him. "You're not here to check on the church, are you?"

Justin's jaw tightened. Then, after a long pause, he whispered,

"No."

The admission hung in the air. Caleb waited, giving him silence rather than pressure.

Justin exhaled, rubbing his temple. "Your town... your service yesterday... I haven't seen anything like it in a long time. Not in rural settings. Not in urban ones either."

Caleb said nothing, letting him find his words.

"It made me think," Justin continued, "that perhaps I... have forgotten something essential. Something I once believed... strongly." His voice dipped. "Faith used to feel alive to me."

Caleb's heart softened. "What happened to that faith?"

Justin shook his head slowly. "I don't know. Life hardens you. Administration hardens you even more. Somewhere along the way... I stopped expecting God to move."

"And yesterday challenged that," Caleb said.

Justin swallowed hard. "Yes. It did."

He looked at Caleb then with an honesty he hadn't shown during the review.

"Pastor, do you believe renewal can spread to someone who hasn't felt anything spiritual in years?"

Caleb smiled gently. "Justin ... renewal always finds the tired first."

Justin closed his eyes, emotion flickering across his face. "I don't know what to do with that."

"You don't need to," Caleb said quietly. "Just don't run from it."

They sat for a long moment in the stillness of the sanctuary.

Before leaving, Justin said softly, "Don't mention this to Mark or Sarah."

"Of course not," Caleb replied.

"And Pastor?" Justin added hesitantly. "I may come again."

"You will be welcomed," Caleb said.

As he watched Justin walk away, Caleb felt the unmistakable confirmation: Renewal was not just confined to Willowend. It was touching those who barely understood what they were seeking.

That afternoon, Caleb visited Mary Kline. She sat on her verandah as always, her Bible open, the wind flipping its pages.

"You've felt it, haven't you?" she said before he even greeted her.

"Yes," Caleb replied. "Everywhere."

"Renewal doesn't stay in one place," Mary said. "It flows. Like a stream. It reaches who it needs to reach."

Caleb smiled. "Even review administrators?"

Mary chuckled. "Especially them."

She leaned forward, lowering her voice slightly. "But streams bring change. And not everyone in Willowend will embrace it." Caleb's expression sobered. "You sense resistance coming?"

"Not resistance," Mary said carefully. "But challenge. Some will misunderstand what God is doing. Others will fear it. Renewal always brings both openness and opposition."

Caleb absorbed her words quietly. "I will pray for wisdom."

"Do more than pray," Mary said gently. "Stay soft. Renewal flows where hearts remain tender."

At sunset, Caleb and Rachel walked the long path behind their home, the sky a deep wash of orange and purple.

Rachel looked up at him. "You look thoughtful."

"I spoke with Justin today," he said. "He's... opening. Slowly. Quietly."

Rachel smiled. "Renewal doesn't spare the visiting officials, it seems."

"No," Caleb chuckled. "Apparently not."

They walked a little further before Rachel said, "What else is on your mind?"

Caleb breathed deeply. "Mary warned me today that challenge is coming. Not big conflict. Just... misunderstanding."

Rachel nodded. "That's part of renewal. Some welcome it. Others fear it."

He touched her hand. "We'll walk through it together."

"We always do," she replied.

As the stars appeared above the ridge, Caleb sensed a quiet assurance: The renewal spreading through Willowend was real.

Beautiful.

Growing.

And the next chapter of it - whatever shape it took - would require grace, courage, and tender steadfastness.

By Tuesday morning, Willowend hummed with a curious blend of normality and expectancy. People went about their work - opening shops, tending gardens, feeding stock - yet something unspoken lingered in their eyes, a softness that hadn't been there weeks earlier.

But renewal, Caleb knew, never unfolded uniformly. Some hearts opened easily. Others resisted or misunderstood. And sometimes, those tensions revealed themselves in the most unexpected ways.

Caleb began the morning with a visit to the bakery. Sheila greeted him with a quick smile.

"You're earlier than usual," she said, sliding two fresh rolls into a bag.

"Couldn't sleep in," Caleb said. "Too much on my heart."

Sheila leaned closer. "Good things or heavy things?"

"A little of both."

She nodded knowingly. "That's renewal."

He raised an eyebrow. "You sound like Mary."

Sheila snorted. "I wouldn't dare compare myself to her …"

She hesitated, then said quietly, "Pastor, you should know - some folks are talking. Not badly. Just confused."

"Confused about what?" Caleb asked.

"Why so many people are suddenly turning up at church. Why young people are meeting. Why Karen prayed out loud. Why the place feels different. Some think it's wonderful. Some think it's... odd."

Caleb absorbed this gently. "Odd?"

"Because it's new," Sheila replied. "New scares people more than fire sometimes."

She handed him the bag of rolls. "Don't worry. The talk isn't malicious. Just uncertain."

Uncertainty Caleb could handle. Uncertainty meant movement.

"Thank you for telling me," he said warmly.

Sheila gave him a small nod. "Keep steady, Pastor. Some will catch up. Some won't. But keep steady."

Later that morning, Caleb headed to the hardware store to pick up supplies for a minor church repair. Inside, he ran into Paul Kensington. Paul is a local businessman and occasional church attendee known for his pragmatic, no-nonsense approach to everything.

"Morning, Pastor," Paul said, but there was an edge in his tone.

"Morning, Paul. How are things?"

Paul shrugged. "Busy. Though apparently not as busy as you've been."

Caleb blinked. "Oh?"

Paul leaned against the shelf, folding his arms. "Town's been buzzing about church lately. People who haven't been in years suddenly showing up. Karen standing up to pray. Kids gathering at the markets. Even the Murrays came out of retirement on Sunday."

There was no hostility in his voice - just confusion and something else buried underneath.

Concern?

Or suspicion?

"You sound unsure," Caleb said softly.

Paul sighed. "I'm not against it. I just... don't understand it. These sudden surges in religion usually come after big events - tragedies, disasters, that sort of thing. But nothing happened here. Not really. The fire didn't even reach town."

Caleb held his gaze. "Something did happen, Paul. Not outside us - inside."

Paul frowned thoughtfully. "I'm not convinced."

"That's all right," Caleb said gently. "Renewal isn't something you force. It's something you recognise when your heart is ready."

Paul didn't respond, but his expression softened just enough to suggest the conversation had landed somewhere meaningful.

"See you Sunday," he said at last, more quietly.

"See you then," Caleb replied.

At midday, Caleb met Rachel for lunch on the church lawn. She had brought sandwiches and fruit, and they sat beneath a large gum tree that cast a cool, dappled shade.

"How was your morning?" she asked.

"Interesting," Caleb said with a small smile. "Sheila told me some folks think renewal is odd. Paul told me he's not sure he believes it."

Rachel laughed softly. "Of course. Renewal always confuses people who prefer straight lines."

"True," Caleb said. "But I want to make sure no one feels pushed or overwhelmed."

"You're not pushing," she reminded him. "You are tending the soil."

He nodded thoughtfully. "I suppose every garden has patches that bloom early and patches that bloom late."

"And patches that resist altogether," she added gently. "But that's not failure. That's normal."

He took her hand. "I'm grateful for you."

"I know," she said, leaning her head against his shoulder.

In the afternoon, Caleb decided to visit the Murrays' bookstore café. When he walked inside, he found Doris rearranging a display of devotionals while Len was seating a customer.

Doris greeted him warmly. "Pastor, we thought you might drop by."

Caleb smiled. "I sensed the coffee calling."

"Or the cinnamon scrolls," Len added from behind the counter. Caleb laughed. "Perhaps both."

As he sat, Doris lowered her voice conspiratorially. "Pastor, I need to tell you something. Yesterday, after church, three people asked where they could find Bibles. Three! In one day!"

"That's wonderful," Caleb said.

"It is," she agreed. "But one of them seemed… troubled."

"Troubled how?"

"He said he felt something in the service but didn't trust it," Doris said. "He said he'd been fooled by emotion before."
Caleb nodded. "People who've been hurt often fear good things."

Doris sighed. "I told him that God isn't trying to trick him."

Caleb smiled. "You're a good evangelist, Doris."

Len called from behind the counter, "She always has been."

Caleb stayed for nearly an hour, listening to them share story after story of customers asking unusual questions, lingering longer than usual, or showing unexpected interest in spiritual things.

"God's stirring something," Len said, wiping a glass. "But it'll take time for some folks to understand it."

Caleb nodded. "That's all right. Understanding can come later. Openness is enough for now."

Later that day, as Caleb returned to the church, he saw a familiar car parked discreetly across the road.

The blue hatchback.

Justin's.

But Justin wasn't inside. Instead, he stood at the edge of the church grounds, not approaching the building - looking at it.

Watching it.

Thinking.

Caleb approached slowly, not wanting to intrude.

"Back again?" he asked gently.

Justin startled, then cleared his throat. "I had a meeting in the next town over. Thought I'd stop by."

Caleb raised an eyebrow. "Twice in one week."

Justin's composure faltered for just a moment. "It… helps. Being here."

Caleb nodded. "You're welcome whenever you need space."

Justin hesitated before saying, quietly, "Does renewal always make people uncomfortable?"

"Yes," Caleb replied. "Because renewal moves at God's pace, not ours."

Justin exhaled slowly. "I'm beginning to understand that."

He didn't elaborate. He didn't need to. Caleb could see in his eyes the flicker of something quietly awakening.

That evening, after dinner, Caleb and Rachel walked the long path behind their house as the sun dipped low behind the ridge. The valley glowed.

Rachel spoke first. "You're sensing the beginnings of tension, aren't you?"

"Yes," Caleb admitted. "Not conflict - just… stretching."

"You're handling it gently," she said. "And that's important."

He looked at her. "Sometimes I worry people will expect too much of me. Or misunderstand the gentleness of what God is doing."

Rachel squeezed his hand. "Caleb, renewal isn't dependent on people understanding it. It's dependent on their openness. Even confusion can become openness."

He breathed deeply. "I hope so."

She looked up at him with a soft smile. "I know so."

They continued walking, the warm dusk settling around them, the air rich with possibility.

Renewal had spread beyond the church walls. Now it was touching hearts that didn't yet know what to do with it.

And Caleb sensed - with deep peace - that while challenge was coming, grace was already ahead of it.

22. GROWING PAINS

By Wednesday morning, the hum of renewal in Willowend had become almost rhythmic - a quiet, steady undercurrent flowing beneath ordinary life. But with new movement came new questions, and with new questions came the first small signs of tension.

Caleb sensed it the moment he stepped into the church office. A note sat on his desk, written in careful, looping handwriting:

Pastor Caleb, Would you mind calling by this afternoon?
We'd appreciate a chat. Blessings, Graham and Julie White.

Graham didn't usually write notes. He preferred phone calls or in-person conversations. The formality of the message made Caleb pause.

"What do you think this is about?" Rachel asked when he told her over breakfast.

"I'm not sure," Caleb said honestly. "But something is weighing on them."

Rachel put her hand on his. "Whatever it is, you'll navigate it gently. You always do."

Before visiting the Whites, Caleb made his usual stop at the community centre. The volunteers were sorting donations, chatting with an unusual sense of joy.

Daniel was there too, stacking boxes of canned food with surprising enthusiasm.

"Morning, Pastor!" Daniel called. "Guess what?"

Caleb smiled. "What's the good news today?"

"Our group from the markets - well, we met again last night. Twice in one week!" Daniel said proudly. "And… three new people came."

"That's wonderful," Caleb said warmly. "How did it go?"

"Good," Daniel said with genuine excitement. "We talked about prayer. Not fancy prayer - just talking honestly to God. It felt real."

Caleb nodded. "That's how it should feel."

Daniel hesitated. "But… someone said we should probably 'run it by you' first. To be official. Do we need to do that?"

Caleb shook his head firmly. "If God is stirring hearts, the last thing you need is bureaucracy. Keep it simple. Keep it sincere." Daniel's relief was immediate. "Thanks, Pastor."

But across the room, Caleb noticed Paul Kensington watching the conversation with a thoughtful frown. Not hostile - just processing. Trying to fit renewal into categories that had never required flexibility before.

Caleb smiled at him. "Morning, Paul."

Paul gave a stiff nod. "Pastor."

He said nothing more.

Another seed of tension - small, barely noticeable, but real.

That afternoon, Caleb walked up the long driveway to the White farmhouse. The air was very warm, cicadas humming in the paddocks. Graham met him at the verandah steps, wiping his hands on a rag.

"Thanks for coming, Pastor," he said, voice steady but serious.

Julie appeared behind him, offering a welcoming but slightly anxious smile. "Come in, Caleb. We've made tea."

Caleb followed them inside, taking the seat they offered at the kitchen table - a place where he had shared joy, sorrow, prayer, laughter. Today the atmosphere held something that was more complicated. Graham cleared his throat. "We asked you here because we're… trying to understand something."

Julie nodded, her hands folded neatly. "We're grateful for what God is doing. Truly. But…"

She glanced at Graham, who continued for her.

"It's all happening so fast."

Caleb leaned forward gently. "Tell me what you're sensing."

Graham hesitated, searching for the right words. "We love seeing new faces at church. We love seeing hearts soften. But some people are worried that things are changing too quickly. Traditions shifting. Young people gathering in new ways. People praying out loud unexpectedly. It feels… unpredictable."

Julie added softly, "And unpredictable things can unsettle those who've been steady for a long time."

Caleb nodded slowly. "I understand. Renewal often feels unruly - not because it is, but because it doesn't follow our familiar patterns."

Julie's voice wavered with vulnerability. "We don't want to stop what God is doing. We just want to understand our place in it." Caleb felt deep affection for them. "Your place is as it's always been - faithful, prayerful, steady. You don't need to lead the new things or reinvent old ones. You simply need to keep your hearts open."

Graham exhaled. "It's the open part we're working on."

Caleb smiled gently. "Then you're already participating in renewal."

They talked for nearly an hour. The Whites weren't resisting at all - they were simply trying to find footing in a movement they hadn't expected, one that asked different things of them than the rhythms they'd known for decades.

Before Caleb left, Julie touched his arm.

"Pastor," she said, "thank you for listening. And for not brushing us aside."

"I would never do that," he said softly.

As he walked back down the driveway, he realised this was renewal's first real growing pain - a gentle stretching of old wineskins to make space for new wine.

Later that afternoon, Caleb visited the school again. Lynette greeted him warmly and led him to the staff room where a group of teachers sat, deep in conversation.

"Pastor," one of them said, "we were talking about something, and we wondered what you think."

Caleb sat down. "I'd be happy to listen."

A younger teacher named Mark spoke up. "We're seeing positive changes in the kids. More kindness. Less tension. But some parents are worried we're becoming 'too spiritual.' We're not - but they're making assumptions."

Another teacher added, "We barely mentioned anything related to church or prayer, yet a parent came in yesterday saying their child was 'acting strangely hopeful' and they were concerned." Caleb kept his expression calm, though the phrase *strangely hopeful* stayed with him.

"How can hope be strange?" he asked gently.

The teachers smiled.

Lynette answered. "When people don't expect hope, anything resembling it feels suspicious."

Caleb nodded. "All renewal does is awaken the good already in people. But yes - some will misunderstand it before they understand it."

As the day drew to a close, Caleb stopped by Mary's home. She sat outside as usual, eyes bright with insight that came not from age, but from depth.

"You've encountered your first growing pains," she said before he even spoke.

Caleb sat beside her. "How did you know?"

"Because renewal always presses gently on those who prefer life to stay predictable," Mary replied. "The Whites, the school, even Paul - they're not opposing. They're adjusting."

Caleb sighed. "I want to shepherd them well."

"And you will," Mary said firmly. "Just remember - renewal is not disruption. It's invitation. Some accept quickly. Some slowly. Some not at all."

"And what is my part?" Caleb asked quietly.

"To keep the door open where God is opening it."

That evening, as the sun dipped behind the ridge, Caleb returned home to find Rachel waiting on the verandah. She looked at him with tender understanding. "Long day?"

"Yes," he admitted. "Beautiful and complicated."

She leaned her head on his shoulder. "That's how you know it's real." He closed his eyes, letting the quiet settle around them.

Renewal wasn't meant to be tidy.

But it was meant to be transformative.

And Willowend was beginning to stretch.

By Thursday morning, Caleb sensed a shift - faint, but present. The renewal in Willowend continued quietly, beautifully, yet questions were beginning to rise like mist from the paddocks after dawn. There was nothing antagonistic. Nothing sharp. Just uncertainty peeking through the cracks.

He prayed longer that morning, journalling reflections with a mix of gratitude and caution.

Lord, give me wisdom to shepherd gently,
ears to hear what lies beneath the words,
and patience for those who fear change.

Rachel touched his shoulder as she passed. "You'll navigate whatever comes," she said. "You're listening - that's all God asks."

Caleb's first appointment was with Bill Turner, the local stock agent. Bill was not a churchgoer, at least not consistently. He attended funerals, special services, and the occasional Easter morning when his heart felt restless.

But today he had asked to meet with Caleb - with no explanation. Bill waited outside his office, hat in hand, leaning awkwardly against the railing.

"Pastor," he said, offering a firm handshake. "Thanks for making time."

"Of course, Bill. Come in."

They sat across from each other. Bill shifted uncomfortably.

"I'll get straight to it," Bill said. "My daughter's been… different this week."

"Different how?" Caleb asked.

"Thinking more. Asking more questions. Talking about prayer. Talking about that young people's thing happening down by the oval. She says she feels something changing 'inside'." Bill made air quotes. "But Pastor, I don't want anyone pushing religion onto her."

Caleb kept his expression soft. "Has anyone pushed anything?"

"No," Bill admitted. "That's the odd part. She says it's her own choice. But I don't know where it's coming from."

Caleb spoke carefully. "Bill, sometimes young people awaken spiritually without anyone prompting. It's not pressure - it's longing. The kind God plants."

Bill rubbed his chin. "I'm not against faith. But I've seen religion tear families apart. Expectations, guilt, all that. I don't want that for her."

"I understand," Caleb said. "And I wouldn't want that for her either. Renewal doesn't bind people. It frees them. If she's seeking hope, let it unfold gently. No pressure from me. No pressure from you. Just openness."

Bill nodded slowly. "I can live with that."

When he left, Caleb sensed another example of the valley stretching - some hearts awakening, others unsure how to respond, all needing tenderness.

By midday, the next ripple of misunderstanding arrived - this time via email.

> *Pastor, I've noticed the tone of the services is changing.*
> *We need to be careful about emotionalism.*
> *Mature faith is steady, not dramatic.*
> *Perhaps we should review our approach.*
> *Respectfully, Anne Parker*

Caleb exhaled. Anne was very faithful, thoughtful, and deeply committed - but cautious by nature. The unexpected always unsettled her. He wrote back with gentle clarity:

> *Anne, thank you for sharing your concern.*
> *Nothing happening at present is being orchestrated.*
> *People are simply responding to God with honesty.*
> *There is no emotional manipulation, only sincerity.*
> *Let's talk more on Sunday if you'd like.*
> *Grace and peace, Caleb*

He prayed for her afterwards. Not because her message troubled him, but because she represented the people whose love for God was sincere yet tightly held - like a flower unsure if it should open.

Later that afternoon, Caleb visited the local aged-care wing again. As he walked down the hallway, he saw a nurse he hadn't met before standing outside Elsie's room, reading her chart.

"Pastor?" the nurse said, recognising him. "I've heard about you."

Caleb laughed softly. "Hopefully good things."

"Mostly," she said kindly. "Though a few residents said things feel 'different' around here lately. One woman said, 'God's stirring the place,' and another said we're turning into a revival centre."

Her tone was light, teasing, but it carried a thread of uncertainty. Caleb answered gently. "Different can be good. People are finding peace."

The nurse nodded, still unsure. "As long as it stays quiet. We don't need any unnecessary excitement - the residents can get unsettled easily."

"I understand," he assured her. "Nothing happening here is disruptive. It's gentle."

She relaxed a little. "Good. I can live with gentle."

Inside Elsie's room, the elderly woman greeted him with her usual soft joy.

"Oh Pastor," she said, "I prayed for you this morning."

"Thank you," Caleb replied, touched. "I've needed prayer."

Elsie leaned forward, lowering her voice as though sharing a secret. "The Lord said, 'Don't fear the whispers.'"

Caleb blinked. "What do you mean?"

Elsie smiled knowingly. "People whisper when they don't understand. But whispers fade. Truth doesn't."

Her words landed more deeply than she could know.

Late in the afternoon, as Caleb walked back through the town centre, he overheard two shop owners speaking near the florist. "I'm not sure what's happening," one said. "Suddenly half the town's talking about church again."

"It won't last," the other replied. "These things never do."

Caleb didn't take offence. He had heard these sentiments before in other contexts. Renewal stirred curiosity long before it stirred conviction.

Still, he prayed quietly as he walked.

When he got home, Rachel was on the verandah pruning her roses. She looked up as he approached.

"You've had one of *those* days," she said.

He exhaled, sitting beside her. "Just… growing pains. Beautiful things happening. And some misunderstandings joining them."

Rachel handed him a small branch. "Feel this."

He took the stem - firm but flexible.

"It bends," she said, "but doesn't break."

"What are you trying to tell me?" Caleb asked with a smile.

"That renewal bends people. And bending is uncomfortable. But you, Caleb - you don't break either. You hold steady. That steadiness helps others stand."

He touched her hand. "You see things in ways I never could."

"That's why we're a team," she said simply.

After dinner, Caleb sat on the verandah again, journalling as the last light faded.

Today brought tension — gentle but present.
Conversations with the Whites, Paul, Bill, Anne.
Misunderstanding is growing, but not in a damaging way
but in a refining way.
Lord, keep me tender.
Let me listen more than I speak.
Let me remain steady without becoming rigid.

He set down his pen as a gentle breeze lifted the pages.
Mary's words echoed softly:

Renewal is not disruption. It's invitation.

He breathed deeply, embracing that truth.

Willowend was being invited into something beautiful. Stretching was part of the journey. And Caleb felt the quiet assurance that God was gently holding every heart - eager, uncertain, resistant, tender.

The growing pains were not signs of trouble.

They were signs of life.

Friday morning broke warm and bright, the kind of morning that gently urged people outdoors. Willowend seemed unusually awake. Dogs barked more cheerfully, screen doors closed less sharply, and conversations outside the general store lingered a little longer. Renewal was still quiet, still unforced, but it was unmistakably growing.

Caleb's plan that morning was simple - spend a few hours preparing Sunday's sermon, visit a few parishioners, and stop by the men's shed in the afternoon. But before he even reached his desk, the day began steering him somewhere else.

He started at the church office with a fresh cup of tea. As he opened his Bible, his eyes fell on Isaiah 30:21:

"Whether you turn to the right or to the left, your ears will hear a voice behind you, saying, 'This is the way; walk in it.'"

The verse settled in his spirit like a stone finding its right place.

Rachel appeared in the doorway, smiling. "You are looking very thoughtful."

"I think God's nudging again," Caleb said quietly.

She came in and placed a hand on his shoulder. "Nudging toward what?"

"I'm not sure yet. But something's unfolding. Something bigger than what we've seen so far."

Rachel's eyes softened. "Then keep listening. God rarely shouts."

Caleb nodded. "I will."

By mid-morning, he visited the home of Elizabeth Payne, a widow in her late sixties who attended church faithfully but quietly. Elizabeth opened the door smiling, but with an unusual brightness in her eyes.

"Pastor, I've been expecting you," she said.

"Oh?" Caleb asked, surprised.

She led him into the sitting room. "Because I've been praying that God would send me someone to share this with."

She picked up a small notebook from the side table. "Three nights this week, I've been waking up at 2am. Wide awake. But not restless - peaceful. Each time, I've had a verse on my mind. Different verses. Encouraging ones."

"That sounds beautiful," Caleb said warmly.

"It is," she replied. "But this morning… the verse was for you."

Caleb blinked. "For me?"

Elizabeth opened the notebook, running her finger down the page.

"'Do not despise the day of small things.' That's what came to me. And I felt… strongly… that you needed to hear it."

Caleb felt a quiet jolt. "That's from Zechariah."

Elizabeth nodded. "God's doing something here in Willowend, Pastor. And it may look small to others. But you must not underestimate it."

Her voice was soft but carried weight.

Caleb left Elizabeth's home with gratitude - and a deeper sense of expectation.

After lunch, he walked to the men's shed, a large tin structure near the railway line. The shed was usually filled with the comforting sounds of saws, radios, and friendly banter - a place where retired farmers, former tradesmen, and a handful of younger blokes gathered to fix things, restore old tools, and drink unpretentious cups of tea.

But today, the usual noise was subdued. Caleb stepped inside, greeted by a few nods. Len Murray waved him over from the back workbench. "Pastor! Good timing."

"What's happening?" Caleb asked.

Len lowered his voice. "Something unusual. The fellas are talking about faith."

Caleb raised an eyebrow. "In the shed?"

"Yes," Len said, half-amused, half-awed. "Out of nowhere. It started earlier when Terry accidentally dropped a mallet on his foot and let out a few words we don't use in church. He apologised, said he'd been trying to 'clean up his mouth.' That opened the door."

Terry, hearing his name, looked over sheepishly. "I didn't know the Pastor was coming! I wouldn't have said that if I knew."

Caleb laughed. "It's all right, Terry. Pain brings out honesty."

The room chuckled, tension easing.

But then Mick - a burly man with a thick beard who rarely attended church - cleared his throat. "Pastor, since you're here… can I ask something?"

Caleb approached him gently. "Of course."

Mick scratched the back of his neck. "All this talk in town about God doing something… is it real? Or is it just one of those 'church buzz' moments that fade after a few weeks?"

Caleb answered slowly, carefully. "It's real, Mick. But it's not flashy or chaotic. It's quiet. Gentle. Like a slow sunrise. You don't notice it all at once, but then suddenly the whole valley is lit."

Mick nodded thoughtfully. "I'm not much of a church bloke. Haven't been since I was thirteen. But… lately, I keep thinking about things I haven't thought about in years."

"What kind of things?" Caleb asked.

"Regret," Mick admitted. "And hope. And whether I've wasted too much time."

Caleb placed a hand on Mick's shoulder. "Hope means the time isn't wasted."

Mick swallowed hard. "Do you think God still looks for blokes like me?"

"Yes," Caleb said. "Especially blokes like you."

Len, hearing the conversation, whispered to Caleb, "This is happening all over the shed. Conversations popping up like wildflowers."

Caleb looked around. Men were talking quietly in pairs. One was wiping his eyes discreetly. Another sat staring at a half-finished project as though contemplating more than wood.

The renewal had reached the men's shed.

Caleb felt the holy weight of that truth.

After the conversations finally settled, Len walked Caleb out to the gravel parking area.

"This is something, isn't it?" Len said, crossing his arms.

"Yes," Caleb replied. "Something profound."

"But," Len added cautiously, "there may be pushback soon."

Caleb looked at him. "From who?"

Len shrugged. "People who fear change. People who think faith should stay in buildings. People who worry when the Spirit starts moving outside their categories."

Caleb nodded. "I've sensed the same."

Len smiled sadly. "You'll navigate it. You've got a steady hand."

But Caleb's spirit stirred at Len's words - not fear, not dread, but a sense of direction.

The nudge from this morning returned.

This is the way; walk in it.

That evening, Caleb sat on the verandah with Rachel, watching dusk fall softly over Willowend.

"I sensed God speaking today," he said.

"What did He say?" Rachel asked gently.

"That something new is coming. Something in the next season of renewal. And I need to be ready to follow where He leads."

Rachel placed her hand over his. "Then we'll walk together into it."

He looked at her, grateful for her unwavering presence.

"Do you think the church is ready for what's coming?" he asked.

Rachel smiled. "The question isn't whether they're ready. It's whether they're willing."

Caleb breathed deeply, the cool evening air filling his lungs.

In the distance, the town rested quietly beneath the rising stars. Renewal had touched the sanctuary. It had touched homes, the school, the café, and now even the men's shed. And Caleb sensed - with a gentle certainty - that the next movement would ask something new of him. Something calling him deeper.

Saturday dawned bright and warm, the air still and golden as it lay across the valley floor. Willowend seemed unusually peaceful, as though holding its breath. Caleb couldn't shake the feeling that the day held something unexpected — not dramatic, but meaningful.

"Feels like a day for God to surprise us," Rachel remarked over breakfast.

Caleb smiled. "Lately that seems to be every day."

She squeezed his hand. "Then let's keep our eyes open."

That afternoon was the monthly community barbecue held in the park near the river - a casual, open gathering where families brought picnic blankets, kids kicked footballs, and someone inevitably overcooked sausages on the communal grill. Caleb attended most months, usually to connect with people who didn't attend church but valued its presence in town.

Today, however, something felt different the moment he arrived. The usual laughter and chatter were present, but beneath it lay an unusual warmth - deeper conversations, fewer distractions, a gentler energy flowing through the mingled groups.

Mary Kline sat near the edge of the picnic area beneath a large gum tree, watching everything with her quiet, discerning eyes. When Caleb approached, she whispered, "Renewal loves gatherings. Even ones with burnt sausages."

Caleb chuckled. "You knew something was coming today."

"I sensed it," she replied. "Not an event. A moment."

"But we won't know what it is until it arrives?"

She smiled knowingly. "That's usually how God works."

The first hint came unexpectedly - through children. A few of the younger kids had gathered near the old wooden bandstand. One girl began humming softly, then another joined, and soon a small group was singing a simple worship chorus they had learned in Sunday school.

They weren't performing. They weren't trying to be spiritual. They were just singing because joy asked for expression. Parents noticed. Conversations softened. People listened. The song was quiet but carried across the park like a soft breeze.

Caleb watched, moved by the innocence of it. Beside him, Mary whispered, "There. The moment begins."

Soon after, something else began unfolding. Graham and Julie White, carrying plates of food, passed by a picnic table where Paul Kensington sat alone. Paul glanced up, gave them a curt nod, and looked away - unsure of how to join the growing warmth around him. Julie paused, nudging Graham. "We should sit with him."

Graham looked uncertain. "He might want space."

Julie shook her head gently. "No one sits alone today."

So they approached him.

"Mind if we join you?" Julie asked.

Paul hesitated - then nodded. As they sat, Paul exhaled. "I'm still trying to understand everything that's happening."

Julie smiled kindly. "So are we."

"And you're okay with not understanding?"

Graham chuckled. "We're learning to be."

Paul stared at his hands. "It feels like something is shifting in town. I just... don't know where I fit."

Julie placed a hand on his arm. "You fit by being here."

The simplicity of her words seemed to settle something in Paul's shoulders.

Caleb watched from a distance, grateful for the gentle courage of the Whites.

Meanwhile, across the grassy area, a group of teens stood near the cricket nets. Among them was Archer - lanky, awkward, but increasingly radiant since joining Daniel's gatherings. He held a football and was explaining something animatedly.

As Caleb walked closer, he overheard Archer say:

"It's weird, but I've actually been praying. Not fancy prayers — just talking to God. And... I feel different. Like I'm not alone anymore."

One of the other boys shrugged. "I haven't prayed in years. Don't see why I'd start now."

Archer nodded. "I get it. I used to think that too. But then... something happened. I can't explain it. But I don't feel empty anymore."

The other boys were quiet. Not converted. Not convinced. Just listening.

Listening mattered.

Caleb silently prayed for them and moved on.

A little later, Len and Doris Murray sat beneath a jacaranda tree with their grandkids. Doris beckoned Caleb over.

"Pastor, sit with us," she said. "We've been talking about the old days."

"Good days?" Caleb asked.

"Some," Doris laughed. "Some absolutely not."

Len leaned back on his elbows. "But you know what's funny? Back then we never imagined God would move like this. Quietly. Gently. Not through big events, but through hearts softening like bread dough."

Caleb smiled. "It's extraordinary, isn't it?"

"Yes," Doris said. "But I think something else might be coming. Something that will ask more of you."

Caleb's breath caught slightly. "What do you mean?"

Doris shrugged. "Just a feeling. A sense. You've shepherded well through the first movement. But renewal rarely stays contained. You might be called to carry it further - or differently."

Caleb felt the earlier nudge return, stronger now - like a distant bell. Rachel approached then, carrying plates. "What mischief are you filling his head with, Doris?"

"No mischief," Doris replied. "Just prophecy."

Rachel looked at Caleb with raised eyebrows. "Prophecy?"

Caleb smiled softly but said nothing.

As afternoon settled into early evening, clouds gathered above the valley, catching the sunlight in pale gold tints. People began packing up picnics, but no one was in a hurry to leave. The sense of peace was too rich.

Then something happened that surprised even Caleb.

Terry - the bearded carpenter from the men's shed - stood up on one of the wooden picnic benches and cleared his throat. "Hey, everyone," he said loudly enough to draw attention. "I, uh... wanted to say something."

Caleb watched with interest - Terry was not known for public speeches.

"I've been thinking a lot lately," Terry said, rubbing the back of his neck. "About life. Mistakes. How I've treated people. And... well... I just wanted to say sorry. To the town. To anyone I've hurt. I'm trying to... do better. Be better."

A long silence followed.

Then someone clapped.

Then another.

Then most of the park.

Terry flushed bright red and sat down quickly, embarrassed but relieved.

Caleb felt tears prick his eyes. Renewal had reached deeper than he imagined.

Rachel stepped beside him. "You're seeing it, aren't you?"

"Yes," Caleb whispered. "A new movement. God's shifting the soil again."

"What do you think it means?" she asked.

Caleb looked at the sky, now filled with warm, fading light.

"I think God is preparing me," he said quietly. "For something more. Something I haven't yet understood."

Rachel took his hand. "Then when the time comes, we'll walk into it together."

Caleb breathed deeply - peace settling over him like a mantle. The picnic had not been planned as anything spiritual. Yet God had woven grace through it like a golden thread.

Renewal wasn't just in the church anymore.

It was everywhere.

And the invitation God was pressing into Caleb's spirit grew clearer:

Be ready.

The next step is coming.

24. WHEN RENEWAL IS NOTICED

Sunday morning arrived with the same quiet expectancy that had characterised recent weeks, but there was something else beneath it - a subtle tension, not negative, but alert. Caleb felt it the moment he woke.

"Today feels... different," he said to Rachel as they prepared breakfast.

Rachel nodded thoughtfully. "The air's heavier. Not in a bad way. Just... full."

Caleb smiled. "That's one way to put it."

They ate in comfortable silence before heading off to church, unaware that the day would open a new chapter in Willowend's unfolding story.

As they approached the church building, Caleb noticed an unfamiliar car parked discreetly across the road. The vehicle's sleek dark finish stood out among the utes and older sedans that normally lined the street.

Rachel followed his gaze. "Expecting visitors?"

"No," Caleb said. "But apparently we have them."

Inside, the sanctuary buzzed with life. Faces both familiar and new filled the pews. Some were residents who hadn't attended in years. Others were quietly curious visitors drawn by whispers of what God was doing in the small rural church.

But one person stood out immediately. Sitting halfway back, with a notebook in his hand, was someone Caleb recognised from denominational gatherings - Andrew Callahan, a writer for the State Baptist Association's ministry journal.

Not a critic.

Not an administrator.

But someone who paid attention.

Andrew caught Caleb's eye and nodded politely.

Rachel leaned close. "Looks like word is getting around."

"Apparently so," Caleb murmured.

The service began simply. A familiar hymn. A prayer. The reading from John's Gospel, beautifully delivered by Mary Kline with her steady, mature voice.

But as Caleb stepped to the pulpit, he sensed a shift wash through the room - a quiet stillness that seemed to say, *Pay attention. Something sacred is happening.*

He opened with no prepared greeting, only a gentle observation.

"God has been stirring hearts in this valley. Not loudly. Not dramatically. But unmistakably."

Some nodded. Others leaned forward, attentive.

"What God is doing here isn't ours to control. It's ours to receive."

He paused, allowing the truth to settle.

"And perhaps," he continued, "it's also ours to share - not with fanfare, not with exaggeration, but with honesty and humility."

He preached from John 15, exploring the theme of abiding - not striving, not performing, but remaining connected to Christ. The message resonated deeply. Not because it was polished, but because it was real. It spoke to exactly what the community was experiencing.

As Caleb closed in prayer, the sanctuary felt thick with peace - tangible, restful, holy. When the final hymn faded, Andrew approached.

"Pastor Caleb," he said warmly. "Good to see you again."

"You too, Andrew," Caleb replied. "So what has brought you to Willowend?"

Andrew smiled, notebook tucked under his arm. "Curiosity. And perhaps something more. Word's been spreading - quietly - that something special is happening here. I wanted to see for myself."

Caleb resisted the instinct to downplay it. "I'm grateful you're here."

"I'd love to talk," Andrew said. "Not for a formal article. Not yet. Just… to understand."

"Of course," Caleb replied.

But another figure caught Caleb's attention - Daniel Strickland standing near the back wall. Unlike Andrew, Daniel didn't approach. He only watched, thoughtful, almost protective.

A complex expression passed briefly across his face before he turned to leave.

Rachel noticed. "He's carrying something, isn't he?"

"Yes," Caleb said quietly. "And I'm beginning to think God brought him here for reasons bigger than the review."

Later that afternoon, Caleb and Andrew walked the path behind the church, passing the old peppercorn tree.

"I want to be clear," Andrew said. "I'm not here to sensationalise anything. Rural churches often experience quiet renewal, but few want attention. I understand that."

"I appreciate that," Caleb replied.

"So tell me," Andrew continued, "in your own words… what's happening here? What is God doing?"

Caleb took a breath, choosing honesty over caution.

"He's softening hearts. Healing old wounds. Rekindling hope. Not through programs or strategies - just through presence. God's presence."

Andrew nodded slowly. "And how are you shepherding it? What's your approach?"

"To stay out of the way," Caleb said. "To listen more than I speak. To encourage without controlling. Renewal dies when leaders try to own it."

Andrew smiled. "That's rare wisdom."

Caleb shrugged. "It's learning. Not mastery."

They walked a little further before Andrew spoke again. "You know," he said, "if this continues, people beyond Willowend will want to know what's happening."

Caleb's stomach tightened slightly. "I'm not sure I'm ready for that."

"You don't need to be," Andrew said gently. "Just be faithful. The story will unfold as it needs to."

After Andrew left, Caleb found himself wandering to Mary Kline's verandah again - drawn there almost instinctively. Mary looked up before he even reached the steps. "Outside attention has arrived, I see."

Caleb blinked. "How did you know?"

"Because renewal grows quietly until God decides it should be seen," Mary said. "And once He decides that, people will notice whether you want them to or not."

"I really don't want Willowend to become a spectacle," Caleb admitted.

"It won't," Mary assured him. "This kind of renewal repels spectacle. It's too gentle. But it will draw people longing for what they sense here."

Caleb sat beside her. "What am I supposed to do as this grows?" Mary smiled, placing her hand over his. "Walk faithfully. Stay small. Listen closely. And be ready for the next thing God asks of you."

"The next thing," Caleb repeated softly. "Everyone keeps saying that."

"Because everyone except you can already feel it," Mary said with a wink.

That evening, as Caleb and Rachel stood outside watching the sun slip behind the ridge, she asked the question he had been avoiding.

"Are you afraid of what's coming?"

Caleb didn't answer immediately.

Finally, he said, "Not afraid. Just aware. God is widening the circle. And that means He may be widening my calling too."

Rachel moved, resting her head on his shoulder. "Wherever God leads next, you won't walk it alone."

Caleb exhaled, peace settling through him like dew on grass.

"I know," he said softly. "And that makes all the difference."

Above them, the sky deepened into a wash of indigo. Willowend slept peacefully - unaware that renewal had just stepped quietly into its next chapter. And Caleb sensed, more clearly than ever:

God was preparing him for something bigger.

Something beyond the walls of his familiar world.

Something he could neither imagine nor avoid.

Monday morning arrived calm and pale, the sky washed in early light. Caleb woke before dawn, not restless but reflective. Renewal had spread gently through Willowend for weeks - first inside the hearts of the faithful, then throughout the community, and now beyond the town's borders.

And with outside attention came new responsibility.

He sat on the verandah with his tea, watching the birds pick at the dry grass. The silence felt alive. Rachel joined him moments later, hair still tousled from sleep.

"You're thinking again," she said softly.

"Always," Caleb replied. "But today… a bit more than usual."

She sat beside him. "It's Andrew's visit, isn't it?"

"Partly," he admitted. "But something else as well."

Rachel waited - calm, patient, knowing he would speak when ready.

"I think God is asking something of me," Caleb said slowly. "Something more than shepherding the local renewal. But I don't know what it is yet."

Rachel took his hand. "Then we listen together."

Later that morning, Caleb received a phone call from someone he hadn't spoken to in months - Mark Jeffries, a regional coordinator for the State Baptist Association.

"Caleb, good morning!" Mark said cheerfully. "Hope I'm not catching you at a bad time."

"Not at all," Caleb replied. "What can I do for you?"

"Well," Mark began, "I've been hearing some very encouraging things about Willowend lately. Nothing too dramatic - just whispers of spiritual renewal. And then Andrew Callahan sent me a message this morning saying he visited your service yesterday."

Caleb's stomach tightened slightly. "Ah."

"Nothing to worry about," Mark added quickly. "Andrew was impressed. He said he hadn't felt such tenderness in a rural congregation in years. Said your leadership was steady. Said the atmosphere seemed 'grace-shaped.'"

Caleb was quiet for a moment.

"That's kind of him," he said.

Mark continued. "I have a question for you - and there's no pressure. But would you be willing to share what's happening in Willowend at our upcoming regional pastors' gathering? Just a fifteen-minute reflection. Nothing formal."

Caleb blinked. "Me? Speak at the gathering?"

"Yes," Mark said. "It doesn't have to be polished. Just share the story. Pastors are discouraged these days. They need to hear a gentle testimony of hope."

Caleb exhaled slowly. "I'll pray about it."

"That's all I ask," Mark replied. "No rush. Let me know by the end of the week."

After the call ended, Caleb sat in silence, turning the invitation over in his heart.

It wasn't a big assignment. It wasn't a promotion. But it was a widening. A step outward. A movement beyond the valley's borders.

A whisper becoming a call.

Later in the day, Caleb visited the café. When he walked in, Doris greeted him with a bright smile. "Pastor! I've just been reading an email from a friend in another town. She said someone told her 'something special' is happening in Willowend."

Caleb groaned playfully. "It's spreading, isn't it?"

"Like wildflowers," Doris said happily. "But don't worry - this isn't sensational gossip. It's real hope moving from one heart to another."

Len appeared beside her. "But with hope comes curiosity. People will want to know how you're leading this without burning out."

Caleb laughed softly. "Assuming I'm not burning out."

Len gave him a knowing look. "You're carrying more than you say."

Caleb didn't deny it.

"But," Len added, "you're also carrying it lightly. And people will want to learn how you're doing that."

Caleb sipped his coffee thoughtfully. "Mark Jeffries asked me to speak at the regional gathering."

Len nearly choked on his tea. "Well! That's a turn."

"Just a brief reflection, they want… encouragement."

Len studied him. "And you're wondering if this is God nudging you toward something."

"Yes," Caleb admitted.

Len patted his arm. "Then don't resist the nudge. At least listen to it."

In the afternoon, Caleb walked to the river - a place he often went when he needed to think, pray, or simply breathe. The water moved slowly, catching pockets of light between the reeds.

He sat under the shade of a large gum, listening to the gentle movements around him - dragonflies skimming the surface, the distant sound of cockatoos, the soft whisper of wind through leaves. As he prayed, he sensed something forming - not a sentence, not a command, but an impression:

Tell the story.
Not the achievements. Not the methods.
Tell of the gentleness of God.

It was very simple. Clear. Unexpectedly freeing. Caleb breathed deeply, letting the clarity settle.

He didn't have to explain renewal.

He didn't have to justify it.

He didn't have to turn it into a strategy.

He only had to tell the truth of what God was doing.

And suddenly, the weight of fear eased.

On his way back to town, he stopped by the general store. Inside, he found two older men - Howard and Frank - discussing something in hushed but animated tones. Howard noticed him and waved him over.

"Pastor, we were just talking about Sunday's service," Howard said. "Don't know how to say this, but… it felt alive. Like church used to feel when we were young."

Frank nodded. "There was something in the air. Something gentle. Something holy. Haven't felt that in years."

Caleb felt a swell of gratitude. "I'm glad it blessed you both." Howard leaned closer. "But let me ask - is something going on? Something bigger than just a good service?"

Caleb hesitated, weighing how much to say.

"God is stirring hearts," he said simply. "Quietly, but deeply."

Howard nodded slowly. "Well… it's stirring mine."

Frank crossed his arms, eyes softening. "Mine too."

Another affirmation. Another confirmation.

Something was happening.

Something real.

Something that wanted to be shared.

When Caleb returned home, Rachel was tending the garden. She looked up, reading his expression instantly.

"You've been given clarity," she said gently.

"Yes," Caleb replied. "I think I know what God wants."

She wiped her hands and came closer. "And what is that?"

"To share the story," Caleb said. "Not to promote Willowend, not to draw attention - but to encourage weary pastors. God is asking me to carry renewal beyond the valley's borders."

Rachel placed her hand on his cheek. "I knew it. I felt it days ago."

He smiled softly. "Why didn't you say anything?"

"I wanted you to hear it from God, not from me."

Caleb folded her into a gentle embrace. They stood together in the quiet evening light as the sun dipped behind the ridge.

Renewal had begun in Willowend.

Then it grew beyond walls.

Now it was reaching beyond the valley itself.

And Caleb sensed, with peace rather than fear: This was the next step.

Not a distraction. Not a burden. It's a calling.

The week leading up to the regional pastors' gathering passed with an unusual mixture of peace and anticipation. Caleb moved through his days quietly, handling his regular pastoral visits, the sermon preparation, and the practical responsibilities of the church. But underneath everything was the growing awareness that he would soon be stepping beyond Willowend to speak into a wider circle.

He found himself waking each morning with the same prayer on his lips:

Lord, let me tell Your story, not mine.

On Tuesday, as he took his morning walk with Rachel, she said gently, "You're quieter than usual."

Caleb smiled. "I'm listening more than usual."

"To God?" she asked.

"And to my heart," Caleb confessed. "Part of me wonders why I was asked to speak. Another part wonders what God might do through it."

Rachel slipped her arm through his. "Your whole ministry has been about gentleness, patience, and faithfulness. That's what other pastors need right now - not strategies, but reminders of God's kindness."

Caleb looked at her fondly. "You always see the heart of things."

"Only when God makes it clear," she replied.

On Wednesday, Caleb spent time at the men's shed again. The atmosphere there had changed subtly since the previous week. Conversations were more open, laughter deeper, silences less awkward. Mick greeted Caleb with a firm handshake.

"Pastor, I've been thinking about what you said last time," he began. "About hope meaning time isn't wasted."

Caleb nodded. "How's that been sitting with you?"

Mick exhaled heavily. "It's like… I'm starting to believe it. Slowly. I even prayed in the car yesterday. First time in decades." Caleb smiled warmly. "God hears whispered prayers as clearly as shouted ones."

Mick scratched his beard. "Well, mine was barely a whisper. More like a grunt. But it felt… real."

Behind them, Terry called out, "Pastor! You should tell him about the barbecue. How half the town cried when he apologised out loud."

Mick groaned. "Don't remind me. I was mortified."

"Don't be," Caleb said. "Your honesty helped others open up too."

Mick shrugged, embarrassed but pleased. "Still figuring it out, Pastor. Still figuring myself out."

"We all are," Caleb replied gently.

That evening, Caleb set aside time to prepare for the pastors' gathering. He opened a blank document on his laptop, but no words came. He stared at the empty page, frustrated.

"What do I say?" he murmured.

Rachel, passing by with a cup of chamomile tea, paused behind him.

"Write what's true," she said. "Don't write what you think they want to hear."

He exhaled. "I don't want to sound like I'm reporting some kind of movement."

"You're not," she said. "You're sharing a story. A testimony."

"But what if they expect something more structured?"

Rachel placed the tea beside him. "Then they'll be surprised by grace."

Caleb smiled. "You're very poetic tonight."

"Maybe because God is writing something in this town," she replied. "And you're just holding the pen."

Her words settled deep in Caleb's spirit.

On Thursday afternoon, as Caleb visited the primary school, he stumbled upon something unexpected.

Lynette met him at the gate with a wide-eyed look.

"You're just in time," she said, gesturing for him to follow.

They walked toward the playground where a group of children sat in a circle beneath a large gum tree. One of the teachers knelt in the centre, holding a picture book.

"They've been doing this every lunchtime this week," Lynette whispered.

"What is it?" Caleb asked.

"A kindness circle," she replied. "Started spontaneously after some of the older children listened to your message last Sunday. They said it made them want to 'spread gentle things'."

Caleb blinked, moved more than he expected.

As they watched, a young boy named Max spoke timidly.

"I want to say sorry to Mia for being mean last week. I didn't mean it. I was upset about something else."

Mia, surprised, nodded shyly. "It's okay. I forgive you."

The circle clapped quietly.

Lynette whispered, "This is what renewal looks like in children. Simple, sincere reconciliation."

Caleb felt a swell of gratitude. Nothing orchestrated. Nothing forced. Just hearts opening - even the youngest ones. Later that evening, Caleb found himself drawn to the river again. The late light shimmered across the surface, the world hushed as though listening.

He prayed:

Lord, if You want me to speak,
let me speak of Your gentleness.
If You want me to encourage,
let me encourage with humility.
And if You are widening my calling,
let my steps remain small and steady.

As he prayed, he sensed God's presence settle around him – it was quiet, steady and warm.

Not a command.

Not a blueprint.

Just reassurance.

You are not carrying this alone.

Caleb breathed deeply, letting the words anchor his heart.

The next morning, a surprise arrived.

A letter.

Handwritten. Delivered by post rather than email.

Caleb opened it at the breakfast table while Rachel watched with curiosity.

Inside was a short note from Marianne, a pastor's wife in another rural town whom Caleb barely knew.

Dear Caleb,
I heard through a friend that God is doing something special in Willowend. I want you to know that your faithfulness has encouraged more people than you realise. Even from afar, your gentleness shines. Thank you for reminding weary ministers that God still breathes life into small places.

Caleb placed the letter down slowly.

Rachel touched his hand. "You needed to hear that."

He nodded, feeling the truth more deeply than he could express.

Renewal was touching more than Willowend.

It was strengthening others through the simple obedience of one rural pastor and a small community awakening to grace.

That afternoon, Caleb walked into the sanctuary to pray. As he entered, he noticed Daniel sitting alone in the front pew, Bible open on his knees.

"Pastor," Daniel said, standing quickly. "Sorry, I didn't know you were coming."

"It's your church too," Caleb said warmly. "So what brings you here?"

Daniel hesitated, then spoke honestly. "I'm nervous about our youth gathering tonight. People keep saying that revival is happening and I… don't know what that means. I just wanted to pray."

Caleb sat beside him. "Revival doesn't mean pressure. It doesn't mean you need to perform. It simply means God is awakening hearts at His pace, not ours."

Daniel exhaled with relief. "That helps."

Caleb placed a hand on his shoulder. "You're doing well. Keep it simple. Keep it real."

Daniel nodded. "Thanks, Pastor."

As Caleb watched him leave, he whispered a prayer: *Lord, raise up the young gently. Let them grow without fear. Let renewal touch them without overwhelming them.*

That evening, Caleb and Rachel sat on the verandah, overlooking the valley. The sky was brushed with rose and amber as the day faded. Crickets began their chorus.

Rachel turned to him. "Are you ready for tomorrow?"

Caleb smiled softly. "I think I am."

"Because you know what to say?"

"Because I know Who to trust," he replied.

Rachel leaned against him. "Then tomorrow will be beautiful."

Caleb closed his eyes as the first star appeared above the ridge. Willowend's renewal had begun as a whisper. Now it was becoming a song - one that others would soon hear. And Caleb sensed, with peaceful certainty: God wasn't expanding his burden. He was expanding his heart.

The morning of the pastors' gathering dawned crisp and clear. Caleb stood on the verandah with his tea, watching the light stretch over the valley. A gentle breeze rustled the gum leaves, carrying with it the faint scent of wattle.

Rachel stepped beside him, adjusting the collar of his shirt like she had done hundreds of times over the years. "You're ready," she said softly.

Caleb smiled. "I hope so."

"You are," she insisted. "You're not going to impress anyone. You're going to share grace."

He kissed her cheek. "I'll be back this afternoon."

Rachel squeezed his hand. "And I'll be praying."

The gathering was held in the hall of a mid-sized church in one of the neighbouring towns. When Caleb arrived, he recognised many faces - pastors he'd met over the years at conferences, workshops, and denominational events. Some looked rested. Many looked tired. A few carried the unmistakable air of those barely holding things together.

Mark Jeffries greeted him warmly near the entrance.

"Caleb! Glad you came. You all right?"

"Doing well," Caleb said. "Thank you for the invitation."

Mark lowered his voice. "There's a heaviness among the pastors today. You may be exactly what's needed."

Caleb nodded, though a part of him wondered how such a quiet man from a small rural town could offer anything meaningful.

The morning opened with prayer, then brief updates from various churches. A few reported some modest encouragements. Others shared their struggles - declining attendance, leadership fatigue, spiritual apathy. The room felt honest but weary.

As Caleb listened, he felt the weight of these stories. They were not failures. They were testimonies of the long, slow obedience that marked pastoral life. And they layered themselves over his heart with compassion.

Near midday, Mark stepped to the front.

"Friends, I've asked Pastor Caleb from Willowend to share something with us today. You've probably heard whispers about what's happening there. I want you to hear it from him directly." There was polite interest, but also some guardedness. Many pastors had been burned by exaggerated reports of revival or overstated ministry breakthroughs. Caleb sensed it – and he understood it.

He walked to the front slowly, carrying nothing but his Bible and a quiet confidence.

"Thank you," he began simply. "I'm not here to present a model. I'm not here to offer strategies. I'm here to tell a story."

A subtle shift passed through the room - curiosity softening into attentiveness. Caleb continued.

"Something has been happening in Willowend. Not a revival in the way some imagine it - no crowds, no noise, no dramatic manifestations. It's something gentler. Something quieter."

He shared about the softened hearts, the children reconciling in the schoolyard, the men's shed awakening, the small circles of prayer forming without prompting. He spoke about Mary's wisdom, Daniel's revival among the young people, the tender confessions coming from unexpected places.

And then he said something he hadn't planned:

"Renewal didn't begin with programs or sermons. It began when our church stopped striving to fix itself and simply sat in the presence of God with open hands."

He felt several pastors inhale sharply - not in disagreement, but in recognition. Caleb continued.

"I didn't lead renewal. I received it. My task has been to stay small, stay gentle, and keep the door open. God has done the rest."

He saw eyes soften. Shoulders relax. A few tears blinked away quietly. He spoke for only fifteen minutes. But every word came from lived experience, not theory. When he finished, the room was still.

Then an older pastor stood - a man Caleb recognised from years of faithful ministry. "Pastor Caleb," he said, voice trembling, "thank you. I've been trying to manufacture life in my church for a long time. I forgot that God moves gently. I forgot that my job is not to generate revival, but to shepherd hearts."

Caleb nodded with humility. "You are not alone."

Another pastor said, "I've been discouraged for months. Maybe years. Hearing your story… it gives me hope again."

Someone else added, "Please keep telling this story. We need to hear it."

And there it was - the confirmation Caleb didn't know he needed.

Not applause.

Not admiration.

Just renewed hope among weary shepherds.

After the session ended, pastors gathered around Caleb, one by one - not to seek formulas, but to share burdens.

A young pastor confessed, "I thought I was failing because my church wasn't growing."

Caleb replied, "Growth isn't the measure. Faithfulness is."

Another said, "I haven't sensed God's presence in months … maybe longer."

Caleb placed a hand on his shoulder. "Then begin with stillness. God speaks into quiet hearts."

Some pastors simply hugged him - long, weary embraces that said more than words could.

Mark approached again, his eyes misty. "Caleb... I don't know how else to put this - that was exactly what we needed. Not a performance. A reminder."

Caleb smiled softly. "I'm glad it helped."

Mark hesitated, then said, "I think you may be called to share this story more widely - when the time is right."

Caleb didn't reject the idea. He didn't embrace it. He only said, "I'll follow wherever God leads."

On the drive home, Caleb felt a deep stillness. Not pride. Not exhilaration. Something quieter. Peace. The landscape rolled by - paddocks, gentle hills, the shimmer of heat rising from the asphalt. He prayed silently.

Thank You, Lord.
Not for using me,
but for letting hope breathe again
in hearts that were tired.

When he arrived back in Willowend, the sun was dipping low behind the ridge. He parked the car, feeling the day's weight fall away.

Rachel met him at the door. "How did it go?"

Caleb wrapped his arms around her, holding her close. "Better than I expected. Gentler than I imagined. And... confirming."

She pulled back to look at him. "Confirming what?"

"That God is widening the circle," he said quietly. "And He's asking me to walk into it - slowly, humbly, but faithfully."

Rachel smiled. "I knew that before you left this morning."

Caleb laughed gently. "You always hear God half a step ahead of me."

"It's one of the perks of the job," she teased.

That night, Caleb couldn't sleep. Not because he was anxious, but because his heart was full.

He lay awake, listening to the quiet breath of the valley outside, aware that something had shifted - not outwardly, but within him.

Renewal was no longer something happening to Willowend.

It was something he was called to steward - not just locally, but beyond the valley. Carefully. Gently. Without spectacle.

A calling born not of ambition, but of obedience.

He whispered into the darkness:

"Lord, whatever You ask, I will walk with You."

And in the stillness, he felt the unmistakable peace of God settle over him like a warm blanket.

The Monday after the pastors' gathering dawned soft and cool, mist hanging low over the paddocks. Caleb woke feeling both rested and reflective, the memory of the gathering still warm in his heart. The encouragement he had witnessed among those pastors lingered with him - a quiet assurance that God was doing something bigger than he could see.

Rachel joined him on the verandah with two mugs of tea. "You're thinking about the gathering again."

Caleb nodded. "It felt... holy. But also humbling. I wasn't expecting that kind of response."

"You weren't meant to," she replied gently. "You were meant to be yourself. And that's what touched them."

He smiled. "Sometimes I think you should be the one giving pastoral talks."

Rachel laughed, brushing a hand through her hair. "No thank you. I'll stay in my lane. But I'm good at seeing what God is doing in you - and in the valley."

Caleb took her hand, grateful once again for the quiet strength she carried. "And that's more than enough."

Later in the morning, Caleb visited the general store for a few necessities. Howard greeted him from behind the counter with unusual enthusiasm.

"Pastor! Heard you spoke at the pastors' gathering. Someone's cousin from another town sent me a message about it."

Caleb blinked. "News travels fast."

Howard chuckled. "It does when it's hopeful. People in other towns are curious. They want to know why Willowend feels... different."

Caleb lowered his voice a little. "It's not something we want to advertise. Just something we want to protect."

Howard nodded. "I know. And don't worry - most people aren't looking for a spectacle. They're looking for reassurance that God still works in small towns."

Before Caleb could respond, Frank entered the store carrying a box of tomatoes.

"Pastor, can I talk to you outside for a minute?" he asked quietly.

Caleb followed him to the verandah, sensing something was off.

Frank scratched the back of his neck. "Pastor… you know I'm not a man who jumps to conclusions. But something happened yesterday that I can't stop thinking about."

"What happened?" Caleb asked gently.

"It was after the service. I was standing outside the church, and two people I didn't recognise were talking quietly near the gum tree. At first, I thought they were visitors. But then I heard them mention the word 'report.' And 'assessment.' And… well… your name."

Caleb felt a slight tightening in his chest. "Did they say who they were?"

"No," Frank said. "But they weren't locals. And they weren't visitors who came for worship. Their tone was… formal. I didn't like it."

Caleb placed a hand on Frank's shoulder. "Thank you for telling me."

Frank nodded, then added, "I might be wrong. Maybe they're harmless. But… just keep your eyes open."

Caleb promised he would.

As Frank walked back into the store, Caleb stood still for a moment, letting the words settle. Renewal had drawn curiosity from pastors and believers - but it could also draw scrutiny from people who didn't really understand quiet movements of God. He breathed deeply. *Lord, give me wisdom. Not fear.*

Later that day, Caleb visited the men's shed.

The atmosphere was lively as usual, with the sound of tools clattering and easy conversation filling the space. But when Mick saw him enter, he approached with an expression that was… conflicted.

"Pastor," he said, rubbing his forehead. "We've been talking. And we've got a question."

Caleb braced slightly. "All right."

"It's not a bad question," Mick said quickly. "It's just something we're trying to figure out."

"What is it?"

Mick exchanged a glance with Len, who stepped forward to join the conversation.

"Some of the blokes are wondering," Len said carefully, "what exactly is happening in town. They feel something changing.

They like it - mostly. But they're… uneasy."

Caleb nodded slowly. "Uneasy how?"

Mick shrugged. "You know men. We don't know what to do with feelings. Especially spiritual ones. We're noticing things in ourselves we didn't expect. Guilt. Hope. Old wounds trying to heal. It's… unsettling."

Caleb smiled softly. "Renewal often begins with unsettledness."

"I get that," Mick said. "But here's the thing - a few of the men want to know what comes next. They're afraid this is leading somewhere they won't understand or can't commit to."

Caleb rested a hand on Mick's shoulder. "Nothing is being demanded of anyone. Renewal isn't a program. It's a gentle awakening. It doesn't force, it invites."

Mick exhaled. "Tell them that."

"I will," Caleb promised.

Len added, "You're shepherding the whole valley right now, whether you like it or not. And some of us need extra reassurance."

Caleb felt the truth of Len's words settle in his spirit. Renewal had widened - and so had the responsibility.

In the afternoon, Caleb visited Mary Kline. She sat on her verandah reading her Bible, the breeze lifting the edges of the thin pages.

"Mary," Caleb began softly, "I think something is shifting again."

Mary closed her Bible with a gentle smile. "Of course it is."

"I spoke at the pastors' gathering," Caleb said. "It was beautiful, encouraging. But now I'm sensing something else - attention from people who may not understand what God is doing. Even men at the shed are unsettled."

Mary nodded knowingly. "When renewal begins to bear fruit, people start to watch. Some people watch with hope. Others with caution. A few with suspicion."

Caleb sighed. "I want to shepherd this well."

"And you will," Mary said. "But just remember – you are not responsible for managing everyone's reactions. Just for walking faithfully."

Caleb sat beside her. "Frank overheard two people after church yesterday. They spoke about 'reports' and 'assessments.' They weren't from town."

Mary's eyes sharpened slightly. "Renewal attracts attention of all kinds. But don't let fear interpret what you don't yet know. Wait. Listen. Trust God's timing."

Caleb nodded slowly. "Thank you."

Mary leaned in. "And Caleb... you must prepare your heart for the next thing God will ask of you. Before long, you will be speaking not only to pastors, but to someone else."

"Someone else?" Caleb asked.

Mary smiled softly. "You'll know when the time comes."

As Caleb walked home that evening, the valley glowed beneath the descending sun. Birds settled into branches. Dust swirled behind the occasional passing car.

Rachel met him at the gate.

"You look thoughtful," she said.

"I am," he replied. "Today reminded me that renewal brings beauty… and weight."

Rachel touched his arm. "God will give you what you need for both."

Caleb looked out across the valley, the soft light brushing the tops of the trees. He knew she was right.

Renewal had awakened Willowend and now it was awakening something in Caleb - deeper, wider, more costly, and more beautiful than he had ever expected. And though uncertainty lingered at the edges, peace held firm at the centre.

The next morning dawned pale and cool, a thin veil of cloud softening the sunrise. Caleb felt unusually alert as he stepped outside with his tea, as though the quiet air itself were waiting for something. He breathed in deeply, praying without words. There were days when prayer sounded like sentences, and days when it sounded like breath. Today was the latter.

Rachel joined him with her mug, eyeing him thoughtfully.

"You slept lightly again," she said.

"I'm thinking," Caleb replied. "And listening."

She leaned against the railing. "Something's stirring. I can feel it."

"Yes," Caleb said. "But I'm not sure if it's something to welcome or something to prepare for."

Rachel gave a soft smile. "Sometimes it's both."

He visited the church shortly after breakfast. As he unlocked the doors, he noticed an envelope that had been slipped under the front entrance.

Unaddressed. Plain. Unsettling in its lack of context. He brought it into the sanctuary and opened it. Inside was a typed letter.

Dear Pastor Caleb,

I recently attended your service. While I appreciate the sincerity of your message, I am concerned about the emotional atmosphere I observed. It seemed overly responsive, perhaps indicative of unhealthy influence or manipulative practices. I intend to look further into this.

Sincerely,
A concerned visitor.

Caleb felt a tightness across his chest - not fear, not anger, but sadness. Sadness that someone could witness gentleness and misinterpret it. Sadness that God's quiet work might be viewed through a lens of suspicion. Sadness that the shadow of misunderstanding had crept into the sanctuary. He sat in the front pew, holding the letter loosely.

Lord, teach me to respond with grace.
Teach me to discern what is genuine concern
and what is unfounded fear.

He remained in silence for several minutes until the stillness settled deep into him. He would not allow one anonymous voice to colour the renewal unfolding in Willowend - but neither would he dismiss it. Wisdom required both courage and humility.

Later that morning, as Caleb walked toward the café, he ran into Paul Kensington outside the newsagent - the man who had been cautiously curious since the early days of renewal.

"Pastor," Paul said, stopping him with a raised hand. "Got a minute?"

"Of course," Caleb replied.

Paul shifted uneasily. "I don't know how to say this without sounding strange, but… things in town feel different. And some people - well, they're starting to speculate."

"Speculate about what?" Caleb asked.

Paul looked over his shoulder as though ensuring no one else could hear. "About you. About the church. About why people are suddenly more emotional. Some think you are leading something. Others think something's happening *to* people."

Caleb kept his voice gentle. "What do you think, Paul?"

Paul hesitated. "I think… something is happening. And I don't understand it. But I also think you're not the type to stir up drama."

Caleb nodded. "I'm not stirring anything. I'm simply making room for God to move."

Paul exhaled. "Well… just be aware. Not everyone sees it that way."

Caleb thanked him. And Paul, somewhat awkwardly, gave his shoulder a reassuring pat before heading off.

Two conversations in one morning. Two reminders that the renewal, once hidden, was now under observation.

Inside the café, Len and Doris were bustling about. The scent of fresh scones filled the air. As soon as Caleb stepped in, Doris hurried over.

"Pastor! Someone was in here earlier asking about you."

Caleb felt his stomach tighten. "Who?"

Doris shook her head. "Didn't give a name. Middle-aged. Sharp-looking. Not unfriendly, but… probing. Asked about the church, the increase in attendance, whether anything unusual had been happening."

"And what did you say?" Caleb asked.

"I told them the truth," Doris replied. "That God is touching hearts. That it's gentle. That nothing strange or theatrical is happening. And then I kindly told them that if they wanted facts, they should speak to you directly."

Caleb smiled despite the tension. "Thank you."

"Pastor Caleb," Len said, stepping forward, "people who don't understand gentleness often fear it. Just be steady. You're doing fine."

That afternoon, Caleb visited the school. As he walked through the playground, several children waved to him from across the yard. It warmed him - but also reminded him why renewal needed protection. Lynette met him near the library.

"Pastor, do you have a moment?" she asked, her tone unusually serious.

"Of course."

She led him into her office and closed the door gently.

"I received a call this morning," she began. "From someone asking if our school had been influenced by what's happening at the church."

Caleb swallowed. "Influenced how?"

"That's the thing," Lynette said. "They didn't say. Just hinted at 'shifts in atmosphere' and asked if we'd noticed any unusual emotional behaviours."

"And what did you say?" Caleb asked.

"The truth," Lynette replied firmly. "That kindness is increasing. That students are reconciling more quickly. That teachers feel a lighter atmosphere. And that none of it is harmful."

Caleb exhaled. "Thank you."

Lynette leaned forward. "Pastor... I don't know who these people are, but I sense the beginnings of something. Not hostility - just scrutiny. Be ready."

Her honesty settled heavily but helpfully.

By late afternoon, Caleb felt the weight of the day pressing down on him. He didn't feel threatened - just aware.

Renewal was a very tender flame. It needed shepherding, not shielding, but shepherding sometimes meant guarding.

He walked to Mary's home almost without thinking.

She sat as always on her verandah, as though waiting for him.

"You've had a day," she said before he spoke.

"I have," Caleb admitted, taking the seat beside her. "A letter. Questions. Visitors with unnamed agendas."

Mary nodded slowly. "It was bound to come. Renewal invites curiosity from those who are hungry - and caution from those who are unsettled."

Caleb stared out at the dust motes floating through the late sun.

"What should I do?"

"Nothing rash," Mary said gently. "Nothing defensive. Nothing fearful."

She placed her hand over his.

"Caleb, when God breathes life into a valley, it draws attention. Your task is not to explain the wind. It's to remain upright in it." Caleb felt tears prick unexpectedly.

Mary continued, "And remember - scrutiny will reveal your integrity, not undermine it."

He nodded slowly. "I needed to hear that."

"I know," she said simply.

As evening settled, Caleb returned home to find Rachel sitting on the verandah with a small smile.

"I've been praying for you all day," she said.

"Thank you," Caleb replied, sitting beside her. "It's been... a stretching day."

Rachel placed her hand on his arm. "Stretching means God is enlarging your heart. Not breaking it."

He leaned back, watching the sky change to shades of rose and gold.

"What if scrutiny intensifies?" he asked quietly.

"Then you will walk through it," Rachel said gently. "Caleb, the same God who breathed renewal into this valley will sustain it. And He will sustain you."

Caleb exhaled deeply, letting her words sink in.

The weight of the day didn't disappear - but it grew lighter. And beneath it all remained the steady pulse of wonder.

Renewal was real.

God was near.

And whatever scrutiny came, it would meet humility, not fear.

The following Thursday began like any other - soft morning light spreading across the hills, kookaburras claiming the dawn, the valley easing awake with familiar comfort. Caleb was seated at the kitchen table finishing his second cup of tea while Rachel prepared breakfast.

"You're settling again," she observed, not looking up from the stovetop. "Yesterday's weight seems lighter."

"It is," Caleb replied. "Mary helped. And so did you."

Rachel placed the eggs on plates and smiled. "Good. You'll need a steady heart. I feel the next few days may bring something new."

Caleb met her gaze. "You sense it too?"

"God rarely gives peace without purpose."

They ate quietly, their unspoken thoughts mingling across the table. Mid-morning, Caleb went to the church office to catch up on emails and prepare for Sunday's message. He had barely sat down when Howard rang.

"Pastor, sorry to bother you," Howard said, sounding flustered.

"There's someone here at the store asking for you."

"For me?" Caleb asked. "Who is it?"

"No idea. Not a local. Said they'd only be in town today and needed to speak with you directly."

Caleb felt a faint flicker of tension. "All right. I'll be there as soon as I can."

He walked to the general store with swift, but steady steps, praying quietly.

Lord, let this be guided by Your hand, not my fear.

When he entered, Howard gestured subtly toward the side aisle. A woman stood browsing a shelf of honey jars, though her posture made it clear she wasn't really reading labels. She looked to be in her late forties, sharply dressed but not imposing, with a posture that suggested both authority and patience. She turned as Caleb approached.

"Pastor Caleb?" she asked, offering a polite smile.

"Yes," he replied. "And you are…?"

"My name is Emily Foster," she said, extending her hand. "I'm with the State Baptist Association."

Caleb shook her hand but felt his pulse tick upward. This wasn't a passing visitor. This was someone official.

"I see," Caleb said calmly. "What brings you to Willowend?"

Emily's smile was warm but purposeful. "Would we be able to speak somewhere quieter? Perhaps a walk?"

Caleb nodded. "Of course."

As they stepped outside, Howard mouthed silently, *Good luck*, though Caleb wasn't sure if Howard meant it humorously or sincerely.

They walked along the footpath toward the park, the morning breeze tugging softly at the leaves.

"Pastor Caleb," Emily began, "you should know from the outset that I'm not here because of a complaint. Nor am I here to audit or assess your church."

Caleb exhaled quietly. "That's good to hear."

"But," she continued gently, "I am here because multiple people have contacted our office - pastors, ministry leaders, even a few laypeople - asking about what's happening in Willowend."

Caleb listened intently.

"Some reports," she said, "have been deeply encouraging. Others... less clear. And when information is vague, people fill the gaps with assumptions."

Caleb nodded slowly. "I understand."

Emily glanced at him. "You look remarkably calm."

"I'm learning to walk gently," Caleb replied. "Renewal teaches you that."

Emily gave a small approving smile. "I've read your messages in the Association newsletter over the years. Even then, your tone stood out. Graceful. Patient. I suspect something of that spirit is shaping Willowend now."

They reached the small park bench overlooking the creek. Emily gestured for them to sit.

"Pastor," she said, folding her hands, "the Association certainly isn't worried … but we are curious. And it's usually better to come and see than to rely on hearsay."

"That's fair," Caleb said.

"So, I need to ask you," Emily said gently, "what *is* happening in Willowend?"

Caleb took a breath.

"God is softening hearts," he said. "Quietly. Tenderly. People are reconciling, opening up, rediscovering hope. Children are forgiving each other in the schoolyard. Men in the shed are talking about wounds they've buried for decades. Nothing dramatic. Nothing artificial. Just... grace."

Emily listened with genuine interest.

Caleb continued, "Attendance has increased, but only slightly. The atmosphere feels a lot lighter. People linger after services, wanting to pray or talk with each other. And everything that's happening is unplanned. No campaigns. No emotional pressure. Just God's steady work."

Emily nodded. "That aligns with the positive reports."

Caleb paused. "There have been concerns too, I gather."

"Yes," Emily said honestly. "Some people who are unfamiliar with spiritual renewal will interpret emotional responses as manipulation. Others will fear anything that doesn't fit their pre-formed categories. It's not unusual."

Caleb nodded. "I received an anonymous letter."

She sighed. "I suspected you might. Every move of God draws both hunger and apprehension."

He looked at her, grateful for her candour. "So, what do you need from me, Emily?"

"Transparency," she replied simply. "Reassurance that what's happening here is grounded, gentle, and healthy. Perhaps… guidance also . Because if this renewal continues, your influence may reach beyond the valley whether you seek it or not."

Caleb swallowed softly. Mary had said the very same thing, but in different words.

Emily continued, "We don't want to interfere in any way. We want to understand, and, if appropriate, offer support."

Caleb felt a wave of relief. Not scrutiny. Not suspicion.

Partnership.

They sat in silence for a moment, listening to the creek murmur beneath the bridge.

Then Emily said something entirely unexpected.

"Pastor, have you ever considered that God might be preparing you for a wider ministry?"

Caleb stared at her, taken aback.

"I'm quite settled here," he said gently.

"I believe you," she replied. "And I'm not suggesting otherwise. But sometimes God uses a quiet valley to shape a voice He intends to share. Your steadiness, your pastoral patience - these are things many rural pastors desperately need."

Caleb inhaled slowly. "It's not something I've thought about seriously."

"Then please pray about it," Emily said. "If Willowend's renewal continues, people will look to you. And you'll need to discern how to steward that without losing the gentleness that birthed it."

Her words felt weighty, but certainly not heavy. It was more like truth spoken in season.

Emily stood. "I'll stay in town for the day, observe quietly, and speak with a few others. But please know - I'm not here to judge. I'm here to learn."

Caleb rose with her. "Thank you for your honesty."

She smiled. "And thank you for yours."

As Emily walked away toward the town centre, Caleb remained by the creek, feeling both grounded and stretched. Renewal had attracted attention - but not all attention was adversarial. Some was simply seeking understanding.

He prayed quietly.

Lord, if You are widening my calling,
help me to walk slowly enough
to hear every step You ask me to take.

The breeze lifted, brushing the back of his neck with a warmth that felt almost like reassurance. And in that moment, Caleb sensed something he hadn't fully realised until now: The valley was no longer the only place where God was at work in him.

Emily moved quietly through the town for the remainder of the morning. Caleb chose not to accompany her - partly because she hadn't asked him to, and partly because he felt it was important that she experience Willowend as it truly was, unfiltered and unaccompanied.

Still, he found himself wondering throughout the day where she had gone, who she had spoken with, and what impressions she was gathering.

At the men's shed, Len and Mick were adjusting a workbench leg when they heard a knock on the open roller door.

"Excuse me," Emily said politely. "I'm looking for Len Turner."

Len straightened. "That'd be me."

"And Mick Andrews?" she added.

Mick raised a hand. "What's this about?"

"My name is Emily Foster," she said. "I'm visiting from the State Baptist Association. I understand you know Pastor Caleb well."

The two men exchanged surprised glances with each other. Then Mick's expression shifted into something more like protective suspicion.

"You're not here to cause trouble, are you?" he asked bluntly.

Emily shook her head. "Not at all. I'm here to understand what God is doing in this valley. Nothing more."

Len softened immediately. "Oh! Well then, pull up a chair."

Mick gave a half-shrug and found one for her.

Emily sat with the two men as the shed buzzed around them - sawdust floating, tools humming, banter rising and falling. It was earthy, loud, and unmistakably real.

"I want to ask," Emily said, "what changes you've seen in the community."

Len rubbed his chin. "Changes? Well… blokes are talking, for one."

Mick laughed. "And sometimes listening."

Len continued, "It's small things. But small things matter in a town like this."

Mick nodded. "There's a lightness - not in a flimsy way, but in the way a man feels when he realises he doesn't have to carry every burden alone. Caleb's part of that. But it's not *about* him."

Emily leaned forward slightly. "What is it about, then?"

Mick hesitated, searching for words. Then he simply said:

"God being kind."

Emily's breath caught at the disarming simplicity of the answer.

Len added, "We trust Caleb. He's steady. And steady men make other men feel safe to open up."

Mick leaned a little closer. "If anyone's been spreading negative whispers, they don't know us. And they sure don't know him."

Emily nodded thoughtfully. "Thank you. That's very helpful."

When she rose to leave, Mick walked her to the door. "Just… tell whoever needs telling that we're not being manipulated. We're being healed."

Emily gave him a sincere smile. "I will."

Next she visited Doris at the café. The bell chimed as she entered, and Doris looked up with the warm familiarity she gave everyone.

"You must be Emily," she said, surprising her.

Emily laughed. "Word travels quickly."

"In this town? Faster than the wind," Doris replied. "Sit down, dear. I'll bring you a cuppa."

While waiting, Emily absorbed the atmosphere. There was a gentle rhythm to the café - people lingering, conversations humming, but never harsh, an ease in the air that wasn't manufactured. When Doris returned, she sat opposite her uninvited but entirely welcome.

"So, what do you want to know?" Doris asked.

"I suppose I want to understand what you're seeing," Emily said.

Doris chuckled. "Oh, I'm seeing plenty. People forgiving each other. Folks staying longer after meals. Kids helping without being asked. And the pastor? Well… he's just being his usual steady self."

Emily smiled. "Do you think anything unusual is happening?"

"Of course something unusual is happening," Doris said matter-of-factly. "We're becoming kinder. That's always unusual."

There was a pause.

Then Doris leaned in with a teasing grin. "Now if you're here to find scandal, you won't. But if you're here to find grace, it's on almost every corner of town these days."

Emily laughed. "Thank you. I think that's exactly what I needed to hear."

As she left the café, she felt both grounded and uplifted - a rare combination.

Her final visit was to the primary school. Lynette welcomed her warmly and showed her the "kindness circle" beneath the gum tree. A few children were gathered there, writing encouraging notes to classmates.

Emily crouched beside them.

"What are you doing?" she asked.

A little girl named Mia looked up at her. "We're writing 'so-kind letters.' That's what we call them."

Emily smiled. "Who taught you that?"

Mia shrugged. "No one. We just started."

Emily felt her throat tighten a little. These were not the fruits of manipulation. These were not signs of emotional coercion.

They were signs of real life.

That afternoon, Emily returned to the church grounds. Caleb, who had been sweeping leaves near the driveway, straightened as she approached. She could read nothing defensive in his posture - only calm readiness.

"How did your day go?" Caleb asked.

Emily stopped a few steps away from him, folding her hands gently.

"It was… illuminating," she said. "Your town is remarkable. Not perfect - but warmed. Softened. Alive."

Caleb exhaled with quiet relief. "I'm glad that came through."

"It did," Emily said. "And more than that, I saw no signs of unhealthy influence. No one's afraid. No one's confused. People are simply being healed."

Caleb felt the weight slide from his shoulders - weight he hadn't realised he'd been carrying all day.

Emily continued, "I also spoke with a few who were initially suspicious. Their concerns weren't rooted in anything real - just uncertainty about what renewal looks like in practice. And that is normal."

She stepped a little closer.

"Caleb, Willowend is experiencing something precious. You're stewarding it well."

He looked down briefly, humbled. "Thank you."

"But," she added gently, "you will need wisdom in the days ahead. Attention will grow. Curiosity will spread. And with it, the need for discernment."

Caleb nodded. "Mary said something similar."

"I'm not surprised," Emily replied. "She seems very perceptive."

There was a moment of comfortable silence.

Then Emily said, "May I ask you something personal?"

"Of course."

"What do *you* want, Caleb? As all this grows?"

The question startled him - both in its directness and its depth.

"I want," he said slowly, "to stay faithful. To remain small. To walk gently. And to never forget that this is God's doing, not mine."

Emily smiled - a genuine, pleased smile.

"That," she said, "is exactly why God entrusted this to you."

As Emily walked back to her car, Caleb remained by the church fence, watching the breeze move through the trees. He felt a curious mixture of gratitude and anticipation.

Emily had not come to scrutinise him. She had come to confirm him. And something in her visit - something subtle and yet unmistakable - felt like the next turning of the page.

Not an ending.

Not a beginning.

A widening.

A gentle widening of calling, influence, and responsibility.

He whispered into the wind:
"Lord… help me walk this with humility."

And in the quietness of his heart, he sensed God's assurance once again.

He was not alone.

He had never been alone.

And the path ahead, though widening, would be guided by the same gentle hand that had led him this far.

Emily left Willowend early the next day, her car disappearing quietly over the ridge road. No one watched her leave except Caleb, who stood for a few minutes outside the church office, hands resting lightly in his pockets. He wasn't anxious - just aware. Something in her visit had shifted the atmosphere. Not in a disruptive way, but in a clarifying one.

Rachel joined him a moment later.

"She's gone?" she asked.

"Yes," Caleb said softly.

Rachel studied his face. "And now you are wondering what comes next."

He smiled faintly. "You always catch me mid-thought."

"I've had a lot of practice," she said warmly.

They stood together in the cool morning air as the town hummed awake. Willowend felt peaceful. But beneath the peace there was movement - gentle, steady, purposeful.

Something was unfolding.

Later in the morning, Caleb walked to the general store for milk. Howard, predictably, intercepted him before he even reached the fridge.

"Pastor! Big day yesterday, huh?"

Caleb chuckled. "News travels fast."

"It floats on the air," Howard said with a grin. Then his expression shifted, softening. "I liked her. She's sharp, but not sharp-edged, you know? Felt fair."

"Yes," Caleb agreed. "She's the right kind of curious."

Howard nodded vigorously. "That's it. Curious without being nosy. Respectful."

He leaned closer. "You should know - a few folks have been asking me whether she came to stir up trouble. I told them no. I told them she listened more than she spoke."

"That's true," Caleb said.

"And that she seemed… I don't know … grateful to see what's happening here." Howard paused. "Because we are grateful, Pastor. You know that, right? Even the ones who don't say it."

Caleb felt something warm settle in his chest. "I do know. And I'm grateful for Willowend too."

Howard grinned. "Good. Just wanted to make sure the air stays clear."

Across town, the men's shed experienced a rare moment of unity. Mick, who had been wrestling with a quiet concern, addressed the morning group.

"Blokes," he began, clearing his throat, "that woman who visited yesterday - she wasn't here to judge us. She was actually here to understand."

A few men nodded slowly, listening.

Mick continued, "Some of us have been feeling uneasy. Not because anything bad's happening, but because anything good feels strange after a long stretch of… nothing."

There were murmurs of agreement.

"But I'll tell you this," Mick said, voice firming. "Whatever's going on in this town, it's making us better. Kinder. More honest. You can't fake that. And if someone from outside wants to check in, I say let 'em. We've got nothing to hide."

Len added, "And the pastor? He's the same man he's always been. He's not pushing anything. He's steady."

Mick nodded. "And steadiness is rare these days."

The message settled like a calming breeze.

Meanwhile, over at the primary school, Lynette found herself speaking with two teachers over morning tea.

"How did your chat go with that lady?" one asked.

"Good," Lynette said. "She wasn't suspicious at all. She was observant. She saw the kindness circle. She saw the shift in the kids. She seemed… heartened."

"And the concerns?" the teacher pressed gently.

"Concerns are just part of anything new," Lynette replied. "But she didn't see anything unhealthy. She saw growth."

The teachers looked relieved.

"It's funny," one said. "This whole valley feels lighter. Not louder. Just lighter."

Lynette smiled. "That's exactly it."

By early afternoon, Caleb walked along the pathway behind the church, reflecting on the conversations he'd had throughout the day. Emily's presence had done something unusual:

It reassured people.

It clarified the renewal.

It steadied the narrative.

It confirmed what many had sensed but couldn't articulate: God was at work - gently, authentically, unmistakably.

Caleb felt a peace about that.

Yet as he reached the old peppercorn tree, he sensed the next layer of awareness rising in him - not anxiety, but a quiet gravity.

Renewal had passed its first moment of scrutiny. Now it was entering a new season - one that would require wisdom beyond the valley.

He made his way toward Mary's verandah later that afternoon. She was already outside, as if expecting him.

"You walked with a new kind of weight today," she said as he approached.

Caleb sat beside her. "Do I?"

Mary nodded. "Not a heavy weight. A purposeful one."

He smiled slightly. "Emily was kind. Thoughtful. Discerning."

"Good," Mary said. "Then she will have seen the truth."

"She did," Caleb replied. "And so did the town. Her presence settled some fears."

Mary tilted her head. "But raised deeper questions in you." Caleb hesitated. "Yes."

Mary folded her hands, her expression soft. "Caleb, renewal never remains still. Once God awakens a valley, He awakens the one shepherding it too."

Caleb exhaled slowly. "I'm realising that."

"And you're not afraid," Mary observed.

"No," Caleb said. "Not afraid. Just aware."

Mary smiled. "Awareness is the doorway to calling."

They sat quietly for a moment, watching the shifting light play across the hills. Then Mary said quietly, "Something will soon be asked of you - something that will widen your ministry beyond Willowend. Not a departure. Not a replacement. A widening."

Caleb listened, not resisting, not reaching - simply receiving.

"And when that invitation comes," Mary continued, "you must hold it gently. Not as a task, but as a continuation of the grace already unfolding here."

Caleb nodded. "I think I understand."

Mary touched his hand lightly. "Then you are ready."

That evening, as Caleb and Rachel closed the curtains and prepared dinner, Rachel paused at the table, watching him. "You've changed," she said softly.

Caleb looked up. "How do you mean?"

"You seem… settled. As if a question you didn't know you were asking has finally been answered."

Caleb considered this, then nodded. "Emily's visit didn't unsettle me. It clarified things. Not about the renewal - but about my role in it."

Rachel stepped closer. "Tell me."

Caleb leaned against the counter, hands lightly resting on the edge.

"I'm beginning to see that renewal isn't something I'm merely witnessing. It's something I'm being prepared to steward - not just here, but perhaps elsewhere too."

Rachel smiled - not surprised, not startled.

"I knew that months ago," she said. "I just needed you to see it too."

He breathed out, a soft, warm exhale. "I suppose I'm slow to catch up."

"No," Rachel said gently. "You're cautious. And God honours caution when it's wrapped in humility."

Caleb's heart warmed at her words.

Renewal was widening.

Calling was deepening.

And he was no longer hesitant to follow.

Later that night, Caleb stepped outside alone. The sky was deep and full of stars. The air cool. The valley peaceful. He whispered into the quiet:

"Lord... I'm listening."

And standing beneath the Southern Cross, he felt it: A shift; a turning; a widening. Not loud; not urgent; but unmistakable. The next stage of the journey had begun.

Two days after Emily left, the rhythm of Willowend settled back into its familiar pattern. Or at least, it looked that way from the outside. Inside, something had changed.

The town moved with the same routines - stock trucks rumbling down the main road, children riding bikes to the park, the regular hum of the café and the servo. But beneath the surface, there was a quiet awareness: Someone had come, seen, and gone again. And their leaving had somehow confirmed the goodness of what remained.

On Monday morning, Caleb sat at his small desk in the church office, the sunlight warming the papers spread before him. He was partway through his sermon notes when his email pinged. He almost ignored it. Most emails could wait. But a subtle nudge prompted him to check. The message was from Mark Jeffries.

Subject: A Thought (or Two) After the Gathering

Hi Caleb,

I've been thinking and praying since you spoke at the pastors' gathering. Your gentle honesty about Willowend's renewal has stayed with me - and with many others too. I've received several notes from pastors who were deeply encouraged by your words.

This may feel sudden, but I wanted to float an idea with you. The Association is planning a small series of regional retreats for rural pastors over the next year - not conferences, not training intensives, but spaces of rest and renewal. We are looking for a few key voices who can help shepherd those spaces.

I believe you might be one of them. I'm not asking you to take on a role away from Willowend. Rather, I'm wondering whether, a few times a year, you would be willing to come and share - simply telling your story, guiding quiet reflection, and modelling the kind of gentle pastoral presence we all glimpsed at the gathering.

This is not a formal job offer, and there is no pressure. Consider this an invitation to pray. If you sense God's leading, we can talk details later.

Grace and peace,
Mark

Caleb read the email twice. The first time as information. The second time as calling. His breathing slowed. The room seemed to quieten further, as though listening. He didn't feel flattered. He felt... sobered. This was the widening Mary had spoken of.

Not a new position.

Not a departure.

A sharing.

An invitation to carry Willowend's gentle story of renewal to pastors who needed it.

He leaned back, closing his eyes.

Lord, is this from You?

The answer didn't come as words. It came as peace - a calm, steady warmth spreading through his chest. Not a push. Not a pull. A quiet *yes*.

He printed the email and carried it home, the single page feeling heavier than its physical weight. Rachel was hanging washing on the line when he arrived. The breeze lifted the shirts like small white sails.

"You're back early," she said, pegging another sleeve.

"I wanted to show you something," he replied.

She wiped her hands on her jeans and took the page, reading it carefully. As her eyes moved down the lines, her expression softened rather than tightened.

When she finished, she lowered the page slowly.

"Oh," she said quietly. "So... this is it."

"This is what?" Caleb asked.

"The widening," she said. "The thing God has been nudging you toward."

He exhaled. "That's what I thought too."

Rachel looked at him with a mix of affection and seriousness.

"How do you feel?" she asked.

"Peaceful," he replied. "And a little overwhelmed."

"Overwhelmed good or overwhelmed bad?"

"Overwhelmed in a way that feels… holy," he said. "As if God is saying, 'This too is part of your pastoral calling.'"

Rachel nodded slowly. "Then we will walk into it. Gently. Carefully. Together."

He smiled, relief flickering through his eyes. "You're not worried about the time away?"

"Of course I'm thinking about it," she said. "But I also know you. You won't say yes lightly. And you won't abandon Willowend. This isn't a choice between here and there. It's an extension of here into there."

He breathed out a quiet laugh. "You should be the one writing to Mark."

"No," she said, handing the paper back. "This is your letter. Your calling. I'm just your echo."

That afternoon, Caleb walked up the familiar path to Mary's house. She sat in her usual chair, knitting something softly coloured, the ball of yarn resting like a small cloud beside her. "You've had news," she said, not looking up.

Caleb chuckled. "At this point, I suspect you know before I do." Mary smiled, eyes still on her hands. "Tell me."

He handed her the printed email. She set her knitting aside and read it carefully, lips moving slightly over the words. When she finished, she looked up with eyes that shone.

"There it is," she said simply.

"You're not surprised," he observed.

"Should I be?" she replied. "We've been watching this coming for weeks. Maybe months."

Caleb sat down, elbows resting lightly on his knees. "Part of me wonders if this is wise. The valley is still tender. Renewal is still early. Is it too soon to step out, even occasionally?"

Mary considered his question with seriousness.

"Caleb," she said, "you're not being asked to leave the valley. You're being asked to carry its story - and its gentleness - into places that have grown weary. That is an extension of your pastoral heart, not a distraction from it."

"But will the church feel neglected?" he asked softly.

"Not if you remain present," Mary replied. "Not if you always communicate clearly. Not if you carry the same humility into the wider work that you carry here."

She paused, then added, "And not if you invite others here into the story - to own the renewal alongside you, rather than watching you carry it alone."

Her words landed with weight and clarity.

"I hadn't thought of that," Caleb said.

"You weren't meant to do this alone," Mary said. "You never were."

That evening, Caleb called Mark. "Mark, it's Caleb," he said once they'd exchanged greetings. "I've read your email. I've prayed. I've talked with Rachel. And... I believe this invitation is from God."

Mark's relief was audible. "I'm so glad to hear that."

"I want to move slowly," Caleb added. "A few retreats a year. Enough to serve other pastors, but not so much that Willowend feels my absence."

"That's exactly what we had in mind," Mark replied. "Small gatherings. Rural settings. No programme pressure - just space for rest and honest conversation. And your voice would help anchor them in grace."

They spoke for a while longer, discussing logistics in broad strokes - dates to be decided, locations yet to be confirmed, no urgent deadlines. When the call ended, Caleb felt strangely light.

He wasn't stepping into something heavy.

He was stepping into something shared.

After the call, he walked outside. The sky was clear and full of stars, the ridge a dark line against the night.

Rachel joined him, wrapping a cardigan around her shoulders.

"Well?" she asked.

"I said yes," he replied quietly. "A gentle yes. A slow yes."

Her face glowed with quiet satisfaction. "Then so did I."

They stood in silence for a long moment, watching the slow arc of a satellite trace across the sky.

"Do you think the church will really understand?" Caleb asked eventually.

Rachel considered her answer.

"I think some will celebrate," she said. "Some will worry. Some won't know what to think until they see how it unfolds. And that's all right."

He nodded. "I'll talk with the church leaders first. Then the congregation. No surprises."

Rachel smiled. "You're a shepherd. You wouldn't move without them."

The following day, at the small leaders' meeting in the church hall, Caleb shared the email and his sense of God's leading. Graham and Julie listened closely.

Sheila folded her arms, eyes thoughtful. Daniel's expression flickered between excitement and concern.

"I want you to hear this from me," Caleb said. "Not as an announcement, but as an invitation to walk with me. I've been asked to help guide a few rural retreats for pastors over the next year. Just a handful. I would be away a couple of weekends. But Willowend would remain my home. My centre."

He looked around the room.

"If this troubles you, I want to know. If you have questions, please ask them. I don't want to rush anything."

Graham spoke first. "Pastor, I think it's wonderful. What God is doing here shouldn't be hidden. Other pastors need to know renewal can be gentle, not forced. We'll support you."

Julie nodded. "We've sensed this coming too. It feels right."

Sheila exhaled slowly. "I'll be honest - my first reaction is to worry. Not because I doubt you, but because any change makes me nervous. But… I can't deny what God is doing here. Or the peace I see in you."

Daniel added, "If you go, some of us can step up more. Help with services. Support the visiting preachers when you're away."

Caleb felt a lump rise in his throat.

"You'd do that?" he asked.

Daniel smiled shyly. "You've been trusting us more. Maybe this is part of that."

The meeting ended not with fanfare, but with a circle of simple prayer - hands joined, heads bowed, hearts quiet.

Lord, lead us.

As Caleb walked home after the meeting, the air cool and clear around him, he realised something.

The widening had begun.

Not with a dramatic announcement.

Not with a grand plan.

But with a single email, a small yes, and a community willing to walk with him.

Renewal had awakened Willowend.

Now it was beginning to awaken something beyond it.

And Caleb sensed, with deep, steady joy:

The story God was writing was far from over.

In the days following the leaders' meeting, Willowend settled into a gentle hum of anticipation. People sensed something was shifting - not in a worrying way, but in a way that made the air feel expectant, like the valley itself was preparing room.

Caleb felt it too.

His decision to accept Mark's invitation hadn't added weight to his shoulders. Instead, it had distributed weight - as though the calling no longer rested solely on him, but flowed outward into the hands and hearts of the community who had quietly grown alongside him.

Early on Wednesday morning, Caleb sat at the kitchen table with his notebook open. The smell of fresh tea curled through the room.

"You're writing already?" Rachel asked as she joined him.

"Not formally," he replied. "Just listening. Trying to discern what these retreats might require."

She glanced at the page - a few simple lines:

Rest, not instruction.

Stories, not strategies.

Grace, not pressure.

Presence, not performance.

Rachel smiled. "Those sound like you."

Caleb chuckled. "Or like what I'm trying to be."

"You already are," she said gently. "That's why they asked."

He closed the notebook. "I just want to honour God in it."

"You will," she said, touching his hand. "One step at a time."

Later that morning, Caleb visited the café. The moment he walked through the door, Doris waved him over.

"Pastor! Sit, sit. I've been waiting to talk to you."

Caleb smiled as he joined her at a small table. "Is everything all right?"

"More than all right," Doris said. "I heard about the retreats. Len told Mick, Mick told Howard, Howard told the baker, the baker told everyone else - so yes, the news is out."

Caleb laughed. "I suppose that was inevitable."

"Absolutely inevitable," she said. "This town leaks information faster than a sieve leaks water."

Then her expression softened.

"We're proud of you, Pastor," she said. "But more than that, we feel… included. Like what God is doing here isn't just for us - but somehow still because of us."

Caleb blinked, moved. "I'm grateful you see it that way."

"We do," Doris said firmly. "And don't worry - we'll take care of things when you're away. We've managed hundreds of days without you before. We can manage two or three now and then." Caleb smiled. "Thank you."

Doris leaned forward conspiratorially. "Just please promise me something."

"What's that?"

"No big city attitude when you come back."

Caleb laughed again. "You have my word."

The men's shed had its own reaction to the news. When Caleb arrived that afternoon, Mick lifted a hand in greeting.

"Pastor!" he called out. "We heard you're becoming a famous motivational speaker."

Caleb grinned. "Not quite."

"Don't lie to us," Len said with mock sternness. "We'll come sit in the front row and heckle."

Caleb shook his head. "These retreats aren't about speeches. Just quiet conversations."

Mick's expression softened. "Good. Because the world really has enough loud voices. What it needs is steady ones."

Several men murmured agreement.

"And Pastor," Len added quietly, "if you ever need us to pray for you, or help with anything while you're away - just say the word. We're part of this too."

Caleb felt a lump rise in his throat. "Thank you. That means more than you know."

At the primary school, the news travelled through slightly different channels. Lynette greeted Caleb at the gate. "I heard you will be helping other pastors," she said, smiling. "That's wonderful."

"The story spreads fast," Caleb replied.

"Oh, that's not why I'm smiling," she said. "I'm smiling because the children are calling it 'Pastor Caleb's sharing days'. They think you're going somewhere to teach people how to be kind." Caleb chuckled. "If only it were that simple."

"Maybe it is," Lynette replied. "Sometimes adults complicate what children understand instinctively."

They walked together across the playground, watching a group of students arranging chairs in a circle beneath the gum tree.

"There's your legacy," Lynette said, gesturing toward them.

Caleb shook his head gently. "No. That's actually God's kindness working in young hearts."

She smiled. "True. But He used you to open the space."

By late afternoon, Caleb felt the day's encouragement settle into his bones. He walked toward Mary's house, sensing she would have something to add. She watched him approach with the same calm expression she always wore.

"So," she said simply, "Willowend knows."

"They do," Caleb replied.

"And how do they feel?"

"Supportive," he said. "Generous. Even excited."

Mary nodded once, as though confirming a fact she already knew.

"And how do you feel?" she asked.

"Peaceful," Caleb answered. "But aware. This is new ground. I want to walk it well."

Mary leaned back in her chair. "Caleb, renewal is never meant to stay in one place. It begins in the heart, then grows outward — sometimes farther outward than we imagine."

"I want to stay rooted here," he said.

"And you will," Mary replied. "Roots don't disappear when branches stretch."

Her words settled over him like a gentle mantle.

That evening, Caleb met with the small worship and leadership team at the church. They gathered in the hall - a simple group: Graham, Julie, Sheila, Daniel, and two newer members, Aaron and Rose.

Caleb explained the retreats again, making sure no one felt blindsided or uncertain.

"If this ever becomes a burden to the church," he said, "I want to know immediately. I will not sacrifice our community for broader ministry."

Graham shook his head. "Pastor, you're not leaving us. You're sharing us."

Julie smiled. "God is writing a bigger story than we realised."

Daniel added, "And we'll fill the gaps when you're away. We're ready."

Sheila surprised everyone by speaking next.

"Caleb," she said softly, "I've been praying about this. At first I was afraid of change. But now... I'm at peace. Maybe this is exactly what we need - not less of you, but more of us stepping forward."

There was a stillness after she finished - the kind of stillness that marks a turning point.

Caleb whispered, "Thank you."

Aaron then said, "Pastor... we'd like to pray for you."

Caleb nodded, humbled.

The group gathered around him - hands gently resting on his shoulders, his arms, the back of his chair. No pressure, no weight. Just presence.

Julie prayed softly:

"Lord, widen our pastor's heart only at the pace You widen his path. Keep him humble, steady, gentle, and grounded. Let the renewal here flow outward, and let the outward calling deepen what's happening here. Protect him, guide him, and remind him always that he is loved - by You and by us."

Caleb felt tears rise as the prayer ended. Not tears of burden, but of belonging. He wasn't stepping into this alone.

That night, Caleb and Rachel sat on the verandah with the stars shimmering above the valley.

"This feels different," Rachel said softly. "Like a new chapter."

"It does," Caleb agreed. "But not a departure from the old one. Just the next page."

They sat together in the quiet, watching the dark silhouette of the hills fade into night.

Caleb breathed very deeply, sensing again that warm, steady assurance of God's leading.

The path ahead was widening.

But his footing was firm.

And the valley - his valley - was with him.

The next morning began with soft rain - a rare gift in the valley. Caleb woke to the gentle drumming on the tin roof, the kind of sound that made the world feel slower and safer. He stood by the kitchen window with his first cup of tea, watching the drops slide down the glass like slow-moving beads.

Rachel came beside him. "Perfect weather to start planning," she said.

Caleb nodded. "I suppose it is."

She rested her head lightly on his arm. "Not planning in a heavy way. Planning in a listening way."

He smiled at her phrasing. "Listening is becoming the main part of my job."

"It always was," she replied. "You're just noticing it more."

After breakfast, Caleb settled into his study. He opened a fresh notebook - one he intended to use for the retreats - and wrote the date at the top. He stared at the blank page for a moment before writing the words:

This is not a program.

This is an invitation.

Below it, he added:

Let the pastors rest.

Let them breathe.

Let them rediscover the gentleness of God.

As he wrote, he sensed a clarity forming. The retreats weren't about teaching methods or theological frameworks. They were about offering what he had been offered in Willowend - room for God to soften hearts.

He jotted down a few simple ideas:

- Guided silence
- Story-sharing circles
- Scripture meditations
- Gentle pastoral conversation
- Unhurried prayer

Each idea felt less like a plan and more like a seed. Halfway through writing, he paused, feeling overwhelmed by a sudden awareness of gratitude.

He whispered, "Thank You, Lord, for letting me carry this."

Later that morning, he walked to the church. The sanctuary felt unusually still - the rain muting every sound. He stepped inside and sat in the second row, near the aisle.

This had always been his listening place - not the pulpit, not the front row, but the quiet seat from which he could see the whole room and feel its pulse.

"Lord," he prayed softly, "let these retreats be extensions of this space. Not in location, but in heart."

He sat there for several minutes, absorbing the peace that seemed to breathe from the walls.

Just then, the door creaked open and Daniel stepped inside, shaking light rain from his jacket.

"Oh-Pastor, sorry," he said. "I didn't know you were here."

"You're not interrupting," Caleb replied. "Come, sit."

Daniel slid into the row beside him. He looked nervous.

"Is everything all right?" Caleb asked gently.

Daniel nodded. "Yes. More than all right, actually. I just... needed to talk to you."

"Of course."

Daniel took a deep breath.

"Pastor, ever since the news about the retreats spread, something has been stirring in me. Not a calling like yours - not yet, anyway - but a desire to help more. To serve more. To step up."

Caleb listened attentively.

"I don't want to take over anything," Daniel said quickly. "I just… feel like God is inviting me into something deeper."

Caleb felt a warmth rise in his chest. "Daniel, that's exactly what renewal does. It awakens people to places of service they didn't see before."

Daniel's voice softened. "Do you think I could help with the services when you're away? Maybe lead a prayer, or read some Scripture, or help organise things?"

Caleb smiled. "Not only do I think you *could*, I think you *should*. Let's talk with the team. We'll find the right steps."

Daniel exhaled, visibly relieved. "Thank you, Pastor."

As he left the sanctuary, Caleb whispered a silent prayer of gratitude. Renewal wasn't just happening through him. It was rising in others.

That afternoon brought another moment of grace. As Caleb walked through the town centre, he noticed a small crowd gathered near the community noticeboard. He was curious, so he approached. Children from the primary school had decorated the board with hand-drawn posters - colourful, uneven, full of sincerity. Caleb was particularly moved by three of them:

"Be Kind - It Changes Everything." - Mia

"Hope Grows When You Share It." - Liam

"Thank You God for Making Our Town Soft Again." - Ella

Caleb felt tears form at the corners of his eyes. They were not from sentimentality, but from recognition.

This was not orchestrated.

This was not promoted.

This was fruit.

Soft, simple, unmistakable fruit.

Lynette appeared beside him. "I thought you might end up here," she said, smiling.

"They did this all on their own?" Caleb asked, voice catching slightly.

"Entirely on their own," she replied. "They said the town needed more reminders to be kind. And they wanted you to know their hearts are changing too."

Caleb stood silently, absorbing the moment. Renewal had reached the smallest and gentlest - and that, he realised, was its greatest mark of authenticity.

Near sunset, Caleb walked home. The rain had stopped hours earlier, leaving the earth fresh and gleaming. Birds swooped low across the wet ground, gathering worms released by the soft soil. When he reached the verandah, Rachel looked up from her seat.

"You look like a man who has seen something beautiful," she said.

"I have," Caleb replied. "Many things, actually."

He sat beside her and told her about his notebook, the sanctuary, Daniel's stirring, and the children's posters.

Rachel listened with quiet awe.

"It sounds," she said softly, "like Willowend is preparing for you to step outward."

Caleb nodded. "Yes. And I think God is preparing Willowend to grow into itself at the same time."

Once again, they in peaceful silence for a few moments.

Then Rachel added, "You know what I think?"

"What?"

"That renewal isn't just happening in Willowend or in you. It's beginning to happen in everyone who hears the story. Even beyond the valley."

Caleb looked out across the town, the gentle light fading behind the ridge.

"Yes," he said softly. "I think so too."

Later that evening, as Caleb wrote a few final thoughts in his retreat notebook, he paused over a new sentence forming in his mind:

The retreats are not about me.
They are about carrying Willowend's quiet miracle
into the hearts of weary shepherds.

He wrote the words slowly.

Then he closed the notebook, feeling the quiet certainty that he was walking the path God had laid before him. Not hurriedly.

Not reluctantly.

Faithfully.

30. THE FIRST STRETCH

The week leading up to Caleb's first retreat felt unusually full - not hectic, but weighted with purpose. The air in Willowend had grown warmer as spring edged closer, bringing bursts of colour to the valley. Each day seemed to carry a fresh reminder that new seasons often overlap with old ones.

Early Monday morning, Caleb stood on the verandah with his notebook tucked under his arm. The retreat was only ten days away, and although he wasn't anxious, he felt the edges of anticipation gathering around him.

Rachel joined him with her usual two mugs of tea. "You're thinking again," she said.

"I am," Caleb replied. "But it's not worry. Just … preparation."

Rachel nodded thoughtfully. "Preparation is holy work. Just don't forget to breathe."

He smiled. "That's why I have you."

Later that morning, Caleb headed to the church office to review some final retreat notes. But before he could reach the door, he saw someone waiting outside - a woman in her late thirties, arms folded, expression tight.

He recognised her immediately. Caroline Miller. She attended occasionally - polite, reserved, but seldom lingering after the service. She was respected in town, but careful. Very careful.

"Morning, Caroline," Caleb said gently.

"Pastor," she replied, her tone clipped but not hostile. "May I speak with you?"

"Of course."

She hesitated before continuing. "I'm concerned about… well… everything that's happening in town."

Caleb opened the office door and motioned for her to enter.

Inside, she sat with perfect posture, hands clasped tightly in her lap.

"Tell me what's troubling you," Caleb said.

Caroline took a slow breath.

"People are changing," she said. "Not badly. Just suddenly. Quickly. The atmosphere feels… emotional. Intense. I suppose I'm struggling to understand it."

Caleb nodded. "Thank you for sharing honestly. What part feels hardest to accept?"

She pressed her lips together. "I have always valued stability, Pastor. Predictability. And now… nothing is feeling predictable. The church is fuller. People I've known for years are crying during worship. Children are writing kindness posters. Even the men's shed is talking about forgiveness and hope. Part of me likes it. But another part… fears it."

"What does it fear?" Caleb asked gently.

Caroline looked away. "Losing control."

Her honesty softened something inside Caleb.

"Caroline," he said, "renewal always unsettles before it settles. It doesn't remove stability - it transforms it. What you're seeing isn't emotionalism. It's softness. People who've been numb for years are feeling again. That can look dramatic, but it's actually very gentle."

Caroline nodded slowly. "I don't want to resist what God might be doing. I just don't want things to get… out of hand."

"Nothing here is being forced," Caleb reassured her. "No one is being pushed into emotional reactions. What's happening is natural. Organic. And very tender."

She exhaled, her shoulders loosening.

"I really needed to hear that," she admitted. "I suppose change is always unsettling."

Caleb offered a reassuring smile. "Even good change requires courage."

Before leaving, she paused at the door.

"Pastor… thank you. I may still feel uncertain. But I trust you."

Her words stayed with him long after she left.

Later in the afternoon, at the café, another small ripple appeared. Caleb was sipping his tea when he overheard two of the locals speaking quietly at the next table - a husband and wife from outlying farmland.

"I'm not sure what's happening at the church," the man said. "People are saying it's revival."

His wife responded, "Well, if it is, it's the calmest revival I've ever seen. Feels more like… gentleness."

"That's what worries me," the man replied. "Gentleness is all well and good, but things spread fast in small towns. Emotions can get out of hand."

The wife sighed. "Sometimes emotions *need* to get out of hand, love. Especially after the drought. The fires. The losses. People are remembering how to feel again."

Caleb didn't interrupt - but he listened, grateful for the balance in their perspectives.

Renewal wasn't being resisted.

It was being *interpreted* - differently by different hearts.

This too was part of his pastoral calling.

When he returned home that evening, he found Rachel in the garden trimming back rosemary sprigs. She looked up.

"You've got that thoughtful look again," she said.

"Caroline came to see me," Caleb replied. "She's unsettled - not opposed, just uncertain."

Rachel smiled knowingly. "Of course she is. Caroline relies on predictability. Renewal always feels unpredictable."

"Yes," Caleb said. "But she was honest. And her honesty gave me perspective."

Rachel went back to trimming. "Every renewal needs a Caroline. Someone who asks the questions others are afraid to ask and ensures that gentleness doesn't drift into carelessness."

Caleb felt a surprising wave of gratitude. "You're right. She wasn't resisting. She was seeking reassurance."

"And that," Rachel said, "is a sign she's on the path too."

That night, Caleb returned to his retreat notebook. He wrote a new heading:

When Renewal Feels Unsettling

Below it, he wrote:

Not everyone trusts gentleness at first.
Not everyone understands softening.
Not everyone knows what to do with tenderness
after years of survival.

And then:

A shepherd's job is not to push people
into renewal. It is to stand with them
while it washes over their hearts
at God's pace.

He closed the notebook with a quiet sense of direction.

The next day brought an unexpected encouragement.

As Caleb entered the sanctuary for morning prayer, he noticed someone sitting in the third pew - Caroline.

She stood when he entered.

"Pastor," she said, her voice steadier than the day before, "I wanted to stop by. Something you said has stayed with me."

"What was that?" Caleb asked.

"That renewal unsettles before it settles."

She paused.

"I think… I'm willing to let it unsettle me a little."

Caleb felt his heart swell a little with gentle joy. "I'm grateful, Caroline."

She sat again, lowering her head.

"Would you pray with me?" she asked.

"Of course."

They prayed quietly, not for certainty, not for clarity, but for trust. When she left the sanctuary, she looked lighter - not transformed, not dramatically changed, but softened at the edges.

A small shift.

A subtle blessing.

A quiet miracle.

Later that afternoon, Mary offered her perspective, as she so often did.

"Caroline came to see you?" she asked when Caleb visited.

"Yes," Caleb replied. "She was unsettled."

"Good," Mary said, sipping her tea.

Caleb raised an eyebrow. "Good?"

"Caleb," Mary continued, "every renewal needs a moment of honest questioning to anchor it. Otherwise people chase feelings instead of roots. Caroline's uncertainty is a gift — it gives you a moment to shepherd the valley back into steadiness."

Caleb considered this. "In a strange way… I think you're right."

Mary smiled knowingly. "I'm rarely wrong on these matters."

He laughed softly. "I've noticed."

Then her tone shifted gently.

"And this - this moment of pastoral steadiness - is what you will carry into all the retreats. Not excitement. Not emotionalism. Steadiness. Integrity. Wisdom. Gentleness."

Caleb breathed out slowly, moved by the truth of it.

"Yes," he said softly. "That's exactly what I hope to carry."

That night, as he and Rachel prepared for bed, she asked, "Do you feel ready for the retreat?"

"Yes," Caleb said. Then he paused. "Ready in the way one can be ready for something gentle but important."

Rachel smiled. "That's the best kind of ready."

Caleb climbed into bed, listening to the faint sound of frogs in the distant creek.

He closed his eyes.

Renewal had revealed its first moment of tension. And instead of shaking him, it had steadied him. And in that steadiness, he felt the quiet confirmation: God was preparing him - not only for Willowend, but for those waiting beyond the hills.

Renewal continued moving quietly through Willowend in the days that followed, softening the edges of people's lives in ways both subtle and unexpected. But as often happens when spiritual tenderness takes root, something arose that required careful shepherding. It began with a rumour. A small rumour. An innocent rumour. But a rumour, nonetheless.

Caleb first heard it from Howard when he stopped at the general store on Thursday morning.

"Pastor," Howard said, clearing his throat in a way that suggested he was bracing for something awkward, "we've got a bit of… well… chatter going round."

Caleb raised an eyebrow. "What kind of chatter?"

Howard shifted uncomfortably. "Some folks - not many - think the church is becoming… emotional. And they're wondering if you're trying to… encourage that."

Caleb blinked. "Encourage emotion?"

Howard raised both hands. "Not me! I said you were the least manipulative person I know. But someone heard someone else say something about tears in worship, and then someone added something about the kids' kindness posters, and suddenly… well… people start building stories."

Caleb nodded slowly. This was not unusual. Renewal always created room for emotion - not emotionalism, but emotion - and people unused to tenderness often misinterpreted it.

"Thank you for telling me," Caleb said.

"I just thought you should know," Howard replied. "It's nothing big. Just little murmurs. But murmurs can grow legs."

Caleb smiled. "Only if we feed them."

Howard exhaled in relief. "Exactly."

At the men's shed later that morning, he encountered the rumour again - this time from Mick.

"Pastor," Mick said cautiously, "I'm hearing some nonsense."

"What kind of nonsense?"

"That you're stirring people up emotionally," Mick said bluntly. "Which is ridiculous, because if anything, you're calming people down."

Caleb chuckled softly. "I appreciate that interpretation."

"But it's coming from a place of confusion," Mick continued. "Some folks don't know what to do with tears - especially their own. Men here haven't cried for decades. Now one bloke tears up while sanding a shelf and suddenly people think there's manipulation in the air."

Caleb nodded carefully. "What do you think I should do?"

"Stay steady," Mick said. "People trust you. They just need some reassurance that gentleness isn't danger."

Caleb felt a warmth of gratitude. "Thank you, Mick. Truly."

But it wasn't until that afternoon that the misunderstanding reached a point requiring action.

Caleb received a phone call from Lynette at the school.

"Pastor, I need to speak with you," she said, her voice tense.

"There's been a complaint."

"A complaint?" Caleb repeated. "Against the church?"

"Indirectly," she said. "A parent is concerned that the kindness circle at school is linked to 'emotional influence' coming from the church. They seem to think we are running some kind of program."

Caleb sighed gently. "I see. Misinterpretation again."

"I know," Lynette said. "But we need to address it carefully before it spreads."

"I'll come by," Caleb said.

Within an hour, he was seated in Lynette's office with a single parent, Mrs. Harrington - a woman who was known for her high standards, earnest opinions, and sincere if sometimes abrupt manner. She wasted no time.

"Pastor, I have nothing against the church," she began. "But I'm concerned that the children's recent emotional behaviours are being influenced by what's happening there."

Caleb looked at her with calm kindness. "Can you help me understand what concerns you most?"

Mrs. Harrington hesitated. "Children crying in kindness circles. Posters about hope appearing everywhere. My daughter saying she feels 'soft' inside. I worry that they're being drawn into something too emotional, too intense."

Caleb nodded slowly. "Thank you for your honesty. May I share my perspective?"

"Please," she said.

"Nothing that's happening in Willowend is about stirring emotion," Caleb explained. "In fact, it's quite the opposite. For years this valley has endured drought, fires, pressure, isolation. People learned to suppress feelings simply to cope. What you're seeing now - in your daughter and in other children - isn't emotional instability. It's emotional healing."

Mrs. Harrington frowned thoughtfully. "Healing?"

"Yes," Caleb said gently. "When a community begins to soften, children lead the way. They express kindness before adults do. They forgive quickly. They feel deeply and recover quickly. That's not manipulation. That's renewal."

Mrs. Harrington softened slightly. "I hadn't thought of it like that."

"And the kindness circle?" Caleb asked.

"That concerns me," she admitted. "They sit and talk about feelings."

"They also talk about apologies, reconciliation, and courage," Caleb said. "I observed them last week. Nothing was imposed. No one pushed them. They created it themselves. I believe it's a sign that the children feel safe again."

Mrs. Harrington took a long breath. "I came ready to argue. But now I just feel... relieved."

Caleb smiled warmly. "Relief is often the first sign that fear is loosening its grip."

She nodded slowly. "Thank you, Pastor."

When she left, Lynette exhaled hard.

"That could have gone very differently," she said.

"But it didn't," Caleb replied. "Grace is steadier than fear."

That evening, Caleb walked to Mary's house once more. She was tending to a pot of herbs on the verandah.

"You've been shepherding today," she said without turning around.

"I have," Caleb admitted. "A few misunderstandings surfaced." Mary smiled. "As they should."

Caleb raised an eyebrow. "Should?"

"Caleb," she said, turning to him, "renewal must be tested gently. Misunderstandings force you to clarify the truth - not just to others, but to yourself."

"I suppose that's true," he said.

"You handled it with grace?"

"I hope so."

Mary nodded. "Then renewal will deepen, not weaken. Every time you respond with steadiness, the valley's trust grows."

Caleb sat beside her. "Sometimes I wonder how you know so much."

Mary chuckled softly. "Wisdom is just long-term listening."

Later, as night fell, Caleb sat on the verandah with Rachel.

"You look tired," she said.

"Tired and grateful," he answered.

"They're a good combination," she replied.

Caleb looked up at the stars beginning to appear. "I think this was the first true stretch of the renewal," he said. "A moment where fear could have taken root."

"But it didn't," Rachel said. "Because gentleness held."

"Yes," Caleb said quietly. "Gentleness held."

He closed his eyes briefly, letting the events of the day settle.

The rumour had not grown.

The misunderstanding had not spread.

The renewal had not fractured.

If anything, it had become clearer.

He breathed out a peaceful, grateful sigh.

God's hand was still steady.

The valley was still softening.

The widening path remained firm beneath his feet.

The morning sun rose softly over Willowend, filtering through the high clouds like a quiet blessing. Caleb stood by the kitchen sink, rinsing his cup, feeling the slow, steady tug of the days ahead. The first retreat was now less than a week away. It was close enough that he could sense its weight, but not so close as to make him nervous. Rather, he felt a kind of holy expectancy - a readiness woven from months of renewal.

Rachel entered the kitchen tying her hair back. "You're calm," she observed.

"I am," he replied. "Strangely calm."

"That's usually a good sign."

Caleb nodded. "I think God is pacing me."

Rachel smiled warmly. "He always has."

Later in the morning, Caleb walked to the church and unlocked the sanctuary. He had decided to spend a few hours simply listening - not preparing content, not writing outlines, but sitting in quiet openness.

He took his usual place in the second pew.

The silence felt like a living thing. Gentle. Present. Patient.

He whispered a simple prayer.

"Lord, let the first retreat carry the same spirit as this place."

A small shift in the air - not a sound, not a sensation - made him open his eyes. It was the way the light fell across the sanctuary floor, catching on the edge of the communion table. It reminded him that everything about Willowend's renewal had been unforced. Completely unmanufactured. That was the heart he needed to carry outward.

After some time, he opened his notebook and wrote only one sentence:

The retreat must offer space for God, not structure from me.

He closed the notebook again.

That was enough for today.

At midday, Caleb walked to the café for lunch. Doris bustled between tables, balancing plates with her usual joyful efficiency. "Pastor!" she called. "Sit anywhere – I will be with you in just a moment!"

Caleb chose a small table near the window. The scent of fresh bread and coffee drifted across the room. As he waited, a familiar figure approached - someone he hadn't expected to see.

It was Tom Gallagher, a retired pastor who had moved to another part of the district many years ago. Tom had served in a number of rural churches and was known as a gentle, wise shepherd.

"Caleb!" Tom said warmly. "I wondered if I'd run into you."

Caleb stood to greet him. "Tom! Tell me, what brings you to Willowend?"

Tom smiled as he sat across from him. "My granddaughter lives here now. I come through every so often. But today, I had another reason."

Caleb raised an eyebrow. "Oh?"

Tom leaned forward slightly. "I heard - through the grapevine, as usual - about the retreats you'll be leading."

Caleb chuckled softly. "News does travel fast."

"It does," Tom said. "But I wanted to see you myself."

There was kindness in the older man's eyes. The kind that recognises calling in another.

"Caleb," Tom continued, "I have been praying for you. Not because you have been struggling - you haven't. But because what's happening in this valley is rare and remarkable."

"And the fact that it's beginning to reach beyond Willowend?" He paused meaningfully. "That's the gentle way God expands a shepherd's heart."

Caleb felt a lump form in his throat. "I don't want to lose my footing here."

"You won't," Tom said confidently. "Your roots are deep. And Rachel is beside you - that's no small thing."

No, it wasn't.

Tom reached into his shirt pocket and pulled out a folded piece of paper.

"I wrote something down for you," he said. "Not advice. Just something that came to me in prayer."

He handed Caleb the paper and stood. "Read it later. And Caleb - I'm really proud of you."

He left before Caleb could reply.

When Doris arrived with lunch, she noticed Caleb staring quietly at the note.

"Pastor? You all right?"

Caleb nodded slowly. "Just… grateful."

Back at home, he unfolded the paper.

Tom's handwriting was neat and steady.

> *When God widens the path beneath your feet,*
> *He does not loosen the soil around your roots.*
> *You will remain grounded while others gather*
> *shade beneath your branches.*
> *Trust the widening.*

Caleb closed his eyes, moved in a way he could not really articulate. The words were not dramatic. They were steady - very much like Tom himself.

He placed the note inside his retreat notebook, just behind the first page. Later that afternoon, Caleb walked to the primary school to check in with Lynette. The misunderstanding from earlier in the week had settled, but he wanted to ensure the atmosphere remained peaceful.

As he approached, he saw a group of children gathered around the gum tree. They were rearranging the circle of small chairs used for their kindness gatherings. He recognised Mia, Thomas, and little Ella among them.

"Pastor Caleb!" Ella called. "Come see what we made!"

He walked over smiling. "What have you created today?"

They pointed to a cardboard sign hanging from the low branch of the gum tree. It was painted unevenly, in bright blue letters:

"This Place Makes Hearts Strong."

Caleb felt a quiet rush of emotion - not because the sign was eloquent, but because it was true.

"That's beautiful," he said softly.

Thomas nodded. "It's for everyone, not just kids. Grown-ups forget to be strong in the right ways."

"Strong in gentle ways," Mia added earnestly.

Caleb crouched down beside them. "You children see things clearly. More clearly than many adults."

Ella grinned. "It's because our hearts are new."

He laughed softly. "I think you're right."

As he walked away, he knew the sign would stay with him - not just as a memory, but as a guiding idea for the retreat.

Strength through gentleness.

Courage through softness.

Renewal through presence.

The children were living the very thing he hoped pastors would rediscover.

On his way home, Caleb stopped by Mary's house. She was peeling apples on the verandah.

"You're carrying something new today," she said without even looking up.

"I suppose I am," Caleb admitted. "Tom Gallagher visited me in the café."

Mary smiled knowingly. "Ah. A seasoned shepherd speaking to a growing one."

"He gave me a note," Caleb said.

"Then treasure it," Mary replied. "God speaks through those who have walked the long road."

She handed him a slice of apple. "Here, eat. You'll need your strength."

"For the retreat?" he asked.

"For the growth," she said. "Growth always asks something of us. But yours will be gentle."

Caleb nodded, feeling her words settle like truth.

That evening, he and Rachel sat by the fire. The night air carried the scent of eucalyptus and the faint hum of crickets.

"I saw the children's sign today," he said.

"Which one?" she asked.

"'This Place Makes Hearts Strong.'"

Rachel smiled softly. "That sounds like Willowend."

"Yes," Caleb said. "And I think it will be the heart of the retreat."

Rachel reached across and took his hand. "You're ready, Caleb. Not because you've prepared enough, but because God has prepared *you*."

He felt the warmth of her words sink deep.

"I hope so," he said quietly.

"I know so," she replied.

Caleb leaned back, feeling a gentle certainty settle into place. Tomorrow, he would begin assembling the final details: travel, accommodation, simple session outlines, prayer times. But tonight was simply a moment of rest before stepping outward. A moment of quiet before the widening path opened fully before him.

The next few days unfolded with a calm sense of purpose. There were no crises, no last-minute interruptions - only steady preparation. Caleb felt as though God had placed a gentle hand on his shoulder, guiding each step without hurry.

On Wednesday morning, he spread his notes across the kitchen table. Rachel stood at the bench filling a small container with teabags and instant coffee for him to take.

"You're sure they'll have food sorted?" she asked.

"Mark said the venue will handle meals," Caleb replied. "I just want to make sure there's enough tea. Pastors survive on tea and prayer."

"Don't forget biscuits," Rachel added. "They help with honesty."

He laughed softly. "I'll pick some up from the store."

She paused, then leaned against the table, looking over his notes.

"What have you planned so far?" she asked.

"Very little, on purpose," he said. "A welcoming circle. Long spaces of quiet. A simple reflection on gentleness. A few Scriptures. The rest will depend on what they bring with them."

Rachel nodded approvingly. "Good. Pastors don't need another program. They need somewhere to put their burdens down."

"Exactly," he said quietly.

He gathered his papers into a neat pile, then placed Tom Gallagher's handwritten note on top. It felt like both a covering and a reminder.

Later that morning, he walked to the church to meet with the leadership team one final time before the retreat.

They gathered in the small hall - Graham, Julie, Sheila, Daniel, and Rose. The sunlight filtered through the high windows, dust motes drifting lazily in the beams.

"I wanted to check in before I go," Caleb said, taking a seat with them in a loose circle. "Not to give instructions. Just to make sure everyone's at peace."

Graham smiled. "We're at peace. We've worked out a simple plan for the Sunday you're away. Daniel will lead the service. Rose will handle the music. We've asked a retired pastor from the next town to preach."

"And I'll make sure the hall doesn't fall down," Sheila added wryly.

They laughed, the lightness in the room unmistakable.

Caleb's expression softened. "Thank you. Truly. This makes it much easier to go."

Julie said, "We've all been blessed by the renewal, Pastor. Letting you carry that blessing to others is part of our response."

Daniel added, "And honestly… it's time some of us stepped up more. You've been gently preparing us for that."

Caleb felt a gentle warmth spread through his chest. "You're all very gracious."

Rose, who had been quiet, spoke next.

"I wanted to share something," she said with hesitation. "I was praying last night and felt God say, 'I'm not sending Caleb away from Willowend. I'm sending Willowend with Caleb.'"

The room grew still.

Caleb swallowed. "That… feels very true."

"We're with you," Rose said simply.

They closed the meeting in prayer, not with long speeches, but with short, sincere requests.

"Lord, keep him gentle."
"Give him words when needed, silence when better."
"Let others taste what we have tasted here."

When they finished, Caleb felt deeply grounded.

At the general store that afternoon, Howard rang up the biscuits, tea, and a few extra items that had somehow found their way into Caleb's basket.

"Looks like you're feeding a small army," Howard said.

"Feeding a few tired pastors," Caleb replied.

Howard nodded, his tone softening. "Do me a favour, Pastor?"

"What's that?"

"When you're at that retreat, remember there's a little town back here praying for you. We might not know how to put it in fancy words, but we're with you."

Caleb smiled. "I think your prayers will be stronger than any fancy words."

Howard then reached under the counter and produced a small paper bag.

"Here," he said gruffly. "On the house."

"What's this?" Caleb asked.

"Mixed lollies," Howard said. "You can't run a retreat without a bowl of them sitting somewhere in the room. Makes the place feel hospitable."

Caleb chuckled. "You're probably right."

"Of course I am," Howard replied. "Now go and do what God's asked of you."

On his way home, Caleb stopped by the men's shed.

Mick greeted him with a wide grin. "We heard you're off to talk sense into some pastors."

"Something like that," Caleb replied.

"We're proud of you," Len added. "And if any of them give you trouble, tell them you've got a whole shed full of men ready to straighten them out."

The group laughed.

Then Mick's expression turned more thoughtful.

"Seriously though, Pastor," he said, "when you talk to them, tell them this from us: if God can soften hard old blokes in a town like this, He can do it anywhere."

Caleb nodded. "I'll tell them."

"Good," Mick said. "And when you get back, we want to hear how it went. Not in fancy terms. Just the human bits."

"You'll get the human bits," Caleb promised.

That evening, Mary was expecting him.

"You always come before you go," she said as he walked up the path.

"I suppose I do," Caleb replied.

She gestured for him to sit. "So .. how does your heart feel?" "Steady," he said. "Not because I have everything planned, but because I don't."

Mary smiled. "Good. Plans can get in the way of listening. You are being sent as a listener, Caleb, not as a fixer."

He nodded slowly. "I know. And I'm oddly comfortable with that."

Mary's eyes softened. "You've grown."

"So have you," he teased.

She laughed quietly. "We all have. This valley has stretched in ways we couldn't have imagined."

There was a pause.

Then Mary said something she had never said to him before.

"I'm proud of you," she whispered.

The simple words struck something deep inside him. He looked down, suddenly overcome.

"Thank you," he said, his voice rougher than usual.

Mary reached out and squeezed his hand.

"Go gently," she said. "Return gently. Let God write the rest."

On the night before he left, Caleb and Rachel packed his small overnight bag together - shirts, a jumper, a Bible, the notebook, Tom's folded note.

"Not much for a man who's going to shape pastors," Rachel said lightly.

"I'm not going to shape them," he replied. "I'm going to create a space where God can."

She smiled. "That's why you're the right one to go."

They sat on the edge of the bed for a moment, bags at their feet.

"You'll be okay?" Caleb asked quietly.

Rachel squeezed his hand. "I'm not fragile, Caleb. I'm rooted too. And I'll be right here when you get back."

He nodded. "I know. I just... don't ever want you to feel left behind."

"I don't," she said. "I feel... included. This isn't your journey. It's ours."

He rested his head briefly against hers. "I'm very grateful for you."

"You'd better be," she replied softly.

The next morning dawned clear and cool. The sky was high and pale, the kind of day that seemed to hint at new beginnings without shouting them. Caleb placed his bag in the boot of the car. As he closed it, he saw a movement near the edge of the driveway.

It was a small group of people from the church - Graham, Julie, Daniel, Rose, and unexpectedly, Caroline.

"We thought we might come and see you off," Graham said, slightly embarrassed.

Caleb smiled, touched. "You didn't have to."

"We know," Julie said. "That's why we did."

Daniel stepped forward shyly. "We just wanted to pray before you left. If that's all right."

"More than all right," Caleb replied.

They gathered in a loose circle near the car. Rachel joined them, slipping her hand into his.

Caroline surprised him by speaking first.

"Lord," she said quietly, "we thank You for our pastor. For his steadiness. For the way You've used him to soften this valley - even those of us who were scared of change. As he goes to bless others, please remind him that he is not going alone. We are with him. And You are with him."

There was a gentle silence.

Then Daniel prayed, "Let the retreat feel like Willowend - simple, honest, gentle, safe."

Graham added, "Bring him back rested, not drained."

Julie finished, "Use his presence, Lord, not his performance."

They ended with a soft chorus of "Amen."

Caleb opened his eyes, feeling both humbled and strengthened. "Thank you," he said simply.

As he climbed into the car, Rachel squeezed his shoulder. "Go gently."

He started the engine. As he drove through the town, he passed the café, the general store, the school, the men's shed, the church - each place carrying a piece of his heart. At the edge of the valley, he glanced in the rear-view mirror.

Willowend lay behind him - familiar, beloved, grounded. And ahead, a winding road led toward something new - not instead of Willowend, but because of it.

He breathed a quiet prayer as he turned onto the highway.

"Lord… let what You've done in this valley flow outward — gently, like a stream."

And with that, the first retreat began.

Not at the venue.

Not in a session.

But here - in the quiet obedience of a small-town pastor driving out of his valley, carrying with him everything he had received.

The retreat centre sat at the edge of a low range, where the hills folded into one another like resting shoulders. It wasn't large or impressive - just a cluster of simple buildings, a dining hall, a small chapel, and a scattering of cabins beneath tall gums. The kind of place that had hosted youth camps and church weekends away for decades.

When Caleb pulled into the gravel car park, he turned off the engine and sat for a moment, listening to the quiet tick of the cooling motor. Birds chattered somewhere in the trees. The air smelled faintly of eucalyptus and dust.

"Lord," he murmured, "You know what these men and women are bringing with them. Help me to carry only what You ask, and nothing more."

He stepped out of the car, shoulders relaxed, notebook tucked under his arm. Mark was waiting near the reception building, hands in pockets, face creased into a wide smile.

"Caleb!" he called. "You found us."

"Not really much chance of getting lost," Caleb replied. "Once the bitumen ended, I knew I was getting close."

Mark laughed and pulled him into a brief, warm hug. "I'm very glad you're here. You're early - that's good. The others will trickle in over the next hour."

"How many are coming?" Caleb asked.

"Twelve," Mark said. "All rural pastors. Some from townships a bit bigger than Willowend. Some from dots on the map you'd miss if you blinked."

Caleb nodded. "I understand that life."

"I know," Mark replied. "That's why you're here."

They walked slowly toward the dining hall as Mark filled him in. These retreats were deliberately small - no big name speakers, no packed program, no pressure. Just space.

"They're tired, Caleb," Mark said quietly. "Some of them are discouraged. A few are on the edge of just walking away. I don't need you to fix them. I just want them to taste what you spoke about at the gathering - the gentleness of God."

"I can offer gentleness," Caleb said softly. "I can't really promise anything more."

"That's all we're asking," Mark replied.

By mid-afternoon, the pastors had arrived. Caleb watched them in the dining hall as they collected tea and coffee, found seats, and made small talk.

They wore the usual collection of ministry uniforms - button-up shirts, jeans, neat but worn shoes. Some carried worn satchels. A few carried more weight in their shoulders than in their bags. He saw it in their eyes - that mixture of faithfulness and fatigue, commitment and quiet question.

How long can I keep going like this?
Is anything changing?
Does anyone really see?

Mark welcomed them briefly, then nodded to Caleb.

"Friends," Mark said, "I've asked Pastor Caleb from Willowend to help guide our time together. Many of you heard him at the recent gathering. What God is doing in his town is simple, gentle, and deeply encouraging. I've asked him not to bring a program - just a story, some Scripture, and space."

He turned to Caleb. "Over to you."

Caleb stood at the front with nothing in his hands but his Bible. He could feel the room's unease - not distrust, but the wary caution of people who had been promised life before and had gone home more tired than when they arrived.

"Thank you," he said quietly. "My name is Caleb. I've been pastoring in a small town called Willowend for many years. It's not special. I'm not special. But God has been gently renewing our valley - and I'm here to tell you that it hasn't come through effort or strategy. It's come through surrender."

A stillness settled.

"I know you're tired," he continued. "Most of you didn't get into ministry because you love rosters and reports. You got into it because you love God and people. Somewhere along the way, that love can get buried deeply beneath expectations, exhaustion, survival."

He paused, letting the words land.

"This retreat isn't about learning new techniques. It's about remembering how to breathe again in God's presence. You don't need to perform here. You don't need to impress anyone. You don't even need to be 'on.'"

A few shoulders visibly dropped.

"We're going to begin with something very simple," Caleb said.

"We're going to sit in silence for ten minutes. No music, no guided prayer. Just you and God."

A couple of pastors shifted uncomfortably at the word *silence*, but no one objected.

"I'll keep track of the time," he said. "If you feel restless, that's all right. If your thoughts wander, that's all right too. Just sit. Just be."

They bowed their heads.

The room quietened.

At first, as always, the silence felt awkward - like a guest that didn't yet know where to put its hands. Chairs creaked. Someone coughed. A bird called outside.

Then the quiet thickened, deepened.

Caleb sat with them, not praying long prayers, not pushing anything, simply resting in the same Presence he knew in Willowend's sanctuary. *Lord, be who You are*, he thought. *That will be enough.*

When ten minutes had passed, he lifted his head gently.

"Thank you," he said softly. "That's all I wanted us to do first. Just stop."

One of the pastors, a man in his fifties with thinning hair and kind eyes, cleared his throat.

"That's the first time I've sat still in months," he said.

Caleb smiled. "You're not alone."

A few quiet chuckles.

"Let's keep things simple," Caleb continued. "I'd like us to go around the circle and, if you're willing, just share one sentence: how you really are. Not how your church is. How you are."

They moved their chairs into a rough circle. It wasn't orderly - more like a huddle. Caleb liked it that way. Ordered chaos felt more honest.

They began.

"Tired. Bone tired," one said.

"Questioning whether I'm still called," another admitted.

"Lonely," said a third, his voice barely more than a whisper.

"Grateful but worn thin," added a woman in her forties.

"Angry at God," someone else confessed, eyes fixed on the floor.

No one jumped in to correct him. No one told him not to say it. The words were allowed to just sit there, breathing in the open. When it came to Caleb, he paused for a moment.

"I'm grateful," he said. "And being stretched. Gently."

There were nods. A few curious glances. Caleb took a breath.

"Thank you for your honesty. You've already done more real work in these few minutes than many conferences manage in three days."

A faint smile passed around the circle.

"For the rest of today," he said, "we're not going to talk about church growth, strategies, or programs.

We're going to talk about your hearts. About hope. About how to live with God in the middle of all the pressures that don't go away."

He opened his Bible.

"I want to begin with a simple picture from my town," he said. "At our primary school, the children created something they call a kindness circle. No adults told them to. They sit under a gum tree and apologise to each other, forgive each other, create simple ways to show care. They even hung a sign on the tree. It says, 'This place makes hearts strong.'"

Several pastors looked up sharply - something in them stirred by the image.

"That," Caleb said quietly, "is what I hope this retreat will be for you. A place that makes hearts strong - not hard, not defended, not numb. Strong in gentleness."

He closed the Bible without reading a verse yet.

"We'll talk Scripture soon," he said. "But for now, I just want to ask you one question: *What has made your heart tired?*"

The room shifted again. A few people drew in long breaths, as if about to swim underwater.

Slowly, one by one, they began to speak.

A pastor from a small town three hours west spoke first. "I'm tired of funerals," he said. "We had three in one month earlier this year. Two were farmers who couldn't see a way through the debt. I preached hope, but inside I felt… empty."

Another followed. "I'm tired of always being the strong one," she said. "In my church, if I crack, everything feels like it will fall apart. So, I don't."

A younger pastor with dark circles under his eyes shook his head. "I'm tired of pretending the numbers don't bother me," he admitted. "They shouldn't. I know that. But they do. Every Sunday I look at the room and count who's missing."

As they spoke, Caleb didn't rush to respond. He simply nodded, occasionally asking a gentle clarifying question.

"How long have you felt that way?"

"What do you do with those feelings?"

"Who knows this about you?"

In many cases, the answer to that last question was simple.

"No one."

After more than an hour of sharing, the air in the room felt different - not lighter exactly, but more honest. As if the masks had been loosened, if not removed entirely.

Caleb finally spoke.

"Thank you," he said. "You have honoured this space with your honesty. I want you to notice something: no one here tried to fix anyone else. You simply listened. That's rare."

He opened his Bible again.

"Later tonight, I want to share some Scriptures that have anchored me through my melanoma scare, our town's drought, the threat of bushfire, and the slow renewal back home. But for now, I'd like to offer you a simple invitation."

He looked around the circle.

"For the rest of today, you don't need to carry anyone's expectations - not your church's, not your denomination's, not your own. In fact, if you'd like, you can imagine hanging them on that kindness tree the children made in my town. Just for a little while."

One of the older pastors smiled gently at the image.

"I might need a whole forest," he said.

"God has a whole forest," Caleb replied softly. "He can handle your expectations better than you can."

A small ripple of laughter moved through the circle - tired, but real.

"We'll break now," Caleb said. "Go for a walk. Sit under a tree. Sleep. Talk to God. Or don't talk at all. There's no assignment. We'll gather again before dinner."

As they filed out, a few paused to squeeze his shoulder or nod in quiet thanks. When the room was empty, Caleb sat alone for a moment, feeling the weight of what he'd just heard

Caleb remained seated in the empty dining hall for a few minutes after the pastors had dispersed. A quiet hum lingered in the air - not noise, but the leftover vibration of honesty. He felt grateful, deeply grateful, that they had trusted him and each other enough to speak from the heart. It reminded him again that God often began His gentlest work by softening the ground before planting anything.

He stepped outside into the afternoon light. The gum trees swayed gently above, their scent drifting across the open space behind the cabins. A small walking trail wound around the property, disappearing into a stretch of thick bushland. Caleb followed it slowly, not with any intention to explore far, but simply to breathe.

Halfway along the path, he found a fallen log and sat. The bush was quiet - the kind of quiet that had texture to it, like a soft blanket settling on the land. He thought of Willowend, of the children's kindness circle, of Rachel praying for him at home. All of it seemed connected somehow, as though the renewal in the valley had stretched far enough to rest its hand on this retreat as well. He opened his notebook and wrote:

These pastors are carrying invisible weights.
Let this space be a gentle unloading, not a forced release.

He underlined "gentle."

When he looked up again, he saw one of the pastors - the older man who had admitted to being tired of funerals - walking slowly along the path. Their eyes met and the man paused.

"Mind if I sit?" he asked.

"Of course not," Caleb said, shifting slightly to give him room.

The man sank onto the log beside him with a soft sigh. "I didn't expect today to hit me like it did."

"How so?" Caleb asked.

The pastor rubbed his hands together. "I think I've forgotten how to stop. How to just be still. How to feel anything that isn't numbness or duty."

Caleb nodded. "Most pastors forget. Sometimes for years."

The man looked down at the soil. "When you talked about the children in your town… something opened in me. I realised I've been telling my church to forgive, reconcile, trust - but I haven't done any of it myself. Not properly."

Caleb didn't rush to respond. The silence held them both.

Finally, the man added, "I think I need God to make my heart strong again. Not hard. Strong."

"That's a good prayer," Caleb said softly. "A humble one."

The man nodded but didn't speak again. They watched the light shift through the trees, each lost in his own quiet conversation with God.

After a short while, the pastor stood. "Thank you for listening," he said.

"I'm glad to listen," Caleb replied.

The man walked back toward the cabins, shoulders slightly more relaxed. Caleb closed his notebook. This was the work. Not sermons, not sessions, not strategies - but presence. Attentive, steady, grounded presence.

Before dinner, Mark approached him in the dining hall.

"How do you think it's going?" Mark asked.

"Gently," Caleb said. "Which is exactly right."

"I sensed something in the room today," Mark said. "A shift. Not big, but real."

Caleb nodded. "They're beginning to trust the space."

Mark looked relieved. "Good. These retreats don't always start so openly."

"Pastors often need permission to be human," Caleb said. "Once they have it, the rest follows."

Mark smiled. "Remind me never to over-plan another retreat."

Caleb chuckled a little. "Planning has its place. But space…" He gestured around the room. "This is where God does His best work."

They set up the evening circle together - simple chairs, a jug of water, a few cups. No centrepiece, no decorations. Caleb wanted the room to feel unadorned, like a blank canvas.

When the pastors began to gather, the atmosphere was different from earlier. Softer. Quieter. Some spoke in low voices, some remained silent. No one looked hurried.

Caleb began the session by opening his Bible to a short passage he had lived inside for months - a passage that had carried him through his own fear and uncertainty.

He read slowly, letting each word land:

"'Come to me, all you who are weary and burdened,
and I will give you rest.'"

He closed the Bible.

"Most of you have preached that passage countless times," he said. "But I want to ask you something simple: when was the last time you actually let Jesus give you rest? Not metaphorical rest. Not spiritualised rest. Real rest."

No one answered. They didn't need to.

Caleb continued. "Rest is not laziness. Rest is surrender. It's trusting that God can hold what you've been trying to hold alone."

He waited.

Then he said something that surprised even himself:

"Tonight, you don't need to be pastors. You don't need to be leaders. You just need to be children in the presence of the Father."

A few faces softened visibly.

"I'm going to give you fifteen minutes to sit or walk outside. No talking. Just breathing. Just existing. And if anything rises in your heart - sorrow, frustration, hope, fear - bring it to God honestly. He's not threatened by your truth."

They rose slowly and stepped out into the twilight. Some walked along the path. Some stayed near the entrance, staring up at the darkening sky. One or two remained inside, heads bowed.

Caleb stayed seated, praying silently for each of them. Not long prayers. Just simple ones.

"Give him peace."
"Give her courage."
"Lift what he cannot carry."
"Let her rest."

When they returned, something had eased. He didn't need them to say it - he could see it.

After they sat, Caleb spoke softly.

"Would anyone like to share what God whispered to you? No pressure. Only if it's right."

A young pastor spoke first. "I felt God say, 'You don't have to keep pretending you're strong.'"

Someone else nodded vigorously. "I felt the same - except in my case I think God actually laughed. A warm laugh. As if to say, 'You've been carrying things I never asked you to.'"

A woman with tired eyes whispered, "God told me, 'I still see you.' I didn't realise how much I needed that."

They shared for twenty minutes - not in dramatic bursts, but in quiet honesty. When the session ended, no one moved quickly to leave. They lingered, talking softly, leaning into the simplicity of the moment.

Mark approached Caleb again.

"You've given them hope," he said.

"No," Caleb replied gently. "God has. I've just given them space to feel it again."

Later that night, Caleb sat alone in his cabin, listening to the faint breeze brushing the window. He opened his notebook one last time and wrote:

Renewal travels lightly.
It arrives quietly. It grows slowly.
It heals deeply.

He closed the notebook.

He felt tired - but it was the good kind of tired. The kind that comes not from strain, but from pouring out something that had been freely given.

Tomorrow, the heart work would begin: conversations, Scripture reflections, and the unravelling of burdens that had been woven into the fabric of these pastors' lives for years.

But for tonight, he felt only one thing.

Peace.

The next morning dawned bright and clear - the kind of morning that felt like a quiet invitation. Caleb walked to the dining hall early and found the kettle already boiling. Someone had arrived before him, though they had left no sign except the warmth lingering in the room.

He made himself a cup of tea and sat by the window. The retreat grounds were still. Even the breeze seemed unhurried. He watched the sunlight creep slowly across the gum leaves outside and prayed a simple prayer.

"Lord… let today be as gentle as yesterday.
And let their hearts be carried, not exposed."

By eight o'clock, the pastors trickled in one by one, offering soft greetings, smiles that seemed easier than the day before, and shoulders that no longer sat quite so high. Something had begun to loosen.

After breakfast, they gathered once more in the meeting room, forming the same imperfect circle of mismatched chairs. Caleb stood, Bible in hand, feeling no pressure to perform or teach anything grand. The retreat didn't need grandeur; it needed presence.

"I want to begin with a simple reading," he said. "Something that held me together during my melanoma scare. Something that held my town together during our hardest seasons."

He opened to Psalm 46 and read slowly, without embellishment:

"'God is our refuge and strength,
an ever-present help in trouble.
Therefore we will not fear…'"

When he finished, he closed the Bible and let silence settle. "Most of us," he said softly, "know those words. Many of us have preached them. But today, I want to ask you to hear them not as pastors, but as people. As children. As sons and daughters who need refuge, not responsibility."

A few eyes already glistened.

"Too often," Caleb continued, "we read Scripture as if it's fuel for ministry. But Scripture was written first for the heart. Not the sermon."

A long exhale rippled around the circle.

"I want to spend this morning talking about the burdens you carry quietly," he said. "The ones you've never said aloud. The ones you've been holding not for months, but for years."

There was a stillness - not fear, but readiness.

He sat down among them, not above them.

"Whoever feels prompted… share one burden you've been carrying alone."

For a moment no one spoke. But then the older pastor from the previous day cleared his throat.

"I'll go first," he said.

He looked down at his hands. "I've been pastoring for thirty years. My congregation loves me. They really do. But I've never told anyone how lonely this work has made me. My wife passed away five years ago, and I kept going because… well, that's what pastors do. But inside, I've been walking through ministry like it's a long hallway with no doors."

His voice cracked. "I didn't come here expecting to say that out loud."

Caleb nodded gently. "Thank you. That hallway doesn't need to stay empty."

Another man - middle-aged, neatly dressed, polished on the outside - leaned forward. "My burden is shame," he said bluntly. "Not because of scandal. But because my church hasn't grown in six years. Every denominational meeting, I feel like a failure. Like everyone else is moving forward and I'm standing still."

Several pastors looked up sharply, tears in their eyes. This was a wound they all knew.

A woman spoke next. She was young - possibly the youngest in the room - and her voice trembled.

"I love my church," she said. "But I feel like a child trying to parent grown adults. They expect me to have wisdom I don't yet have. I pretend I'm confident because they need me to be. But truthfully… I'm scared most days."

Her honesty broke something open. Not dramatically, but deeply. The group didn't rush to comfort her; they simply sat with her in the pain.

Then, unexpectedly, the quietest pastor in the room spoke. He had barely said a word since the retreat began.

"My burden is something no one knows," he said quietly. "I'm tired of being angry. Angry at God. Angry at people. Angry at the constant demands. Angry at feeling unseen. I've prayed for the anger to leave, but it sticks to me like dust."

He lowered his head. "I'm afraid one day it will swallow me."

There was no judgment in the room. Only compassion.

Caleb waited a few long seconds, then spoke softly.

"Thank you. All of you. You've done something sacred this morning. You've spoken truth in a place designed to hold it."
He leaned forward, resting his elbows on his knees.

"You're not alone. Not one of you. Pastors carry burdens no one sees - and we often think we're the only ones struggling. But struggle is not failure. It's humanity."

The room softened.

"And I want to tell you something I learned in Willowend," he continued. "Renewal begins when we stop pretending we're unbreakable. God works most deeply in the cracks."

He paused, letting the words breathe.

"We're going to take some time now. Not to fix anything. Not to counsel each other. Simply to sit in God's presence with what you've shared. Openly. Honestly."

He pointed to the door leading outside. "If you want solitude, walk the trail. If you want to stay, stay. But let your heart be held, not hidden."

They dispersed quietly.

Caleb remained seated for a moment, watching them leave. Their burdens were heavy - but they were no longer *silent.* That alone was a beginning.

He stepped outside into the cool air. The sky had turned a vivid blue, the kind of clear that made everything beneath it seem sharper and more alive. As he walked toward the trail, he saw one of the pastors - the young woman - standing alone beside a low wooden fence, arms crossed, staring at the horizon.

"May I join you?" Caleb asked.

She nodded without speaking.

For a while they simply stood together. He didn't fill the silence. He didn't offer advice. He just shared the space.

After a minute she whispered, "I didn't realise how afraid I was until I said it out loud."

Caleb nodded. "Speaking truth frees space inside us."

She brushed a tear away. "I want to be strong. But not hard."

"That's exactly the right desire," he said. "Strength without harshness. Leadership without armour."

She breathed deeply. "Do you really think God can use someone as unsure as me?"

"God has always used people who are unsure," Caleb replied. "The overconfident ones rarely let Him."

Her tears returned - not from sorrow, but from relief.

"Thank you," she whispered.

He smiled softly. "You're going to be a good shepherd. A gentle one."

After the session, Caleb took a walk alone through the gum trees, needing time to absorb the weight of what he had heard.

The pastors' confessions echoed in his heart - loneliness, shame, fear, anger. They weren't unusual. But hearing them spoken aloud reminded him why he was here. Not to lead a conference. Not to offer expertise. He was here because God had softened a valley - and now God was using that softness to soften shepherds.

A realisation rose quietly inside him.

This calling is not temporary.

The thought startled him.

He had seen the retreats as an extension of Willowend's renewal - something he would do occasionally, occasionally offering help to others. But now, standing in the bush with his notebook tucked under his arm, he sensed something deeper forming.

This is part of your ministry now.
Part of your identity.
A widening, not a detour.

He didn't resist the thought. He didn't fear it either. It settled in him like a small, glowing truth.

Rachel had seen it.

Mary had hinted at it.

Even Tom Gallagher had spoken into it.

But now he felt God impressing it gently on his own heart.

You are being called to shepherd shepherds.

Not instead of Willowend.

Not apart from it.

But *because of it* - flowing from it, supported by it, strengthened through it.

He closed his eyes.

"Lord… if this is what You want, I'm willing."

The breeze lifted softly, rustling through the leaves. Nothing supernatural, nothing dramatic - just a quiet affirmation, like the hush that comes when a heart finally aligns with truth.

Caleb opened his eyes and took a slow breath.

Something had shifted.

Not outwardly.

Not visibly.

But deeply.

He turned back toward the retreat centre, ready for the next session.

When each of the pastors gathered again after their quiet time, something unspoken had changed. They moved differently, took their seats differently, even breathed differently - as though the stillness had seeped into their bones.

Caleb recognised the look. It was the same look Willowend carried when the renewal first began to take hold. He waited until everyone had settled, then spoke with gentle clarity.

"I want to invite you into something sacred," he said. "Not dramatic. Not pressured. Simply sacred."

The room seemed to tighten slightly, readying itself.

"This morning, you named burdens you've carried alone for months or years. Now I want to create space for you to let God carry them with you. Not away from you - with you."

He paused, letting that distinction settle.

"God rarely removes all burdens," he continued. "But He does lift the weight of carrying them alone."

Several pastors nodded slowly, as though understanding this truth in a new way.

"I want to read something to you," Caleb said, opening his Bible to Psalm 34. He read in a quiet, steady voice:

*"'The Lord is close to the broken-hearted
and saves those who are crushed in spirit.'"*

He closed the Bible.

"Broken-hearted," he said softly. "Crushed. These are not signs of spiritual failure. They are places where God becomes most present."

A long silence followed. Not uncomfortable - more like the air holding its breath.

"I want to give each of you the chance to pray aloud if you wish," Caleb continued. "Not polished prayers. Not pastoral prayers. Just honest prayers. You can speak a single sentence or simply sit in silence. Either is enough."

The group remained still for a moment. Then the young pastor who had spoken of fear earlier lifted her head.

"Lord," she whispered, "I don't want to lead with fear anymore." Her voice trembled, but the words held steady.

Another pastor followed. "God... I'm tired of pretending. Please give me courage to be real."

A deep breath moved through the circle like a shared heartbeat.

The older man - the one who spoke of loneliness - prayed next. "Father... I'm tired of walking that hallway alone. Would You open a door?"

Caleb bowed his head, feeling each prayer settle over the group like dew. One by one, quietly, without pressure or expectation, they prayed.

"Help me not to compare my ministry to others."

"Teach me how to rest again."

"Lift this anger that keeps clinging to me."

"Help me forgive myself for not being enough."

Every confession, every request, wove the room together more tightly. When the last voice fell silent, Caleb looked up.

"Thank you," he said softly. "You've just created a sanctuary. Not made of walls or windows - made of honesty."

Some wiped tears. Some closed their eyes. Others simply sat, shoulders lowered, breathing more deeply than when they had arrived.

"We're going to do something simple now," Caleb continued. "I invite each of you to take your notebook - or a sheet of paper - and write a single sentence. Not a sermon point. Not a plan. Just a truth your heart needs to remember."

He paused.

"Something God whispered today."

The room grew quiet again except for the soft sound of pens moving across pages.

Caleb wrote his own sentence:

You are being called to shepherd shepherds.

The words made his chest tighten, not with fear, but with recognition. The truth had been forming for weeks - months, even - but now it had stepped into the light. He didn't try to explain it. He simply let the sentence sit there.

When the pastors finished writing, he invited them to fold their papers.

"These sentences are between you and God," he said. "No one here needs to read them. But I encourage you to keep them. They are seeds."

He placed his own folded paper inside his Bible.

"Would anyone like to share what God said to them today?" he asked gently. "Only if you feel you need to."

One pastor held up his folded page without opening it.

"God told me, 'You're not failing.' I didn't realise how much I needed that."

Another said, "I wrote, 'Rest isn't weakness.'"

A third, the man who had confessed his anger, whispered, "God told me, 'Let Me soften what you've hardened.'"

Caleb felt a deep affection for these weary shepherds.

He sensed God nudging him to say one last thing before they broke.

"You know," he said softly, "renewal in Willowend didn't begin with a meeting or a sermon. It began when a few people allowed God to break open something inside them. Not dramatically. Gently. And then others began to soften too."

He looked around the circle.

"What I'm seeing here… feels very similar."

The pastors exchanged quiet looks - perhaps hopeful, perhaps uncertain, but open.

"We're going to take a break," Caleb said. "When you return, we'll simply talk - pastor to pastor, friend to friend - about what it means to lead gently, to lead from rest, to lead with softness instead of strain."

They stood slowly, some stretching, some wiping their eyes. But every single one of them walked with a lighter step. As they dispersed into the bright morning air, Caleb remained in the circle for a few moments, alone. He let everything settle.

The prayers.

The confessions.

The honesty.

The unexpected unity.

Then, quietly, he whispered the prayer rising in his own heart:

*"Lord… thank You for trusting me with this. I didn't ask for it.
I didn't expect it. But if this is where You're leading,
I'm willing to walk the path."*

He closed his Bible gently.

Outside, laughter broke through the air - soft, tired laughter, but real. It was the first time he'd heard it since arriving.

Caleb stepped out of the room and into the sunlight, feeling the unmistakable warmth of God's presence resting on the retreat like a hand of blessing.

He knew this one day would stay with him for the rest of his ministry.

The final morning of the retreat began quietly, with soft fog hugging the ground beneath the trees. Caleb walked slowly toward the dining hall, the dew soaking the edges of his shoes. He could hear the faint murmur of voices inside - not hurried, not heavy, but warm. A different kind of sound from the first morning.

When he entered, several pastors were already gathered around the long table, sipping tea and talking in low tones. Their faces looked different. Not transformed in a dramatic sense, but loosened, relieved, more rooted. As if each had been carrying invisible weights for so long that their bodies had forgotten how to stand without them - until now.

"Morning, Caleb," Mark said from the far end of the table.

"You're up early."

"Looks like I'm not the only one," Caleb replied.

Mark scanned the room with quiet satisfaction. "They're doing what pastors rarely do - resting."

Caleb nodded. "Let's hope they remember how to keep doing it once they go home."

"That's the challenge," Mark said. "But I think this group will. Something's shifted."

They had breakfast together, not as a formal session, but as a shared meal among friends. Stories emerged - light ones, earthy ones, the kind of stories that revealed something of each pastor's personality. Laughter surfaced easily, as though it had been waiting for permission.

At one point the older pastor - the one who had confessed his loneliness - turned to Caleb.

"I slept last night," he said, sounding surprised. "Properly slept. Haven't done that in a very long time."

Caleb smiled warmly. "I'm glad."

He nodded slowly. "I think I needed to be reminded that I'm not the only one carrying things."

"You never were," Caleb said gently. "But hearing others say it helps the truth sink in."

The man exhaled deeply. "It does."

Later that morning they gathered in the meeting room for the final session. The chairs formed the familiar imperfect circle. Caleb took his seat among them rather than standing at the front. He wanted the closing to feel communal, not instructional.

"Friends," he said, "we're not going to end with a sermon or a charge. I have no final list of lessons or actions. Renewal doesn't grow from lists. It grows from softened hearts."

They listened quietly.

"I want to ask one final question," he said. "You don't have to answer aloud. Simply hold it before God."

He paused.

"What has God restored in you this week?"

The silence that followed carried weight. Not heaviness, but depth - like deep water settling after being stirred.

One pastor finally spoke. "Hope," he said simply. "I didn't realise how close I was to losing it."

Another added softly, "Courage. The courage to actually rest. The courage to stop performing."

A third pastor wiped his eyes. "God restored something tender in me. I'd forgotten tenderness was allowed."

The woman who had spoken of fear earlier said, "Confidence - but not the kind I thought I needed. A quieter confidence. The confidence to be gentle."

Stillness held them again.

Caleb nodded slowly, his heart full.

"If you leave here with anything," he said, "let it be this: God doesn't need your strength nearly as much as He desires your surrender. He is not asking you to lead with pressure, but with presence."

He reached for his Bible and opened it.

"I want to read one final verse," he said.

He chose Isaiah 30:15 - a verse he had prayed over Willowend many times:

*"'In repentance and rest is your salvation,
in quietness and trust is your strength.'"*

He closed the Bible gently.

"That is my prayer for you," he said. "Quietness. Trust. Strength born of rest."

They ended the retreat with a simple time of prayer. No hands raised, no music, no intense moments. Just a circle of tired, softening pastors sitting in the presence of God.

At the end, Mark thanked Caleb with quiet sincerity.

"You've given them something rare," he said. "Not instruction. Permission. Permission to breathe."

Caleb shook his head. "God did the work. I only held the space." Mark smiled. "You did it well."

Before leaving, Caleb took a very slow walk around the retreat grounds. The sun had fully broken through the morning fog, casting long golden shafts across the dirt paths. Birds darted in and out of the trees, scattering leaves that drifted gently to the ground.

As he reached the edge of the property, he noticed a faint smell on the breeze - not strong, not alarming, but unmistakable.

Smoke.

He turned his head toward the distant hills. A thin line of haze hovered above one ridge far off, so faint that someone unfamiliar with the bush might have missed it entirely.

Caleb inhaled slowly.

Bushfire season was approaching once again. Early yet. But it was approaching. He didn't feel fear - only awareness. The same awareness which he felt when he sensed renewal beginning in Willowend many months earlier. A kind of gentle alertness. A whisper: *Pay attention.*

He stood for a long moment, watching the distant haze shift subtly in the breeze. Then he turned back toward the cabins to collect his bag. The smoke wasn't close at all. It wasn't urgent. But it was real. And Caleb knew instinctively that the days ahead would require that same gentleness, that same steadiness, that same quiet trust he had been learning to live in.

Renewal had softened Willowend.

Retreats were softening weary pastors.

But something - something on the edge of the horizon - would soon test that softness.

Not to break it.

But to prove it.

As Caleb loaded his bag into the boot of the car, the pastors gathered around to say their goodbyes. There were no dramatic partings, no emotional scenes. Just handshakes, nods, and simple, honest gratitude.

"Thank you for letting us be human," one pastor said.

"Thank you for reminding us that God is gentle," said another.

"Thank you for not giving us a program," said a third with a weary smile.

Caleb shook his head. "Thank you for trusting the space."

As he got into the car, Mark placed a hand on the open window frame.

"I hope this isn't your last retreat," he said.

"It won't be," Caleb replied without hesitation. "But I think the next one might look different."

"How so?"

Caleb paused, searching for the right words.

"I think God is preparing something… wider. Not bigger. Not louder. Just wider."

Mark smiled. "Then I look forward to seeing it unfold."

When Caleb turned onto the highway leading back toward Willowend, he glanced in the rear-view mirror. The retreat centre was already fading into the landscape.

Ahead, the road stretched long and quiet.

He felt a deep calmness settle inside him - the kind that told him God's hand remained steady upon his shoulder.

He whispered a simple prayer.

"Lord, let what happened here take root. And prepare me for what's coming."

The sunlight glinted off the windscreen.

The valley waited for him. And so did the next chapter of his life.

The drive back into Willowend always felt like slipping into a familiar armchair - the landscape softening, the road narrowing, the town easing into view between tall gums and low roofs. As Caleb crossed the small wooden bridge at the edge of town, he felt a wave of affection rise within him. It wasn't the relief of escape or the pride of accomplishment. It was something deeper: belonging.

He was home.

He pulled into the driveway and saw Rachel already waiting on the verandah. She stepped down the front steps before he had even turned off the engine.

"You're back early," she said warmly.

"Traffic was light," he replied as he got out of the car.

But Rachel saw more than that. "You look… peaceful."

"I feel peaceful."

She walked closer and gently touched his cheek. "God used you?"

"I think He used the space," Caleb said. "I just held it open."

Rachel smiled. "That's still being used."

After unpacking, they sat together at the kitchen table, and Caleb shared the story of the retreat - the honesty, the prayers, the softening hearts. Rachel listened without interrupting, her eyes reflecting both pride and understanding.

"Do you think this is the beginning of something bigger for you?" she asked softly when he finished.

"Yes," Caleb said without hesitation. "But not bigger in the sense of visibility or responsibility. Bigger in the sense of… reach."

Rachel nodded thoughtfully. "You've always pastored beyond your words. Perhaps now you'll do it beyond your valley."
Caleb reached across and took her hand. "Only if you walk with me."

"I wouldn't dream of doing anything else," she replied.

That afternoon, Caleb took a long, slow walk through town. He wanted to reconnect with the rhythm of Willowend, to see how the renewal had continued while he was away. His first stop was the café. Doris greeted him with her usual enthusiasm.

"Pastor! There you are. Come in, come in. You've been missed."

"Just a few days, Doris," Caleb chuckled.

"A few days is enough. Tea?"

"Tea would be perfect."

As she poured, she lowered her voice conspiratorially.

"So," she said, leaning on the counter, "did those pastors behave themselves?"

"They did," Caleb said. "More importantly, they opened their hearts."

Doris nodded approvingly. "Good. Pastors need soft hearts. Hard hearts make hard sermons. And hard sermons make hard people."

Caleb laughed. "I'll take that wisdom with me."

But before he left, Doris added something more quietly. "I think something's shifting here again," she said. "Not big. Just… deepening. The renewal hasn't slowed while you were away."

Caleb felt the truth of that settle inside him like a warm stone.

"I'm grateful," he said.

At the primary school, Lynette waved him over immediately.

"Caleb! Welcome back. The kindness circle survived without you."

"It was never mine to supervise," he said with a grin.

"No, but they did make something for you."

She handed him a small, folded card, decorated with uneven marker lines and fingerprints.

On the front, it read:

"Welcome Home Pastor Caleb!"

Inside, written in the shaky handwriting of at least a dozen children, were the words:

"Thank you for helping people be kind."

Caleb felt his eyes sting.

"They really wrote this?" he asked.

"They did," Lynette replied. "And not because I suggested it.

One of the kids said, 'Pastor Caleb helped our hearts. Now he's going to help other pastors' hearts.'"

He swallowed hard.

"Children see more clearly than we do," she said.

"Yes," Caleb whispered. "They do."

At the general store, Howard was stacking shelves when Caleb walked in.

"Ah! Pastor's back," he said. "Did you sort those pastors out?"

"Something like that," Caleb replied.

Howard grinned, but then his expression shifted. Not with concern, exactly. More with curiosity. "You know what I've noticed?" he said. "People are talking differently."

Caleb waited. Howard wasn't a man who rushed to conclusions, and when he spoke this way, it usually meant he had been paying attention.

"In town," Howard continued. "At the café. Outside the post office. Even down at the oval. It's not about the retreat as an event. It's about what people are asking each other now."

"What are they asking?" Caleb said.

Howard shrugged. "Real things. Not just 'How're you going?' but 'How are you really holding up?' I heard two blokes the other day talking about prayer like it wasn't an awkward word anymore. Didn't feel forced. Just... natural."

Caleb felt something settle quietly in his chest.

"I've lived here a long time," Howard went on. "Long enough to know when something's just a mood and when it's deeper than that. This feels deeper."

They stood for a moment, watching people move along the footpath and across the green. A few lingered in conversation, reluctant to rush home.

Voices were quite low. Laughter rose occasionally, not loud, but genuine.

"It's as though people have permission now," Howard said.

"Permission to slow down. To speak honestly."

Caleb nodded. "I've felt that too."

Howard looked at him, his eyes very thoughtful. "You didn't orchestrate this, you know."

Caleb smiled faintly. "That's a relief."

Howard chuckled. "I mean it. If you'd tried to engineer it, it would've collapsed under its own weight. But this... this feels like something that grew."

Caleb thought of the retreat - of Mary's words, of Rachel's steady discernment, of the way those days had unfolded without urgency or spectacle.

"Yes," he said quietly. "Grown is the right word."

As the afternoon wore on, people began to drift away. There were no dramatic farewells, no declarations. Just nods held a moment longer than usual. A few quiet thank-yous. One or two brief embraces that surprised even the people offering them.

Rachel came to stand beside Caleb as the last of the light softened across the town.

"You all right?" she asked softly.

"Yes," he said after a moment. "More than all right."

She smiled. "You're seeing it, aren't you?"

"I think so." He glanced around the now-quiet street. "This didn't end today."

"No," she agreed. "It started."

They walked back toward home together as the late afternoon light stretched across the paddocks beyond the houses.

The air was calm - not expectant in the way it had been during the fire days, but settled. Grounded.

"Do you think people will want more?" Caleb asked.

Rachel considered the question. "Not more events. More space. More honesty. More room to breathe."

He nodded. "That I can do."

That evening, Caleb sat at his desk, not to prepare a sermon or respond to emails, but simply to reflect. He found himself thinking less about plans and more about people.

Amelia's tentative courage.

Graham's quiet return to prayer.

The way strangers had begun to speak to one another like neighbours again.

It struck him that renewal rarely announced itself. It arrived disguised as ordinary faithfulness - people choosing gentleness when no one demanded it, choosing openness without knowing where it might lead.

Later, as the sun dipped below the horizon, Caleb stepped outside. The valley lay before him in its familiar stillness, unchanged in shape but somehow different in spirit.

He realised then that the retreat had not been a peak to descend from, but a threshold crossed.

What came next would not require him to push, to drive, or to prove anything. It would require him to stay attentive. To notice. To trust that what God had begun in quietness would continue the same way.

Behind him, Rachel joined him at the door.

"Thinking again?" she asked gently.

"Yes," he said, smiling. "But not worrying."

"Good."

They stood together, watching the last light fade from the hills. Somewhere within Willowend, something had taken root.
Not loud enough to draw attention.

Not fragile enough to be lost.

Just strong enough to grow.

And Caleb sensed - with a calm he hadn't felt in a very long time - that the work ahead would not be about holding things together, but about allowing them to be given away.

The midweek gathering did not feel like an event, and Caleb noticed that almost at once.

There was no sense of arrival, no nervous energy hovering at the door, no quiet checking of watches as people slipped into their seats. Instead, people came as though they had been expected - not by him, but by the space itself. They arrived in twos and threes, greeting one another without hesitation, settling into chairs as if they had done this many times before, even though they had not.

Caleb stood near the door longer than usual, holding a mug of tea he had already forgotten to drink. He watched faces more than movement. The guarded expressions he had grown used to over the years were largely absent. People were not bracing themselves. They were present.

This was new.

The chairs were arranged loosely, not in straight lines, and the Bible lay open on a chair near the centre, as though someone had placed it there without thinking too much about it. There were no printed outlines. No carefully framed questions. Caleb had deliberately resisted the urge to prepare something structured. He had learned, especially in recent weeks, that structure could sometimes crowd out what needed room to breathe.

Amelia arrived early and chose a seat toward the edge of the circle. She kept her jacket on, though the room was warm, and sat with her hands folded loosely in her lap. The small prayer card Caleb had written for her peeked from her pocket. When she noticed him looking her way, she gave a quick nod-more acknowledgment than reassurance. She did not look anxious. She looked settled.

Graham arrived next, later than Caleb expected. He hovered briefly near the back before choosing a chair close to the wall, positioning himself so that he could leave easily if he needed to.

Yet there was nothing defensive in his posture. He sat upright, attentive, his hands resting loosely on his knees.

Julie followed a moment later. She rested her hand on Graham's shoulder as she passed, just briefly, then took a seat nearby. It was a small gesture, but it carried years of shared history, and Caleb found himself grateful for it.

Rachel joined Caleb near the door and leaned in slightly.

"They're coming because they want to be here," she said quietly.

"Yes," he replied. "Not because they feel they should."

That distinction mattered more than it might have once.

When it felt right - not when the clock suggested it was time - Caleb moved to the centre and spoke. He did not begin with an opening prayer or a welcome. He simply named the space.

"We'll keep tonight simple," he said. "There's no pressure to speak, and no expectation that anyone needs to pray out loud. We're just here to listen. To one another. And to God, if He chooses to speak in the quiet."

No one nodded vigorously. No one shifted awkwardly. They seemed to settle more deeply into their chairs, as though relieved by the absence of performance.

Caleb read a short passage of Scripture - a few verses, familiar and unadorned, about rest and trust and the nearness of God. He did not explain it. He did not draw out points. He closed the Bible and placed it back on the chair, then waited.

The silence that followed was not strained. It carried weight, but not pressure. It felt attentive, as though the room itself were listening.

Eventually, Margaret spoke.

She did not raise her hand or clear her throat for attention. She simply spoke into the space when she felt ready.

"I didn't realise how tired I was," she said slowly. "Not in my body. In my spirit. I think I've been tired there for a long time."

No one rushed to respond. No one tried to fix her words or turn them into something else.

"When everything slowed down during the fire," she continued,

"I was afraid at first. But then… I noticed how much noise I'd been living with. Inside. I don't think I want to go back to that." A few people nodded, almost imperceptibly.

Graham shifted in his chair, then cleared his throat.

"I don't usually talk in groups," he said, glancing briefly at Julie before looking back down at his hands. "But I think I know what you mean."

Caleb watched him carefully, not with the attention of a leader guiding a moment, but with the attentiveness of someone witnessing something holy.

"I've filled every quiet space with work for years," Graham went on. "When everything stopped, it scared me. I thought the quiet would swallow me up." He paused, choosing his words. "But it didn't. It… settled me."

Julie reached for his hand, and he did not pull away.

"I don't have the language for prayer anymore," Graham added quietly. "Not like I used to. But I think God's been listening anyway."

Caleb felt a warmth rise in his chest, unexpected but very steady. This was not testimony shaped for encouragement. This was recognition spoken without agenda.

The conversation unfolded slowly after that. No one dominated it. People spoke of ordinary things - sleep returning, neighbours checking in, the strange relief of not pretending to be fine. Someone mentioned praying without knowing what to say. Another spoke of feeling less defensive when faith came up in conversation.

Caleb said very little.

When the evening eventually drew to a close, it did so naturally.

No one checked the time. No one asked whether this would happen again. Chairs were stacked without instruction. Cups were washed without direction. Two people lingered to ask whether they could help someone else during the week - nothing official, just something practical.

As the last of them drifted out into the cool night air, Rachel slipped her arm through Caleb's.

"You didn't lead that," she said.

He smiled. "I noticed."

"That's not a criticism."

"I know."

They stood together for a moment, looking at the now-quiet room. Caleb felt a quiet gratitude - not the kind that swells and demands expression, but the kind that anchors.

Something had happened here that could not be repeated on command. And that, he realised, was exactly how it was meant to be.

By the end of the week, Caleb began to notice that the change was no longer confined to gathered moments.

It was showing up in the spaces between.

Amelia started arriving early on Sundays - not to help, not to speak, but to sit. She chose the same pew each time, near the back but close enough to hear the small sounds of the sanctuary settling into itself. She sat with her hands folded loosely in her lap, eyes often closed, as though she were learning how to inhabit stillness without apology.

One morning, as Caleb passed her on his way to unlock the side door, she opened her eyes and smiled.

"I like it when it's quiet like this," she whispered. "Before everyone comes."

He nodded. "So do I."

She hesitated, then added, "It feels like God isn't in a hurry."

Caleb smiled. "He rarely is."

During the service, Amelia did not sing every hymn. Sometimes she stood, sometimes she was seated. There was no calculation in it, no self-consciousness. She was simply present. When the service ended, she stayed behind to talk with a woman she had never met before, listening more than speaking.

Caleb noticed that too.

Graham rang one afternoon and asked whether Caleb might come by the farm - for a conversation, he said, but for a walk. They walked the boundary fence slowly, the late afternoon sun casting long shadows across the paddocks. Graham spoke in fits and starts, as though testing words before trusting them.

"I keep thinking prayer has to sound a certain way," he said eventually. "Like if I don't get the words right, it doesn't count." Caleb stopped and rested his arms on the fence.

"When you listen to Julie," he said, "do you need her to phrase everything perfectly before you know what she means?"

Graham considered that. "No."

"God is better at listening than we are."

They resumed walking. After a while, Graham said quietly, "Sometimes all I manage is sitting on the verandah and saying nothing."

"That counts," Caleb replied. "Often more than we realise."

Later that afternoon, Caleb stopped in briefly at the Thompsons' place. Mrs Thompson asked whether there was "something small" she might do. She said it as though she were apologising for not offering more.

Caleb suggested she check on Margaret Ellis, who had stopped driving the previous year and rarely saw visitors. Mrs Thompson nodded, thoughtful.

"I can do that," she said. "I've been meaning to."

She did not ask for instructions.

What struck Caleb was how little coordination was required. There were no rosters to manage, no announcements to make, no structures demanding upkeep. People were responding to nudges that felt personal and unforced.

This was not enthusiasm.

It was attentiveness.

One morning, as Caleb walked through town, Mary Kline stopped him outside the post office. She leaned on her walking stick, her eyes bright with recognition.

"You're watching them," she said.

"I am," Caleb admitted.

"And you're resisting the urge to gather it all back to yourself." He laughed softly. "With some effort."

"Good," Mary said. "Don't interrupt what's growing."

They stood together for a moment, watching people come and go, greeting one another by name.

"This is what fruit looks like before it's named," Mary added.

"Messy. Quiet. Unimpressive."

Caleb nodded. "I keep thinking I should do something."

Mary smiled. "You are. You're staying out of the way."

The words settled with unexpected clarity.

The most telling moment came late in the week, when someone came to Caleb not for help, but for blessing.

Daniel stood in the doorway of the church office, his posture straighter than Caleb remembered. He no longer shifted his weight nervously or avoided eye contact.

"Mum and I talked," he said. "About what comes next."

Caleb gestured for him to sit.

"She wants to help with meals," Daniel continued. "Not just church stuff. Anyone who needs it. She said she's tired of waiting until she feels ready."

Caleb felt his throat tighten slightly.

"She asked me to ask you if that was okay."

"It's more than okay," Caleb said. "It's generous."

Daniel nodded. "She doesn't want to be invisible anymore."

Caleb leaned forward. "She isn't."

After Daniel left, Caleb remained seated for a long time. The familiar rhythms of the office - tick of the clock, distant traffic, the rustle of leaves outside the window - newly significant.

This was not revival as he had once imagined it. There were no crowds, no sense of arrival, no clear moment he could point to and say, This is it.

But there was movement. Not toward him, but through the community.

That evening, as he and Rachel sat together after dinner, Caleb found himself speaking what had been forming quietly within him.

"I think my role is changing," he said.

Rachel looked at him, attentive but unsurprised.

"I'm not stepping back," he continued. "But I'm not standing at the centre either. It feels like I'm walking alongside something that's learned how to walk."

Rachel smiled. "That sounds healthy."

"It feels right," he said. "And a little unsettling."

She reached for his hand. "Growth usually is."

They sat in silence for a while, the house settled around them, the valley quiet beyond the windows. Caleb realised then that the work ahead would not really require more effort, only more attentiveness. Not more vision, but more trust.

Willowend was no longer simply receiving care.

It was beginning - slowly, quietly - to give it.

And that, Caleb knew, was how this chapter of the story was meant to deepen.

The real question Caleb could no longer avoid was not *what* was happening in Willowend, but *how he was meant to respond to it.*

Years of ministry had trained him to recognise moments like this as opportunities for leadership. There was an instinctive pull toward naming the change, giving it language, offering some direction. He could already imagine the outlines of a full plan - gatherings shaped around discernment, teaching that articulated what people were experiencing, structures that could carry it forward without losing momentum.

And yet, each time he considered doing so, something in him resisted. It was not reluctance born of fear or fatigue. It was discernment. The kind that does not shout but steadies.

One evening, as he and Rachel walked the familiar track behind their home, Caleb spoke the unease aloud.

"I don't think I'm meant to gather all of this into myself," he said.

Rachel slowed slightly, giving his words room.

"What makes you say that?" she asked.

"Because it isn't flowing toward me," he replied. "It's flowing through the people. If I try to contain it, I'll change its nature."

She nodded slowly. "So what *are* you meant to do?"

He smiled faintly. "Pay attention. Protect space. Say yes when it matters. Stay quiet when it doesn't."

Rachel laughed softly. "You've always been better at the quiet than you think."

"I'm learning," he said.

The thought stayed with him through the week. He found himself listening more carefully - just to words, but to timing. When to respond. When to wait. When to trust that something would unfold without his intervention.

Late one afternoon, an email arrived from a pastor Caleb barely knew. He recognised the name, but only distantly - a man from a town several hours away, someone he had met briefly years earlier at a conference.

The message was simple, almost hesitant.

I've heard that Willowend has become a place where people can sit without having to perform. Would you be open to meeting for a day of prayer and conversation? No agenda. Just space.

Caleb read the message once, then again. He did not feel flattered. He did not feel anxious.

He felt attentive.

Instead of replying immediately, he walked down to the church and sat alone in the sanctuary. The afternoon light filtered gently through the side windows, dust motes drifting lazily in the air. The room felt familiar, but not static - as though it were learning how to hold more without becoming crowded.

He thought of the fire weeks earlier, of how fear had driven people inward. He thought of the quiet that followed, of how gentleness had drawn them outward again. He thought of Margaret's careful question, Graham's halting words, Amelia's growing confidence, Mary's steady wisdom.

He thought of Rachel - always beside him, always discerning, never demanding centre stage. This was not something to protect or possess.

It was something to steward lightly.

When Caleb finally returned to his office and opened his laptop, his reply was brief.

Yes. We would welcome that.

He closed the screen and sat back, a deep sense of rightness was settling over him. It was not excitement. Not apprehension. Just alignment.

Willowend was still Willowend - the same valley, the same people, the same unhurried rhythms. But it was no longer a place that existed only for itself.

It had learned how to open its hands.

And Caleb, standing quietly at the edge of what was forming, understood that this too was part of his calling. Not to be the centre of a widening circle, but to help ensure it remained gentle as it grew.

The reach beyond the valley had begun.

Not loudly.

Not urgently.

But with the unmistakable strength of something given freely, and therefore able to endure.

The invitation from Barrow Creek did not arrive with urgency. That, more than anything, caught Caleb's attention. It came as a phone call one quiet morning while he was sorting through paperwork at the church office. The voice on the other end introduced itself carefully, as though uncertain whether the call was welcome.

"This is Ellen Hayes," the woman said. "I'm one of the deacons at Barrow Creek."

Caleb leaned back slightly in his chair. "Yes. I remember meeting you some years ago."

"That was before," she replied. There was a pause, then she added, "Before everything changed."

He waited.

"We're still meeting," Ellen continued. "Not well. But faithfully. Since Mark left, things have been… a little thin." She hesitated. "Someone mentioned Willowend. Said it had become a place where people were allowed to breathe again."

Caleb did not correct her.

"We're not asking for you to come and fix anything," Ellen said quickly, as though anticipating resistance. "We don't want a program or a guest preacher. Just… company. Perhaps a few people who know what it's like to keep showing up when things feel small."

Caleb felt the words settle into him with a familiar weight. This was not flattery. This was need spoken without expectation.

"I can ask," he said simply. "Not for myself. But for the church."

"That's all we hoped," Ellen replied. "Thank you."

After the call ended, Caleb did not move immediately. He sat with his hands resting loosely on the desk, noticing the quiet in the room. The instinct to decide quickly - to say yes or no, to assess capacity - rose up, then receded.

This was not his invitation to accept.

It was Willowend's.

That evening, he mentioned the call almost casually as he and Rachel prepared dinner together.

"Barrow Creek," Rachel said thoughtfully. "That's a long drive."

"Yes."

"And they're not asking for leadership."

"No."

She smiled faintly. "Then it sounds like exactly the kind of invitation you wouldn't want to answer alone."

Caleb nodded. "I was thinking the same."

The following Sunday, Caleb spoke briefly at the close of the service. He did not frame the conversation as an opportunity or a challenge. He simply named what had been offered.

"A small church in Barrow Creek has asked whether a few people might visit one Sunday afternoon," he said. "Not to lead anything. Just to sit with them. Listen. Share a meal."

There was no immediate reaction.

Caleb let the silence breathe.

"If that stirs something in you," he added, "I'd love to talk with you. If it doesn't, that's all right too."

He stepped back, resisting the urge to say more.

After the service, several people lingered - not clustering, not conferring, just waiting their turn. Margaret spoke first. "I was the one who mentioned Barrow Creek weeks ago," she said. "I think I should go."

Caleb smiled. "I thought you might."

Julie joined them. "Graham won't say it," she said, "but he's already asked which Sunday."

Graham stood a little behind her, hands in his pockets. "I'm not promising to talk," he said. "But I can sit."

"That's more than enough," Caleb replied.

Amelia approached hesitantly. "I don't know if I'd be any help," she said. "But I could come. If that's okay."

Caleb met her eyes. "It is."

By the end of the morning, five people had quietly offered themselves. No one volunteered publicly. No one asked for assurance. They simply came, one by one, each responding to something they recognised.

Caleb did not organise a meeting. He did not create a plan. He simply told them when and where they would leave and reminded them to bring food.

The drive to Barrow Creek the following Sunday unfolded without fanfare. They travelled in two cars, the road stretching long and pale ahead of them. Conversation came and went naturally - sometimes reflective, sometimes light. There was no nervous anticipation, no rehearsed explanations.

They arrived to find the small church already open. The building was older than Willowend's, its paint faded, its garden overgrown in places. Inside, the sanctuary felt tired but cared for, as though someone had refused to let it be abandoned even when hope had worn thin.

Ellen met them at the door, relief softening her face.

"Thank you for coming," she said, more sincerely than formally. They sat together without ceremony. There was no service to follow, no agenda to keep. Someone put a kettle on. Someone else arranged chairs. Slowly, conversation found its way into the room.

A man spoke about the exhaustion of keeping faith alive when numbers dwindled. A woman admitted she had considered leaving altogether. Someone else spoke of prayer feeling hollow, of Scripture sounding distant.

No one from Willowend responded with advice.

They simply listened.

Margaret asked questions. Graham nodded more than he spoke. Amelia sat very quietly, attentive, her presence was steady and unassuming.

At one point, Ellen looked at Caleb and said, "This is different from what we expected."

He smiled gently. "It's different from what we expected too."

When they shared the meal later, it felt less like hospitality and more like fellowship rediscovered. Stories overlapped. Laughter surfaced unexpectedly. For a while, the weight that had settled over the small congregation lifted - not completely, but enough to let light in.

As they prepared to leave, Ellen walked with Caleb to the door.

"You didn't bring answers," she said.

"No," he agreed.

"But you brought hope," she replied quietly.

Caleb shook his head. "I think you already had it."

She smiled, unconvinced but grateful.

As they drove away, the group from Willowend sat quietly for a time. Finally, Amelia spoke. "I thought I was coming to help," she said. "But I think I needed that too."

Caleb nodded. "That's often how it works."

He glanced at the road ahead, the horizon wide and open. Willowend had taken its first step beyond itself.

Not with strategy.

Not with confidence.

But with open hands and listening hearts.

And Caleb sensed, with calm certainty, that this was only the beginning of where that widening path might lead. The effects of the visit to Barrow Creek did not manifest immediately. There was no surge of enthusiasm on the drive home, no talk of doing more or going further. In fact, the return journey was marked mostly by silence. It was the kind that followed something meaningful but unresolved, where words felt either too small or too soon.

When they reached Willowend, they parted without ceremony. No one suggested a debrief. No one lingered to analyse what had happened. They simply went home.

It was only over the following days that Caleb began to notice what the visit had stirred.

Margaret rang first.

"I've been thinking about Ellen," she said. "Not in a worrying way. Just… holding her in mind. I wondered whether it would be strange to write to her. Not with advice. Just to say we're praying."

"That wouldn't be strange at all," Caleb replied. "It would be kind."

"I thought so," Margaret said. "I'll do that then."

Julie mentioned, almost in passing, that Graham had been quieter than usual since they returned. Not withdrawn, just thoughtful.

"He keeps saying he didn't realise how heavy things could get without anyone noticing," she said. "I think it unsettled him. In a good way."

Amelia came by the church one afternoon, hesitating at the door before stepping inside.

"I didn't expect that to affect me," she said. "I thought I was past all that."

Caleb waited.

"I've spent years telling myself I don't need people," she continued. "But sitting there… listening to them… I realised how lonely faith can get when you try to carry it alone."

She paused, searching for words.

"I don't want to live like that anymore."

Caleb nodded. "You don't have to."

What struck him was not the emotion in her voice, but the steadiness beneath it. This was not a reaction. It was a decision. The following Sunday, something subtle but unmistakable shifted in the gathered worship.

Caleb could not have named it if asked, but he felt it in the way people prayed, in the way Scripture was received. There was less urgency to be moved, and more willingness to be shaped. The service did not run long. No one lingered at the end for dramatic conversations. Yet there was a sense of shared attentiveness that had not been there before.

As people drifted out, Howard caught Caleb's eye.

"They brought something back with them," he said quietly.

"Yes," Caleb replied. "Perspective."

Howard nodded. "And compassion."

Later that week, another message arrived - this time from a town Caleb did not recognise immediately. The pastor wrote briefly, explaining that he had heard about Willowend through Barrow Creek. He did not ask for help, only for prayer.

Caleb forwarded the message to a few others, without comment. Within hours, replies came back - asking what to do, but offering to pray, to write, to listen if needed.

No one asked Caleb to organise it.

That night, as Caleb and Rachel sat together, he spoke what had been forming slowly.

"This is bigger than a visit," he said.

Rachel nodded. "It's changing how people see themselves."

"Yes," he replied. "They're no longer asking, 'What does our church need?' They're asking, 'Who needs us?'"

Rachel smiled. "That's a dangerous shift."

"In the best possible way," Caleb said.

The real test came a fortnight later.

Ellen rang again.

"I wanted you to know," she said, "that something has lifted here. Not everything. Not all at once. But enough to breathe."

Caleb smiled, unseen.

"We didn't do anything special," she continued. "But people are talking again. Listening. A few have even said they'd be willing to take turns leading prayer."

"That's good," Caleb said. "Very good."

She hesitated. "There's something else."

He waited.

"One of the nearby churches has asked if we would like to meet together sometime. Just to share a meal. I don't think we'd have had the courage to say yes before."

Caleb leaned back in his chair, a quiet sense of awe settling over him.

"I think you should," he said.

After the call ended, Caleb sat for a long time, hands resting loosely on his knees. He was not surprised. And yet, he was deeply moved. This was how it worked, he realised. Not by multiplying effort, but by multiplying courage. One small act of presence loosening something that had been bound elsewhere.

That evening, he walked through Willowend as dusk settled over the valley. Lights flickered on in houses. A few people waved as he passed. The town felt the same - yet not. It was no longer inward-facing. It was learning how to look outward without losing itself.

Caleb paused near the church and stood for a moment, listening to the quiet. He thought of the seasons of ministry he had known - times of strain, times of stability, times of exhaustion. He had not expected this stage, this gentle widening of responsibility that did not centre on him.

And yet, it felt truer than anything that had come before.

When he reached home, Rachel was sitting on the veranda.

"You're thinking," she said.

"I am," he admitted.

She smiled. "About how far this might go?"

"Yes."

"And about how little control you have over it."

He laughed softly. "That too."

She stood and joined him. "That's all right, you know."

"I know," he said. "It just feels like standing on the edge of something."

Rachel rested her head briefly against his shoulder.

"Then stand there," she said. "And watch."

As night settled over Willowend, Caleb felt no urgency to move ahead. No need to define the next step.

The path was already opening.

Quietly.

Patiently.

One faithful act at a time.

The widening of Willowend's life did not come with a grand announcement. There was no meeting to explain it, no sermon to frame it, no language that tried to name what was unfolding. It simply continued, one invitation at a time, carried by people who were no longer waiting to be told what faithfulness looked like.

Caleb noticed it most clearly in the way questions changed.

People no longer asked him what the church should do. They asked who might need company. Who might need prayer. Who might need space.

One afternoon, as he sat at his desk answering emails, he became aware of how few of them required decisions from him. Most were updates - small notes of connection offered freely.

I visited Ellen today.
We're praying for Barrow Creek.
I rang someone I hadn't spoken to in years.

Caleb read them slowly, with a growing sense of gratitude. This was not delegation. It was maturity.

That evening, Howard dropped by, leaning casually against the office doorway.

"You've noticed it too," he said.

"Yes," Caleb replied.

Howard smiled. "You're becoming less necessary."

Caleb laughed softly. "That's one way to put it."

"It's a good way," Howard said. "Churches don't grow healthy by becoming dependent. They grow healthy by learning how to give."

Caleb nodded. He had learned that lesson many times in theory. Seeing it lived out was something else entirely.

A week later, another message arrived - this time not asking for prayer or presence, but offering it.

A small group from Barrow Creek wondered whether they might come to Willowend for a quiet day. Not for teaching. Not for renewal. Just to sit, walk, and pray together.

Caleb read the message twice before passing it to Rachel.

She smiled as she read. "You won't be able to stop this now."

"I wouldn't want to," he replied.

They spoke about logistics briefly, then let the conversation drift. Neither of them felt the need to manage the moment. Later that night, Caleb stepped outside and stood beneath the open sky. The ridge beyond the town lay dark and still, the memory of fire now distant, almost unreal. The valley breathed quietly, settled into itself.

He thought back to the early days of his ministry, to the certainty he had once carried about what leadership required. He had believed that clarity meant control, that faithfulness meant visibility, that growth meant expansion in all the obvious ways. None of that had prepared him for this.

What was unfolding now was slower. Quieter. More demanding in its own way. It required trust without applause. Discernment without urgency. Leadership that resisted the need to be central. Caleb realised then that this season was not an extension of his ministry, but a refinement of it.

On a Sunday morning not long after, Mary Kline took her usual seat near the front. She greeted Caleb with a knowing smile as he passed.

"You look settled," she said.

"I feel it," he replied.

She nodded. "That's how you know it's real."

After the service, as people lingered in conversation, Mary waited until the room had thinned.

"You won't always see where this leads," she said quietly. "Some of it will happen beyond you."

"I know," Caleb said.

"And you're all right with that?"

He smiled. "I think that's the point."

Mary patted his arm. "Then you're doing it properly."

That evening, as the light faded and Willowend settled into its familiar rhythms, Caleb and Rachel sat together on the veranda. They spoke of ordinary things - the week ahead, people they had noticed, letters yet to answer.

Eventually, Rachel said, "Do you miss being at the centre of it all?"

Caleb considered the question carefully.

"No," he said. "I don't think I ever belonged there."

She smiled. "You belong where you are now."

"Yes," he said quietly. "Watching. Walking. Trusting."

They sat together as night deepened, the town resting around them like a field after sowing. Nothing dramatic marked the moment. No sense of completion or arrival.

Only the quiet assurance that something good had taken root. Willowend was no longer simply a place of refuge.

It had become a place of sending.

And Caleb, standing within that gentle widening, knew that this was not an ending - but it was enough of one.

For now.

The following Saturday morning arrived with the kind of mildness that made Willowend feel almost unchanged, as though the last few months had been no more than a season of weather. The air was cool but not cold, the sky a clean blue, and the valley rested in that quiet, ordinary way that had once seemed permanent.

Caleb stood near the church door with Rachel as the first car turned in through the gate.

"They came," Rachel said softly.

"They said they would," Caleb replied, but he felt the weight of it all the same.

Two vehicles pulled up beside the hall. Ellen stepped out first, her posture a little uncertain, as though she were still surprised to find herself here. Behind her came three others - faces Caleb recognised from their visit to Barrow Creek, and one he didn't. A younger man, perhaps late twenties, with a worn backpack and the quiet look of someone who had been carrying too much for too long.

Margaret was already there, setting cups out on the table without fuss. She saw Ellen and lifted a hand in greeting, then moved immediately toward her as though there were no gap to bridge. "Welcome," Margaret said simply. "We're glad you came."

Ellen's shoulders softened. "Thank you. It feels… strange being the one visiting."

"It's only strange if we make it," Margaret replied, and guided her inside.

Caleb watched that exchange with a small, private gratitude. It wasn't his moment. It didn't need to be. He stepped forward as the younger man lingered at the edge of the group, glancing around without committing to any one place.

"I'm Caleb," he said gently.

The man looked up, a flicker of caution in his eyes. "Luke."

"Welcome, Luke," Caleb said with a warm smile. "You are safe here. Nothing complicated. Just tea, and a bit of space."

Luke nodded once, as though he had been offered something he wasn't sure he deserved. Rachel approached him then, her manner calm and unhurried.

"I'm Rachel," she said, offering her hand. "You don't need to do anything today except breathe."

Luke hesitated, then shook her hand. "Thanks."

They moved into the hall together. No one tried to organise the morning. There was no agenda pinned to the noticeboard. Chairs were arranged loosely in the shape they seemed to choose by habit now - open, unforced. The kettle boiled. Biscuits appeared. Conversation began in small pieces, then widened as people found one another.

Caleb sat back slightly and watched.

It was not that he had nothing to do. He could have filled the space with guidance, offered a reading, suggested questions. But he had learned that some kinds of ministry were not about adding something, but about keeping the space clear enough for something else to happen.

Ellen sat with Julie near the window and spoke quietly. Caleb caught only fragments - weariness, relief, the long slog of Sunday after Sunday with too few helping hands. Julie listened without interrupting, her expression steady.

Graham stood outside with Howard for a time, leaning against the verandah railing. They said little, but their silence did not feel empty. It felt companionable, grounded in an understanding that did not require explanation.

Amelia moved in and out of the room, more comfortable now in her own skin than she had been at the beginning. She refilled cups without being asked, but she did not bustle. She simply served as though service had become a natural expression of being here.

At some point Luke drifted toward the doorway, his eyes fixed on the paddocks beyond the church grounds. Caleb followed at a distance, not to corner him but to be available.

Luke stood with his hands in his pockets, shoulders slightly hunched, as though bracing against something that wasn't really present.

"You can stay out here if you like," Caleb said, stopping beside him.

Luke nodded. "It's quiet."

"It is," Caleb said. "Sometimes that's the best gift a place can offer."

Luke didn't reply immediately. Then, without looking at Caleb, he said, "Ellen told me you didn't try to fix them."

Caleb smiled faintly. "I wouldn't know where to start."

Luke's mouth twitched, almost a smile, almost not. "Most people start anyway."

Caleb let that hang for a moment.

"You're a pastor," Caleb said, not as a question.

Luke's shoulders tightened. "Was."

Caleb didn't correct him. He had learned not to rush for titles.

Luke breathed out slowly. "I didn't leave because I stopped believing," he said, his voice low. "I left because I couldn't carry it anymore. Every Sunday felt like I was pretending to be strong so everyone else could keep leaning. And then I started resenting them for it. And then resenting myself."

Caleb listened, the familiar ache of recognition stirring. He had heard versions of this before, but never lightly.

"You did the right thing by stopping," Caleb said quietly.

Luke turned his head slightly, surprised. "Most people tell me I should push through. That it's the calling."

"The calling isn't to break," Caleb said. "The calling is to belong to Christ. Sometimes the faithful thing is to step back until you can breathe again."

Luke stared out over the paddocks, his eyes brightening despite himself. He swallowed.

"I don't even know what I am without it," he admitted.

Rachel's voice came from behind them, gentle and steady. "You're still you."

They turned. Rachel stood a few steps away, holding two mugs of tea, as though she had simply noticed the moment and responded naturally.

Luke looked at her, wary but drawn.

Rachel offered him a mug. "You don't have to solve that question today. Today can just be today."

Luke took the mug with both hands. "Thanks."

Caleb glanced at Rachel and saw the quiet strength in her face - the kind that never demanded attention but changed the atmosphere simply by being present.

They stood together for a while without speaking. The breeze stirred the tops of the gums. Somewhere in the distance a bird called, and Willowend felt like itself - ordinary, unthreatened, steady.

Inside the hall, laughter rose just briefly, then softened again. Someone was telling a story - nothing dramatic, just something human. Caleb could hear the cadence of ease. A month earlier, that ease would have felt improbable.

After a time, Ellen stepped out onto the verandah and looked at Caleb.

"Is it all right if we walk?" she asked. "Just a few of us. No talking if we don't want to."

Caleb nodded. "Of course."

So they walked - along the track behind the church, and down toward the creek line, then back again, the group stretching out naturally as people found their own pace. Some spoke quietly. Some didn't. The land did what it always did: it offered space.

When they returned, Margaret had laid out food without fanfare. Sandwiches, slices, fruit. The kind of spread that suggested care rather than occasion.

They ate together under the shade. Conversation deepened without being pushed. Ellen spoke of the fear of failing her people, and Mary, sitting nearby, said simply, "You're not failing. You're learning what you can't do alone."

Howard asked Luke a plain question - where he grew up, what he missed most. Luke answered cautiously at first, then more freely as he realised no one was collecting his words to judge him.

Caleb sat among it all, not hovering, not directing, simply present. More than once, he caught himself thinking that this was what the retreat had been preparing: not the experience itself, but the capacity to host the next person who arrived weary.

Late in the afternoon, as shadows lengthened across the church yard, Ellen approached Caleb again.

"We didn't know what we needed," she admitted. "But it wasn't advice. It was… this."

Caleb nodded. "A reminder you're not alone."

"Yes," she said. Her eyes softened. "And maybe permission to be small without being ashamed."

Caleb felt the truth of it settle.

As the Barrow Creek group began to gather their things, Rachel moved among them with quiet warmth, hugging one woman, clasping Ellen's hands for a moment longer than necessary. Luke lingered near the car, glancing back toward the church as though he were taking a mental photograph.

Caleb stepped beside him.

"You're welcome back any time," he said.

Luke nodded. "I might."

There was no drama in his voice, but there was something else - possibility.

As the cars pulled away, Caleb and Rachel stood together near the gate, watching them disappear down the road that led out of the valley.

Rachel slipped her hand into his.

"That mattered," she said quietly.

Caleb nodded. "Yes."

And as the dust settled and the familiar stillness returned, he realised something with a kind of calm astonishment: Willowend had not been diminished by giving itself away.

It had been strengthened by it.

The days following the visit unfolded more slowly than Caleb expected. He had half-anticipated an emotional aftershock - people needing reassurance, questions demanding answers, some sense that what had happened required explanation. Instead, Willowend returned to its ordinary rhythms with remarkable ease. The town went about its business. The church calendar remained largely unchanged. And yet, beneath the surface, something had shifted again.

Caleb noticed it first in the way people spoke about the visit. They did not describe it as something they had *done*, but something they had *shared*.

Margaret mentioned Ellen in passing while they were packing chairs away after Sunday service. "She rang me yesterday," she said. "Just to talk. About nothing in particular."

Julie told Rachel that Graham had prayed out loud that week - quietly, without preamble, as though he had always done so.

"He didn't even notice," she said. "That was the thing."

Amelia came by the church late one afternoon, hovering at the doorway before stepping inside.

"I keep thinking about Luke," she said, once she was seated. "About how tired he looked."

Caleb nodded. "I noticed that too."

"I didn't realise pastors could get that tired," she said. "I mean… I suppose I did. I just never saw it up close."

Caleb leaned back slightly. "Most people don't."

She was quiet for a moment, then added, "I'm glad he came. I think he needed to see a church that wasn't asking him to be anything."

Caleb felt the weight of that settle.

Luke himself rang two days later. The call came mid-morning. Caleb recognised the number immediately, though he couldn't have said why.

"I wasn't sure if I should," Luke said, after an awkward pause.

"I'm glad you did," Caleb replied.

There was silence on the line, not uncomfortable but uncertain.

"I haven't been able to stop thinking since I left," Luke said finally. "Not in a bad way. Just… things seem to be rearranging themselves."

Caleb waited.

"I don't want my old job back," Luke continued. "Not like it was. But I don't think I'm finished either. And that scares me more than quitting did."

Caleb considered his words carefully.

"You don't need to decide what comes next," he said. "Only whether you're willing to stay open."

Luke exhaled. "I don't know how to do that without slipping back into the same patterns."

"That's a fair concern," Caleb said. "Which is why you shouldn't do it alone."

They spoke for quite a while - not about ministry structures or timelines, but about rest, identity, and the slow work of untangling calling from expectation. When the call ended, Caleb sat quietly, aware that something had been entrusted to him - not to solve, but to hold.

That afternoon, Howard dropped by.

"You look like someone's been thinking too hard," he said.

Caleb smiled faintly. "Possibly."

"Luke?"

"Yes."

Howard nodded. "That's how it starts. Not with a vision, but with a person."

Caleb leaned forward, elbows on his knees. "I don't want to create another dependency."

Howard met his gaze steadily. "Then don't. Create a rhythm instead."

The idea stayed with Caleb longer than he expected.

Not dependency. Rhythm.

He found himself noticing how often the conversations now circling Willowend were not about growth, but about sustainability. About faith that could endure rather than impress. About ministry that did not consume the one offering it.

A week later, Caleb mentioned Luke to Rachel as they walked in the early evening.

"He's not asking to come back," Caleb said. "Not really. He's asking whether there's a way forward that doesn't break him."

Rachel was quiet for a moment. "And do you think there is?"

"Yes," Caleb said slowly. "But it wouldn't look like anything we'd recognise straight away."

Rachel smiled. "That sounds familiar."

Caleb laughed softly. "It does."

They walked on in silence, the track beneath their feet worn smooth by years of use. The land had learned how to hold weight without cracking.

Later that week, another message arrived - this time from Ellen.

Luke seems lighter, she wrote. *Not fixed. Just less alone. Thank you.*

Caleb closed the message and leaned back in his chair. He was beginning to see that what Willowend was offering was not a model to replicate, but a posture to inhabit.

Presence.

Permission.

Patience.

That evening, as he sat in the sanctuary alone, Caleb found himself praying without words. Not for outcomes. Not for clarity. Simply for faithfulness in the next small step.

He sensed - again, not as a voice but as a steady knowing - that this widening work would cost him something. Time. Energy. Attention. Perhaps even the comfort of staying known only in one place. And yet, there was no resistance in him now.

Only readiness.

Willowend had opened its hands.

Caleb was learning to do the same.

The clarity Caleb had been waiting for did not arrive as a decision. That surprised him.

For most of Caleb's ministry, clarity had come with a sense of direction - an understanding of what needed to be done next.

But this time, it arrived differently. It came as a loosening rather than a tightening. A quiet assurance that he did not need to move ahead faster than the work itself was moving.

Luke visited Willowend again the following week, arriving alone this time. He did not come on a Sunday. He came midweek, parking his car near the hall and sitting for a while before stepping inside. Caleb noticed him through the window and waited, resisting the urge to go out and greet him immediately.

When Luke finally knocked, it was tentative.

"Come in," Caleb said.

Luke stepped inside, glancing around as though reacquainting himself with the space. "I wasn't sure if this was all right," he said. "I just needed somewhere… quiet."

"You're welcome," Caleb replied. "You don't need a reason."

They sat together for a time without speaking. The silence was not awkward; it was exploratory, like someone learning the contours of a room they might one day inhabit more fully.

"I've been thinking about identity," Luke said. "About how much of mine was wrapped up in being useful."

Caleb nodded. "That's a hard knot to untangle."

Luke looked down at his hands. "I don't know how to serve God without burning out. Or whether that's even the right question anymore."

Caleb considered his words carefully.

"Perhaps the question isn't how to serve," he said, "but how to stay human while you do."

Luke let out a slow breath. "No one's ever said it like that to me."

Caleb smiled gently. "That doesn't make it new. Just neglected." They spoke for a while, not about plans, but about rhythms - walking, prayer without language, the slow reintroduction of Scripture without obligation.

When Luke left, he did so with a quiet gratitude that needed no explanation.

That evening, Caleb told Rachel about the visit as they prepared dinner.

"He's not looking for a role," Caleb said. "He's looking for permission to heal."

Rachel nodded. "And you're not trying to become his answer."

"No," Caleb replied. "I don't want to be."

She smiled. "Then you won't."

The following Sunday, Caleb found himself standing back more deliberately than usual. He preached as he always did - carefully, thoughtfully - but he noticed how little the sermon seemed to matter compared to what was happening around it. People listened, but they were also watching one another. Attending to one another.

After the service, a small group gathered near the back of the church, not waiting for Caleb to join them. Margaret was speaking quietly. Amelia was listening intently. Graham stood nearby, hands relaxed at his sides.

Caleb felt no need to insert himself.

Later, as he walked through town, he ran into Howard outside the bakery.

"You look like someone who's given something away," Howard said.

Caleb considered that. "Maybe I have."

Howard nodded approvingly. "Good. That's usually when the real work starts."

Toward the end of the week, Caleb received another email - this one from a pastor in a coastal town he had never visited. The message was brief and cautious.

*I've heard about what's happening in Willowend.
I don't know if it's appropriate to ask, but would you
be open to a conversation sometime? No expectations.*

Caleb stared at the screen for a long moment.

This, he realised, was the edge of the widening circle. Not an invitation to build something new, but a question about how to remain faithful when the familiar structures no longer held.

He did not answer immediately.

Instead, he walked down to the creek line behind the church and stood watching the water move slowly over stones. The creek did not rush. It did not attempt to be more than it was. And yet, over time, it shaped everything around it.

That night, sitting with Rachel on the veranda, Caleb spoke what had been forming quietly within him.

"I don't think this season is about expansion," he said. "I think it's about accompaniment."

Rachel leaned her head against his shoulder. "Walking with people instead of leading them."

"Yes," he said. "And trusting that God will do the leading."

She smiled. "That sounds like something you've been moving toward for a long time."

Caleb nodded. "I just didn't know what it would cost."

"And now?"

He smiled faintly. "Now I know it will cost comfort. And clarity. And the safety of staying small."

Rachel was quiet for a moment. Then she said, "And it will give life."

"Yes," Caleb said. "It already is."

They sat together as dusk settled over Willowend, the town resting into itself once more. There was no sense of urgency pressing in on him now.

Only the steady awareness that something had been entrusted to his care - not as a possession, but as a responsibility to hold lightly.

Caleb did not feel as though anything had been settled that evening. There were no conclusions to circle, and no plans demanding definition. Instead, he sensed something quieter taking shape within him - a steadiness that did not depend on knowing what came next. Whatever lay ahead would unfold in its own time.

He looked at Rachel and felt again the gift of standing on shared ground. He did not need to explain everything he was carrying; she understood without being told. That, too, was part of the calling - not to move ahead alone, and not to rush clarity before it was given.

As the house settled into silence around them, Caleb felt no urgency to force the future into focus. It was enough, for now, to remain attentive, faithful, and willing - trusting that the next step would come when it was needed.

38. HELD LIGHTLY

The letter arrived without ceremony.

It was handwritten, addressed carefully, and postmarked from a town Caleb had driven through more than once, but he had not stopped. He noticed it among the usual envelopes late one afternoon, its presence unassuming but persistent. He carried it home rather than opening it immediately, setting it aside until after dinner.

Rachel noticed, as she always did.

"That one feels different," she said.

"Yes," Caleb replied. "I don't know why."

They opened it together later, sitting at the kitchen table as the light faded from the windows. The letter was not long. The handwriting was neat but uneven, as though the writer had paused often to consider each sentence.

The writer introduced herself simply as Ruth. No mention of how she had heard of Willowend, only that she had. She wrote of a church that was still meeting, though fewer each month. Of a pastor who had grown tired and stepped aside without anger or scandal, just weariness. Of a small group who had continued to pray, unsure whether they were being faithful or simply stubborn.

We are not asking you to come, we are asking whether there is a way to learn how to keep walking without losing heart.

Caleb read the letter twice before folding it again.

Rachel sat quietly, her hands resting on the table. "You're not surprised," she said.

"No," Caleb replied. "But I am sober."

She nodded. "That's appropriate."

They did not discuss what he should do next. They had learned, over the years, that discernment rarely emerged through immediate analysis. Instead, they let the letter rest between them like a shared responsibility, neither urgent nor dismissible. That night, Caleb slept deeply.

In the days that followed, he became increasingly aware of how much had changed in Willowend without announcement or intention. He noticed it in the way people prayed - not louder, not longer, but with less performance. He noticed it in the way conversations lingered after services, not because people needed answers, but because they had learned the value of presence. He noticed it in how often his own voice was no longer required.

One Sunday morning, he arrived early and found Margaret and Amelia already in the sanctuary, sitting several rows apart, both in quiet prayer. They looked up briefly as he entered, smiled, and returned to their stillness.

Caleb took a seat at the back and waited.

He realised then that this had become his preferred place - not out of weariness or retreat, but out of trust. The church no longer required him to hold it together. It had learned how to stand.

Later that morning, Howard joined him near the door.

"You've noticed," Howard said.

"I have."

Howard smiled. "It's a good thing. Not an easy one."

"No," Caleb said. "But a true one."

Howard hesitated, then added, "You won't always be able to be here like this."

Caleb met his gaze. "I know."

The acknowledgement passed between them without anxiety. It felt honest, not ominous.

Midweek, Caleb invited a small group to gather - not as an announcement, but as a conversation. He did not frame it as a meeting. He simply said he wanted to listen.

They sat in the hall with mugs of tea, chairs loosely arranged as they had become accustomed to. There was no expectation placed on anyone to speak.

Eventually, Graham broke the silence.

"I think I know what you're going to say," he said, not unkindly. Caleb smiled. "I'm not sure I know yet."

Graham nodded. "Fair enough."

Julie spoke next. "If this is about you being away sometimes… we'll be all right."

Amelia looked up. "I don't feel like I need to hold on to you anymore," she said, then flushed slightly. "I hope that doesn't sound wrong."

"It doesn't," Caleb replied gently. "It sounds healthy."

Margaret leaned forward. "You didn't make this about you," she said. "So don't be afraid to let it grow beyond you."

Caleb felt the weight of their words - not as pressure, but as confirmation. This was not abandonment. It was trust offered freely.

He did not promise anything. He did not outline a plan.

He simply thanked them.

That evening, Caleb and Rachel walked the familiar track behind their home. The land lay quiet, the paddocks silvered by late light. The creek moved steadily, unchanged by the seasons it had outlasted.

"I think the ending is beginning," Caleb said quietly.

Rachel smiled. "That's usually how it works."

He glanced at her. "I don't feel like I'm leaving."

"No," she said. "You're being sent. Gently."

They walked on in silence, the kind that no longer asked to be filled.

Caleb understood now that this final chapter would not be about conclusion, but about recognition. Naming what had already taken shape. Trusting what would continue beyond the page. Willowend had not become something else.

It had become more fully itself.

And in that fullness, it had learned how to open outward without losing its centre.

The letter from Ruth remained on the table at home, unanswered for now. Not because Caleb was uncertain, but because he was listening - the pace of the work, to the people entrusted to him, to the quiet leading that had shaped this season from the beginning.

There would be time.

For now, it was enough to stand within what had grown, and to recognise it for what it was: not an achievement, not a movement, but a faithful response. And that, Caleb knew, was how the story was meant to draw toward its close.

The conversation that followed did not happen all at once.

It emerged slowly, in pieces, over days rather than hours, as people spoke when they were ready and held silence when they were not. Caleb did not press it forward. He had learned that forcing clarity too early often distorted what was being discerned.

The letter from Ruth remained on the kitchen table for several days, moved occasionally to make room for meals, then returned to its place as though it belonged there. Rachel did not ask him whether he had replied. She trusted that he would know when the time was right.

Instead, she asked different questions.

"How does it feel?" she said one evening as they washed up together. "Not the idea of going - the sense of it."

Caleb considered carefully. "It feels like being asked to walk more lightly," he said. "Not to carry more, but to carry differently."

Rachel nodded. "That's a good distinction."

"Yes," he agreed. "And a costly one."

They spoke then about what it might mean in practical terms - being away occasionally, sharing responsibilities more openly, trusting others to hold what he had once guarded instinctively. None of it felt threatening. It felt grown.

One afternoon, Luke returned to Willowend again, this time with less hesitation. He sat with Caleb in the office, his posture more relaxed, his voice steadier.

"I'm not ready to lead anything," he said plainly. "And I don't want to pretend that I am."

"That's wise," Caleb replied.

"But I've started meeting with a couple of people from Barrow Creek," Luke continued. "Not teaching. Just walking. Talking. It's... enough."

Caleb smiled. "It sounds like you're discovering a different pace."

"Yes," Luke said. "And I don't want to lose it."

"You won't," Caleb said gently. "Not if you protect it."

Luke nodded, then hesitated. "I don't know what this makes me," he said.

Caleb leaned back slightly. "It makes you human," he said. "Faithful. Becoming."

Luke laughed quietly. "I can live with that."

As Luke left, Caleb felt a quiet gratitude. This, too, was part of the work - not directing outcomes, but witnessing restoration as it found its own shape.

The next Sunday arrived with the same sense of, 'What is God doing today?' which had been felt my most the congregation for some time now.

Caleb preached as he always did - thoughtfully, without urgency - but he was conscious of how little weight the sermon needed to carry. People listened, but they were not leaning on his words to hold them up. They were listening as people who had learned how to stand.

Near the end of the service, Howard led the prayers, his voice steady and unhurried. He did not pray for growth or success. He prayed for faithfulness, for gentleness, for courage to follow where God led - even when the path was unclear.

Caleb felt a deep sense of agreement rise within him.

Afterwards, people lingered, not in clusters around him, but in small conversations scattered through the space. Margaret laughed with someone near the door. Amelia sat with a young couple, listening intently. Graham stood quietly nearby, content to be present.

Caleb remained where he was, watching, aware that this was not distance but trust made visible.

Later that afternoon, he and Rachel drove to the ridge beyond town. The road wound gently upward, offering a familiar view of the valley spread wide below them. Willowend lay quietly in the late light, unchanged and yet profoundly different from the place it had been months earlier. Rachel switched off the engine and they sat for a while without speaking.

"This feels like a good place to look back from," she said eventually.

"And forward," Caleb replied.

He thought about Ruth's letter. About Ellen. About Luke. About the quiet questions now coming from places he had never expected to be part of his story.

"I don't think the work ahead will be dramatic," he said. "I think it will be slow. Relational. Costly in ways that don't show." Rachel smiled. "Those are usually the ones that last."

They sat until the light began to fade, the valley softening into shadow. Caleb felt no rush to return. The stillness did not demand movement. When they finally drove back down toward town, he knew what he would write to Ruth - not a promise, not a plan, but an invitation to walk together at a pace that honoured their shared humanity.

That night, Caleb sat at his desk long after the house had quietened. He took out a sheet of paper and began to write - not quickly, not carefully, but honestly. He wrote of listening. Of learning. Of a community that had discovered how to carry one another without fear. He did not offer answers. He did not outline a future.

He simply wrote, *You are not alone.*

When he finished, he folded the letter and placed it beside Ruth's. He would send it in the morning.

For now, it was enough to have named the truth that had been forming all along: that the work God had begun in Willowend was not confined to one place or one man but was teaching him how to walk with others into spaces where faith needed room to breathe. And that, Caleb sensed, was the heart of what remained.

The letter went into the post early the next morning. Caleb walked it down himself, the air cool and still, the town only just beginning to stir. The main street was quiet except for the distant hum of a ute somewhere near the servo and the soft clink of a flagpole rope against metal in the slight breeze. He carried the envelope loosely, not re-reading what he had written, not rehearsing how Ruth might respond. He had learned that second-guessing honest words rarely improved them. The letter was not a promise. It was an opening.

That felt right.

On the way back, he paused outside the bakery. Sheila was already inside, lights on, moving with the early-morning efficiency of someone who had spent her life making warmth out of flour and patience. She looked up and lifted a hand through the glass.

"Up early, Pastor," she called when he stepped in.

"Just posting a letter," he replied.

She nodded as though she understood far more than he'd said. "Good day for it. Air feels clean."

Caleb smiled. "It does."

As he walked home, he noticed the small, ordinary signs of Willowend waking - someone hosing down a verandah, a dog trotting along the footpath with a contented gait, a magpie calling from the top rail of a fence. The town had not become dramatic. It had become steadier.

The days that followed were ordinary in the best sense of the word. Caleb visited people, returned calls, sat in conversations that wandered without needing to arrive anywhere. He noticed again how rarely he felt the old pressure to be the one who carried the emotional weight of every room. People still came to him, yes, but more often they came already carrying something themselves - prayer they had learned to speak, courage they had learned to practise, gentleness they had learned to offer.

One afternoon, Amelia met him outside the hall as he was unlocking the side door. She had a grocery bag in one hand and a list in the other.

"I've got meals for Barrow Creek," she said, as though this were the most natural thing in the world. "Margaret said they've had a rough week."

Caleb looked at the bag, then at her. "That's generous."

Amelia shrugged, but her eyes were clear. "It's not hard. It's just... time."

He nodded slowly. In her voice, he heard something that had not been there months earlier: a quiet confidence that faith could be expressed without proving anything.

A few days later, Luke rang.

"I'm coming through town," he said. "Just for a coffee. If you're around."

"I'm around," Caleb replied.

Luke arrived mid-morning and sat with Caleb on the veranda at home, the sun warm but not sharp, the breeze carrying the smell of eucalyptus from the paddocks beyond. They spoke about small things at first - roadworks, the way the season was turning, how Barrow Creek seemed to be breathing again. Then Luke went quiet for a moment, staring out into the valley.

"I still don't know what I'm meant to be," he said.

Caleb waited. He had learned that the most important words often came after the pause.

"I used to think I had to go back to a pulpit," Luke continued. "Like anything else didn't count. But I've been meeting with two blokes from Barrow Creek, just walking and talking. One of them prayed for the first time in years last week. Not because I told him to. Just because… it felt possible."

Caleb smiled softly. "That sounds like ministry."

Luke let out a breath that was almost a laugh. "It does, doesn't it? Without the machinery."

"Without the weight," Caleb said.

Luke nodded. "I don't want the weight again."

"You don't have to take it," Caleb replied. "Not all at once. Not alone."

When Luke left, he did so without the old hesitancy. He didn't look like a man who had been fixed. He looked like a man who had been given space to become.

That evening, Ruth rang.

Her voice was steady but careful, as though she were still surprised he had written back at all.

"Thank you," she said. "For not rushing us."

Caleb leaned back in his chair, the phone warm against his ear. "There's no need."

"We don't know where this leads," Ruth continued. "But it helps to know we don't have to know yet."

"That's something Willowend has taught us all," Caleb said. "Walking without answers isn't the same as walking without hope."

There was silence on the line, and then a quiet exhale. "We'll walk for a while," Ruth said. "And see."

When the call ended, Caleb remained seated, not because the conversation demanded analysis, but because it confirmed what he had already sensed. This widening work would continue, not through solutions, but through real companionship. Not by gathering attention to one place, but by releasing courage into many.

When Sunday arrived, Caleb felt a certain tenderness in it, as though the valley itself knew the season was shifting. He arrived early and found Margaret already in the sanctuary, moving quietly among the chairs. She wasn't arranging for appearance. She was arranging them for welcome.

Amelia arrived soon after and began filling the kettle in the kitchen without being asked. Graham came in behind them, nodded once at Caleb, then went outside to check the side gate, as though practical care were his way of praying.

Caleb stood for a moment near the back and watched. He realised again that this had become his preferred place - not out of detachment, but out of trust. The church no longer required him to hold it together. It had learned how to stand.

The service itself was simple. The hymns were sung without strain. The Scripture was read without flourish. Howard led the prayers, his voice steady, asking for faithfulness and gentleness and courage to follow where God led, even when the path was unclear. Caleb preached, as he always did, but he sensed - without resentment and without pride - that the sermon was no longer the main pillar holding the morning upright. The shared life of the people was.

Afterwards, they lingered, not in a cluster around him, but in scattered conversations that moved like water around stones. Julie spoke with Ellen on the phone near the doorway, giving her time without making it a performance. Amelia sat with a young couple and listened intently, saying very little, her attention itself a gift. Graham stood near Luke, who had arrived quietly and stayed at the edge, and the two of them talked in low voices like men who did not need to pretend.

Howard approached Caleb near the door as people drifted out.

"You've noticed," Howard said.

"I have," Caleb replied.

Howard smiled. "It's a good thing. Not an easy one."

"No," Caleb said. "But a true one."

Howard hesitated, then added, "You won't always be able to be here like this."

Caleb met his gaze without flinching. "I know."

The acknowledgement passed between them without anxiety. It felt honest, not ominous.

That evening, Caleb returned to the church once more before night settled fully over the valley. He did not tell Rachel he was going; she didn't need an explanation. He walked the short distance alone, the air cooling as the light faded, the streetlights beginning to blink on one by one.

Inside the sanctuary, the quiet was familiar and welcoming. The chairs were neatly arranged. The lectern stood where it always had. The building smelled faintly of old wood and hymn books and tea - ordinary things that, over years, had become holy by association.

Caleb sat near the back and let the stillness rest around him. He thought of the first weeks - how fear had pressed in, how people had arrived carrying smoke in their clothes and worry in their eyes, how the church doors had been opened not as a strategy but as an instinct of refuge. He thought of the midweek gathering that had seemed so small at the time, and of how something had quietly begun to grow there. He thought of Mary's steady words, of Rachel's discernment, of the way leadership had shifted outward without being forced.

He had once believed leadership meant standing at the centre, holding a shape together through effort and clarity. Now he understood something gentler and far stronger.

Leadership, at its best, was not about becoming indispensable.

It was about helping others discover that they could stand too.

Caleb rose, turned off the lights, and stepped outside. Above him the stars were bright, scattered across the sky like promises that did not hurry. The ridge beyond town lay dark and still. Willowend rested beneath that wide, quiet canopy - unchanged in the ways that mattered, transformed in those that would endure.

Rachel was waiting on the steps at home when he returned, as though she had known without asking. She stood and slipped her hand into his.

"Ready?" she asked.

"Yes," Caleb said.

They went inside together, their pace unhurried, their path familiar. The work ahead would take them beyond the valley at times, into places marked by weariness and quiet hope.

But Willowend would remain - not as an anchor holding them in place, but as a home that had taught them how to live lightly and faithfully. Caleb did not feel he was leaving. He felt, in the deepest sense, that he was being sent - gently.

And as the house settled around them and the valley outside fell silent, he knew with a steady assurance that this story did not end in a neat conclusion. It ended the way true things often do: with a life that had learned how to keep walking.

In the weeks that followed, nothing extraordinary happened. No crowds arrived. No headlines were written. No new programs were announced. And yet, something continued to move.

Caleb noticed it in the way conversations deepened without being prompted, in the way people prayed with less self-consciousness and more honesty, in the way leadership no longer gathered at the centre but surfaced quietly at the edges.

He noticed it in himself, too - a loosening of old assumptions, a growing trust that God did not require him to manage outcomes in order to be faithful. The church did not become larger. It became truer.

From time to time, Caleb would receive a call or a letter from beyond the valley - a pastor asking for space to breathe, a congregation seeking gentler ways of listening, a leader unsure how to carry weariness without surrendering hope. He did not arrive with answers. He arrived with presence. Often, that was enough.

And Willowend remained what it had learned to be:

a place of refuge without possessiveness,

a community shaped more by prayer than by fear,

a church willing to follow God without needing to know the whole road ahead.

Some evenings, as the light faded over the ridge and the town settled into its familiar quiet, Caleb would stand with Rachel and look out across the valley. He no longer asked what would come next in precise terms.

He asked only to be kept attentive - to the Spirit's prompting, to the people entrusted to him, to the possibility that God was always doing more than could be seen at first glance.

The story of Willowend did not conclude. It learned how to listen. And perhaps, somewhere beyond the valley - in another small church, in another weary community, in another season marked by uncertainty - God was already beginning the same quiet work. Not through fire. Not through noise. But through faithfulness, offered one open heart at a time.

Yet even as Willowend learned to listen, it also learned that listening sometimes reveals more than comfort. There were conversations not yet finished. Names spoken only once, then remembered. A letter still unopened on Caleb's desk, its contents deferred until the right moment - or perhaps until courage caught up with calling.

Rachel sensed it too: that the stillness they had come to cherish was not an ending, but a threshold. Faithfulness, Caleb had discovered, does not always lead to rest. Sometimes it leads to readiness.

The valley would look the same tomorrow. The church doors would open as they always had. Familiar faces would gather, sing, pray, and return home again.

But beneath the quiet rhythms of ordinary days, something was stirring - not urgent, not loud, but persistent.

God rarely finished His work all at once. And so Willowend stood, neither resolved nor restless, but poised - grateful for what had been given, alert to what might yet be asked.

What shape that asking would take ... what cost or calling it might bring...what roads might open beyond the ones already walked...

Well, that's another story for another day.